**"Hayden, what's wrong? What happened?"**

Hayden rested both palms on the windowsill. He swallowed once, then twice.

Kate curved her fingers around his hand. "What's going on?"

"Nothing's making sense. I can't get my head around this case, and I need to." He looked down at their hands and must have noticed the bone-crushing grip because he let up the pressure. "I need to because I need to keep you safe."

Hayden, the wall of granite, had cracked. And it scared her. A glacial cold, like the waters of the lake outside her window, washed over her. "The Butcher's still on the loose. And we're no closer to finding out where he's hiding between kills or who he is or…"

For a week she'd lived and breathed this case with Hayden, who now stood before her, his face twisted in anger and something more unsettling: fear.

"Oh, God," she said with a gasp. "He has to finish the job." Her finger slid along the scar on her neck from the first attack and to the scar on her breast from the second. "I've been out in the open for days. At some point he'll find out and come for me because I'm the job he never finished."

# THE BROKEN

## SHELLEY CORIELL

FOREVER

NEW YORK    BOSTON

Forever
Hachette Book Group
237 Park Avenue
New York, NY 10017

www.HachetteBookGroup.com

Printed in the United States of America

First Edition: April 2014
10 9 8 7 6 5 4 3 2 1

OPM

Forever is an imprint of Grand Central Publishing.
The Forever name and logo are trademarks of Hachette Book Group, Inc.

The Hachette Speakers Bureau provides a wide range of authors for speaking events. To find out more, go to www.hachettespeakersbureau.com or call (866) 376-6591.

The publisher is not responsible for websites (or their content) that are not owned by the publisher.

*To Mom*

# ACKNOWLEDGMENTS

Special thanks to the staff and guest lecturers of the Tempe Citizens Police Academy and to FBI Special Agent Jeff Thurman (Ret.) for opening the door to the criminal justice world and teaching me that law enforcement officers' greatest weapons are their hearts.

Humble gratitude to Lauren Plude and the team at Grand Central Publishing/Forever for your expertise and enthusiasm, and to Jessica Faust, the agent who refused to give up on Smokey Joe and the Apostles.

Hugs to writerly friends and mentors who had a hand in getting this, my first romance, out the door: Jennifer Ashley, Susan Colebank, Connie Flynn, Anastasia Foxe, Susan Lanier-Graham, Varina Martindale, Sarah Parkin, Erin Quinn, Laurie Schnebly-Campbell, and Pat Warren.

As always, my heart to Lee and The Girls for loving me despite my habit of looking at blank walls and discussing plot holes with the dog.

Finally, a heart full of love and gratitude to Diana Davidson, a woman of strength, courage, and wisdom. Early on she recognized that not every little girl was meant to be a cheerleader or ballerina. Thanks, Mom, for taking me out of gymnastics and enrolling me in that book club. You, more than anyone, taught me the power and promise of a good story.

# CHAPTER ONE

*Tuesday, June 9, 1:48 a.m.*
*Mancos, Colorado*

The cry was low and tortured, pulled from the gut of a man who'd been to hell and back.

Kate Johnson threw off her covers and grabbed the box of paper clips she kept on her nightstand. "I'm coming, Smokey Joe," she called even though the old man couldn't hear her. He was too far away, trapped in a time and place known only to his tormented mind. She tore down the steps of the cabin and into Smokey's bedroom.

"Safety pins! Where the hell are my safety pins?" Smokey's hands clawed at the covers she'd tucked around him four hours ago. "Dammit to hell! I need those pins."

Kate took one of his hands in hers and dropped a handful of paper clips onto his palm. "Here you go."

His knobby fingers clamped around the bits of metal, and he dipped them in a frantic but practiced rhythm. Eventually his cries died off and gave way to moans. Then came the sobs. They were the worst.

As she had done dozens of times over the past six months,

she sank to her knees beside his bed and gathered him in her arms. Papery skin over old bones. The sour-sweet smell of cold sweat. Her cheek rubbed against the sprigs of gray hair on his head. As the sobs tapered off and his trembling ceased, she looked at her arms and shook her head. How could a hug, nothing more than two arms, *her arms*, stop a war?

When the old man's breathing returned to normal, he opened his sightless eyes. "That you, Katy-lady?"

She squeezed his bony knee. "Yes."

Relief smoothed the lines of terror twisting his face.

She left his bedside and opened the top drawer of the bureau. "Who was it?"

He inched himself to an upright position. "Never got a name on this one. He wasn't talking by the time ground grunts got him in the chopper. Mortar round blew off half his neck."

"What do you remember about him?" This was another thing she didn't understand, Smokey's need to relive the pains of the past. Yesterday's horrors should be bundled up and tucked away. They had no place in this world. She reached into the drawer for a clean nightshirt.

"He had red hair, color of a firecracker, and he held a picture of his momma in his hand. We lost him before we got to Da Nang, but I made sure the hospital crew got the picture and told them to tell that boy's momma she'd been right there with her son when he needed her, offering comfort only a momma can."

*Mommas don't offer comfort.* The thought snuck up on her, a jarring uppercut to the chin.

"Katy-lady, you okay?"

The bureau drawer slammed shut. "I'm fine."

She handed Smokey Joe the clean nightshirt and sat on the foot of the bed. That's when she noticed the soft voices coming from the radio on the nightstand. A late-night talk show host was talking to William from Michigan about a school shooting in New Jersey that left two eleven-year-olds dead. "This!" She jabbed a hand at the radio. "What is *this*?"

"Don't know." Smokey raised his gaze to the ceiling. "Can't see."

She snapped off the radio, silencing the voices. "You were listening to the news before bed again, weren't you?"

"You going to start nagging me? I don't pay you to ride my ass."

"No, you pay me to take care of you, and if you don't want to take out any new help wanted ads, listen to me. Your doctor said no news before bedtime. Those stories from the Mideast bring back too many war memories." And trigger nightmares of a time when he desperately tried to save bloody and broken bodies with only a handful of safety pins and a heart full of hope.

His gnarled fingers fumbled with the buttons of his sweat-soaked nightshirt. She reached over to help.

"I wasn't listening to no war news. There was another one of them Barbie murders. This one right here in Colorado. All the stations are yammering about it."

Barbie murders? What an insane world, filled with criminals without conscience, a public fascinated by the gory and gruesome, and media ready to unite the two for the sake of ratings. She didn't miss the crazy world of broadcast news and had no regrets that she hadn't seen a newscast in almost three years, not since she'd *been* the news.

She unfastened Smokey's next two buttons. "So a *Barbie* was killed?"

"Yep. Course the coppers don't call 'em Barbies. That's just my name, but I think that makes six now, all TV gals, all stabbed to death in their homes."

She grew still. "Broadcast journalists? Stabbed?"

"Yeah, not too pretty, either. Each gal had more than fifty knife wounds. Now why the hell does someone need to stab a body fifty times?"

Her hand sought the scar between her right eye and temple. *Because twenty-five isn't enough to kill?*

"I'll tell you why." Smokey jabbed a crooked index finger at his temple. "He ain't right in the head."

Kate slipped the shirt off Smokey's bony shoulders, her own shoulders relaxing. As an investigative reporter she'd seen up close the machinations of the criminal mind. She knew the mean and twisted and evil that perpetuated crimes against humanity. There were plenty of bad people in this world, plenty of knife-wielding crazies, and the twenty-five scars that crisscrossed her body had nothing to do with Smokey's *Barbies*. "Haven't we both determined the world in general isn't right in the head?"

"But this guy's sick, scary sick. He does that creepy thing with the mirrors."

The curtains on Smokey's window shifted with the night breeze, and the hairs on the back of her neck stood on end. "Mirrors?"

"After he kills them Barbies, the screwball goes around breaking every mirror in the house. Shatters every single one. You ever heard of such a crazy thing?"

Sounds ricocheted through her head. The swoosh of a hammer. The crack of glass. The obscenely happy tinkle of falling mirror fragments.

Smokey's shirt, soaked in sweat and terror, fell from her hand.

\* \* \*

*Tuesday, June 9, 2:20 a.m.*
*Colorado Springs, Colorado*

Hayden Reed stared at the shards of mirror that once covered an entire wall in Shayna Thomas's entryway. The largest piece was no bigger than two inches square.

Insanity was one hell of a wrecking ball.

He squatted to study the destruction, looking for trace—blood, footprints, hairs, fibers, anything that would lead him to the killer he'd been tracking for five months. All he saw in the broken mirror were distorted bits of his face, a macabre reflection of a man who'd been slammed by a wrecking ball of his own.

Parker Lord's voice echoed through his head. "Hold off on the Colorado slaying," his boss had said. "Hatch can cover for you and bring you up to speed when you get things wrapped up in Tucson with your family."

Hayden stood. His family was fine.

Time to hunt for the Butcher. But first he needed to track down Sergeant Lottie King.

A uniform directed Hayden through the living room and down a hallway where he came face-to-face with a short, round African American woman. Her crinkly gray hair hugged her head in a tight knot, and she wore a simple navy suit and a Glock 22 holstered under her left arm. On her feet were the highest, reddest heels he'd ever seen outside a whorehouse.

"Chief warned me some FBI hotshot was coming in, and you got hotshot written all over you." The sergeant crossed her arms over her chest. "My boys said you're one of Parker Lord's men, a fucking Apostle. That true?"

Hayden noticed the tone. It happened often at the mention

of Parker's Special Criminal Investigative Unit, a small group of FBI specialists known for working outside the box and, according to some, outside the law. Some media pundit nicknamed them the Apostles. Like Parker, Hayden didn't care about names, only justice. "Yes."

"Heard you boys play by a different set of rules."

He clasped his hands behind his back. "We don't play."

Her jaw squared in a challenge as she jutted her chin toward the shattered mirror in the hallway. "So tell me, Agent I-Don't-Play, what's your take?"

Shayna Thomas had been found dead in her bedroom four hours ago. Multiple stab wounds. No signs of sexual trauma. Shattered mirrors. All the earmarks of another Broadcaster Butcher slaying. Hayden pointed to a spot three feet down the hall. "The unsub stood there. One strike. Used a long-handled, blunt instrument he brought with him. Carefully positioned his body out of the glass trajectory. You'll find no blood near this or any of the other broken mirrors. You'll also find no footprints, no fingerprints, no trace, and no witnesses." The other Butcher crime scenes had been freakishly void of evidence.

The sergeant locked him in a stare down. He studied the wide, steady stance of those high heels, the indignant puff of her chest, and the single corkscrew of hair that stuck out above her right ear.

"And your take, Sergeant King?"

The police sergeant's nostrils flared. "I think we got us one fucked-up son of a bitch, and I can't wait to nail his ass to the splintered seat of a cold, dark cell where he'll never see the light of day."

Early in his law enforcement career, he'd learned there were two kinds of people behind the shield: those seeking personal gain—a paycheck, ego strokes, power—and those seeking justice. Like him, the woman in the red shoes was one of the latter. Hayden unclasped his hands. "And I can't wait to hand you a hammer."

A smile wrinkled the corner of her eyes, and he saw what he needed: respect.

"Damn glad you're here, Agent Reed."

"For the record, Sergeant King, I hear you aren't much of a slouch, either."

"Ahh, a pretty face *and* a smooth talker. I think I might be able to work with you." The smile in her eyes dimmed as she motioned him to follow her down the hall.

"Timeline?" Hayden asked.

"A man out walking his dog hears breaking glass as he passes Thomas's house. He calls the station at 10:32. Beat officer arrives at 10:37. He makes repeated shout-outs, but no one responds. He looks through the front window, sees the broken mirror, and calls for backup. When the second uniform arrives, they enter and discover the victim in the master bedroom."

"Positive ID?"

"Confirmed. Shayna Thomas. Homeowner."

"Current status?"

"Crime Scene Division's still processing." Sergeant King's red shoes drew to a halt. "This is one mother of a scene."

"Blood." Hayden didn't frame the single word as a question. They'd found excessive amounts of blood at the other Butcher crime scenes, five since January.

"It's the fucking Red Sea in there. You better watch those shiny shoes of yours." Lottie pointed to the door in front of them. "I'm warning you. It ain't pretty."

Wrongful death never was.

Inside the bedroom, blood peppered four walls, striped

the white down comforter, and clung to the fan centered on the ceiling. The victim lay on the ground in front of a dresser. Blood soaked her T-shirt and jogging shorts and matted her hair. She was a brunette, slim, probably attractive. Hard to tell. Lacerations decussated her face, arms, neck, and abdomen, but as he expected, the V at her legs was blood- and injury-free.

He saved the hands for last. He always did. It was hard to think clearly after seeing them, hard to stop being the dispassionate evaluator. Drawing air into his tightening lungs, he turned to Shayna Thomas's bloody hands. They rested on her breasts, fingers intertwined as if in prayer, a gesture of peace amidst the chaos of murder.

For a moment he lowered his eyelids and calmed the rage that simmered in a place he refused to acknowledge.

Those bloody hands beckoned him, pulled him in, and wouldn't let go. His boss, Parker Lord, was wrong. Hayden needed to be here.

\* \* \*

*Tuesday, June 9, 2:23 a.m.*
*Mancos, Colorado*

Run. Fast and far.

Kate's hands shook worse than Smokey Joe's as she yanked the saddlebags out of the closet and slammed them on her bed. From the bureau, she hauled out the few things she called her own: underwear, scarves, T-shirts, chambray overshirts, jeans, and her leathers. She jammed all but the leathers into the bags and threw in her brown contacts and hair dye. Meager belongings compared to her on-air days, a time when she wore a different face. A face not yet hacked by a madman. A madman who hadn't stopped after the butcher job on her.

The wooden floor creaked behind her. She dropped her leathers and spun. Something shifted in the shadow of the doorway. She reached for the ceramic lamp on the night-stand then set it down when Smokey stepped out of the darkness.

He cleared his throat with a rough cough. "You taking off?"

Her hand dropped to her side, and she tried not to look into his sightless eyes, eyes filled with confusion and something else. *Oh God, please don't let him look at me like that.* "Yes." What more could she say? *I'm sorry for disappointing you. I'm sorry for leaving because there's a madman roaming the country who vowed to kill me and who has since murdered six other women.*

She yanked the saddlebag zippers closed. How stupid to think she could stop running, stupid to stay in one place so long, and stupid to put an old, blind man like Smokey Joe in danger. She picked up the leather pants and jammed her legs into them. The Shayna Thomas attack had occurred in Colorado Springs, only three hundred miles from Smokey Joe's cabin in southwestern Colorado.

Smokey scratched the stubble on his chin. "That big order? You got it done?"

"Order?" She grabbed her helmet from the top shelf of the closet.

"That gal out of San Diego who wants all them angels. You get 'em done?"

Kate couldn't think about their online jewelry store or tourmaline angels. She thought only about getting away. "Order's done. It's boxed and on the table."

"I'll ship it." One of Smokey's slippers, the color and texture of beef jerky, whisked across the floor. "Where should I
send your cut?"

"You keep it." She needed no connections to Smokey Joe,
no trail that could put him in the sights of a knife-wielding
madman.

Smokey nodded and shuffled away. The sound of his ratty
slippers on the floor she polished weekly pounded in her
head and tugged at her heart.

The past six months with Smokey Joe had been peaceful,
and after being on the run for more than two years, she'd
needed the rest and recharge. During her time here in the
scrub canyons and pine forests of southwestern Colorado,
she hadn't thought about the past or the future. She'd been
simply living, living simply.

She flung her saddlebags over her shoulder—amazing
how little a person needed to live—and rushed down the
steps to the bottom floor. She bolted through the kitchen but
ground to a halt at the backdoor.

Turning quickly, she set the timer for Smokey's morning
coffee, flicked on the bread machine, and left an urgent voice
message with his case manager. Only then did she slip out of
the house, deadbolt the lock, and escape into the safe cover
of darkness.

# CHAPTER TWO

*Tuesday, June 9, 5:07 a.m.*
*Colorado Springs, Colorado*

What's wrong, Pretty Boy?" Sergeant Lottie King sat on the foot of the bed next to him.

Hayden pointed to the beveled mirror on the wall in Shayna Thomas's spare bedroom. "It's not broken." Its wholeness slammed him in the gut, momentarily throwing him off balance.

"Maybe our killer thought eighty-four years of bad luck was enough," Lottie added. "The SOB shattered the hell out of twelve others."

Hayden shook his head. "It's not consistent with his MO. He breaks every mirror in the house. In the Santa Fe slaying he even broke two mirrors in a model dollhouse. This mirror should be broken."

"*If* it's your guy." Lottie kicked off her right shoe and rubbed her instep. "You think this might be a copycat?"

"It's him." For the past five months, Hayden walked in the Butcher's shoes, invited the evil into his head. He knew how this offender worked. "Too many similarities. Victims' professions and general looks, manner of death, complete lack of traceable evidence, and"—Hayden blinked hard, refusing to see the red—"the folded position of the hands is a holdback."

Air rushed over Lottie's lips. "Damn. We got us a monster right here in Colorado Springs."

*Monsters.* That had been Marissa's term for the violent criminals he spent most of his career chasing.

*I'm always sharing you with monsters!* Marissa had screamed at him. *You never let go. Those killers you hunt are in our home, at our dinner table, in our bed.*

He winced at the flash of memory and blamed it on Tucson.

Lottie poked her foot into her shoe. "Okay, Mr. FBI Profiler, get out that crystal ball of yours. Where the hell do we go now?"

In his line of work there was a proper order of things, a clear course of observation, analysis, and application. The process fortified him and drew him further away from that Tucson grave. Hayden motioned with his hand to the door. "The beginning."

In the foyer they found Detective Scott Traynor. If Sergeant King was the head of the operation, Traynor was her hands and feet. The lead investigator was tall and lanky with straw-colored hair and freckles across his nose. Hayden pictured him sitting on a tractor in the eastern Colorado hayfields, but he wasn't fooled by the easygoing farm-boy appearance. Lottie's right-hand man carried a cell phone in his shirt pocket, a walkie-talkie clipped to his belt, and a small tablet in his hand. He wore a ring of sweat around his collar and dusty loafers. Scott Traynor was plugged in and running hard.

"Offender's point of entry?" Hayden asked.

"No signs of force," the detective said. "At this point we're speculating he came in through the front door."

Speculation did not solve murder investigations bathed in blood. That's why he was here. Time to do his job. Time to become the monster.

Hayden walked to the front porch, where cool air crowded the charcoal night. "I'm Thomas's attacker." Hayden positioned himself in front of the door. "It's after ten and dark, but the porch lights illuminate me. Thomas has a peephole. What do I do?"

"Is the door locked?" Detective Traynor asked.

Criminal investigative analysis started with studying the victims and their behaviors, and in the past five months, he'd spent hundreds of hours learning about the five murdered broadcasters. "Smart, successful women like Shayna Thomas don't take safety risks. The door is locked. How do I get in?"

"You have a key," the detective said.

Hayden reached into his pocket and took out his own set of keys, which jingled in the pre-dawn stillness. "How do I get the key?"

"You steal it."

Lottie caught the detective's attention. "Find out if Thomas had a recent issue with lost or stolen keys, and find out who had access to her purse both at work and home."

"Good." Hayden stuffed the keys in his pocket. Now from another angle, always a second angle, sometimes a third, sometimes a fourth or fifth or sixth. "I have no key. How do I get in?"

The detective frowned. "You knock on the door, and she lets you in?"

"Why would she do a dumb-ass thing like that?" Lottie asked.

Hayden asked himself that same question at the other five crime scenes, and now, like then, he faced the same chilling answer. "She knows me or has reason to trust me."

Sergeant King opened her mouth, but before she could speak, the radio at her waist squawked. "Hey, Sarge, we need you out back. You aren't going to believe what we found at Thomas's bedroom window."

\* \* \*

*Tuesday, June 9, 5:34 a.m.*
*Mancos, Colorado*

A pair of ratty, old slippers padded into the kitchen.

"Coffee's on," Kate said, her voice as soft as the early morning light slipping through the muslin curtains on the window over the sink.

Smokey Joe shuffled to the table and sniffed. "Tuesday."

Yes, it was Tuesday, her baking day, and she was in Smokey's kitchen, where swirling scents of cinnamon and yeasty bread warmed the air. A golden loaf, speckled with raisins, sat on the counter.

She poured a mug of coffee from the steaming pot and set it on Smokey's placemat in the number three spot, right where he liked it. She pulled a serrated knifed out of the drawer, her hand tightening on the hilt as the sun glinted off the jagged metal blade. The flash of silver blinded her, but she blinked and cut two thick slices of bread, which she dropped in the toaster. "You have a doctor's appointment this morning at nine, so we'll need to leave here by eight."

If Smokey was surprised she was still in the cabin, he didn't show it. He sat and grunted. "Doctor Collins?"

"Yes."

He took a long draw from his coffee. "Don't like him. Pain in the ass."

She smiled in spite of herself. "You're going anyway."

"Hell of a day," Smokey said into the rim of his mug. "You riding my ass and Doctor Collins poking up it."

A laugh joined her smile.

Smokey Joe took another swig. "You gonna tell me about it?"

The toast popped. So he wasn't going to pretend last night never happened. She placed the toast on two plates. Nor could she.

When she had tried to leave, her bike wouldn't start. Grounded until the parts store opened this morning, she'd tried to get some rest for the road trip ahead, but the anger coursing through her veins left her wide-eyed and wired. She ended up using Smokey's computer to go online and learn about the Broadcaster Butcher murders. She'd discovered each attack mirrored hers except for one thing: She survived.

"Do we need to call the coppers?" Smokey continued in his worn, scratchy voice.

"No." She'd gone that route in the beginning, and look where it got her. "Not yet." But she would. She had to. She took the butter from the refrigerator, hacked off a chunk, and dropped it onto Smokey's toast. But who to contact? The Colorado Springs Police would be the logical choice, but she'd relied on the local police after her own attack. Not only had they failed to capture her attacker, but also they hadn't taken her story seriously. They all but called her a liar. More importantly, they failed to protect her when she needed them most.

"Why didn't you take off last night?" Smokey asked when she set his plate in the number seven position.

She'd never been good at hiding her emotions, and right

now, if Smokey weren't blind, he'd see a massive dose of what was under her anger: fear mixed with guilt and shame. "Honestly?"

"Shoot straight or ditch the rifle."

"My bike needs repair work. Ignition's shot." Shameful, to think she'd be taking off again if the mechanical gods hadn't conspired against her. She'd be running from her past, from her responsibilities with Smokey, and from the fact that her attack was not the private nightmare she'd believed for three years.

Six women had died. Her stomach twisted.

Smokey Joe poked at the toast but didn't eat. With a grumble he reached for the small glass dish that sat in the middle of the kitchen table. The little dish had an illustrated donkey and read LOST MY ASS IN LAS VEGAS.

He picked up the set of car keys that always rested there. "Here," he said, his voice gruffer than normal.

"I can't take your car, Smokey." *And I can't involve you any more than you already are.*

"I don't plan on doing no driving this week."

She couldn't chuckle this time.

"You don't got to keep it," he said. "Just go into town, buy what you need at the parts store, then git."

She started pacing. If only it were that easy. She'd stopped in Mancos because she'd run out of money and out of steam, but even with a wad of cash in her saddlebags and six months to rest her legs, she had things she needed to take care of, things that couldn't be handled from the seat of her bike on a scenic road to nowhere.

Smokey picked up his toast. "You staying?"

She stopped behind his chair, noticing his hand shook. "For a while." At least until she got Smokey a new aide and figured out who to talk to about her attack.

Smokey shoved back his plate of uneaten toast. "Then I got something for you." Suddenly spry, he darted to the dented file cabinet in the corner of the kitchen and pulled out a small plastic case. Inside was a gleaming hunk of metal. "Ever shoot before?"

"No."

"Wanna learn?"

Kate stared at the gun in the old soldier's hand. After her attack, she'd thought about getting a gun, but that meant background checks, paperwork, lessons, all trails leading to her. Plus it meant fighting, something she'd been doing most of her life. For once she'd opted to run, and, in the end, that wrong choice had led to the horrific deaths of six broadcasters.

"Yes, I need to know how to handle a gun."

Smokey's fingers, steady and strong, reached for the box of ammunition in the case. "Good. I'll teach you how to load, and we'll head out back for target practice." He took out five rounds and laid them in a straight line next to his coffee mug. "Then we'll get the place ready."

"Ready?"

"For war."

\* \* \*

*Tuesday, June 9, 5:35 a.m.*
*Colorado Springs, Colorado*

The Crime Scene Division tech pushed aside a sun-crisped shrub, giving Hayden a clear view of the silty ground below Shayna Thomas's bedroom window.

"By the size and shape, I'd say the print's from a man's

running shoe," the tech said. "Fresh. Hasn't been disturbed by insects or wind."

"Get a cast made." Hayden raised both eyebrows. "You said there's more?"

The tech directed his gaze to the windowpane above the shoeprint. "Picked up a bunch of good prints. Looks like he may have been rubbing the dirt off the glass, trying to get a better look."

Lottie pressed her lips together. "Did some Peeping Tom work before he went in and hacked the hell out of her."

Hayden had seen these types of guys in action, knew what was going on in their heads. Brushing back branches, he peered through twigs and studied the underside of leaves. At last he found it. "He did more than peep." Hayden pointed to a thick, white substance on a bush to the right of the windowsill. "Ejaculate."

"Pervert," Lottie said with a growl.

Hayden slipped his hand in his pocket. "But one who isn't too bright."

Lottie nodded. "So let's call him Mr. Stupid. He leaves behind a fucking trifecta of evidence. Shoe impression as he stands at the window. Fingerprints as he wipes the dust for a better view. And ejaculate after he gets his rocks off watching Shayna Thomas in her bedroom. Why the hell didn't he just leave us a business card?"

Hayden's hand curled into a fist. "Something's not right." Like the mirrors.

"Not right?" Lottie aimed her right hand pistol-style at the window. "Pretty Boy, we just got a helluva lot closer to finding us a butcher."

"Have we?" Those shiny, intact mirrors winked at him. Mocked him. "No one has ever found trace or contact evidence at any of the Butcher crime scenes."

"Maybe he's getting sloppy."

Hayden wanted to believe they had something on the Butcher, but he knew too much about the sick art of serial killing. "With each victim, serial killers refine their methods. They don't suddenly get sloppy."

"I'm assuming you already worked up a profile of Mr. Stupid," Lottie said.

Hayden nodded. He had created the initial profile after the second murder, when the FBI had been brought on board because they were dealing with a serial killer working across state lines. Over the past five months, he added to and refined the profile. He knew this man inside and out. "We're looking for a male between the ages of twenty and forty. Thin or small in stature. A social misfit who may live alone or with his parents or an older relative. High school education. Few if any physical relationships with women. Not gainfully employed or has a job with a good deal of flextime. Has some kind of disfigurement or handicap, possibly unseen, such as a stutter, or visible, such as acne scars or a limp. Home and person are meticulous, and he thrives on clear, written instruction. Carries around a small spiral notebook everywhere he goes. He's methodic and craves order. There's nothing sloppy about him." Hayden pointed to the prints and ejaculate. "These should not be here. Something went wrong."

* * *

*Tuesday, June 9, 6:00 p.m.*
*Colorado Springs, Colorado*

The El Paso County morgue smelled of rotting flesh and vanilla air freshener. Hayden had smelled worse, but as he looked at the shredded body on the steel autopsy table, he could honestly say he'd never *seen* worse.

He and Lottie stood across from Dr. Maryanne Markoff, the thirty-something medical examiner who'd spent all day with Shayna Thomas's corpse.

"Sixty-two distinct puncture wounds made by an eight-inch, double-edged knife," Dr. Markoff said with a slight shudder. Overkill like this was hard to witness, even for the seasoned ME who daily stared death in the face. "Twenty-two lacerations to the face and head, seven to the neck, and the remainder to the arms and torso. Also noteworthy are the areas free of puncture wounds. Breasts unmarred."

"Same as the others?" Lottie asked.

Hayden nodded. All bodies were free of puncture wounds on both breasts, another fact they'd withheld from the public, another reason to doubt this was a copycat.

"What do you make of that, Pretty Boy?"

Just like in a good piece of art, negative spaces were as important as splashes of color. They told a story all their own, and there was story behind those unmarred areas. "Two schools of thought," he said. "The offender could revere female sexual organs, wanting to kill the victims but preserve what makes them female, shades of a Madonna complex. Or he could despise the female species and those organs that make them women, too filthy or unworthy of his knife."

"This is one fucked-up prick." Lottie rubbed at the furrows deepening across her forehead.

The ME held up her hand. "But a smart one. Single stab wound to the base of the neck severed the spinal cord and caused instant immobilization but not immediate death. Two subsequent stab wounds to the carotid and radial arteries led to death by exsanguination."

"So the son of a bitch paralyzed her and bled her to death?"

"Yes," Hayden said, "with only three thrusts of his knife. The remainder of the puncture wounds are postmortem."

"That true?" Lottie asked the ME, who nodded. The sergeant let out a long hiss. "So he's a smart butcher. Rape?"

The ME turned to Hayden. "I have a feeling you already know, Agent Reed."

"Rape kit came back negative," Hayden said. "No defensive wounds, either. No traces of blood or skin fragments under the nails. No bruising indicative of struggle."

"Give the man a gold star," Markoff said with her first smile of the meeting. "You know your stuff."

Yes, he already knew what the ME's report would say. He knew the scenario, or at least part of it. Shayna Thomas's murder went according to the Butcher's proper order of things. He gained easy entry into the domicile. A single immobilizing stab wound, delivered unexpectedly from behind, felled Shayna Thomas. The two subsequent stab wounds drained her of blood and life. Then the knife frenzy began, more than fifty stab wounds to a body that couldn't fight back. Blood flew. Rage soared. After stabbing Thomas's lifeless body, the Butcher, a meticulous sort, put his blood-soaked clothes in a plastic bag, maybe two for containment, and changed into fresh clothes. Then came act two, a purposeful trip through the house to break every mirror. But in the Shayna Thomas murder, something went wrong in that second act. He failed to break all the mirrors.

A sharp itch clawed between his shoulder blades. The killer should have destroyed *all* the mirrors. Something—or more likely someone—stopped the Butcher and sent him running. Was it the man walking his dog or the patrol officer at the door? Or was it someone else, someone in the picture but still unknown at this point in the investigation? The key right now was to step back and study as much of the picture as he could.

Lottie's red toe tapped against the gray speckled linoleum of the morgue floor. "I don't get it. The Butcher entered Shayna Thomas's home without apparent struggle. Then he gets close enough for a quick, almost effortless kill. Think she knew him?"

"It's possible," he said. "Trauma to the head and neck is common in attacks where the offender knows the victim."

He'd been contemplating this possibility for months. The Butcher murders were not random assaults on high-risk victims but rather highly organized attacks on carefully sought-out women. They occurred like clockwork every four weeks with no variation in means or mode. The key: finding out why *these* women. Why were they important to the Butcher?

It was after eight by the time he and Lottie left the morgue and climbed into her stifling car. She cranked the air conditioner, and as they waited for the car interior to cool, Lottie turned to him. "You want this Butcher's ass in the worst way. On most days, he's all you think about."

The seatbelt Hayden stretched across his chest stilled. How could she tell? Few had ever been able to read him.

*Do you ever feel anything, Hayden? Do you know what it's like to hate? To love? To hurt so bad you will do anything to end the pain? I can never tell what you're* feeling, *and it's killing me.* Marissa. She'd crept into his head again.

He clicked the seatbelt in place. "So you moonlight as a profiler?"

"Nope. But I know how to make peanut brittle." Lottie smacked her lips.

Hayden turned to the police sergeant. "Excuse me?"

"Peanut brittle candy. My oldest grandson loves it. We

make it every Christmas, with peanuts, mind you, none of them pansy-ass macadamia nuts. You're like peanut brittle, all shiny and polished, hard as hell, too, so hard no one can read you. In order to get to that stage, you got to boil the shit out of it. So I figure you've done some boiling in your life, including some serious simmering over this jerk-off."

Simmered? Yes. Boiled? That, too. The Butcher heated his blood.

He blamed the bloody hands.

"I want him." The words rushed over his lips, much like the air now pouring out of the car vents, dry and chilled. "And I'm going to get him."

Lottie jammed the car in reverse. "I'm liking you more and more, Pretty Boy."

As they drove to the station, Hayden knew both he and Lottie weren't done for the night. People like them didn't call it quits when the sun went down. "Dinner?"

Lottie shot him a half smile. "You got a half dozen women back in the station and even that pretty young medical examiner we just met who'd shit in Macy's front window to have dinner with you, and you want to wine and dine an old bag like me?"

"Yes."

A frown tugged the smile off her lips. "If you're up to ordering in and going over case notes in my office, you got a date, and while you're ordering dinner, why don't you order us a witness? Our lives would be a whole lot easier if we could find somebody who's seen this butchering SOB in action."

That low simmer bubbled in Hayden's gut. "We have one."

# CHAPTER THREE

*Tuesday, June 9, 9:30 p.m.*
*Dorado Bay, Nevada*

He raised the crimson-filled glass to the star-studded sky outside his office window and toasted the gods other people believed in.

"To power," he said. "And to those of us who have it."

He swirled the glass of lush, red liquid.

When he'd taken Shayna Thomas's life, he'd taken her power.

It had been almost twenty-four hours, but heat still curled about him, warmed him. Tongues of flames licked his insides as he thought about that knife going in and out, in and out.

He tilted the glass, allowing a few precious drops of Shayna Thomas's blood to land on his semi-erect penis. Those few drops furthered his arousal.

Power. He slicked it over himself.

*There's power, power, wondrous working power in the blood...*

The hymn from the steepled building near his childhood

home in the seediest section of Las Vegas pulsed through his head. He saw his neighbors—the whores who reeked of heartless sex and the users and abusers who smelled of despair—singing and praying for power from above to mend their pathetic lives. He'd been at the church, a skinny kid with a bad limp, outside the window watching and calling them fools.

Power came from within.

He fully recognized that at age twelve when he'd reached into a place that went deeper than his soul and made his first kill, taking power from those who controlled him, from his whore of a mother and from the john of hers who used his asshole like a pincushion.

Those had been his first two kills. There had been many since, and there would be at least one more. He stared at the photograph he'd centered on the windowsill to catch the glow of moonlight.

His hand pumped faster. He pictured red spilling out of his latest kill's body. He pictured Shayna's wavy dark hair, creamy white skin, brown eyes that he pretended were green.

His body jerked and he bit his tongue so hard he tasted blood. Spasms rocked him as wave after wave of heat blasted through his veins. It was minutes, maybe hours later that the heat subsided to a nice cocoon of warmth.

Yes, the blood empowered, but in the end, it soothed.

He took a tissue from his pocket and wiped. After zipping his pants, he folded the tissue and blotted the creamy drops that had dribbled to the floor.

Just as he stood, the door of his office swung open, the lights blazed on, and an off-tune rendition of "Moon River" warbled through the room.

He blinked away the bright light, snatched the small glass

of blood he'd placed on the table, and slipped it behind his back.

"Oh, you scared me!" Glenda, the cleaning woman, took a step back, her hand to her chest. "I didn't expect anyone to be here at this hour. Would you like me to come back later?"

Stupid bitch. She was supposed to clean from six to nine Wednesdays and Fridays. Six to nine. Wednesdays. Fridays. She wasn't following the schedule. Anger burst behind his eyes.

But he kept his words calm. "No. I'm leaving."

When he reached the door, she called out, "Excuse me, is this yours?"

He turned and looked at the picture she'd picked up from the windowsill, the one of a smiling, living Katrina Erickson. Holding the blood that should have been Katrina's, he walked toward the cleaning lady, took the photo, and left.

\* \* \*

*Tuesday, June 9, 9:30 p.m.*
*Colorado Springs, Colorado*

A whistle slid over Lottie's puckered lips. "This is the witness you were talking about? A regular little Miss America."

Hayden stacked the empty Thai takeout containers and put them in the trash can next to Lottie's desk. Then he turned to see her studying the eight-by-ten glossy of the woman he'd been hunting for five months. "She's a broadcast journalist last working in Reno, but she did some modeling in her college days. Name's Katrina Erickson." He ran his finger along the right side of the photo. "Three years ago the Butcher attacked her."

"Three years? I thought the first Butcher attack occurred six months ago."

"That was the first *murder*. When I started researching similar cases, I discovered Erickson's attack. A significant number of stab wounds. Folded hands. Broken mirrors. A near carbon copy."

"Except Miss America didn't die."

"Her attacker stabbed her twenty-four times with an eight-inch, double-edged knife. We believe he thought she was dead, and she would have been if not for an anonymous nine-one-one call directing police to check her home. She was stitched up and underwent inpatient rehab for a number of months, but the day she left the hospital, she disappeared. No one has seen her since."

"You think the Butcher found her?"

"No. If he had, he would have left her body where others could find it. His killings are brutal and meant to be seen—and admired—by others. Katrina Erikson is still alive but off-grid. She's strong, resourceful, and smart. I'm fairly confident she's not being held against her will but in hiding by choice."

Lottie turned from the photo of Katrina Erickson to a four-foot corkboard on the wall of her office. More than fifty photos dotted the surface, all of Shayna Thomas, all predominately red. "I don't blame her. The Butcher's one sick SOB." She leaned back in her chair and propped her bare feet on her desk. "Got a handle on where Miss America is hanging out these days?"

He took out a large manila envelope from his briefcase and tipped its contents onto the desk. Out tumbled a brochure from a motorcycle shop in New Mexico, a picture of Katrina taken seven days after her attack, and a small pendant in the shape of a fairy.

Lottie looked skeptical. "You gotta explain this one."

He pointed to the brochure. "Katrina Erickson loved scenic rides, and before her disappearance, she was a member of a motorcycle club. Small community of hardcore biker enthusiasts. I'm hoping one of them will come through and admit to seeing her."

Lottie pointed to the close-up photo, which showed a fresh wound snaking from Katrina's right eye to the upper portion of her right ear. "What's this all about?"

"Katrina Erickson is beautiful, and, as a broadcaster, she took great pains with her appearance. It's possible she'll try to have this lone facial scar surgically reduced. We've contacted hundreds of plastic surgeons. Nothing yet."

The police sergeant studied the fairy. "And this?"

He picked up the silver-winged pendant with the bright green stone. "Tourmaline jewelry. Katrina Erickson's hobby. Before her attack, she was the creator of a line of handmade jewelry called the Fairy Shoppe. Made quite a bit of money at it. So it's possible she's making and selling jewelry somewhere. I've been jewelry shopping but haven't found anything yet."

"Motorcycle clubs, plastic surgeons, and little glass fairies. This is all we have to help us track the only woman to survive the Butcher's knife?" Lottie looked at the ceiling. "Lord, help us."

The fairy pendant slipped from his fingers and clattered to the desk. No, Lord, help another beautiful, dark-haired broadcast journalist because he finally figured out what was bothering him about the mirrors. The Butcher, who craves order and routine, hadn't broken the final two mirrors in Shayna Thomas's house. He hadn't finished the job, which means he wasn't going to wait a month between killings.

The Butcher could and would strike at any time.

\* \* \*

*Wednesday, June 10, 12:30 a.m.*
*Colorado Springs, Colorado*

Hayden left the station around midnight and checked in to his hotel room. He looked at the mound of pillows on the bed and the small bottle of lavender spray and the relaxation CD on the nightstand, all designed to help hotel guests slumber long and peacefully. Not him. Not tonight. Frankly, not ever.

*You're a friggin' freak of nature*, one of his bunkmates had said the first week at boot camp. *Normal people don't function on three hours of sleep, Reed, not with the hell we're going through.*

Maybe that's why he was so successful at chasing abominations of the human condition. Because he was one. He could go weeks with only a few hours of sleep per night, which was a good thing because tonight he had no plans of sleeping.

After loosening his collar, he called up his folders on Katrina Erickson and clicked on a video file. A picture of the former broadcast journalist at KTTL-TV in Reno popped onto the screen, and the audio streamed.

"Using a metal spoon he filed to a razor-sharp point, convicted felon Devon Morales escaped from the Nevada State Prison at dawn this morning," Katrina was saying in the clear, authoritative voice she used when on the air.

This broadcast clip, one of her "Justice for All" reports, was shot in mid-February four years ago and featured Katrina standing in near-blizzard conditions outside the prison gates. Even with her hair flying in the frosty winds and her nose red from the cold, Katrina Erickson was exquisite.

Hayden stilled the video stream, and for a moment he stopped studying the victim.

And appreciated the woman.

He'd learned somewhere that models and actors had a symmetry to their faces that drew people to them. That must be the case with Erickson, because he was drawn to her, to the perfect order of her features, to her heart-shaped face softened by heavy, brown waves of hair, to the fair skin of her graceful neck and spray of freckles across her nose, and to full, pink lips and intense green eyes.

Eyes that had seen a butcher.

The beautiful woman fled. The victim returned.

Hayden wanted Katrina Erickson, needed her. She alone had witnessed the Broadcaster Butcher in action. And she alone survived.

In his efforts to track her down, Hayden spent the past five months studying everything about her. He created spreadsheets of people who may have wanted to harm her, including subjects of her "Justice for All" reports, and he personally interviewed dozens of people who knew her.

Her coworkers said Katrina was a top-notch journalist and on the fast track to landing a job with one of the networks. "Katrina clearly had a mission, and she had the fire and the smarts to get there," the general manager at KTTL-TV had said.

Those who knew her as a youth were blunter. "At times my sister could be explosive," her younger brother had admitted to Hayden after a good deal of prompting and patience. "The night she ran away from home, she got in a fight with our mother and ended up stabbing me." As proof, her bother lifted the cuff of his shirt and showed him a raised scar in the shape of a check mark on his right wrist.

"Katrina was feisty as a kid, a real scrapper who got more

than her fair share of fat lips and black eyes," the pastor of her childhood church said. "We prayed for her often."

So why had a scrappy, ambitious, talented, successful woman who could clearly take care of herself disappeared off the face of the earth? And, more importantly, where was she?

Hayden turned back to his computer screen and called up his e-mail, clicking on the one from Hatch Hatcher. His teammate had been digging into a tourmaline jewelry store Hayden spotted last week online.

Hatch's message read: *Store ships out of Durango, Colorado. I talked to a local postal clerk who said he had a customer who frequently mailed small, jewelry-size boxes. But when I e-mailed him a photo of Katrina Erickson, the clerk couldn't give a positive ID. He said it was hard to tell because the woman always wore dark glasses, scarves, and long-sleeved shirts. I'd offer to head to Durango, but this is your party. Let me know when you need me to RSVP.*

\* \* \*

*Wednesday, June 10, 7:30 a.m.*
*Mancos, Colorado*

Hayden couldn't imagine Katrina Erickson in a town where elk outnumbered residents, but after his phone conversation with Hatch, he dug into the Durango lead and discovered the woman with the online jewelry store lived in a remote cabin in Mancos, a small mountain town in southwestern Colorado and the heart of elk country.

Hayden pulled his car off Highway 184 and drove along a twisting dirt road through the dense pine forest. Winter and spring had been dry in the mountain states, and the air smelled of dust and drought. After four miles he came to a small A-frame cabin, owned by one Joseph Bernard, a veteran who'd served two tours in Vietnam and claimed a chestful of medals. Records from the VA showed he was legally blind, had battled and defeated colon cancer one year ago, and had a live-in aide, Kate Johnson. Was Kate Johnson an alias for Katrina Erickson? That simmer Lottie talked about started to bubble.

The minute Hayden stepped out of his car he spotted the first wire. Seconds later he spied two others, one along the front of the house three inches above the ground and the other across the lower-level windows. Trip wires, but, interestingly enough, there'd been no attempt to camouflage their presence. Given the remote location, he could be looking at an individual suffering from paranoia, irrational fears, PTSD, or, more likely, a combination. Hayden knocked on the front door and called out, "FBI."

A tufted-ear squirrel in a pine tree near the door made a series of sharp clicking sounds, almost as if scolding him for disturbing inhabitants of this remote part of the forest.

When no one answered, he made his way around the side of the house, inspecting the ground before each step so as not to trigger any of the wires. Out back he got another surprise: a pile of aluminum cans with bullet holes. He unholstered his Sig 45 and flattened himself against the back of the cabin. A low hiss struck the air followed by a pop.

He spun just in time to see the wooden doors of a shed ten yards east of the cabin splinter and blow. Dust and debris rained through the air.

"What the—" Something slammed the back of Hayden's head.

* * *

"Did I git him?"

Kate gaped at the man below. Dirt and splinters of wood covered the dark suit that stretched across his broad shoulders and long legs. A deep red stain soaked through the collar of his shirt, and next to him tongues of fire licked at the door-frame of Smokey's toolshed. He claimed to be with the FBI. Isn't that what he'd shouted when he banged on the door?

Kate swallowed the boulder in her throat. "Exactly what happened down there?"

"I wired the shed with C-4," Smokey Joe said. "Not enough to kill, just enough to slow down the enemy so we can take off. Now, did I git him with the log?"

"You got him." Oh God, did Smokey get him. Blood pooled in a dark red disk on the thick carpet of pine needles beneath the man's head.

"Is he down?" Smokey asked.

"Down." And possibly dead. Kate steadied her hands on the hood of Smokey's car.

She should have run. She should never have involved Smokey in something this dangerous. They'd spent the past twenty-four hours at target practice and "safeguarding" Smokey's house with security sensors and booby traps. What had she been thinking?

"Okay, time to git." Smokey fumbled for the door handle of his car, which sat on the mountain road that snaked above the cabin.

Kate didn't move, her gaze glued to the tongues of flame wicking a corner of the shed below. "The shed's on fire, it might spread." And kill the man if he wasn't already dead.

The rainless spring left the ground cover dry and brittle, prime tinder for the sparks popping off the shed. She couldn't leave that man down there with the fire. She was already responsible for the deaths of six women. "Stay here, Smokey. I'm going down to make sure he's okay and put out the fire."

She scrambled down the side of the mountain, gravity yanking her along pin-sharp needles and rocks. Her feet landed with a knee-jarring thud. A grumble sounded above her along with footsteps. She looked up and cried out, "Stay put, Smokey! You can't—"

Too late. Smokey was tumbling down the mountain in a cloud of silky dust and twigs. He landed at her feet, stood, and jammed a finger in her face. "Ain't no one gonna tell me what I can and can't do." He shifted the waistband of his baggy trousers. "You git the man, and I'll git the fire."

Kate wanted to tackle Smokey Joe and tie him to a pine tree, but she and the pine tree would most likely suffer injury in the process. Plus they didn't have time. The flames now licked at the shake roof of the shed. "The hose is ten paces forward, five left," she said. "Shed will be to your right. Aim at two o'clock."

She rushed to the man on the ground. He was deathly still except for the shallow rise of his chest and the line of crimson trickling from the side of his head. A red spark popped off the shed and landed next to his shiny Italian leather lace-up. She crushed the ember with her palm and jammed her hands beneath his wide shoulders, the jacket weave fine and smooth against her trembling fingers.

"Okay Mr. FBI Agent in the really nice suit, let's go." She rolled him over and dragged. His body slid easily along the dry needles, a steady trail of red snaking in his wake. When she got him next to the cabin, she yanked off her overshirt and slid it beneath his head. His breathing was shallow, his skin was chalky, and the blood continued to trickle. Carefully poking through his matted hair, she gasped when she spotted the inch-long gash.

He needed medical help ASAP. Reaching inside his suit coat pocket for a cell phone, she found a wallet. A spasm rocked her hand as it fell open, displaying a shiny badge. Hayden Reed was legit FBI. She continued to root through his jacket pockets and found a pen, a pair of handcuffs, and a small cinnamon candy. The candy was shiny red, the same color as the large circle of scarlet soaking her shirt beneath his head. She dug into his pants pockets. Keys. A tricked out utility knife. Another piece of candy. "Where's your damn phone?"

"You talking to me, Katy-lady?" Smokey Joe asked. He stood next to the shed, aiming the hose at the now smoldering wooden doors. Good. One crisis averted. One more to go.

"No, I'm talking to our guest, who I'm trying to keep from dying in your backyard." She reached into his back pants pocket, her fingers finally clamping around a phone. She aimed for the number nine when a hand snaked out and grabbed her wrist.

Before she could scream, Agent Hayden Reed shifted from under her and pinned her to the ground. His hands clamped down on her arms. His legs were leaden weights on her lower body. She was paralyzed. For the first time in two and a half years, she couldn't run.

A wave of fierce heat shot through her veins. But she could fight. She squared her shoulders, tensed her neck, and slammed her forehead into his stunned mouth.

\* \* \*

"Come on, Katy-lady, jist squeeze and squirt."

Kate looked at the gaping wound on the back of Agent Hayden Reed's head and at the bottle of Super Glue Smokey

Joe handed to her. They sat in the cabin's kitchen, Smokey perched on the edge of one chair, his eyes bright, Agent Reed in the other, his face expressionless.

Sweat slicked her hands, and she almost dropped the glue. "Smokey, are you sure this stuff is safe for cuts?"

"Do it," Agent Reed said with a quiet so loud she took a step back. "Now."

Her fingers tightened around the glue. At age sixteen, she left home for good and swore no one would ever talk to her in that tone of voice again. She opened her mouth but snapped it shut. She didn't need to be slapped with another count of assault and battery on a federal agent. She just needed to get Special Agent Hayden Reed patched up. Then she could run and get her Broadcaster Butcher business taken care of.

She tugged a curl of hair over the right side of her face and bent over Agent Reed's head. He didn't flinch as she squirted a stream of glue along the gash and pressed together the two pieces of flesh. Nor did he wince when she dabbed a warm washcloth at the small cut on his lip, compliments of her forehead. He'd taken off his suit coat and wore a soft, creamy shirt of Egyptian cotton. He smelled of laundry starch and cinnamon.

And blood. She smelled his blood.

She grabbed the crimson-soaked cloths on the table and tossed them in the sink. Then she picked up the glue and ground on the lid. Through it all, Agent Reed sat stone still. How could someone so silent say so much?

At last she turned toward him, her throat dry and tight. She didn't believe in coincidences. An armed FBI agent had landed on her doorstep twenty-four hours after another Butcher slaying, this one less than three hundred miles from her home. "What do you want?"

"Katrina Erickson."

Her legs gave way, and she backed into the counter in an effort to keep herself upright.

He didn't say anything but continued to look at her with that rock-hard expression. No, there was something beyond the cold stone, something hot and molten burning in the steel gray of his eyes.

Her fingers tightened on the counter's edge. Was this a man she could trust? Hell, would he even believe her? That had been the problem before. "And when you find her, this Katrina Erickson, what will you do?"

"Talk to her." His lips barely moved.

"About what?"

"About the man who attacked her three years ago."

The kitchen was cool, but sweat coated her palms. "What if she says she saw nothing, that the attacker was wearing a mask and dark bulky clothes?"

"I'll ask her to try to remember anything." For the first time since he took a seat in Smokey's kitchen chair, Agent Hayden Reed shifted his body. He leaned toward her, resting his elbows on his knees and holding out his hands as if to catch something. "I'll take anything, the color of his eyes behind the mask, the brand of his shoes, the sound of his voice, the way he smelled." His voice softened, a low but steady rumble. "Anything, Katrina, I'll take anything." The rawness shocked her. This man wanted the Butcher desperately, enough to bare his soul.

She dug her teeth into her bottom lip. "And when you get this information, what will you do?"

His outstretched hands curled into fists. "Hunt him down."

Kate could see this imposing, commanding man tracking down the evil that attacked her and killed six others. And she realized then that this FBI man in the fancy suit, great shoes, and crazy cinnamon scent would serve her purpose. She pried her fingers off the edge of the counter and picked up a pad of paper and a pen from the LOST MY ASS IN LAS VEGAS candy dish.

"Let's save us both a lot of time and energy," she said. She scribbled two lines, tore out the page, and tossed it on the table. "Here you go. The name and address of the man who attacked me. Now get out of my life."

# CHAPTER FOUR

*Wednesday, June 10, 11:31 a.m.*
*Mancos, Colorado*

Who in the Sam Hill is Katrina Erickson?"

Hayden didn't answer Smokey Joe, nor did the woman standing in front of him, her face bone-white except for the tiny slash of raised skin near her right eye.

A tremor rocked his hand as his fingertips traced the spiky series of letters and numbers on the paper Katrina Erickson had thrown on the table. He recognized the name and the address. He'd met the man, had interviewed him, could call a colleague and have this guy collared in the next fifteen minutes. He pictured six sets of bloodied, folded hands. Was this the beginning of an end? Or was a woman who would do anything to get back on the run manipulating him?

Hayden placed the paper on the table and flattened it with his palm. "You're telling me the man who stabbed you is Jason Erickson, your brother?"

"Yes." The word trembled on her lips.

"You're sure?"

"Yes," she said with more force.

His leg muscles tensed. He had to go slow, be thorough, follow the steps. He'd acted rashly only once in his life, although, in the end, that had served him well. "How do you know for certain your brother attacked you? You told police your attacker wore a mask and dark, bulky clothing."

Katrina picked up a dishtowel and scrubbed at the spotless counter. "I recognized his scar," she told the counter. "Three inches long with a jag at the right wrist. It showed above his glove as he stabbed me."

Hayden had seen that scar on the day he visited Jason Erickson at his workplace in Dorado Bay, Nevada. Time to establish Katrina's physical reaction to truth. Or lack of it. "How did he get the scar?"

"I gave it to him." No hesitation.

A truth teller. Good. Next step. "Why?"

The heel of her hand ground into the wadded dishtowel. "I hate him."

Another truth. In his careful study of Katrina Erickson, Hayden learned she was estranged from her family. Was she now unjustly fingering her brother because of the family rift? Go slow. Dig deeper. "How do I know you're not lying?"

"Kate Johnson don't tell no lies." The old man with the cloudy eyes had been still during the exchange, but now he jumped up, knocking over the kitchen chair. Smokey Joe lunged toward him but tangled his feet in the overturned chair rung.

Kate dropped the dishtowel and ran to Smokey Joe's side, grabbing him before he hit the floor. Then she righted the chair and helped him sit.

Smokey Joe stabbed a finger at him. "You hear me, G-man?" A tremor grabbed his hand and shook it, the bones rattling in the quiet kitchen. "She. Don't. Lie!"

Katrina's gaze fell to the ground, but not before Hayden read her face. It was a face he'd studied for hundreds of hours, one he saw when he lay in bed and didn't sleep. But her eyes were greener today and warmer, like the leaf color of a palo verde tree, and there was an odd sheen to them. That dampness looked as out of place as water puddles in the desert. She cared for Smokey Joe, which would work to his advantage.

"But she has lied, Smokey Joe. To you." Hayden paused just long enough to watch Katrina swallow. "Ask the woman who's been living with you for six months what her real name is."

Katrina's fingers wrapped around the back of Smokey's chair, her knuckles whitening.

"What's this pup yapping about, Kate? Why would G-man here call you a liar?"

"She'd lie to get away from here," Hayden went on. There was a time to go slow and a time to push. A brutal killer was on the loose, one who wasn't going to wait a full month between murders because he needed to complete the job. He needed to break all the mirrors. "She wants me gone, so she can run. Come on, *Katrina*, tell him. Tell your friend why you're on the run and who you really are." He paused again, another chance to let the power of his unspoken words thunder through her head. "Or I will."

Her gaze snapped to him, and despite the distance, he felt her burning anger. Taking a breath, she straightened her spine and squared her shoulders. He'd seen the move often, just before she began her "Justice for All" reports.

"My name is Katrina Erickson. Three years ago a man named Jason Erickson, my brother, attacked me in my home in Reno, Nevada. He stabbed me twenty-four times and left me to die. And I would have, except someone called nine-one-one. I got to the hospital and underwent surgery." She kept her voice smooth and modulated, as if reading from a teleprompter. This was the reporter, not the victim. "Two hours after the surgery, Jason came to me in the hospital. My head was covered in bandages so I couldn't see him, but I *felt* his dark, angry presence. And I heard him. He whispered in my ear that there'd been a terrible mistake, that I was supposed to die and that next time he'd do it right. I was intubated and half loopy with pain meds, but I remember him holding my hand, his hot breath against my ear."

The lines on Smokey Joe's face doubled as he leaned toward her voice.

"A few days later, when the doctor removed the tube from my throat, I told the lead detective that my brother, Jason, was my attacker, and that he'd been in my room. The detective said no one had entered my room other than medical personnel and that he had had an officer at the door the whole time. The doctor and nurses agreed, adding that the narcotics I was given for pain had most likely caused hallucinations. So the detective, who followed up with Jason just enough to discover we weren't on the best of terms, didn't even mention my brother in his formal report."

Something warm and prickly traveled up the back of Hayden's neck. The evidence and facts of the case *could* support Katrina's version of the attack. She and her brother had a violent history. But more than that, Hayden believed her. This story, told with details and clarity and a detachment that spoke volumes about pain and terror, wasn't told to entertain or obfuscate. She was telling the truth, the truth as seen through her eyes. He rubbed the skin along the back of his neck. The problem was, he'd heard a different truth from her brother, a truth that had been equally compelling. When Hayden interviewed Jason Erickson five months ago, he looked Katrina's brother in the eye as the younger man professed absolutely no insider knowledge of the Broadcaster Butcher slayings or of his sister's current whereabouts. Jason had been an open book, the reading easy. Nothing about Katrina's brother had set his internal radar blipping. And he was rarely wrong.

*I hate that you're never wrong. Hate that you're practically perfect, and you damn well know it.*

*Not now, Marissa*, he told the voice.

Had Jason attacked Katrina and the six other broadcasters? Had Hayden been wrong?

"Are you saying the coppers called you a liar?" Smokey asked.

"The technical term was *unreliable witness*," Kate said with a harsh laugh. "At one point, the detective and medical personnel had me believing I'd imagined the whole thing. I *imagined* seeing Jason's scar during the initial attack. I *imagined* the voice whispering in my ear and threatening to kill me. In the end, I figured my time and energy would be better spent fighting to get healthy and get my career back on track. So, I worked my butt off in rehab. Meanwhile, the police searched for clues, hunted for witnesses, looked for suspects..."

"...and found nothing," Smokey Joe said when she trailed off.

"Yes, Smokey, they found *nothing*." For the first time, Katrina's voice faltered, a quick hitch in her breath. "But Jason found me again, right after I left rehab."

Katrina turned to Hayden, her green eyes as sharp as shards of glass. With jerky hands, she yanked her chambray shirt from her shoulders, standing before him with tumbled hair and wearing a tight white tank top.

An unexpected warmth spread down his torso as his gaze

slid over the small swells of her half-exposed breasts, at their tight, stiff centers, the shadowed valley, the creamy curve of—

The clock above the sink stopped ticking. The shadows filtering through the window stilled. And his hot awareness of a beautiful woman's half-naked chest chilled.

"What the hell's going on?" Smokey Joe banged a fist on the table. "A man's got a right to know what's happening in his own kitchen."

Hayden closed the distance between him and Katrina, who was once again a victim. His fingers slid along the upper curve of her breast, where he slipped away the fabric just short of exposing her right nipple.

She sucked in a breath but didn't flinch.

Smokey Joe jumped to his feet. "What's going on, Katy-lady? You okay?"

"No." Hayden's lips barely moved as his finger slid along a pale red line etched in her breast. "This scar, it isn't supposed to be here. It wasn't in your medical records. It wasn't in the official police report. All reports indicated twenty-four stab wounds. Breasts noticeably untouched." On the surface, he kept his voice calm, but underneath, words and questions and scenarios started to hiss and bubble. "Were those reports wrong?"

She pushed away his hand. "No."

His jaw tensed as he pointed to the scar on her breast. "So this..."

"...is number twenty-*five*. From the second attack."

"What second attack?" Hayden asked. "There was no official report about a second attack. None of the investigators in Reno mentioned a second attack."

A harsh laugh fell from her twisted lips. "Trust me, Agent Reed, there was definitely a second attack." Once again, she turned toward Smokey Joe, directing her words at him. "Before I left rehab, I had a new security system installed in my condo, and Reno PD escorted me home. They assured me they were still on the hunt for my attacker and that they wouldn't stop until they found him. They promised to put an extra patrol in my neighborhood those first few days. They told me they were doing their job. They were doing everything possible to keep me safe. But that night Jason, dressed in the same dark clothes and mask, got into my condo. He stood over my bed. He stuck a knife into my chest." Her chest heaved and shoulders jerked.

Smokey Joe fumbled through the air and took her hand in his.

Hayden took a breath and processed this new information. It was logical that the Butcher attacked a second time. His MO had always been to kill. What surprised him was her reaction. He'd studied Katrina Erickson, he knew her type. She was strong and smart. "Why didn't you go to Reno PD? Why didn't you report the second attack?"

"What would the police say? 'Ooops! Sorry we screwed up. We'll do better next time'?" Katrina patted Smokey Joe's hand and guided him back into the chair. "I didn't report the attack, Agent Reed, because it wouldn't make a difference." This final statement had no force, no fire. The absence of anger spoke volumes.

"I see," Hayden said.

A flare fired in Katrina's eyes as she yanked her shirt over her breast. "What the hell do you *see*?"

"I see a woman who doesn't trust authorities, who was let down by those meant to protect her." His head dipped in a sober nod. "I see a woman who no longer believes in justice."

The last word hung between them, a fragile thread. For

years, her career in broadcast news revolved around justice.
Her reports had uncovered wrongs done to ordinary people,
crimes against society, and heinous acts against the human
spirit. Like him, she'd thrown her heart into the pursuit of
justice.

"Well, you're blind, because what you see standing before you right now, right here"—she stabbed a finger at her
chest—"is a stronger, smarter woman who refuses to be anyone's victim. All those months of rehab, of physical and
mental fortification, made me strong. So had being used as a
sharpening stone for a knife blade." She squatted in front of
Smokey Joe, taking his hands in hers. "After the second attack, I emptied my savings, hopped on my bike, and became
Kate Johnson. For two years I rode all over the country, just
me and my bike and lots of winding roads. I stayed in small,
out-of-the-way places where people didn't ask questions. I
paid cash for everything and went months without talking to
other human beings. Six months ago my savings ran out. I
was in Durango at the time, and I needed a job."

"And you found me." Smokey lowered his gaze to their
clasped hands.

"I found you." She brought their intertwined fingers to
her lips. She'd been the pro and told the tale. For Smokey.
When she turned from Smokey Joe to him, her face lost
all tenderness. *There, are you happy? Are you happy I hurt
Smokey? Are you happy you made me relive that hell?*

Hayden knew this story hadn't been easy, but they were
chasing evil, which invariably meant a walk through hell.
"Katrina, I'm sorry you—"

"You're *sorry*?" She dropped Smokey's hand and bolted
upright. "For what? For the scars that disfigure my face and
body? For the ineptitude of your law enforcement brothers?
For believing in a system that doesn't work?"

"It works."

"Like hell it does! It's a broken system, a broken world, Agent Reed, shattered and ugly and full of evil."

The force of her words, the power of her emotion, slammed him like a heat wave rolling across the desert.

Hayden worked with enough victims to know that no matter how loud he talked and how long he offered valid, substantiated arguments, Katrina wouldn't hear him, not at that moment. She wouldn't hear that the scars had faded, that law enforcement had not failed because he was still working the case, and that she was safe. Full of anger and fear, she was as deaf as Smokey Joe was blind.

Smokey scratched a spring of hair at the back of his head. "So this slasher fella, your brother, he has something to do with the Barbie murders?"

Katrina tilted her chin toward Hayden in a dare. "Absolutely."

Smokey pounded his fist on the table, the Las Vegas candy dish rattling. "Then stop your yammering at Kate, G-man, and git on that damn government-issued phone of yours and call someone to nab this guy."

"That's my intent, Mr. Bernard," Hayden said. He reached into his pocket and took out a set of handcuffs. Before anyone could blink, he slipped one circle of silver around Katrina's wrist.

"What the hell do you think you're doing?" she cried, trying to pull away.

He clicked shut the cuff. "I've been chasing you too long to let you out of my sight now."

She yanked her arm, the metal digging into her flesh. "I'm not going anywhere."

The second cuff locked around the rung of a kitchen chair. "I know."

He pulled out his phone, made his way to the living room, and dialed Parker Lord's direct line, his heart beating triple-time. Was this it? Was he finally closing in on the Butcher?

As he waited for his boss to answer, he spotted movement out of the corner of his eye, and he ducked just in time to see a candy dish with a picture of a donkey go flying past his ear. It slammed into the wall, where it shattered into hundreds of jagged tiny pieces. He turned and looked at the kitchen table where Katrina glared at him and Smokey Joe grinned.

* * *

*Wednesday, May 10, 2:30 p.m.*
*Colorado Springs, Colorado*

"It's like fucking Cinderella without the glass slipper, only shoeprints."

Lottie stared at the terraced set of planters that made up the slope of Shayna Thomas's backyard and shook her head. CSD already made a cast of the print found below Thomas's bedroom window, and now they were making a few more.

Detective Traynor pointed to the disturbed earth next to the red flag. "We found these large prints throughout the backyard. Looks like some kind of work boot."

"Check Thomas's bills. Find out if she has a lawn man and what size shoe he wears."

Detective Traynor brushed aside a leafy fern with brown, brittle tips. "But this one has us stumped. You're the shoe queen. What do you think?"

Lottie squatted, her old knees creaking as she stared at the boxy footprint comprised of wavy lines and the letters O and K. "I ain't ready to bet the grandkids' college education fund, but I think it may be some kind of orthotic. Line of ugly shoes called Ortho King. My doc keeps nagging me to get a pair." She'd hurt her back two years ago playing ball with one of the grandsons, and her doctor told her to get shoes with more support, but she couldn't give up her flashy heels. For the first twenty-two years of her life, she wore hand-me-down shoes, walking through this world in threadbare soles, scuffed toes, and other people's sweat. Her old hoofers deserved better. She gave her foot with its four-inch cheetah-print slingback a little jiggle.

Traynor squatted next to her. "Didn't Agent Reed say that the killer may have some kind of handicap or disfiguration?"

"Yeah, he did. Said it could be something unseen, like a stutter, or visible, like a limp." Lottie pointed to the odd shoeprint. "Get a cast made."

* * *

*Wednesday, June 10, 8:30 p.m.*
*Mancos, Colorado*

Agent Reed walked into Smokey's kitchen, a key dangling from his finger. "If I take off the cuffs, are you going to run?"

Kate eyed the key, debating if she should grab for it first or knock him off balance with a shoulder to his midsection and *then* snatch her ticket to freedom. "No."

He rubbed his swollen lip. "Are you going to head-butt me again?"

Only rookies would use the same offense twice. She would lunge for his legs. That would bring him down fast and hard. "No."

He laughed and dropped the key in his pocket. Kate stiffened in the chair. She hadn't expected the laugh. It was a low and rusty sound, as if he didn't do it often.

"If you're going to lie," he said when the chuckle tapered off, "you can at least try to be a little more convincing. You may want to work on the blinks. Two quick ones before each lie was a dead giveaway."

Pompous know-it-all. But he was right. She was a horrible liar, which is probably why she ended up in investigative journalism. She'd spent her on-air days in pursuit of truth. Now she just wanted to pursue any long and winding road that would take her far away from Agent Organized and Efficient.

Agent Reed had spent the past nine hours in Smokey's living room on the phone, issuing orders, mounting the cavalry, and trying to close in on a butchering madman. Early on he'd offered to take off her cuffs if she agreed to go to the local police station so he could work without worrying about her safety, but she'd made it clear she'd rather be shackled to one of Smokey Joe's kitchen chairs. From what she could tell from Agent's Reed's phone conversations and teleconferences, her brother, Jason, was missing from his home in Dorado Bay, a small resort town on the Nevada shores of Lake Tahoe. Police had found a week's worth of mail crammed in the mailbox, and neighbors hadn't seen him for days. Their mother, who lived in the same house, was also AWOL. No one at Jason's work had seen him for two weeks. With each dead end, she found herself one step closer to the edge of terror. Jason could be outside Smokey's cabin at this very moment.

Hayden didn't seem fazed. He made calls, took notes, and, when he reached a dead end, headed off in another direction without losing speed. On his last phone call she heard him make arrangements for him and his team, an elite FBI group out of Maine, to descend on Dorado Bay tomorrow. She should feel relieved. The power, the efficiency, the might of the U.S. government manifested in one Special Agent Hayden Reed was on the case, but all she felt was the need to run fast and far. She yanked at the cuff around her red wrist.

She'd sworn at age sixteen she would be in charge of where she went and what she did, but from the moment the FBI agent pinned her beneath him, she'd felt powerless, and in her world, there was nothing worse.

"I'm not the enemy," Agent Reed said softly as he sat in the chair next to hers.

She hadn't expected that either, the softness. Everything about Agent Reed was hard—the razor-sharp creases in his suit pants, the square jaw, the gunmetal eyes.

He reached for her face, as if to smooth back the curl hanging over her eye, but she jerked her head away. "I'm not either." She meant for her words to come out as a barb, but they landed in the air between them on a sigh. Today had been exhausting. Telling Smokey about her attack and reliving her past had been an emotional roller-coaster.

But she'd get through this, past Agent Reed, and back on the road, and sooner rather than later.

A feather-light set of fingers slid along her wrist.

"If you try to run, I'll catch you," Agent Reed said as if he could he read her mind. "You realize that, don't you? I'll find you and keep you safe until the Butcher is behind bars. Don't fight me on this."

Fight? The mighty Agent Reed had obviously never run across someone like her. She fought monsters in her childhood, scrapped and scraped her way through college, and battled her way to a coveted anchor spot in broadcast news before age thirty. She may have been on the run the past two years, but that didn't change who she was at her core.

She faked a yawn and held up her wrist, metal clanking against metal. "I'm too tired to fight tonight. Just take off the cuffs so I can go to my room and go to bed." But only after she checked the window in the cabin loft. It was probably too small to slip through, but she had to try.

Agent Reed checked his watch then reached into his pocket and took out the key. "Actually, you will go to your room and *pack*. Tonight I'm taking you to the FBI field office in Denver. You need protection."

"I don't think so." Law enforcement had already failed her twice. "In case you haven't noticed, I'm doing much better on my own. I don't need your buddies in snappy blue suits."

"But I need you." He stood and pushed in his chair. "If your brother is behind these murders, you're important to me and the U.S. government. As a material witness in a capital crime, you'll need to testify against him. There's no way I'm letting you run away."

For a moment she had the urge to laugh. There was no way Hayden Reed or anyone else was going to get her in a courtroom full of people who'd stare at her, point, whisper, and turn their heads when she met their gazes straight on. It happened to her countless times since she'd been stabbed. The grotesque was fascinating.

"I'm not going to Denver," she said matter-of-factly. Agent Reed so loved facts. "I can't leave Smokey alone."

"He can go with you."

"And disrupt his life even more than I already have?" Smokey Joe had dropped into bed right after dinner, emotionally and physically exhausted. He didn't even ask for a rain check on their nightly domino game. "If you have any ounce of compassion behind that man-of-steel persona, you will not drag him into this any more than he is."

He stood motionless for the longest time, and she pictured the gears in his brain whirring and clicking as he weighed the facts and analyzed their options. "You care about him." There was his non-question thing again. It drove her nuts, and so did the fact he didn't know what he was talking about.

"This is just a job," she insisted.

"A *job*?"

"Something to pay the bills." She straightened the dominoes on the table and made a note to tell Smokey's caseworker that he liked his nightly game. "So what happens with Smokey?"

"I'll call social services and get them out here first thing in the morning."

She shook her head. "They'll put him in a temporary group home. He doesn't do well in institutional settings. He flooded the last one he was in, and it wasn't an accident. He needs one-on-one attention, someone to be with him, but not to micromanage his days." Someone like her. But her time with Smokey was over. For now she'd resigned to go with Agent Reed to the Denver field office. She pictured that upstairs window. Unless she got a chance to run.

"Don't worry about Smokey Joe. I'll find him a safe place."

"Not a group home?"

"Not a group home."

"And you'll make sure he ends up in a place where he's not surrounded by buildings and cars and noise. He needs room to breathe." Smokey had spent two years in a hole in the ground in a North Vietnamese prison camp and had an insatiable need for fresh air and wide open spaces.

"I'll find a place with plenty of space." She opened her mouth, but he held up a hand. "I'll take care of everything."

And she believed him, because Special Agent Hayden Reed was the kind of man who'd take care of Smokey and the rest of the free world.

He finally circled his hand around her wrist and turned it so the lock was faceup. "Give me his caseworker's number, and I'll make arrangements for tomorrow."

"What about tonight?"

He inserted the key and turned, the cuff clicking open. "We'll stay here."

"We? You're *sleeping* here?"

"No, I'm *working* here." The cuff slipped off, but his fingers remained circled about her wrist. "I have plenty to keep me busy."

She hopped to her feet. "But—"

"Would you prefer I set up a team of deputies from the sheriff's department to stand guard?"

She tried to shrug off his hand, but his fingers tightened, a golden manacle that was stronger than tempered steel. Agent Efficient was enough. "Fine. Work here. If you get tired, there are pillows and blankets in the hall closet." When he finally let go, she took off up the stairs to her loft. Footsteps sounded behind her, and she spun and glared at him. "Is this really necessary?"

He answered with a pair of raised brows. She stood in the doorway with her arms crossed as he searched under her bed, in her closet, and through her drawers. He tugged at the tiny glass window at the V of the loft.

She let loose an exasperated sigh. "You're being ridiculous. The Butcher can't get through that window."

"I'm not worried about someone trying to get *in*." Damn him. And damn those eyes. "I promise, Katrina, if you make any attempt to leave this place, I'll cuff you to the bed."

She wanted to swipe off the unbearably confident look on

his face, but it was his world, his way. He wasn't giving up control. He was Mr. Unflappable.

Oh yeah? She'd seen that flash in his eyes when she'd taken off her shirt in the kitchen. He was Super Agent, but he was also a man.

Kate uncrossed her arms and slipped off her overshirt. A half smile slipping onto her lips, she tossed her shirt to the ground and sunk onto the quilt covering her bed. She slid her fingers along her thighs and up her torso. Finally, she raised her hands to the brass headboard. "I'd love for you to cuff me to this bed." She licked her lips. "Pleeeease."

Agent Reed's entire upper body tensed. She saw it in his shoulders, in his jaw, and in his hand as he slid his palm along his tie as if to straighten the brilliant splashes of yellow and orange scattered across the length of silk. His gaze slid from her bare feet and up her legs. An unexpected tingle coursed through her midsection as he lingered on her breasts before sliding to her wrists. A soft breath caught in his throat, and she didn't need to be a mind reader to know he wasn't thinking about the Butcher.

With her hands still in the bound position, she waggled her fingers at him.

He blinked and took a step back. Then he spun on his shiny Italian lace-ups and practically raced down the stairs.

Mission accomplished. She'd just shaken the unshakable Hayden Reed, and if she wasn't so damned furious at him, she'd laugh.

\* \* \*

Hayden sat on the couch and waited for exhaustion to roll over him like a bulldozer, because between Tucson and the latest Butcher slaying, he must be suffering the effects of serious sleep deprivation. That's the only explanation for his reaction to Katrina as she begged him to handcuff her to the bed. If he'd been sharper, he wouldn't have been struck speechless. Granted, he still would have noticed the swells of her breasts, the tumbled curls of her hair, and curvy hips straining against her low-riding jeans. And appreciated it all. Any man with eyes would have. But he was the lead investigator in the hunt for the Butcher. She was a victim and a witness, and, as his teammate Hatch would say, never the twain shall meet.

He unbuttoned his cuffs and snapped back the fabric. Time to get his head off Katrina and onto the Butcher. He picked up his phone and punched in a number.

"Shouldn't you be in bed, or do pretty boys like you not need beauty sleep?" Lottie's throaty voice cackled on the other end. "But I'm glad you called, Reed, 'cause I got something that's going to knock you on your ass."

Like sassy Katrina stretched out on a bed and inviting him to join her? He blinked away the vision, and focused on Sergeant King. "Shoot."

"Got us a witness," Lottie said with a note of triumph.

"What?" Witnesses had been nonexistent at all the other crime scenes, but then again, Shayna Thomas's murder wasn't like the others. He pictured those unbroken mirrors.

"You heard right, a witness. A fourteen-year-old kid who lives across the street saw someone on Thomas's front porch the night she died, and I don't think he's shitting us. The kid snuck out of his house through his second-story bedroom window to go meet his thirteen-year-old girlfriend. He swaps spit for a while and comes home around ten fifteen. He climbs the trellis and shimmies in through the window. After he gets inside, he turns to shut the pane and sees someone on the porch across the street. Light's on so the kid gets a pretty good look at her."

Hayden almost dropped the phone. "Her?"

"Thought you'd pick up on that one. Yep. The witness swears that Shayna Thomas opened her door and let a woman into her house. Looked like a granny. Gray shoulder-length hair. Shapeless pink dress with flowers. He never saw a face and could only describe her build as average, not fat, not thin."

Hayden blinked, trying to process this information. "A woman. Are you sure?"

"The kid was serious, and he was putting his ass on the line, admitting he'd snuck out."

When Hayden hung up the phone, he slid a finger along the sharp crease of his pants.

Most serial killers were men, yet the young boy across the street swore he saw a woman. It's possible the unsub could have entered the house in drag. Women like Shayna Thomas would be much more inclined to open the door to a woman than to a man. Or it's possible the killer could have a female accomplice. Most serial killers worked alone. They were social deviants and craved singular power. However, he'd studied a few cases of partner serial killings, and in those cases, there was clearly a dominant/subservient dynamic. It's possible the woman in the pink dress could gain them entry, and the Butcher would perpetuate the criminal act.

Was he looking for two people? Like Jason Erickson and his missing mother? It would explain the contradictory signals, the raging number of stab wounds but the folded, peaceful hands, the broken mirrors but the spotless crime scenes.

Had he been wrong? Searching all this time for a single offender when he should have been hunting for two?

# CHAPTER FIVE

*Thursday, June 11, 9 a.m.*
*Tucson, Arizona*

Y ou've done gone and brung me to hell."

"The locals call it Tucson," Hayden said as he took the duffel from Smokey Joe's hand and put it in the trunk of his SUV, which was parked in long-term parking at the Tucson airport.

"How hot is it?" Smokey wiped at the sweat beaded on his forehead.

"About 110 degrees. But it's a dry heat." Hayden shut the trunk and walked to the passenger side, where Kate reached for the rear door. He grabbed her wrist. She jumped, her pulse spiking beneath his fingertips. Quickly, he dropped her hand, refusing to contemplate at length the spike in his own pulse. "The handle," he said. "It's hot." He took a handkerchief out of his pocket, lined his hand, and opened her door. "Give it a minute. I'll get the AC going."

She hugged her bag to her chest and looked the other way.

She'd given him the silent treatment all morning. He figured part of the reason was that she was still mad at him for putting her in protective custody. The other part: She hated being out in the open. The moment they turned onto the highway, she popped on her sunglasses and ducked lower in the seat, a clear reminder that she was a victim and that her sexual come-on last night was designed only to get a rise out of him because, right now in her mind, he was one of the bad guys.

"You've spent some time in hell?" Smokey asked as Hayden cranked the engine and air conditioner.

"Some."

Smokey turned to Kate, who was climbing into the backseat. "Did you know about this, Kate? You know G-man here was going to leave me in a furnace?"

"He told me he was going to bring you someplace safe."

Early this morning he'd talked with Smokey Joe's caseworker and an advocate at the veterans hospital, and both agreed with Katrina that Smokey did not do well in group situations. After exhausting a number of alternatives, Hayden made arrangements with Maeve, his mother-in-law, to house Smokey Joe as a guest for the next few days. Smokey would be safe and out of the way, and, frankly, after the accident, Maeve could use the company. Hardly a conventional move, but Parker's team was known for its unconventional approaches.

He'd explained to Kate that Maeve was a close family friend who lived in the desert outside of Tucson and had cared years for her husband, who suffered from Alzheimer's. "She knows how to handle people with special needs," he'd assured Kate. "And there's plenty of open space and not many people. He'll be safe." Kate reluctantly agreed only when the caseworker told her that the only other option right now was a group home.

With Smokey Joe sulking in the front seat and Kate stone-faced and staring out the window in the backseat, he guided the SUV away from the airport and into the foothills of the Catalina Mountains. They followed the road through scrappy desert and heat waves to a sun-baked adobe house with a hummingbird garden out front.

When his mother-in-law opened the door, she hugged Hayden and smiled at Kate and Smokey Joe. "I'm glad you're here, Mr. Bernard," Maeve said. "Please come in."

Smokey didn't budge, and Katrina grabbed his elbow and dragged him into the entryway.

Maeve led them to a sunroom. "Can I get you some coffee, Mr. Bernard? Or how about a lemon muffin or fresh strawberries?"

Smokey crossed his arms over his chest and scowled like a two-year-old. Kate, who took a seat in a wicker chair near a large potted palm, looked like she wanted to give him a swat.

Maeve poured a cup of coffee and handed it to Hayden. "How was your flight, Kate? I'd ask Hayden, but I'm sure he spent the whole time working."

"Uh…fine," she said, sinking further into the shade of the palm. Hayden knew being out in public today would be difficult for loner Kate, but Maeve was good with difficult situations and people. Hayden studied his mother-in-law, noting that she looked tired this morning, her face thin and waxen behind her carefully applied makeup. Unlike Kate, his mother-in-law wasn't good at being alone.

As for him, he hadn't been alone for days, thanks to the voices booming through his head.

*Found another footprint. Some kind of orthotic.*

*Got us a witness…woman in a pink dress.*

*Here you go. The name and address of the man who attacked me. Now get out of my life.*

Katrina's voice, the last, echoed the loudest, probably because it went nicely with the vision of her that refused to
leave his head, the one of her stretched across that bed. He
straightened his tie and reminded himself she was the key to
stopping the Butcher. That's why he kept thinking about her.
His quasi-obsession was quite logical.

"And why do they call you Smokey?" Maeve was asking
when he turned his attention back to the group seated in the
sunroom.

"Smoked a lot of weed. Got any?" The wiry tuffs of the
old soldier's eyebrows narrowed, and Hayden swallowed a
laugh.

"Smokey!" Kate said through pinched lips.

"No, I'm afraid I don't," Maeve said.

Smokey snorted. "Didn't figure a broad like you would."

"Perhaps you'd like to put your things away," Maeve
went on, unruffled. "Let me take your bag."

"Ain't no invalid. I can carry it myself."

"Well then let me show you to your—"

"Can't see a damn thing, lady. Why the hell would you
show me anything?"

Hayden watched as Katrina's creamy white skin drained
of all color but for the splash of freckles across her nose. She
opened her mouth, but Hayden shook his head.

Next to him, Maeve's polite smile didn't waver. "I'm
fully aware of your disability, Mr. Bernard."

"I'm blind, lady. Call it what it is."

Maeve set her coffee cup on its saucer with a louder-than-
expected clank. "Okay, blind man, grab your damn bag and
follow me."

Smokey's upper body rocked in a small jolt, and something that sounded suspiciously like a laugh tripped over his
lips. "You always this bitchy?"

"Only when the people around me are acting like jack-asses."

\* \* \*

*Thursday, June 11, 10:10 a.m.*
*Colorado Springs, Colorado*

Lottie felt the gears moving notch by notch, and today she and her navy stilettos with yellow polka dots were behind the wheels of justice pushing hard. Last night the wheels got a bit of grease from that kid who claimed to see a woman in a pink dress standing on Thomas's front porch the night she died, and this morning justice got another little nudge when Lottie had an unexpected visit from one of Shayna Thomas's coworkers.

"Tell me everything you know about the slug," Lottie told the blond-haired woman with the plastic boobs.

The woman sitting in front of her was Sue Mathis, a weathergirl from the television news station where Shayna Thomas had worked. Lottie couldn't help but think the buxom journalist had a bit of plastic in her brain, too. Thomas had been killed more than forty-eight hours ago, and the question had been asked over and over, "Did Shayna Thomas ever complain about anyone stalking her?"

Silicone Sue finally had a lightbulb moment. "You know, I didn't think it was important at first, because Shayna didn't make a big deal out of it."

Lottie took a deep breath. "Ms. Mathis, at this point, everything is important. Please tell me what you know about the stalker."

"I don't think I ever heard Shayna call him a stalker. She

mentioned that she kept bumping into him, at the grocery store, the bank, clubs. Kind of creeped her out."

"Did she know him?"

"She didn't say. She just said he'd been popping up more and more."

"Did she ever tell you anything about him? What he looked like? What kind of car he drove? How he was dressed?"

"Nothing. She mentioned him two weeks ago while we were at a coworker's retirement party. It was a pretty light conversation, cocktail chatter. She made a joke about the whole thing."

Lottie continued to drill Sue Mathis until Detective Traynor poked his head into her office. "Hey, Sarge, time for the press conference. Chief wants you front and center."

\* \* \*

*Thursday, June 11, 10:15 a.m.*
*Tucson, Arizona*

"Can I get you more coffee, Kate?" Maeve asked when she returned to the sunroom.

Kate sunk deeper into her chair. "No, thank you. I'm fine." It was odd, being in this strange, sun-filled house, try-ing to chat with a stranger. As a broadcast journalist, she had been able to talk to strangers, hold her own against politi-cians and powerbrokers, and make small talk to put sources at ease, but the social muscles that had served her well in broadcasting had atrophied in the past three years. Now she felt like her brain and mouth suffered a serious disconnect.

Kate pulled a lock of hair over the right side of her face.

"Hayden, uh, went to check on the drip system in the garden. He noticed that a few plants looked dead."

"He's a good boy." Maeve poured herself a glass of orange juice from the frosted carafe. "Ever since my husband died, Hayden's been so good about fixing things around this place."

An image of Hayden with a tool belt around his waist popped into Kate's mind, and she almost giggled. The image was silly because Hayden Reed wasn't a hammer-and-nail kind of guy. He tackled bigger things, like people. She slid her thumb along the rim of her coffee cup. That's what Hayden liked to do, fix people.

In the single day they'd been together, she'd spotted him looking at her often, as if trying to figure out how to fix her broken world, but there weren't enough tools in anyone's tool belt to put her back together. Not that she wanted her old life. Despite always looking over her shoulder, she'd found an unexpected contentment as she traveled the back roads on her bike and settled in with Smokey Joe. She realized that for once in her life she wasn't fighting against someone or for something. She hadn't known peace as a child or in college and certainly not in her broadcast news days, but the past two and a half years had been oddly fulfilling. Until Agent Reed snatched it all away.

As she took another sip from her coffee cup, a loud thud sounded from the back of the house followed by "Dammit to hell" and a very Smokey Joe–like growl.

Kate swallowed a groan. "Smokey's really not that bad, not once you get past the rough edges."

"Oh, we'll get on fine." Maeve smiled over the rim of her glass. "Hayden's right. It'll be good for me to have some company right now, especially after the funeral last week."

Kate's cup stilled halfway to her mouth. "Funeral?"

Maeve set down her juice with a clank, lines marring her forehead. "I'm sorry, dear. I assumed Hayden told you about Marissa and the accident? It's consumed both of us the past two weeks."

Buttoned-up Hayden was hardly the show-and-share type. "Marissa?"

"My daughter." At Kate's look of confusion, Maeve added, "Hayden's wife."

"Wife?" Coffee sloshed over the cup and burned her fingers. "Hayden's married?" She couldn't imagine Hayden married to anything but his job.

"The marriage ended long ago. It's probably been at least seven years." A wash of sadness slipped over the older woman's face, and Kate could tell she still had fond feelings for her daughter's ex-husband. "Anyway, two weeks ago Marissa died in a car accident and—"

"Drip system's fixed." Hayden walked into the room, wiping his hands on a paper towel. "Three of the sprinkler heads had snapped off."

Maeve planted an accusing look on him. "I was just telling Kate about Marissa's accident."

Hayden folded the towel and set it on the table next to the tray. "It doesn't concern her," Hayden said, his words clipped and cool. "Time to get back to the airport. Flight to Denver takes off at noon."

Maeve's frown deepened, and Kate's own lips turned down. Hayden straightened his cuffs three times before he headed out of the room, his shoulders a degree or two less than erect, and Kate wondered what weighed him down. Regret? Sadness? Her entire life she hadn't been shy about releasing her emotions, and she couldn't imagine the weight a man like Hayden, the type of person who kept things close to the chest, must carry beneath that exquisitely tailored, buttoned-up suit. He seemed very human.

"Katrina!" Hayden called from the entryway. The steely edge was back, reminding her who he was and why he was in her life.

As she thanked her host, the sound of shattering glass rent the air. She and Maeve rushed down the hallway to a big, light-filled bedroom along the back of the house. Smokey stood next to the window, bits and pieces of what had been a porcelain teapot at his feet on the tile floor.

"Damn old hands," he muttered.

Kate couldn't wrench her gaze from the broken pieces of glass: a bodyless spout, cracked handle, and dozens of splintered slivers and chunks. Another broken mess.

"It's okay." Maeve swished her hands through the air. "Just an old garage-sale teapot." She waltzed out of the room and came back with a dustpan and broom. Kate helped the older woman sweep the glass into a trash can she'd found in the attached bathroom.

When Maeve left with the trash can, Kate said, "Clear."

Smokey remained at the window, and he raised his hands and fumbled at the latch. "I didn't mean to break her teapot." He tugged harder at the window, his hands and body shaking. "You tell her that, okay? Tell her I'm sorry."

Kate settled her hand on his. Together they pushed the latch until the window swung open. "I will."

Smokey Joe stood at the window breathing deeply, and the tremors released the hold on his body.

"I need to leave now," she said.

He mumbled something about living in an oven and then something with the word *safe* in it.

As she stared at his stooped back, she realized this was probably the last time she'd see him, except perhaps when she stopped by his cabin to pick up her bike. "Be nice to Maeve. She seems like a good person."

This didn't merit even a grunt from the old man. She turned to go when he muttered, "On the nightstand. Something for you."

She found a small teal tourmaline angel sitting next to an alarm clock. Her throat tightened as she traced its single wing. She'd planned to toss the pendant last month when she'd accidentally broken off the other wing and cracked the stone, but Smokey wouldn't hear of it.

"Ain't nothing wrong with a one-winged angel," he'd said and put it in the zipper pocket of his wallet. "Kinda like the idea of a few gimps up above."

She'd laughed with him then, but now she wasn't laughing. "This is yours."

"No, you take it. So you don't forgit me."

Her fingers tightened around the angel. Then she carefully set it on the nightstand. "No. You keep it." A character like Smokey would be impossible to forget.

She hurried out of the room and met Hayden, who was talking softly with Maeve in the foyer, his hand resting on her shoulder. Tears pooled in the corners of the older woman's eyes.

Kate must have made some noise or movement, because Hayden's head popped up. When he spotted her, he gave Maeve's arm a squeeze and kissed her cheek.

Kate headed for the door but stopped and reached into her bag. "Here." She handed Maeve a small box of paper clips. "You might need these. If Smokey has a nightmare, hand him a few."

Maeve took them, her forehead lined.

"He worked in transport on a medical evac helicopter in Vietnam. A few times he used safety pins to keep body parts together. In his nightmares, he asks for them. I didn't want to give him sharp pins, so I gave him paper clips. They seem to help."

Maeve nodded thoughtfully. "I'll remember that."

"And if you're okay with it, give him a...a...hug." Her throat tightened. Two arms. Her arms. With the power to stop a war. "That helps, too."

* * *

*Thursday, June 11, 1:05 p.m.*
*Dorado Bay, Nevada*

He turned off the television and smiled.

Chaos was everywhere—in the Mideast, on Wall Street, and in Colorado Springs, where a short, fat black woman who looked more like a grandma than a cop was leading the charge to find Shayna Thomas's murderer. Sergeant Lottie King had been on the news for two days straight, promising that her ever-growing team of able-bodied law enforcers would crisscross the globe until they found the vile creature who killed Shayna Thomas.

Silly old woman. He wasn't a vile creature. He was actually quite meticulous, and he was rather close by, a few states away in a picture-perfect town on the northern tip of Lake Tahoe in Nevada. And for the record, there was no chaos in his little corner of the world. All was going according to plan. Broadcasters were dying, and law enforcement officials everywhere were hunting for the Broadcaster Butcher.

He didn't like the name the news media had assigned to him. It was too coarse and brutish. He possessed much more finesse than a butcher, a precision worthy of admiration by the masses. He stretched out his right leg, which was bothering him again. When it was all said and done, it wasn't about the attention, or even the power he got from the blood of the six women he'd murdered. It was all about Katrina. This one woman eluded him, but not for long. FBI Special Agent Hayden Reed would see to that.

Yesterday, while watching a news report from Colorado Springs, he'd spotted Agent Reed, who, as usual, stood in the background, watching and waiting. Reed had been the first one to connect the Santa Fe and Boise slayings to Katrina Erickson's attack three years ago. Such a brilliant man and a valuable ally. He had high hopes that Agent Reed would track down Katrina, because in the end, it really was all about her, about finding her and silencing her.

His right leg twitched.

The one thing he couldn't control—his anger—uncurled and clawed its way through his body. He pictured his knife plunging in and out of Katrina's lifeless body and the blood frothing over lips that would never talk again.

*"And this is Katrina Erickson, reporting for KTTL's 'Justice for All.' "*

Never again. No, never, ever again.

He drew in a deep breath, the oxygen fanning the fire that lived within his belly. The fire spread lower, licking at his groin and heating the blood rushing to his midsection. Yes, he would find Katrina and take pleasure—his greatest—in killing her. His hand stroked the front of his trousers. He imagined a world without Katrina. He stroked harder, faster. A world without fear.

His hand froze. His anger, the hot pulsing inferno within, was dashed by that wave of glacial fear, the blood-chilling realization that she knew the truth.

He pried his hand from his now limp dick and reached for his phone. His hand shook as he dialed Jim—Just Jim. Jim didn't have a last name or a conscience. What he did have was a love for money. People like Jim came in handy because they were so easy to manipulate.

The phone buzzed eight times before Just Jim picked up. "'Lo," said a groggy voice.

"It's me," he said. "You failed to call this morning at nine with your status report."

"I was on a fucking plane, surrounded by too fucking many people headed for the hellhole of Tucson."

Tucson? "Your assignment is to follow Agent Reed, who is in Colorado Springs."

A sharp laugh cut through the phone line. "You obviously haven't checked your e-mail."

He despised people laughing at him, almost as much as he despised anything that got him off schedule. He hadn't checked his e-mail because it wasn't four yet.

"Well, you may want to check. I sent you a picture. I think your FBI guy found *her*."

His hand grew slick with sweat. "Are you sure?"

"I've been on his tail for two days and finally got a look at her in the airport. She fit the basic description. Slim, about five-foot-eight. Her hair wasn't dark brown, but reddish-brown with loopy curls to her shoulders. She wore a long-sleeved shirt, a scarf, and big sunglasses. I'm pretty sure it's the woman you want."

He didn't need *pretty sure*. He needed absolute certainty. He flexed his fingers, once, twice, three times before he could convince them to flick on his computer screen three hours before schedule.

"Now don't forget you owe me another five grand. I expect it tomorrow in—"

He stopped listening and stared at the woman captured by Just Jim's camera.

It was Katrina.

The one person who still held power over him.

\* \* \*

*Thursday, June 11, 3 p.m.*
*Reno, Nevada*

"You ready to call it quits, Robyn? It's so damn hot my shoes are sticking to the concrete."

Robyn Banks ignored her cameraman, who had been complaining about something or other for the past three hours. She'd been staked out at the Reno airport, trying to get a glimpse of Katrina Erickson, who she was sure was coming back to town.

Robyn was the only reporter so far to make the connection. Jason Erickson, the man the FBI wanted for questioning in conjunction with the Broadcaster Butcher slayings, was Katrina's brother. Katrina had left northern Nevada after the Butcher—possibly her brother—attacked her three years ago. When the FBI nabbed little brother, Katrina would be free to return home. Robyn licked her lips, careful not to smudge her lipstick. Katrina Erickson coming home would be the juiciest story on the nightly news. Robyn wanted this so bad she could taste it. Katrina served in a crystal bowl. Whipped cream and a cherry on top.

Katrina's attack was big news three years ago, and so was her disappearance. Rumors ran rampant when Katrina fell off the face of the earth. Some speculated her attacker found her after she was released from rehab and hacked her body into such minuscule pieces that no one could identify her. Others buzzed about Katrina having a nervous breakdown and being locked up in a mental institution. Hell, Robyn even heard someone say Katrina lived in BF, Kentucky, and made beaded jewelry for a living.

She had no idea where Katrina had been for the past two and a half years, but every instinct that made her a damn good reporter told her Katrina Erickson was coming home, which was a good thing, because Katrina owed her. The bitch stole something right out from under her.

Robyn wanted something in return.

A nice, fat, juicy news story covering the reappearance of Katrina Erickson would do just fine. It had been a long time since one of Robyn's stories led off the news hour. Hell, it had been a long time since she'd covered the biggies and the breakers.

She wanted Katrina Erickson's story. No. She needed it.

"Are you sure Erickson is going to show today?" her cameraman asked.

"No." All she knew was Katrina would have to come home eventually, and Robyn would be here to greet her.

"Let's knock off then."

Robyn shook her head. "One more hour. There's another plane landing in thirty minutes from Chicago. We'll stick around for that, and if Katrina doesn't show, we'll leave."

Her cameraman grunted. "Tell me again why you're so anxious for me to shoot this woman?"

"Because shooting her with my nine millimeter would land me in jail."

# CHAPTER SIX

*Thursday, June 11, 3:30 p.m.*
*Denver, Colorado*

**K**ate sat in the small conference room on the second floor of the FBI's Denver Field Office and pretended to ignore the people pretending not to stare at her.

"Can I get you a cup of coffee?" Agent Sankey asked. He was the young FBI agent Hayden had ordered to babysit her. "Or how about a bottle of water?"

"No, thank you." *But you can stop staring at me.* She pulled the collar of her shirt around her neck and pushed her sunglasses farther up the bridge of her nose. What was taking Hayden so long?

"We should be getting you out of here soon," he continued in an overly serious voice.

She gave him an absent nod. Away from Smokey Joe's cabin, she felt exposed, a walking target for the Butcher's knife and the object of stares and whispers. The airports and planes today as she and Hayden traveled to Tucson and then to Denver had been hellish, teeming with thousands of people. The all-seeing Hayden recognized her panic early on, and he staked himself at her side, literally, her body tucked into his most of the day. In a cloud of cinnamon-scented air, she'd felt safe. And she hadn't felt that way in almost three years. She took comfort in the loaded gun hidden beneath his fancy suit coat, in the sheer size of him, but mostly in his eyes. Nothing would get past that steely stare, including the Butcher.

And she knew Hayden was right; Smokey was safe. Grumbling, but out of danger. Now there was a brilliant move. On the flight to Denver, Kate realized that Maeve, who had just lost her daughter, needed someone just as much as blind Smokey did. Hayden, a master of reading and fixing people, took care of them both with a single swift, efficient move. Really, he was amazing if you could get over the fact that he was controlling and almost inhumanly focused on his job.

If she were still in the broadcast business, she'd be digging into the quiet, controlled FBI profiler's past, because there must be a juicy human interest story behind his granite façade. She'd seen that moment when he begged her for information about the Butcher, when he'd bared his soul, and she'd seen a flicker of desire when she'd stretched out on her bed begging for handcuffs. People so buttoned up were usually hiding something.

At that moment, the man in her thoughts walked out of an office at the far end of the corridor. As he made his way toward her, she noticed she wasn't the only one getting stares.

Hayden was more than easy on the eye. She took off her sunglasses and set them on the table. He could have had a career in front of the camera. He had hard, chiseled good looks with eyes the color of a storm just before it shook the skies and a tall, muscled body, all wrapped up in a shiny suit of quiet but bone-deep confidence.

But it was funny—for a man who made his living as an observer, he seemed unaware of the effect he had on women. He was oblivious to the flirty smile of a barista in the airport coffee shop, the casual touch of the flight attendant, and the come-hither look of one of his colleagues down the hall.

Was Hayden that consumed with his work? With the Butcher? Or was he reeling from the recent death of his ex-wife? She could ask him, but he'd quip out his standard, "It doesn't concern you." Unfortunately for her, everything in her life right now concerned Agent Reed, because he was making arrangements for her protective custody.

When he walked into the conference room, his face was more serious than normal. "Are you ready?"

Ready to give up her freedom? To hand over control of her future to a system that had failed her? She sunk deeper into the chair. Like she had a choice.

Hayden handed a folder to Agent Sankey then turned to her. "In ten minutes Agent Sankey will take you downstairs to meet agents Schupp and Gant, who will take you to a safe house. Either Schupp or Gant will be on duty around the clock. Listen to me, because this is key. You won't be able to go outside on your own, nor will you be allowed to contact anyone by phone or e-mail, including Smokey Joe."

Her fingertips bit into the leather chair as he rattled off more directives. He might call it protective custody, but she called it prison. Already, the walls closed in on her, and she snagged in a long breath.

"I know it will be hard for you to be cooped up in the house," Hayden went on. "So I've arranged for the custody team to take you out for a daily drive along a secure route."

Perfect. Agent Efficient had thought of everything. "Care to tell me what time I can change my underwear?"

Agent Sankey hid a laugh behind a cough.

Something flashed in Hayden's cool, gray eyes. Anger? Confusion? Desire? She couldn't tell because he reached into his pocket, took out his wallet, and slipped out his card. "I like to be thorough."

"Agent Obscenely Thorough," she said with a smile. "Maybe you should have a new badge made up." His jaw ticked, and she took perverse pleasure that she'd found a way to shake this granite-faced man who'd taken control of her foreseeable future, because right now she was powerless. For more than two years she'd taken care of herself, kept herself safe, but now her life was in someone else's hands. And her brother, who already killed six other women and who promised to finish the butcher job on her, was on the loose.

Hayden handed her his card. "If you need anything at any time, no matter where you are, contact me."

"And you'll don your superhero cape and come to my rescue," she said without a hint of humor.

His hand settled on her shoulder. The touch should have been steely and cool, but it warmed her to her toes. "I'm going to keep you safe, Kate."

Kate. He'd called her Kate in a voice steady and strong but softened by a hitch of breath. Why did he have to call her Kate? And why did she take so much comfort in the sound of her name on his lips and the warmth of his touch? It was easier to dislike him when he called her Katrina, the name assigned to her by the woman who gave birth to her.

"I know," she said. As much as she hated his controlling ways, she knew Hayden was not the enemy. He wanted Jason behind bars as much as she did.

Jason. This all came back to Jason, to catching him so he wouldn't kill again. Would this special agent from his specialized elite FBI team be able to catch her attacker, to end the nightmare? She wanted to believe it. Damn, did she want to believe it.

Hayden took a step closer, raising his other hand and sliding his fingers along her cheek. More soothing heat. His palm cradled the side of her face, his thumb sliding to her right temple, to the scar.

An iceberg slammed into her. She ducked from his touch and smoothed the hair along her temple back in place. What now? Should she thank him for his efforts? Wish him luck? Next to her, Hayden hadn't moved. He stared at his hand with an odd expression.

"I'm ready," she said. Because he needed to get going so eventually she could get going.

Her words snapped him from whatever thoughts had turned him to stone. With a nod, he slipped his hand in his pocket and took out another business card. "Here, call me—"

She held up his card. "You already gave one to me."

His forehead lined. With a final nod, he spun on his polished Italian lace-ups and headed for the door. With each step he took, the room grew colder. A shudder wracked her body, and she clasped her arms about her chest.

"You okay?" Agent Sankey asked, putting his hand on her shoulder.

She jerked at the touch, and he stepped back as if she'd sunk a set of venomous fangs into his flesh. She wanted to throw her hands in front of her face, just as she had countless times over the past three years. Like the time a little boy pointed at her during her first week in rehab and said, "Look, mommy, a real live monster." And like the time a well-meaning, elderly volunteer at the hospital squeezed her shoulder and said, "Don't worry, dear, you're young. All those ugly scars will fade."

Most had. A few, like the one on the right side of her neck, the one near her right eye, and the one across the bottom of her belly, still served as visual reminders of the ugliness of her attack.

She stared out the window, which overlooked a courtyard below. She longed to throw it open and gulp in fresh air.

Agent Sankey nodded toward the chair. "Why don't you have a seat, Ms. Johnson? It's probably not a good idea to stand by the window."

Because Jason, the Broadcaster Butcher, her brother, may see her. He'd already had a hand in taking away her career and her peace of mind. Now he was taking away her simple, basic need to stand at a window and breathe fresh air.

Ten minutes later, her escorts arrived, and Agent Sankey led her through the communal office area. A man talking to a uniformed officer stopped in midsentence when she passed them. Two women near a printer craned their necks, their gazes glued to her as she walked the length of the hall. A huddle of blue suits dropped their voices as she walked by but not low enough for her to miss certain words: butcher, knife, scars. She wanted to run, to flee from the stares and whispers. Instead, she focused on slowing her breathing and her heart, which hammered against her constricted chest.

In the parking lot at the back of the building, shimmering waves of heat rose from the asphalt, and a swell of baked air slammed into her. She shielded her eyes from the bright glare and stopped. "I left my sunglasses in the conference room."

"I'll go back," Agent Sankey offered.

She raised her head and turned her face so the agent could see the gash near her right eye. "I'm scarred, not helpless."

The force behind her words stopped the agent, and she cringed. She knew it was wrong, lashing out at him for her panic. She was so much better off when it was just her and Smokey Joe.

"I'm sorry," she said in a softer tone. "It's been a rough twenty-four hours."

The young FBI agent's face grew old and weary. "I know, but Agent Reed will get him. He's one of our best."

He was Agent Efficient, Agent Know-It-All, Agent Obscenely Thorough, and Agent with the Really Nice Suit and Italian Shoes. Kate breathed in calm and strength. "I know."

With the baby-faced G-man on her heels, she went back into the office. Again, she tried to ignore the stares and whispers. Her glasses were right where she'd left them on the table in the conference room. She jammed them in her bag with a shaky hand. Sweat slid along the sides of her face. It was crazy, getting so worked up about people staring at her. After all, she used to make her living from people watching her.

She smoothed her hair along her neck. "You know, I think I'd like a water bottle before we go."

She must have looked like hell, because the agent nodded and took off. The minute he was out of sight, she shut the door on the stares and whispers. There was probably something else going on here, something to do with her re-entry into the world, and Agent Know-It-All would probably be able to explain it. Unfortunately, or fortunately, Hayden was gone, off to find her knife-wielding brother.

Pacing the room, she stopped at the second-story window overlooking the crisped grass of the courtyard below, which was thankfully empty. No Jason. She unlatched the lock and pushed open the window. The breeze, although far from cool, felt good sliding through her hair and into her tightened lungs. She envisioned herself roaming mountain roads on her motorcycle, just her and Smokey, and the wind. A different picture, one of her trapped in a safe house and surrounded by guards, flashed behind her eyes, bright and sharp, like a knife slashing into her skull.

Her fingers gripped the windowsill.

She thought about the other guards in the hospital and near her home who didn't protect her. She thought about her brother's threat to finish the job. And she thought about Hayden. About his palm on her cheek, his promise to keep her safe, and the sound of his shoes as he disappeared from her life.

That's when she stopped thinking.

She hitched her saddlebags on her shoulder and pushed off the screen. Throwing herself over the ledge, she hung by the tip of her fingers, sucked in a breath, and dropped. When her boots hit the ground, she ran.

She took off with no plan, no destination. She simply had to put distance between herself and the FBI agents who would soon be hunting her down and putting her in a cage. She ducked out of the courtyard and sprinted through the parking lot.

Her legs pumped faster. She reached a nearby office complex and ran along the back row of cars, keeping low. She rounded a dumpster. Footsteps pounded behind her.

Her hair flying, she turned and saw a flash of black. *Oh, God, no!* She ran out of the parking lot toward a grassy hill and bolted toward a shallow ditch. A hand grabbed at her. Fingers sunk into her chambray shirt.

"Nooooo!" she cried over the hiss of tearing fabric.

She careened forward, but someone tackled her from behind. Her chest slammed to the ground. Her teeth rattled. A boulder settled on her legs, pinning her to the grass. She jammed her elbow back.

"Ooaf!" Her attacker winched her arms behind her.

Pain ripped through her shoulders, but she couldn't scream. Fear closed her throat.

*Jason is not here*, she told herself as hot breath slid along the back of her neck. He couldn't have found her. Hayden wouldn't have left her in a place where the Butcher and his knife lurked.

Her breathing slowed, and so did her attacker's. A set of hands, cold, hard shackles, turned her over. Her eyes closed. She didn't want to see the face. His face.

She tried to picture Hayden. His surprisingly warm hands. His gaze that said stronger than his words, *I'll keep you safe*.

When she opened her eyes, her racing heart stilled, and she swallowed the terror clogging her throat. Safe. She was safe.

As she let loose a long breath, two hands clamped down on her shoulders and fingers dug into her flesh. Her relief gave way to irritation that skyrocketed to anger, more at herself than the oaf sitting on her.

"What the hell are you still doing here?" Kate asked.

For the second time in as many days, Agent Hayden Reed said nothing as he straddled her, pinning her to the ground. But this time, he didn't wear a face of granite. He was livid.

* * *

*Thursday, June 11, 4:15 p.m.*
*Colorado Springs, Colorado*

Detective Traynor handed Lottie a pair of orange sneakers with yellow zebra stripes. She turned them over. Size nine.

"Ain't my size." She tossed them on her desk. "And I look like shit in orange."

"But apparently Shayna Thomas's stalker liked them," Traynor said. "We had a shoe guy check the casts, and a pair of shoes like these made the print in front of Shayna Thomas's bedroom window."

"I'll let Hayden know ASAP. We need to find out if this Jason Erickson he's hunting down has size nine feet and shitty taste in sneakers." She nodded to the papers in his hands. "What about the other prints?"

"Boot print confirmed. Matches shoes worn by Thomas's lawn man."

"Got a location on him for Monday night?"

"At home in bed with his wife."

"And the other print from that orthopedic-looking shoe?"

"Still working on that one." Traynor held out a stack of papers that listed orthotic shoe vendors. "You up to some shoe shopping?"

* * *

*Thursday, June 11, 4:30 p.m.*
*Denver, Colorado*

"You know, Reed, my ass is on the line, letting you take her," Agent Wulbrecht said. "Officially she's in our custody, not yours."

"Officially she's alive, and I plan to keep her that way." Hayden shut the passenger side door and walked around to the driver's side of his rental car. "She's coming with me."

"You're in the middle of a case," Agent Wulbrecht said.

"Exactly. I'm in the middle of a case, and that woman"—

he jabbed a hand at the passenger side of the car, noticed his fingers shaking, and jammed his hand in his pants pocket— "is a vital part of it. You and your team were assigned to watch her, and you failed. You jeopardized the investigation and put Kate's life in danger."

"We left her for less than two minutes. How the hell were we supposed to know she would jump out a second-story window?"

"You," Hayden said, pulling out the rental car key and aiming it at Wulbrecht's chest, "obviously don't know her."

"But she never would have gotten away, Cisney was out that window seconds after her."

"Like I said, you don't know her."

"And you do?"

Hayden pictured the hundreds of files, dozens of video clips, and stacks of interview transcripts he'd gathered on Katrina Erickson. And he compared them to the woman he knew as Kate Johnson. He heard Kate's voice, sharp as broken glass as she talked of her brother but soothing as she held Smokey Joe. He saw her hands, fisted at him but gently holding Maeve's. "Yes."

Wulbrecht offered Hayden his palms. "Fine, have it your way, but you're going to have to answer to the SAC."

There'd been only one other time in his FBI career Hayden refused so blatantly to play by the rules. Six years ago, when he was working for the Behavioral Science Unit in Quantico, he worked up a profile of a suspected serial killer targeting homeless men in Little Rock, Arkansas. The commander of the Arkansas State Police's Criminal Investigation Division, a grandstander with political aspirations, refused to release Hayden's profile because it was clearly at odds with their investigative course of action. With seven dead men in the city morgue and an investigation stymied by lack of evidence, Hayden went to the press on his own and released the profile. The Arkansas State Police denounced his profile and started a flame-throwing war with the bureau. In a bid for jurisdictional harmony, Hayden's supervisors demanded that he recant his profile. Hayden refused, was yanked out of the field, and immediately turned in his resignation. Twenty-seven hours later, two Little Rock police detectives who just wanted to get a bad guy off the streets tracked down the killer using Hayden's profile. Six months later, FBI legend Parker Lord visited his classroom at the University of Arizona, where he was teaching psychology, and invited him to be part of a new team he was starting.

Hayden pointed to the pen in Agent Wulbrecht's pocket. "Write the report. I'll sign it."

Hayden got into the car, clicked the door shut, and stared straight ahead. Next to him, Kate squirmed in her seat. He placed his hands on the steering wheel. "You have to stop running, Kate. Do I need to remind you again what we're up against?"

She shot a hand toward the building. "Do you really think the Butcher would come after me so close to an FBI office?"

No, the Butcher would never try anything that bold or stupid. Stupid right now belonged to him. Hayden made an error. He should never have entrusted Kate to the care of someone he didn't know and trust implicitly because *she* was anything but stupid.

It was no sixth sense that made him turn around to check on her. It was his intimate knowledge of her psyche. She was a victim, but at her core, she was a survivor. He pressed his arm to the tender spot of his side where she'd jammed him with her elbow fifteen minutes ago. She was also a fighter. He'd made the colossal error of forgetting this, which is why she was going to the Box, the SCIU's home base on the coast of northern Maine. There'd be hell to pay from FBI higher-ups for breaking protocol, but Parker would stand by him. Hayden promised Kate he'd protect her, and he was going to keep that promise. The Butcher spent too much time in Hayden's head for him to be worried about conventions.

Hayden was also mad at himself. He'd demanded her trust but gave her nothing in return. He unclenched his fingers from the steering wheel. Maybe it was time to trust her. Kate was a journalist, someone who cared about justice and truth. Maybe Kate needed to see the truths of this case.

He reached into the backseat for his briefcase and took out a folder. One by one he set six eight-by-ten glossy photos on the dash in front of Kate.

Color drained from her face.

"They don't even look human, do they?" Hayden asked.

Her teeth dug into her bottom lip, but she didn't take her gaze off the photos of blood and bone and shredded flesh. "Why are you showing me these?"

"So you know what we're dealing with."

"I know, more than anyone else, I know what kind of vile creature Jason is. I lived with him."

He banged a fist on the dash, shaking the photos. "Then why the hell do you keep running away?" The volcano he'd kept a lid on let out a fiery spurt. This woman, unlike anyone he'd ever met, had the uncanny knack of pushing his buttons.

Hot sparks shot across her cheeks as she jabbed her thumb at the FBI building behind them. "That was hell for me back there. Hell. Do you know how many people I've talked to in the past six months? I can count them on one hand. One. Hand." Her hand, hovering between them, visibly shook. She shoved it under her thigh. "I needed to get away, Hayden, and I'm not going to apologize for it."

Knowing they needed balance, he calmed his racing heart

and gathered the photos. "This isn't time for alone. That will come later. Right now you need to be patient with the process, and you can't forget who's after you."

Her finger traced the scar near her right eye, which was no bigger than a grain of rice. "I won't forget," she said. "He made sure of that."

He reached for the envelope. "Now there's one more picture you need to see." He pulled out another eight-by-ten, but it wasn't a face.

"A mirror?"

"It's from Shayna Thomas's guest bedroom. It's proof that the Butcher didn't finish the job. He didn't break all the mirrors. Which means..."

She inched back from the glossy photo of the unbroken mirror. "Oh God, he's going to kill again. Soon."

"Exactly. As much as he likes order, he won't wait a full month between killings. He needs to right his wrong. He needs to break all the mirrors, which is why I need to be focusing on him and him alone, not you, Kate. I've wasted precious time this afternoon."

"I'm sorry, Hayden. I didn't realize...I..." She fidgeted with her seatbelt and slipped it in place. "Okay, I'm ready to help."

"With what?"

"The investigation. I'm going to help you find my brother."

"That's my job. Right now all you need to do is stay put and stay safe. I'm taking you to the airport, where I'll be handing you off to Finn Brannigan, one of my teammates. He'll take you to SCIU headquarters in Maine. The Box is completely secure. You'll be safe there. I'll even send for Smokey Joe if you like." The Box was on the edge of the Atlantic Ocean with plenty of open space and fresh air.

"No." She picked up the photo of the unbroken mirror. "I'm not going to Maine." Her pale cheeks gave way to a fiery wash. "You need me."

"I know this is hard on you, that you feel horrible about those broadcasters' deaths, maybe even responsible, but I assure you we'll catch the Butcher and bring him to justice. We have hundreds of trained law enforcement officials on this."

"I can help. I'm a trained investigator and researcher."

"You're a journalist."

"But I'm also the Butcher's sister." He opened his mouth, but she waved the photo of the unbroken mirror in his face. "You can get a hundred more *trained law enforcement officers* on this, but they won't be able to do what I can do." The green of her eyes brightened, a look he'd seen so often in her "Justice for All" reports.

"What are you talking about?" Hayden asked.

Kate jammed the photo into his briefcase and buckled her seatbelt. "I can take you to Jason. If my brother isn't at his house in Dorado Bay, I know where he's hiding."

# CHAPTER SEVEN

*Friday, June 12, 6:15 a.m.*
*Fallon, Nevada*

Hayden pulled the rental car out of the EZ-Rest Motel parking lot and aimed it in the direction of the rising sun. Kate noted that not one hair on his head, still damp from his morning shower, moved out of place. How the hell did Agent Reed manage to look so put together when she was falling apart?

She smoothed the hair along the side of her face, but it sprung back in defiance. Probably had something to do with the nervous sweat on her palms. For only the second time since her attack, she was back in her home state of Nevada. Six months ago, she had made a dead-of-night stop at her condo in Reno to pick up a few small pieces of jewelry to sell because her money had run out. Now, in the bright light of day, every inch of her itched to run, to get away from this place where her terror started. But she knew the terror wouldn't end until Jason was stopped, and Special Agent Hayden Reed, the man leading the charge to stop Jason, needed her.

Yesterday afternoon, Hayden had threatened to send her off to Maine to be babysat by his SCIU teammates, but she convinced him that if time was of the essence, he needed her because she alone knew the one place Jason Erickson would go if he needed to hide, a hunting cabin in north-central Nevada. The problem was, she didn't remember exactly where the cabin was, so she couldn't give Hayden directions, or even a town. Since his search team found no trace of Jason or any hint of where he may have gone, Hayden had no choice but to bring her along on his investigation, which suited her fine because six broadcasters had died, and she'd do her part to make sure no more were silenced by the Butcher's knife.

She took out the road map sandwiched between her seat and Hayden's. Yesterday she explained to Hayden that in her youth, her family spent a few vacations at a small hunting cabin somewhere east of their home near Lake Tahoe. Thankfully, Hayden hadn't pressed her to talk about Jason and her childhood, because she sure as hell didn't want to amble down memory lane. Looking for the cabin was bad enough. The cabin belonged to some distant relative in her father's family, and Kate remembered it as a quiet, desolate place, more brown than green, swept by small trees and shrubs, a place scrubbed with dust and sun. In her youth, she had hated going to the cabin. It was too remote, and there was nothing to do. Her brother, on the other hand, had loved the solitude and serenity of the place.

She remembered that it took her family about two or three hours to drive to the cabin from their home in Dorado Bay and that there was a small general store with a life-size fiberglass elk out front with only three legs.

"A three-legged elk isn't much to go on," Hayden had

said last night as they mapped out their plans. "But it's something."

Hayden's optimism, his unwavering belief that her brother would be caught and justice would prevail, continued to surprise her, and some small piece of it must have rubbed off on her, maybe as he pinned her to the ground or maybe as he cradled her cheek, because a tiny part of her was hoping that this road trip to find a three-legged fiberglass elk would be the beginning of the end. Hayden had narrowed the initial search to about twenty small towns. His plan was to drive east, stopping at every town, hoping she'd recognize something, possibly the three-legged elk.

This morning Hayden was impeccably dressed, and one would never guess he'd been awake most of the night putting together a plan of attack. She'd drifted off to sleep in one of the motel's sagging double beds as he pecked away at his computer and talked softly on the phone, both soothing sounds. When she awoke, he wore another dark, exquisitely cut suit and bright silk tie, which she was sure was custom painted, this one with black and white and red swirls. His jaw was shiny and smooth, his damp hair combed neatly off his forehead. For a moment, she longed to ruffle his hair, not to dust up Mr. Perfect, but simply to assure herself that he was real and at her side.

"Do any of the towns sound familiar?" Hayden asked as he nodded at the notepad sitting between them.

Her finger traveled along Hayden's neat list. "It's been so long." She closed her eyes as she tried to picture riding in the car with her parents, but the canvas remained white, no color, no images, which was no surprise. She'd spent her entire life trying to block out childhood memories. "I'm sorry."

Agent Reed's hand settled on her leg, which she hadn't

realized was shaking. "It's okay." His fingers pressed down, his calm seeping into her.

"Okay," she repeated. Again, she looked at the list of towns Hayden compiled. "Carroll Summit. Lester Flats. Danaville. You know, I think the cabin may have been located in a town with a person's name. I keep coming back to these three."

"We're closest to Lester Flats. We'll start there."

The day was clear and bright, and heat shimmered on the sagebrush-covered flats. Game birds chucked, and small animals scampered through the brown-tipped grasses. Was Jason out here planning his next hunt? She shivered despite the heat slicing through the car's front windshield.

"Anything look familiar?" Hayden asked.

She stared past the flats to the rim-rocked mountains. She'd traveled these roads as a child with her father, but now nothing looked familiar. She shook her head. They drove through Lester Flats, and although it had a general store, it wasn't the one with the three-legged elk.

The elevation rose, and the flats gave way to hills and washes dotted by sparse juniper and pinyons. Again, she tried to dig into the dark pit of her childhood memories. Trees, yes, she could picture trees around her father's cabin, smell the tangy bite of pine.

"We're getting closer," she said.

The highway stretched on, and the road bisected a small canyon with elongated rocks that looked like . . .

"The people canyon," she said with an intake of breath. "I remember this." She had driven along this stretch of road with her family many times, and on each drive, she and her father would point out rock formations that looked like people. "That's the granny with the bun, and over there is the Indian chief," she told Hayden despite her pulse slamming the hollows of her neck. "The town, it's up ahead and over the hill."

In less than five minutes they reached the small town of Danaville with its two gas stations, three churches, and one general store, complete with a life-size fiberglass elk with three legs.

"Are you sure?" Hayden asked.

She wanted to laugh. Her nerves tried to catapult her into the heavens, but Hayden, obsessively thorough, pulled her back to earth with a single question. "Yes. To get to the cabin, drive through town and look for a road on the right. It should go for a few miles then loop around a small reservoir."

He motioned to the notepad. "Draw me a map?"

"No, I'm not that clear, but I'll know the cabin when I see it."

"Which isn't going to happen." Hayden pulled the car into the parking space in front of the three-legged elk. "I'm calling for backup."

\* \* \*

*Friday, June 12, 10 a.m.*
*Danaville, Nevada*

"What the hell happened to your lip?"

Hayden ignored Hatch's question and lowered the binoculars. No signs of life in the hunting cabin, and there hadn't been for the past hour.

"Time to move in." Hayden slipped the binoculars over his head and set them on the hood of his rental car, which sat atop a hill overlooking the cabin Kate ID'd as her brother's reclusive getaway. He turned to Hatch Hatcher, his SCIU teammate who'd arrived an hour ago along with his teammate Evie Jimenez, a SWAT team from the Las Vegas Division, and six deputies from the Churchill County sheriff's department. "You ready?"

Hatch stroked the stubble along the side of his jaw and pointed to Hayden's swollen lip. "If I didn't know you better, I'd say someone nailed you a good one."

Hayden reached for the two-way radio.

"Not so fast, Professor." Hatch popped him on the arm. "If I'm storming that place with you, I need to know where your head is." Hatch, with his shaggy blond head and lazy Southern drawl, appeared easygoing, but the agent was a pit bull, the kind who locked jaws and didn't let go. "What happened to your lip?"

Hayden wanted to collar Jason Erickson now. He'd been patiently waiting for this moment every minute of every day for the past five months, but Hayden knew Hatch was right. People putting their lives on the line with each other needed to be in sync. "I got into a little scuffle when I first got to Mancos. I'm a hundred percent now."

A slow smile spread across Hatch's face. "Kate got to you, didn't she?"

Hayden stared at the radio in his hand. Kate had gotten to him in more ways than one. She got him mad as hell and worried when she took off on her own, and she got him thinking about handcuffing her to a bed, but that's not what Hatch was referring to. "Kate butted me in the head after I caught her trying to escape from Joseph Bernard's cabin."

Hatch chuckled. "Someone finally messed up that pretty face, and a woman at that. Now that's a first."

Hayden didn't tell his teammate that Kate had struck twice. His side still ached from the elbow she'd planted in his side yesterday during her escape from the Denver field office. Right now she was down the road about a quarter mile with Evie and two sheriff's deputies, all fully armed.

Hatch took off his own set of binoculars and set them next to Hayden's. "Let's sail."

Hayden held the walkie to his mouth. "Carranza," he said, addressing the SWAT team commander, "get your men on the service road. Martinez, you and Arnold take the perimeter. Reisenauer, go ahead and set up for the long shot. It's time."

Hayden and Hatch unholstered their sidearms. "It'd be a hell of a lot easier if this place had a phone," Hatch said. As the SCIU's crisis negotiator, Hatch had a proven track record of talking down everyone from hijackers to suicide jumpers.

Hayden agreed. Making contact by phone would enable them to determine first if Erickson was indeed in the cabin. Plus it would give Hatch the flexibility of negotiating in private, which would be less threatening to Erickson.

One of the deputies who just walked up to the car offered a bullhorn.

Hayden shook his head. "Too dictatorial. Erickson is the type who needs to control, not be controlled. Anyone shouting at him through a horn would just get him worked up."

"You think he's really in there?" the deputy asked.

Hayden patted the paper in his suit coat's inner pocket. "Search warrant says we can find out."

The hunting cabin was a small, slump block structure with a high-sloped metal roof surrounded in the back and along one side by scrubby pinyon pines. To the other side sat a ramshackle shop with splintered paint and a sagging roof.

He and Hatch left the top of the rise and hurried down the hill toward the pines. Upon reaching the trees, Hayden bent low, scrambled across the driveway, and flattened himself against the front of the cabin while Hatch looped around to the back. He inched toward the door and looked in the window. Single room with a small bathroom. No visible occupants.

A long whistle then a short sounded in the air. Hatch's signal. Clear. Hayden answered with a long and short whistle.

"FBI!" Hayden hammered the door. No answer. He lowered his shoulder and pushed, leading with his Sig. The back door burst open, and Hatch rushed in.

They searched under the bed, in the tiny closet, behind the shower curtain.

"The shop," Hayden said.

Outside they ran toward the small, windowless building with the sagging roof. Locked door. *On three*, he mouthed to Hatch. They lowered their shoulders and pushed open the door and dropped to the ground, shouting in unison, "FBI!"

A cheesy, sweet odor rolled out on a wave of moist heat. Sharp lances of light sliced the shadowy interior. In the center of the shed on a long table was a mound, completely black but vibrating and making soft clicks, like hundreds of miniature metal scissors snapping.

Up close he could see the shiny dark lump wasn't a single item but a mass of hundreds of small beetles. He waved them away, and like a blanket of black, they lifted, revealing a pile of flowers. Roses. In every shade of pink, from the palest blush to a deep magenta.

Below the sea of pink lay a grossly decomposed body.

# CHAPTER EIGHT

*Friday, June 12, 11 a.m.*
*Danaville, Nevada*

The cheesy odor of decayed flesh rolled in thick, hot waves through the shed. One of the deputies stood twenty yards away, puking up his breakfast, while another stood at the door wearing a sickly shade of green. The smell didn't bother Hayden, nor did the click of flesh-eating beetles or the sweltering heat. Right now all that mattered was the gathering and analysis of information. He straightened one cuff, then the other.

"What can you give me at this point?" Hayden asked the tech from the coroner's office, who stepped in after the crime scene team had photographed, measured, and bagged physical evidence, including the shriveled remains of seventy-two long-stemmed pink roses.

"Female, between forty and sixty years of age. Caucasian."

"How long has she been here?"

"She's in the final stages of butyric fermentation, so I'd guess around fifty days. But there are burn marks on the torso, indicative of freezing, so given the cold winter and cool, dry spring, decomposition could have been delayed by as much as three or four months. At this point, I'd say death occurred between late January and April of this year. We'll have a better idea after we run labs. Do you think it's one of his broadcasters?"

Hayden shook his head. While CSU processed the scene, he had stood quietly in the corner and slipped on the Butcher's shoes. In those shoes, he walked through the dark, airless shed, stood over the body, even placed fresh pink roses on rotting flesh. "The broadcaster murders are all about the show, a public statement of power and control. This body wasn't meant to be found or viewed by anyone but the killer. Given the elevated body and flowers, the presentation of the victim is ceremonial in nature. This has a very different signature than the broadcaster killings."

"Do you think it's a different killer?"

The hands. It came back to the hands. This woman's hands were clasped, thumbs interlocked, and centered on her chest. "Same killer or someone with intimate knowledge of the killings."

"I wonder who she is."

A shadow moved across the door, blocking the sun. "I know."

Hayden's jaw clenched. "What are you doing here? You're supposed to be on the hill with Evie."

Despite the smell, Kate didn't gag, nor did she gaze in horror at the flesh-dotted bones. Her face was oddly composed. "Hatch needed Evie to look at something they found in the cabin."

Hayden reached for her elbow and tried to turn her around. "You need to get out of here. This is no place for—"

"Agent Reed, didn't you hear her?" the tech asked. "She said she can identify the body."

The sunglasses on Kate's nose slipped as she nodded once. "It's Kendra Erickson."

For the first time that morning, the hairs on the back of Hayden's neck stood on end.

"Who?" the tech asked.

"My mother," Kate said with a hollow but steady voice. "I recognize those pink shoes."

* * *

*Friday, June 12, 11 a.m.*
*Colorado Springs, Colorado*

"That is one butt-ugly pair of shoes." Lottie jabbed Detective Traynor in the ribs and pointed to a pair of lace-ups the color and texture of chunky peanut butter.

"Ugly to the eyes, but heaven to the feet," a deep voice said behind her.

Lottie spun and came face-to-face with a man with a rusty mop of hair on his head and an equally unruly red mustache. This must be Rusty Coswell, the manager of the orthotic shoe store. "I'm sure that's a wonderful shoe," she said.

"But you'll be dead before you'll be caught in a pair of these, right Sergeant King?" He tipped his gaze to her shoes, a pair of denim stilettos with tiny swinging cherries.

She'd taught her grandkids to stand up for and speak their truths. Ain't healthy for a soul to back off on her truths. "I'm afraid so." She offered him her hand. "Thanks for meeting with us on such short notice, Mr. Coswell. We have the casts."

The smile beneath his bushy mustache fell away, and the shoe salesman ushered them to his office. "I still can't believe something like that happened here."

Colorado Springs, a town of a half million people, wasn't a stranger to violent crime, but it had never seen a murder like this. Thomas's celebrity status combined with the carnage and Butcher's notoriety had her town on edge. She was hoping orthotic shoe man here could help take off a bit of that edge. She took out the cast of the odd shoeprint found in Shayna Thomas's terraced garden and handed it to the man, who put on a set of bifocals and studied the print.

"Custom orthotic," the shoe salesman finally said. "Ladies size eight and a half wide. Manufactured by Ortho King out of Michigan, which distributes nationwide." He reached into the file drawer of his desk, took out a catalog, and pointed to a big, black chunky shoe.

"This shoe could have been fitted and sold anywhere in the United States?" Lottie asked.

"Yes."

"Who would wear this type of shoe?"

"Diabetics often wear orthotic devices, as do patients suffering from arthritis, those with some type of foot deformity, or individuals with general foot fatigue or discomfort caused by everything from obesity to stress from rigorous sports."

"It could be anyone?"

"Probably a woman."

Traynor made notes on his notebook. "We have a woman with a size eight and a half wide foot. That narrows our search."

"Numbers, how many are we looking at?" Lottie asked.

"Of this size and brand, probably a couple thousand over the past ten years," the shoe store manager said. "That'll be a lot of prescriptions to check."

"Prescriptions?"

"Patients need a prescription for these types of shoes."

"And prescriptions are attached to names." The cherries on Lottie's shoes jiggled.

\* \* \*

*Friday, June 12, 11:05 a.m.*
*Danaville, Nevada*

Hayden placed his hands on either side of Kate so she couldn't escape his words. "Do not move."

She nodded and sat on the hood of the sheriff's cruiser parked in front of the cabin. She'd refused to get inside the car, despite the fact that a body she believed to be her mother's lay in the final stages of decomposition not fifty feet from her.

He put a finger under her chin and lifted her gaze to his. "Give me a minute to talk with Evie, and then we'll go."

Again, she nodded, but he wasn't sure if she was listening. A part of her had checked out, shut down, but given that Erickson was still on the loose, he preferred shut down to on the run.

He motioned to Hatch to come over to the patrol car. "Don't let her out of your sight. Cuff her if you need to."

He walked to the hunting cabin and wondered if that body really could belong to Kendra Erickson. He'd wanted to interview Kendra five months ago when he first went to Dorado Bay, but Jason said his mother was out of town, and Hayden believed him. The young man displayed no signs of dissembling. He'd said his mother had been at...A quick rush of air shot over Hayden's lips. Jason said his mother was at the family's hunting cabin, which was obviously the truth. Had Erickson killed his mother as early as January and brought her here? Did he come here regularly and drape her body with fresh roses? Hayden needed to spend some time with those thoughts, move the pictures around in his head, but first he needed to talk with Evie.

Inside the cabin, Hayden found Evie Jimenez in the kitchen, poking into the drawer next to the sink and swearing. Evie was the SCIU's bomb and weapons specialist. She had a notoriously short fuse and could swear in two languages.

Hayden looked in the drawer and pressed his lips together. "A match?"

Evie nodded. "An eight-inch double-edger, same as the asshole used on all the victims."

Hayden studied the razor-sharp length of metal. He'd dreamed about this knife, about the Butcher's hand holding it, but he needed more than a knife. "Get it bagged and printed." If this knife belonged to the Butcher, it would most likely be clean. The man he hunted wouldn't leave prints behind, but Hayden had to be thorough. Obscenely thorough. "And get someone to take the drains apart. I want them sampled."

If they found Shayna Thomas's blood in that drainpipe, they had their link, although, honestly, he didn't hold out much hope for trace blood. The Butcher, being the meticulous sort, didn't leave blood trails. Hayden needed something more, proof that they were on the right track.

"Did you find anything else?" Hayden asked Evie. "Any souvenirs?"

"*Nada*. No jewelry, hair, or clothing, nothing we can tie to Thomas or any of the other broadcasters. Place is spotless."

Which fit the profile. They were looking for a neat freak, someone who thrives on order and routine and...

"The mirrors," Hayden said.

"What?" Evie asked.

"Did anyone check the mirrors?" Hayden didn't wait for an answer. He ran to the small bathroom and stared at dull grayish-yellow paint and a faint outline of an oval where a mirror had once hung above the bathroom sink. He yanked open the drawers, checked the small dresser near the cot in the corner. Not a single mirror.

The knife, the absence of mirrors—they both pointed to the Butcher.

\* \* \*

*Friday, June 12, 1 p.m.*
*Danaville, Nevada*

"Are you okay?" Hayden asked.

"I'm fine." Kate felt no horror, no disgust, no loss, and no sadness at the knowledge that her mother's rotting corpse had just been packed into the back of a coroner's van. She didn't even feel a lick of anger. Or triumph, which, on second thought, made her anything but fine. "I'm a monster, aren't I?" Kate ground the heel of her boot into the dried grass near the sheriff's cruiser where she'd been sitting, waiting for Hayden to finish in her father's old hunting cabin.

"Kate—"

"I mean, I can't be human, right? Because right now I should feel something." A sliver of panic pricked her midsection. "A normal person would feel something after seeing that, wouldn't she?"

"You are you, and you feel what you feel," Hayden said

with an infuriating calm. "Don't fight it. Accept it, along with the fact that your feelings may change when the shock wears off."

She opened her mouth to argue, but he placed a firm finger under her chin and tapped her mouth closed. Her skin tingled at his touch, and she allowed that warm quiver to rush along every inch of her skin. No, she wasn't an unfeeling monster. That wash of heat from Hayden's touch was proof of that.

"It's okay," he said.

*It's okay.* She breathed in the low, deep calmness of his voice, his soft cinnamon scent. Hayden. Hayden was here. For two days he'd been at her side and in her head, and right now she was grateful. She scrubbed her hands down her face. "You think I'm a nutcase, don't you?"

"I think you're too hard on yourself."

"Just picking up where my mother left off." Despite the midday sun beating down on them, a biting cold crept from the sun-baked earth to her feet.

"Are you ready to talk about her?" Hayden asked.

She kicked at the dried grass. "Will you believe me?"

"I'll believe the truth."

"And do you think I'll tell you the truth?" The words fell sharp and bitter from her tongue. A fight brewed. There was something comforting in the fight, perhaps because she spent the first half of her life fighting the monster in her own living room.

"I know you," Hayden said with his unflappable calm. "You have no reason to lie."

"Maybe you don't know me as well as you think. Maybe I lied about the scar on my attacker's wrist. Maybe you're wrong for trusting me. Maybe you're a piss-poor profiler, a sorry excuse for an FBI agent." Once, just once, she wanted to see him one shade less than perfect, because right now, in the shade of the shed where her mother had been rotting, she felt anything but perfect.

He took both of her hands in his and pulled her away from the hood of the cruiser. Nudging her with his arm, they walked away from the cabin. "Talk to me, Kate."

Here she was doing her best to drive Hayden away, but he was patiently standing by her side. Smokey was right when he said this world was one crazy place. She rolled her head along her shoulders and squinted at the bright sun flooding the sky. "Where were you three years ago, when I needed someone to believe me?"

"I'm here now."

Yes, Mr. Fix-It had arrived on her doorstep. "Headline or in-depth version." She didn't want to go where he was asking her to go, but it was vital to the case. And right now, it was vital to her well-being. The cold was growing, an arctic glacier crushing her chest.

"Your choice," he said.

"You're pulling some psychobabble stuff on me, aren't you? Letting me control where this goes, how it unfolds."

"And if I am?"

"It's working, because, yes, I want to tell you about Kendra. I think in knowing her, you'll better understand Jason." *And me.* No, Hayden, didn't need to understand her. He just needed to catch a killer.

"Technically all my mother wanted was happily ever after," Kate said. "Kind of strange, isn't it, starting a story with happily ever after?" She pulled in a long breath.

"My mother lived her entire life in Dorado Bay. She grew up in a fancy house on the lake with two parents who doted on her. She was pretty and popular. After high school, she was supposed to go to some prestigious all-girls college on the East Coast, but her senior year she met my father and things changed. Her parents didn't like him, called him a transient bum who was beneath her. My father worked as a blackjack dealer, and my grandfather got him banned from all the casinos and run out of town. Deeply in love with him, Kendra took off after my father and soon got pregnant with me. She was ecstatic. My father, who was a self-professed free spirit and dreamer, reluctantly settled down with her in Dorado Bay, but he hated being tied down, hated living in a town that looked down on him. They fought all the time. Kendra would scream and rant, and my dad would take off. As the years went on, she grew more angry and depressed. He grew to hate her, and my mother, shunned by her parents and the whole town, began to hate everyone."

Hayden's arm brushed hers, the expensive cloth of his suit coat soft and smooth. "Doesn't sound like a healthy place for a young girl."

Hayden didn't know the half of it. "When I was five, Jason was born, and two years later Kendra, in a fit of rage, attacked my father with a kitchen knife. That night my father came to me and said he was leaving and that he'd come back for me when he found a better place where we wouldn't have to deal with dragons like her. But he never came back, and she blamed me. Maybe because I looked so much like him or because we were so close. Or maybe because I was a free spirit, wild like him." Was. Right now she was anything but free.

"As for Jason," she went on, "Kendra adored him. As sick as it sounds, I think she turned all of her love and attention that should have been for my father onto Jason. She doted on him, but in a twisted way. He had no friends, no interests of his own. They were inseparable. What she liked, he liked. What she didn't, he didn't." Something hard and prickly clawed up her throat.

"Including you."

Her fingers traced the scar along her earlobe, another one Hayden didn't know about, the one that a butcher hadn't carved into her. "Yes, just like my mother, my brother hated me."

\* \* \*

*Friday, June 12, 7 p.m.*
*Dorado Bay, Nevada*

Agent Hatcher took a blue silk handkerchief out of his pocket and unfurled it with a flick of his wrist. The motion stirred the air in the too-hot, too-still break room of the Dorado Bay Police Department.

"You don't have to entertain me." Kate watched the blond-haired FBI agent, the latest of Hayden's dutiful babysitters, tuck the blue silk into a tiny hole atop his fist.

"But it's my pleasure." A slow smile slid across Agent Hatcher's mouth, conjuring two deep dimples. With the blue silk completely hidden, he waved his hand in the air before her in slow, sweeping arcs. Then finger by finger he opened his fist and showed her his empty palm. His blue eyes widened. He slipped his hand into the folds of hair near her left ear and pulled out a white silk scarf with a print of a single red rose. He handed it to her and bowed.

"Nice trick, Agent Hatcher."

His hand clutched his chest. "Are you calling my amazing feats mere tricks? My dear, skeptical Miz Johnson, don't you believe in magic?" His drawl was slow and sugary but wasted on her.

She dropped the white silk on the table. "Magic exists only in children's storybooks." She offered him a small smile. He was, after all, trying to get her mind off the horrors of the day, trying to ease her soul, much like Hayden, but instead of steel and masterful control, Agent Hatcher was pretty scarves, dimpled smiles, and thick Southern charm. Hayden said Hatch was his team's crisis negotiator. She could see this man diffusing dangerous situations. Something about Hayden's teammate invited closeness.

"Call me Kate," she said.

Agent Hatcher hopped off the back of the chair he'd been perched on. "You, Miz Kate, are a cynic in need of serious conversion."

"I'm a realist."

"You're also a tough lady." He squatted before her and took her hand in his. "Hayden filled me in. You've been through a lot today, and you're still going strong. Pretty admirable."

She unwound his fingers from hers, picked up the white silk scarf, and began kneading it. "There are six other women who've been through worse. They—"

"The proper response to any compliment, according to my very wise Great Aunt Piper Jane," Hatch interrupted, "is 'thank you.'"

She wrapped the white silk about her fingers.

The slashes of his dimples deepened, his sugary grin widened, and his blue eyes sparkled. Label him Agent Charming and Disarming.

"Okay, thank you," she said with a half smile. "Does anyone ever win an argument with you?"

"Very, very few." Hatch hopped up and sat on the table,

his legs swinging. "Although your man Hayden has been a formidable opponent."

Hayden Reed wasn't *her* man. He belonged to no one, but she did agree he was a force to be reckoned with. "He's hard-headed, consumed with order, and a control freak," she said.

Hatch took three silver-dollar-size silver rings from his pocket. "You know him well." He slid the rings in and out of his fingers, and they appeared to pass through each other, defying their solid shape.

"I don't know him at all," she said.

The silver rings continued to clink as he formed a chain. "Hayden's good at holding things inside. At headquarters we call him the man of steel."

The image fit, the vision of a superhero. But Hayden Reed was very much honed of flesh and blood. She'd seen the human, hungry look in his eyes the night she invited him to handcuff her to the bed.

"I don't think he's as tough as he makes out to be," she said. "He hasn't been sleeping lately."

"Some times are harder than others," Hatch said.

"It's Tucson, isn't it?"

The rings stilled. "Hayden told you about the accident?"

"His mother-in-law did."

"You met Maeve?" Hayden's teammate seemed incredulous.

"Briefly." Because of Smokey Joe. She'd hadn't talked to him since she left Tucson two days ago. She'd call him tonight.

"Well, Miz Kate, if you're aware of his sleeping habits, I think you know Hayden better than you're letting on." Hatch waggled his eyebrows.

Kate squirmed. "We've been together because he doesn't

trust me. He's afraid I'll take off. So I've seen he's not sleeping, that he's obsessed with finding the Butcher, and I wonder if he's avoiding thinking about the accident in Tucson. People need to grieve. It's part of moving on."

She was a master of moving on. She'd grieved over her father when he left and over the monstrosity of her mother when they'd parted ways when Kate was sixteen. Maybe that's why she hadn't felt anything over the dead body in the shed. She'd already grieved, not so much for the woman, but for the mother/daughter relationship that never was.

"Something has to give eventually with Hayden," she continued in an effort to get her mind off Kendra. "He can't keep going like he does."

Hatch put the rings in his pocket. "Maybe you can knock some sense into him."

"Me?"

"Did you or did you not knock him in the mouth with that beautiful little head of yours?" The ocean blue of Hatch's eyes sported little whitecaps of mirth.

She wasn't proud of that move, but the picture was funny, she taking on a man with the size and agility of Hayden Reed.

"Guilty," she said with a laugh.

Hayden appeared in the doorway and drew to an abrupt stop.

Hatch waved him in. "Just talking about boxing matches." Hatch winked at his teammate. "Keep your gloves on, Professor, and perhaps you, Miz Kate, should start believing in magic." He pointed to her hands.

The white silk cloth with the red rose that never left her fingers was now a different color. Pink. A soft, blushy, horrible pink.

She dropped the silk as if it were a red-hot coal.

Hatch chuckled and walked out the door while Hayden picked up the scarf.

She inched back from him, not seeing Hayden, not seeing anything but pink. "Get it away."

Hayden jammed it in his pocket. Good. It was gone. The pink was gone. She wiped sweaty hands on her denim-clad thighs.

"Are you okay?" Hayden asked.

"I hate pink." *Try to make sense out of that, Mr. Head Guy.*

If he did, he said nothing. Instead, he reached for her saddlebags. "Time to go. I have a place for us to stay."

\* \* \*

*Friday, June 12, 8 p.m.*
*Reno, Nevada*

"That lying, butchering son of a bitch!"

Robyn Banks stormed into the hallway that snaked through KTTL's crowded newsroom. No one said a word to her as she made her way to Wayne's office, but nothing unusual in that. Ring the bell. Out of the way. Here comes the town leper. No one wanted to catch what she had.

She threw open the door of the news director's office, not bothering to knock. Eighteen years at this place had earned her some privileges. "Fifteen seconds," she said, spit shooting through her lips. "You slashed the hell out of my woolly mammoth tooth story, gave it a measly fifteen seconds, and put it at the bottom of the running order."

Wayne didn't look up from the monitor where video rolled of a raging forest fire.

She slammed a palm on his desk. "You promised me four times that."

The news director stopped the streaming image and made a note on the pad in his lap. "Your story was shit."

She knew it was shit when she turned it in, lacking an interview from a scientific source and relying on the overly cute five-year-old kid hugging the giant fossilized tooth his dad found while dove hunting, but she deserved more than fifteen seconds. Interns with skiing squirrel stories got more than fifteen seconds. "You promised me sixty seconds on that piece."

Wayne put his notebook on the desk. "You give me sixty seconds worth of solid news or gut-wrenching human interest, and I'll run every second of it."

She slumped into the chair across from his desk. "I gave you what I could in the time I had." Her renewed hunt for Katrina Erickson consumed her.

"Exactly." The news director leaned back in his swivel chair. "And it wasn't enough. Again."

The nuclear blast of that last word slammed Robyn. "If you're referring to the wrinkle paint story—"

"The wrinkle paint story, the bald cocktail waitress story, and the kitchen fungus story. Take your pick, Robyn. You're kicking out shit, and you have been for the past year. I have younger, hungrier reporters out there kicking your ass."

Like Katrina Erickson. Robyn had been news anchor at KTTL for eight years when Katrina arrived. Eight years of rock-solid reporting, writing, and producing. She was the entire package, gaily wrapped in pretty paper.

"You know what I'm capable of, Wayne." Robyn tried to keep the whine out of her voice.

"What you *were* capable of."

"If this is about my age—"

"Don't throw that sacred cow at me. This isn't about a forty-something woman getting a few wrinkles—"

"Thirty-five."

"Whatever. It's about a news reporter failing to report news of interest and import."

She pressed at the sides of her head. This was not the way she envisioned this conversation. Hell, her life was not what she envisioned, what she carefully planned, but there were still parts of her life she could control, like this pissant job. She stood. "Fine, I'll dig deeper. Meet with old sources. I can—"

"Sit." Wayne ran a hand over his bald head. He looked old, like she felt, old and used up. "I was going to save this for later, at a time when you're less emotional, but I don't think I'll be seeing that anytime soon. Bottom line, Robyn, is your contract is up next month. KTTL isn't renewing."

"No." She couldn't leave KTTL. Not now. "Anything. Tell me what you need me to do. You want me to take the weekend field assignments? The one-man-band jobs? The—"

"Robyn, please, groveling doesn't look good on anyone. You're done here. GM wants it"—he paused—"and I agree."

Wayne flicked the switch so the forest fire images exploded again on the screen. That's how she felt inside, like old, dry tinder, sparked by a carelessly tossed match. This was an injustice. She hated injustice, and she despised those who caused it.

"What would you say if I said I could deliver Katrina Erickson?"

Wayne's head snapped up.

"An in-depth feature, where she's been, why she left, and what she knows about the Butcher murders."

Two days ago the FBI had landed in Dorado Bay in search of Jason Erickson, who was a person of interest in the Broadcaster Butcher slayings. The search was now statewide, and authorities had submitted Erickson's photo to media outlets like KTTL.

"You've been in touch with Katrina?"

"We've always been like sisters." Like sisters who fought. Sharp nails. Hair-pulling. Or at least the adult, civilized version of it. "What do you say?"

"I say you deliver Katrina Erickson, and I'll get the GM to extend your contract. You get me a scoop on the Butcher, and hell, I'll get you the weekend anchor position."

# CHAPTER NINE

*Friday, June 12, 10 p.m.*
*Dorado Bay, Nevada*

Hayden stood on the deck of the lakeside cottage, looking not at the bay stretched out before them but at Kate's face as she leaned over the railing. Her features, like the water, were dusted with golden moonlight, but unlike the bay, Kate's face was anything but placid. He searched for words, something casual or even light-hearted, because after seeing her mother's decaying body, Kate needed light. Unfortunately, he'd never excelled at light.

*You're always so serious, Hayden*, his first-grade teacher had told him. *It's okay to smile once in a while.* She hadn't known then that he'd just buried his mother.

*Hayden, you'd be so much easier to live with if you'd just let loose*, Marissa had said right after they were married. *You need to walk naked in the rain, dance in the cereal aisle at the grocery store, and get rid of all those stodgy blue striped ties.*

His fingers slid along his tie, a deep purple silk with hand-painted yellow, black, and teal waves. He settled his elbows on the railing next to Kate and gazed at the moon-speckled water. "Isn't *dorado* Spanish for gold?"

Over the night chatter of bullfrogs and crickets, she released a soft "Mmm-hmm."

"I see."

Her mouth quirked in a half smile. "What do you *see*?"

He splayed his fingers, gesturing to the dappled bits of golden moonlight bobbing on the water. "When I first saw the bay, it was bright blue and clear. I couldn't figure out why it was named Golden Bay, but here in the moonlight, it looks like millions of gold coins sprinkled across the water."

The smile reached the other side of her mouth. "As a kid, I'd sneak out of the house at night and come down to the bay just to look at the water. I'd pretend all the little golden ripples were coins I could scoop up to buy a fancy car to take me away from here." Kate's fingers curled around the railing. "Even as a kid, I had running on my mind." She kicked a twig from the deck into the smooth pool, and tiny droplets of gold tinkled on the night. "I hated this place."

Hayden rested his palm on her white knuckles. As much as she hated her hometown, she cared enough about stopping a serial killer to come back. Lottie had called her Miss America, but there was so much more to her than a pretty face and beautiful body. Kate had exquisite strength, and she was a woman not afraid to fight, and he was thankful to have her at his side. He could have rented them a hotel room in town. It would have been practical, closer to Erickson's home, to the people Hayden needed to meet with, but he knew Kate needed the solitude of the cottage on the bay's isolated eastern shore.

He told the FBI field agent in Denver that he knew Kate because he studied her for the past five months, but he was finding she was also an easy read. She was more than a feisty, cynical fighter. Today he'd seen her laughing with Hatch. A spike of irritation stabbed at his chest. Everyone loved Hatch with his silly magic tricks and lazy Southern drawl. Hatch knew how to do light. He knew how to make her laugh. The sweet, chiming sound of Kate's laughter had shocked him into stillness. All Hayden received from Kate were glares, angry shouts, a head-butt to his mouth, and an elbow to his ribs.

"Are you thinking about the Butcher?" Kate asked, breaking the silence. She was no longer gazing at the bay, but at him, her eyes clear and curious. She wasn't tugging her hair across her neck. She wasn't ducking into the shadows. She wasn't searching the deck for a quick escape. She trusted him to do his job.

He stood, his spine straightening one vertebra at a time. No, he hadn't been thinking about Erickson, but he should have been. It didn't matter that Hatch could make Kate laugh or that Hayden couldn't get that sound out of his head. The case mattered. For the first time in five months, all the bits of information he'd been gathering and analyzing were finally starting to come together.

He checked his watch and figured it was still early enough to call Lottie. "Let's head inside. I have work to do."

Kate didn't argue, and he realized that she, too, wanted to get out of this place that dredged up painful memories and opened old wounds.

"How long will we be here?" she asked. The rental had a high-tech security system, three bedrooms with storm windows, a small kitchen so they wouldn't have to dine out in restaurants, and a single great room with a wall of windows giving million-dollar views of the bay. The curtainless wall of windows was not optimum for his efforts to hide and protect a witness, but the summer season in this resort town had started, and he was able to book this secluded cottage only because of a last-minute cancellation.

"A few days, possibly a week," he said. But this time, he didn't have the luxury of time. The Butcher hadn't broken all of the mirrors at Shayna Thomas's house. He was going to strike again soon with the intent to get it right. The fact that Jason wasn't at his home or the family cabin meant he was on the hunt.

"What are we going to do?" Kate asked.

*We.* After she led him to the hunting cabin, Hayden finally made peace with the word. His head told him he should tuck Kate into the Box in Maine, where she would be safe, but something deep in his gut, the part of him that would do anything to stop the Butcher, the part of him that made him one of Parker's Apostles, told him he needed Kate.

"We're going to walk in Jason's shoes," he said. "Get into his head." Who better to have at his side than the monster's sister, who had lived with him for almost half his life? "I plan on talking to Jason's employer, his coworkers, his neighbors, friends, and relatives. I'm going to re-create Jason's days, his routines, his complete existence."

"Sounds like a plan, Agent Obscenely Thorough." On her words floated a hint of a laugh, and it shocked him at how much he enjoyed that sound.

\* \* \*

*Saturday, June 13, 6 a.m.*
*Dorado Bay, Nevada*

Kate stood in the bathroom of the lakeside cottage the next morning frowning at a tube fisted in her trembling hand. "Stop being such an idiot," she told herself. With a shaky breath, she uncapped the tube and raised her gaze to the mirror.

It had been almost three years since Kate had seriously studied her face in a mirror, and after three years little had changed. The left side of her face was untouched by Jason's blade, but the right side showed signs of his wrath. The Butcher's knife had sliced along the right side of her neck and near her right eye.

Last night Hayden told her she'd spend the day with him as he interviewed those who knew Jason, and she wasn't about to go out looking like a monster. With the tip of her finger, she dabbed the cover-up cream on the scars. After applying the cover-up, she sponged on foundation and translucent powder. Stepping back from the sink, she surveyed her work. With the brown contacts and the scarf around her neck, she looked almost normal.

She found Hayden at the dining table in front of the wall of windows overlooking the lake. A plate of Danish and a cup of coffee sat next to his laptop. He wore another crisp white shirt and neatly pressed trousers, this pair a nice, dark gray, the color of his eyes. A matching jacket and a beautiful tie with red poppies sat on the back of one of the empty chairs. His hair was slicked back, and his jaw was smooth.

Perfect, as usual.

"Coffee cups are in the cupboard by the sink," Hayden said as he tapped on his laptop.

She poured herself some coffee and sat in the chair next to his. Her face reflected in the laptop's lid. She noted the scarf completely covered her neck, and, unless she squinted, she couldn't see the scar near her eye. She jabbed a fork at the top of a sugary Danish and scraped the crumbs into a small hill of white.

Hayden continued to click away on his computer. She continued to scrape.

*Scrape. Click. Scrape. Click.*

"Well?" The fork clanked to her plate.

"What?"

"What do you think?" She pointed to her face.

His fingers paused. "The brown contacts cover the green."

She jammed a hand at her right eye. "And this."

"What?" His face twisted in bafflement.

"The scar, Hayden, what about the scar?"

He shrugged and turned back to the computer screen. "It looks fine." *Click. Click.*

"Fine? You can see it?" Her voice rang out in a screech.

He closed his computer, crossed his arms over his chest, and leaned back his chair. He looked almost…casual. Well, as casual as a man as uptight as Hayden could look. "No, Kate, the scar isn't noticeable, but it wasn't before."

She gnawed the Danish. This was more of his psychobabble crap: mock nonchalance to give her confidence to go out into the world of light and the living.

Hayden righted his chair and leaned toward her. He was close enough for her to see the cool gray flecks in his eyes, smell that sweet cinnamon scent that shouldn't smell like trussed-up Hayden. "I'm serious, Kate. Unless they're looking closely, most people won't even notice the scars, even without the makeup. Only in your head are they this huge, ugly disfigurement."

She wanted to believe him. He was an analytical observer, a man who saw everything. And he believed in justice and truth. For so long she'd been running from her past. Maybe he was right. Maybe part of her was stuck in the past, the part that refused to see beyond those first few weeks when her face had been swollen and disfigured and colored by scarlet and purple. Maybe time had worked its healing magic.

Damn, he was doing it again, getting into her head. It drove her nuts. She'd rather have him in her bed than in her head.

A picture of Hayden sprawled on her bed with a sheet draped low on his hips flashed through her mind. In this image, moonlight slipped in the window and tugged at his hair, mussed by her fingers. A silky glow of sweat coated his chest where her tongue slid. The vision was so bright, so clear, it sent a geyser of warmth surging through her midsection.

Across from her Hayden pulled in a sharp intake of breath. He stared at her, his customary staid expression one of bafflement and... heat.

The Danish dropped from her hand. *Please don't tell me he saw that in my head.*

No, that was ridiculous. Hayden couldn't read her mind. He was just a man, albeit a man with keen powers of observation. There was no way he could get into her head. Nor was he ever going to get into her bed. Men like Hayden Reed were control freaks, and at age sixteen, on the day she ran away from her dragon of a mother, she swore no one would ever control her again.

She brushed the glazed sugar from her fingertips and stood. "Let's go look for a butcher."

\* \* \*

*Saturday, June 13, 7:10 a.m.*
*Dorado Bay, Nevada*

Hayden pulled the rental car in front of Hope Academy, a two-story lodge made of warm cedar, native stone, and huge glass panels reflecting the brilliant expanse of morning sky. Fifty-six boys stood in six arrow-straight lines doing jumping jacks. Ten jumping jacks per rep. Five reps. He counted every one, anything to get the vision of Kate sitting at the breakfast table out of his head.

Didn't work. He pictured her tongue dart out and capture the fleck of glazed sugar on her lower lip. He saw the pulse at her neck stutter. He saw heat flooding her cheeks. All of which sent a rush of hot blood through his veins. Absolutely unacceptable given she was his witness and currently facing the demons of her past, not to mention the uncertainty of her future.

He focused on the boys in Hope Academy T-shirts. They moved on to lunges. One lunge up. Two lunge up.

*Hayden, you work too hard. This Broadcaster Butcher case is consuming you.* Maeve.

*Take a few days off, get some R & R, and come back fresh.* Parker.

*You know what you need, Hayden? A good fuck.* Hatch.

Hayden pushed the voices aside along with the vision of Kate at the breakfast table. What he needed was to get his hands on Erickson. Kate's brother should be his focus. Not Kate's sugar-dusted lips.

He turned off the car and jammed the keys in his pocket.

Next to him Kate scrunched her forehead. "Where are the barbed wire and the tower with armed guards? This looks more like a church retreat than a home for delinquent boys."

Good. Kate, who was employing a few more brain cells than him today, had gotten over the awkward moment at breakfast. "Looks can be deceiving." He pointed to the white post fence that bordered the property. "See that thin wire above the top rail? Electrically charged." Then he lifted his hand and motioned to a small wooden box in the spruce tree at the corner of the main house. "There's a camera in there, and there was one at the gate we passed off the main highway. We've been watched since the moment we entered the property."

A shiver rocked her body, and he rested his hand on her thigh, giving it a squeeze that had nothing to do with breakfast. Kate couldn't stand people watching her because she considered herself disfigured. The scars near her eye and along her neck were faded and no longer raised, but he'd studied enough victims of violent crime to know that in her mind she saw a monster, which was ridiculous. This was also a good reminder that Kate was also a victim and that he was obligated to protect her, not ogle her over morning coffee.

They walked up the neatly manicured gravel drive to the academy, a ten-acre residential treatment center for emotionally and socially troubled teenage boys. According to the school's website, the academy accommodated sixty boys, ages twelve to seventeen, and a residential staff of fifteen. Jason had worked as a Hope Academy cook for the past five years.

"Do you really think someone here may know where Jason is?" Kate asked.

They stopped in front of an oversized pair of cedar doors. "No, but they will help us get a better picture of his routine and interests."

"And you want that because…"

"Only Jason is going to be able to tell us where he is." And that meant walking in his shoes, slipping into his skin, and becoming the monster.

Before they knocked, the door swung open to frame a short woman with a smudge of silver glitter on her cheek.

"This is private property. You'll need to get off, or I'll call the police."

Her words and expression were as sharp as the scissors she held in her right hand. In her early forties, she wore a yellow polo shirt that read HOPE ACADEMY STAFF; shoulder-length, no-fuss brown hair; and a frown. No jewelry but for a lanyard noosed around her neck with a half dozen keys. She reminded Hayden of a tiny, angry sparrow.

He took out his credentials. "And this is Kate Johnson. We have an appointment with the camp director, Kyl Watson."

The woman studied him and slipped the scissors into her pocket. "My apologies. Kyl didn't mention you were coming."

They stepped into a great room with an oversized fire-place flanked by large leather sofas and groups of comfortable chairs. In the center of the room were four card tables, each littered with buckets filled with sequins, feathers, ribbons, and glitter. Two teenage boys sat at each table, and most were gluing baubles onto papier-mâché masks with long stick handles.

One boy had written FUCK HOPE in glue on the table and was sprinkling the words with silver glitter.

"Get it cleaned up, Bradley," the woman said. "If it's not gone by the time I get back, you'll get bricks. Do you hear me?"

The boy nodded.

"Excuse me?" she said with unexpected force.

"Yes, Miss Watson, I hear you, and I understand what you're saying."

She pointed to a long table beneath one of the windows where at least twenty masks, bedecked in sequins and feathers, were drying in the sun. "The boys are making masks for a fundraiser we're hosting next weekend."

"We're ar-teests," said one of the boys, who was crafting a bright sun of red, orange, and yellow onto one of the mask shells with sequins.

"They're lovely," Kate said. "I like your colors."

"Some of the masks will sell for up to five thousand dollars," the woman explained. "It's our biggest fundraiser of the year." She motioned them to follow her down a hallway. "I'm Beth Watson, the assistant director. I'm sorry about the junkyard dog routine. I thought you were the press." Her gaze slipped to Kate, who, in her blue jeans, blazer, and neck scarf, really did look like the intelligent, attractive broadcast journalist she'd once been. "We've had them hounding the place for days, ever since word got out that Jason is wanted for questioning in the Broadcaster Butcher slayings." Her lips pinched in a little beak as she swung open a door marked DIRECTOR. "This Butcher stuff must come to an end."

"That's why I'm here, Ms. Watson. To find him and stop the killings."

Beth Watson shuddered and took off at a clip. The woman didn't waste time or energy. Everything about her was purposeful.

The director's office was not much bigger than a broom closet with file cabinets covering every inch of the walls. Within seconds, a man wiping his hands with a damp paper towel walked in and introduced himself as Kyl Watson. In his mid-thirties, he had the look that most social service providers wore: overworked and underpaid, but dedicated to his cause.

"I'm afraid you caught me working on the plumbing this morning. Clogged sink in team five's dormitory." Watson folded the paper towel and dropped it in the garbage can near his desk. "As I told Chief Greenfield yesterday, I'll give you everything I have on Jason. I need this nightmare to end."

"This has been hard on you," Hayden said with a tilt of his head.

"On the entire academy." Watson shifted the pad on his desk, aligning it a quarter-inch from the edge. "I have sixty boys here, troubled boys struggling with everything from low self-esteem to drug addiction. We're trying to provide a safe, healthy, nurturing environment where they can make positive life changes, but with all the media attention and talk of the brutality of the crimes, our campus has been disrupted to say the least."

"The boys have been upset?"

"We're a small staff here, Agent Reed. Jason may have been the kitchen manager, but he also interacted with the boys, supervising activities and helping with homework."

"Reaction from parents?"

Watson dropped his hands in his lap. "Concern from most. Outrage from a few. Two families pulled their boys."

"I'm sorry." And Hayden was. Serial killing—any killing—had a ripple effect that reached far and wide.

"Not half as sorry as I am." He straightened the desk phone then folded his hands in his lap. "So what can I do to help?"

"Help me paint a picture of Jason. Give me the colors and textures of his days, his work, his relationships."

"Jason was an exemplary employee. He started as a kitchen hand and within a year had worked his way up to kitchen manager. He kept meticulous records, never complained, and willingly took on new and challenging tasks." The director handed him Jason's file, the contents nothing short of glowing.

"What was Jason's schedule like?" Hayden asked.

"As a live-in, he worked three weeks on, one week off."

"Was he ever late? Did he ever miss any work?"

"Until this week, he had a perfect attendance record." Watson pulled out the work schedule and handed it to Hayden. "I'm sure this will interest you."

It did. Each of the Butcher attacks occurred while Erickson was off work.

"Has he contacted you at all since he took off two weeks ago?"

"Not a word. He was due back here on Monday." Five days ago.

"And you weren't concerned about his failure to show?" Hayden asked.

"We were, but Beth mentioned that he'd been going to his family's cabin during his weeks off, and she got the impression he was having some family issues. Since Jason had plenty of vacation time banked and a great work record, we were going to give him until Monday before doing anything, including contacting the police. Honestly, we were beginning to think he might have been the victim of some crime."

Hayden set aside the schedule. "How did Jason get along with others here?"

"Everyone liked him. Staff, students, even visiting parents said kind things about him." Beside him Kate stiffened. "Jason was quiet and shy, but he was always pleasant and respectful."

"Did he have any close friends or confidants?"

"None. He was a lonely kid, but a good one."

*Kid.* Interesting word choice to describe Jason, a man in his mid-twenties. Shades of paternal feelings. "Girlfriend?" Hayden asked.

"I think he had a special girl in his life. I never met her, but I remember him picking flowers from the academy gardens to take to her."

"Did he ever talk about his childhood, his family?"

"No, I think he spent his weeks off with his mother, but I never met her. I heard in town that she's a bit of a recluse, hadn't been out of the house in five or six years."

Kate's entire body tensed, and her leg started to bounce. He casually reached over and set his hand on her knee. He knew this was hard on her, but there was no way he'd leave her alone at the cottage. Plus, her intimate knowledge of Jason might give him a different insight.

"About six months ago, around January, did you notice any changes in Jason? Or were there any changes here at the academy?" Hayden was fishing for triggers, anything that would explain the onset of the slayings in January.

"No. Jason was very much an even-keeled individual, very predictable."

"Do you have any idea where he may be?"

"Not a clue. As I said, he was very quiet and private."

Hayden went fishing and came up with an empty net. "I'd like to see Jason's things and the places where he slept and worked."

The Hope Academy kitchen smelled of pine cleaner, and the stainless steel appliances were so clean Hayden could see the tight lines of Kate's mouth reflected on their surfaces. Likewise, Jason kept his dorm room tidy and unadorned, except for one small picture. On his nightstand sat a photo of a little brown-haired girl dressed in a blue princess costume with a tall gold crown. She held a baby dressed as a pumpkin on her lap. Both smiled at the camera with chocolate-smeared faces.

Next to him Kate gasped. He pictured her eyes without the brown contacts: green, the same color as the little girl in the photo.

Other than the picture, which needed much further thought, he found nothing significant. No calendars, address books, notebooks, and no souvenirs from six dead broadcasters.

The director escorted them to the main house and down the hall. As they passed the door marked INFIRMARY, Watson stopped.

"You know, there's one more thing," Watson said. "Earlier this year Jason started taking some kind of prescription medication. Because we're very strict around here about any drugs, he kept the meds in the infirmary."

"What was he taking?"

Watson shook his head and took out a set of keys that jingled on a large silver loop. "Our staff physician, Dr. Trowbridge, keeps track of that type of stuff, but he's out of town at a conference." He opened a small locked cabinet. "Here we go."

The prescription bottle label read ANAFRANIL.

Kate nudged closer. "What's it for?"

"Antidepressant," Hayden said. "A drug historically used to treat obsessive-compulsive and panic disorders. When exactly did Jason start taking the Anafranil?"

Watson tapped the bottle against his palm. "January. I'm sure it was January because we had some changes in our employee health insurance plan, and I remember Jason checking to make sure prescription drugs were still covered."

"January," Kate repeated. "The same month the first broadcaster was murdered."

# CHAPTER TEN

*Saturday, June 13, 8:15 a.m.*
*Dorado Bay, Nevada*

A little girl in a sherbet-orange sundress with green slime running from her nose screamed into Kate's ear. Kate dropped the *Field & Stream* magazine she'd been pretending to read and grabbed the side of her head.

"Oh, Pammy, come here, doll baby." The little girl's mother picked up the screaming child and held her to her chest and started to rock. "I'm so sorry," the mother said to Kate. "She has an ear infection, and she's miserable."

Kate mouthed "Oh" and settled the magazine in front of her face.

She and Hayden sat in the Dorado Bay Medical Center, a small operation with a part-time doctor and one nurse, as they waited to meet with the physician who prescribed the antidepressant to Jason six months ago. On the waiting room chair next to her, Hayden pecked away at his laptop, jotting page after page of notes from their meeting at the academy. She continued to be amazed at Hayden's total focus. If she hadn't seen that flare of heat in his eyes at breakfast, the one that still warmed her cheeks when she thought about it, she'd swear he was some kind of super secret robo-agent.

"Do you two have any kids yet?" the woman asked when the little girl stopped screaming and climbed off her lap.

"Kids? Him, me, us?" Kate asked with a start. "No!" The idea of her and Hayden being a couple was insane. She didn't do "couples." In college, she'd dated but never more than two or three dates with the same man, and she'd never slept with any of them, mostly because she never found a man she connected with. It was ironic. In college her classmates called her "everybody's girl" because she dated so much, but they'd been wrong. She'd belonged to no one. And never would. As for kids? Not in this lifetime. The Butcher's knife had done too much physical damage.

"Just wait," the mother in the doctor's office said. "Kids will change your life. Mostly for the better." She smiled at the child who toddled over to a fish tank, where she took a long green string of mucus from her nose and wiped it on the front of the glass.

"Oh, Pammy, don't do that!" The mother whipped a tissue from her purse and swiped at the child's nose, which sent Pammy into another nuclear meltdown.

Still Hayden typed on his computer without missing a stroke. Was he human?

A nurse in a smock with blue monkeys poked her head into the reception area. "Dr. Gray will see you, Pammy."

"No!" The little girl kicked as her mother picked her up and carried her toward the exam rooms. As the door shut, Kate watched Pammy run to a man in a white coat and kick him in the shin.

"Dr. Gray will see you after this patient," the nurse said before she shut the door.

Twenty minutes later, the nurse led them to one of the exam rooms, where Dr. Gray was rubbing his shin. He sported two Pammy-size sandal prints on his pants.

"Agent Reed. Ms. Johnson." The doctor nodded as he began washing his hands.

"Why did you prescribe an antidepressant to Jason Erickson?" Hayden asked. No foaming the runway, no greasing the skids. Hayden could read people well, and it was obvious that he knew they didn't have much time with Jason's doctor.

"Panic attacks," Dr. Gray said.

"When did they start? How did they present?"

"I prescribed the antidepressant after the first of the year. Classic case. Palpitations, sweats, chest pain, nausea, feelings that he didn't exist."

"Was this Erickson's first time on antidepressants?"

"That I know of." The doctor rinsed his hands and dried them with a paper towel from the dispenser. "I've only been seeing Jason for the past five years."

"Why a tricyclic? It's an older class of antidepressant and not widely prescribed now, given that selective serotonin reuptake inhibitors do the same job with fewer side effects."

The doctor dropped the towel in the trash can. "Are you a physician, Agent Reed?"

"Forensic psychologist."

The doctor put his hands in the pockets of his white coat and tilted his head in thoughtful contemplation. "A man who spends a good deal of time in the criminal mind. Tough calling."

Hayden pointed to the shoe marks on the doctor's pants. "So is dealing with patients like Pammy."

For the first time, the doctor smiled, and Kate realized

again how good Hayden was at figuring out how to get into people's heads to get what he needed.

"It's challenging." The doctor walked gingerly down the hall toward another exam room.

"So why put Jason on a drug with undesirable side effects?" Hayden asked.

"Because Jason insisted on the tricyclic, even after I warned him of the accompanying dizziness and vision problems."

"Why?"

"Apparently his mother took the same drug when she was younger and suffering from anxiety attacks. Jason said the drug worked for her and insisted on taking what she used."

Kate remembered Kendra's panic attacks. Screechy affairs with flying dishes, destroyed books, and overturned furniture that ended with the panicked woman cowering in a corner. Even now, the skin on Kate's forearms pebbled at the memory of her out-of-control mother.

"I've been monitoring Jason for the past six months, and he is doing very well. No complaints, and he said his panic attacks all but disappeared."

They reached exam room two. Kate saw the tick in Hayden's jaw. Time was running out.

Hayden asked, "In your professional opinion, Dr. Gray, do you think Jason was of a mindset to murder those six broadcasters?"

The doctor picked up the chart on the plastic inbox of the exam room. "Absolutely not. I can't see Jason stabbing those women. He may have had a few panic attacks, but in my opinion, he's no killer."

\* \* \*

*Saturday, June 13, 8:30 a.m.*
*Carson City, Nevada*

"Get me a goddamn drink."

The tone, more than the words, made Robyn Banks cringe. Mike hadn't always talked to her that way. Three years ago he'd treated her like a queen. No, like a goddess. She'd been the center of his celestial universe.

Until Katrina Erickson ruined everything.

Mike stumbled over the hole in the carpet of their living room, where she sat at the card table that served as her computer desk, trying to decide if she should really hire a private investigator with the company name Cheap Dicks. But she needed cheap right now. She had to track down Katrina Erickson. Her job at KTTL-TV depended on it.

"I said get me a goddamn drink. Jack and water."

Robyn turned from her computer but refused to see the wreck of a man before her. Instead she concentrated on her wreck of a home, specifically at the wall that once held two Cassatts but now featured only two holes, the exact size and shape of Mike's fist. "It's too early for whiskey," she said.

"Then make it a fucking Bloody Mary."

She forced a smile. "How about pancakes?"

"You cook like shit."

She ran her hands through her hair and massaged her scalp. She was trying. Didn't anyone see that? The news director at work? Mike here at home? She pressed the sides of her head. Didn't they see she was trying to hold it together? "I'll get us cereal, make some juice."

"For Christ's sake, Robyn, stop pretending."

"Pretending?"

Mike threw his arms wide. "That we're fucking normal."

She straightened her spine. No, they weren't normal. They never had been. Not now. Not in the past. They'd been special at one time. Not so long ago they were destined to be northern Nevada's Golden Couple. She held the nightly anchor spot, the shiniest of all stars, at KTTL-TV for eight years, and Mike Muldoon was the star of his own shining universe. He had been king of all pension administrators and had amassed a horde of golden treasure that suited her lifestyle.

"We could be more normal." This morning she didn't hold back the bitterness. "You could try to get a job."

"Newsflash, baby. People don't want to hire an ex-con to handle their precious retirement dollars, especially one charged and found guilty of embezzling six million bucks."

No, it was $6.8 million, and the charges included not only embezzlement of health and welfare plans, but also the defrauding of pension funds. When Mike screwed up, he did it in a grand way. Justice had been swift for Mike. He had spent two years in prison. When he came out, he was a changed man. But Robyn had stayed at his side through it all. Even as the U.S. government had stripped away everything she and Mike owned: the Cassatts, vacation homes, her Jag. But they hadn't taken their home, a Victorian fixer-upper they had no money to fix.

She blinked back memories of what they no longer had and held out her hand. "Come on, Mikey, let's go get some breakfast."

Mike smacked her hand and limped by her. "I'll get myself the damned drink."

* * *

*Saturday, June 13, 9:30 a.m.*
*Dorado Bay, Nevada*

Jason's home squatted in a row of small, cheap tract houses in downtown Dorado Bay. Kate hadn't been to that house in fifteen years, not since the night of her junior prom, the night she turned her back on her home and the people DNA deemed her family. She fingered her left ear and the scar there. It wasn't as big as the ones Jason had given her, but now, as she walked up the driveway of her childhood home with Hayden, it burned, reminding her that this place had been her own brand of fiery hell.

Hayden had called ahead, and Dorado Bay police chief Mitt Greenfield waited for them on the porch. He wore gray-skinned cowboy boots and a frown that reached his eyes.

"We're glad you're here, Agent Reed. You, too, Ms. Johnson. We've been through this place top to bottom and found some odd things."

Hayden opened his mouth, but a loud screech sounded behind him.

"Holy crap!" Kate spun toward the noise. "What was that?"

"Jason's cat," Chief Greenfield said.

"Jason owns a cat?" Hayden asked before she could.

"That's what the neighbor across the street said," the chief added. "Said the cat's been caterwauling for two weeks. And she won't leave the place, either. It's like she's waiting for Erickson to come home."

Kate watched as Hayden jammed a hand in his pocket. "What's wrong?" she asked him.

"The cat—it's not in the profile. The Butcher does not

have close attachments. He's isolated and cares exclusively for his own pleasures. If the Butcher had a pet, it would be dominated, most likely caged. Such an animal would instinctively fight to escape."

*Escape.* The single word blasted away thoughts of Jason's cat. Kate's earliest memories of this house were of escape. She felt the tug now.

Hayden's hand rested at the base of her spine. Her shoulders jiggled with a silent laugh. Of course he knew she was panicky, and of course he had her back. She headed up the steps.

Nothing about her childhood home had changed. The entire house smelled of bleach and stale air caused by permanently sealed windows. Plastic sheeting covered the furniture. Alphabetically arranged books sat in razor-sharp rows on the bookcase. In the kitchen all food had been taken from original containers and placed in plastic storage canisters and labeled. As a child, she'd been consumed with running from this place. Jason had sought to bring order to it.

"What was he like when you were growing up?" Hayden asked.

She'd been expecting this question and was surprised it took Hayden so long to ask. But Hayden was a patient man, and it was time to walk through this house and look back on her childhood. A distasteful and daunting task, but head-guy Hayden would point out that only then could she move on. Yes, this man had gotten into her head, and right now she welcomed his presence.

"When Jason was born, Kendra rarely let me touch him," she started. "He was her special child. He was shy and never brought friends home. He was a neat freak and insisted on everything being organized."

"Did he ever show interest in animals?"

"He was always bringing home strays, which Kendra would toss out of the house."

"Do you ever remember him mistreating any animals, pulling feathers off birds, torturing dogs or cats?"

"No, why?"

"As children many future serial killers exhibit sadistic tendencies toward animals. Many are also fascinated with fire and wet their beds, even into their early teens."

Kate shook her head. "That doesn't sound like the kid I grew up with." Although after what Jason did to her, she couldn't bear to think of what he might have done to the cat still screeching outside.

Hayden thrust a hand over the right side of his head, ruffling the neat wave of hair.

"What is it?" she asked.

"Sometimes I think I'm chasing two people. There's so much about Jason that fits the profile of the Butcher. He's a male between the ages of twenty and forty. Small build. Lives with his mom when not at work. No college education. Loves order. Then there are times where it doesn't fit. The cat. He's well liked by everyone. He had a girlfriend and picked her flowers." His hand dropped to his side, and she had an insane desire to smooth his wayward hair.

Instead she clasped her hands behind her back. "You said a witness saw a woman in a pink dress on Shayna Thomas's front porch. Maybe he has a partner."

Hayden fisted his hand and slipped it in his pocket. "Maybe."

Jason's bedroom was as neat as the rest of the house, with a closet full of clothes arranged by color and a collection of video games organized alphabetically.

"Check out the nightstand," the chief said. "That's when things get really weird."

Hayden opened the drawer, and inside was a stack of underwear. Young-girl underwear. A half dozen pairs, white with little blue flowers and worn.

Kate opened her mouth, but only a choky gasp spilled out.

"Yours?" Hayden asked.

She nodded, her skin crawling. "Why would he keep piles of my old underwear next to his bed?"

Hayden's eyes squinted, like he was reading fine print in a dense book. But isn't that what profilers did? They read the fine print on evidence and people. "He had deep feelings for you," Hayden said. "The location is significant, too. Your things aren't in a box in the attic or under his bed. They're next to him as he sleeps, within arm's reach and literally at the level of his heart."

Kate waved a shaking arm at the nightstand. "But it's not right. He didn't even like me. He stabbed me twenty-four times that first time, threatened me while I was in the hospital, and stabbed me again the night I got out of rehab. He tried to *kill* me."

Hayden moved to stand in front of her, a granite wall between her and the sickening contents of her brother's nightstand. She matched her breathing with his, and her heart slowed.

"What do you know about Jason's sex life?" Hayden continued. "Do you remember any pornographic magazines, or do you remember him masturbating or sometimes staring at you?"

She shook her head. "Like I said, he was very quiet, and I left when he was eleven. But I don't remember him being overtly sexual. Although"—her stomach churned—"he never slept in his own bed. He always slept in the master bedroom. With her."

Before they reached the master bedroom, Kate smelled

the flowers: stale roses. Worse than the smell was the sight. Pink was everywhere: a frilly pink comforter, pink striped wallpaper, pink paint on the ceiling, and pink throw rugs in the shape of roses. Her stomach heaved, and she grabbed onto the highboy dresser with the pink crocheted doilies.

"You okay?" Hayden asked.

She was fine. She could deal with this search of her childhood home if it meant getting closer to a killer, but as it turned out, Hayden found nothing significant in Kendra's sea of nauseating pink.

In the kitchen, Hayden poked around cupboards and the walk-in pantry.

"Check out the freezer," Chief Greenfield said, his voice wobbling for the first time.

It was empty, except for a frozen bloodstain.

"Oh, God," Kate said with a hitch of breath. The stain, the width of the freezer and half the length, was hardly blood seepage from a package of hamburger.

"We're getting it typed," Chief Greenfield said. "Seeing if we can get a match on any of the broadcaster victims. If that's the case, we have our link."

Hayden studied the freezer for a good five minutes. She didn't know how he could stand the cold. The icy air pouring out of the freezer made her knees quake.

When he at last raised his head, he brought out a brick-red chunk of ice. "He didn't have a broadcaster in here." Two threads poked out from the ice. Pink.

She reached for Hayden's arm to steady herself. "You think he stored Kendra's body in this freezer?"

For a moment, Hayden didn't say anything. Then he nodded.

The cold intensified. "Why?" Kate asked.

"He wanted to keep her close." He turned to her. "Just like he wanted to keep you close."

* * *

The picture was getting clearer.

Hayden saw that Jason had been a boy torn in two. He was a little boy trying to please his overbearing, mentally ill mother, who was deathly jealous of Kate, a jealousy brought on by Kate's father's attention. Jason was also the little boy who adored his daring, pretty older sister, and he was sensitive enough to know the injustice being done to Kate. Had that rift as a child sent Erickson into a bout with dissociative identity disorder? Hayden had wondered from the beginning if he was chasing one person with a split personality because there were such disparities at each crime scene. However, people who genuinely suffered from the disorder were barely able to function, to dress themselves and get through the day and its normal challenges, let alone plan and execute six successful murders.

He jammed a fist in his pocket. The tesserae in the mosaic that was Jason Erickson were numerous, and they were starting to come together, but there were still a number of missing pieces. He had one more room to check before he could get Kate away from the hell house of her childhood.

When he started up the steps to the attic, Kate grabbed his hand, her fingers cold and hard. "We don't need to go there," she said with a sudden sharpness.

"What's up there?"

"Nothing." Two fast blinks.

He raised an eyebrow.

"I can't stop you, can I?"

"Should you?" He kept his words soft.

"No." Her shoulders curved in as if she were trying to disappear into herself. "You probably need to see it."

A band of something clamped around his chest, containing his growing anger at Kate's mother and a society that allowed horrible wrongs against children. The staircase was narrow, the ceiling low. "Do you want to go in first, or do you want me to?"

A growl rolled over her lips and collided with her strangled laugh. "This is another one of your psychobabble things, isn't it? Giving me some control in a place where as a child I had no control?"

He admired her astuteness and that laugh. "And if it is?"

"It's still bugging the hell out of me." With another little growl, she rushed passed him and shoved open the door. "Welcome to my world."

The minuscule room with high-pitched ceilings held a twin bed with a plain blue blanket and a three-drawer dresser. On the floor in front of the bed stretched a blue and brown circular rag rug. Nothing else. No pictures on the walls, no knickknacks or books, but there were bars on the window.

She circled the room, touching nothing. "You know, she never physically abused me." Kate stopped at the window, and the silhouette of her against those bars made him flinch. The surest way to kill a spirit like Kate's was to cage it. "But she never let me truly live. I couldn't have friends, join school clubs, read popular books or magazines, or wear pretty clothes. She was miserable in life, and she wanted the same for me."

Her voice trailed off, and she squatted, pulling back the rag rug. On the faded maple floor spilled a brown stain. "Remember that scar on Jason's arm, the one I gave him?" She didn't wait for him to answer. "It happened right here. It was the night of my junior prom, and I was determined to go. Kendra refused to buy me a dress or shoes and wouldn't let a boy on the property, but for once I wanted to be a normal high school girl in a pretty dress going to a fancy party. So I put together an elaborate scheme. I sewed an outfit from old cocktail dresses I'd found at Goodwill and told my date I'd meet him at school.

"Long story short, Kendra found me getting ready and went ballistic. She was particularly upset I wore a pair of small gold earrings my father had bought me before he left." Kate massaged the jagged welt on her lobe. "The earrings set her off. She yanked one out, and while I stood in shock holding my bleeding ear, she picked up a pair of scissors and headed toward my dress laid out on the bed.

"That's when I lost it. I ran toward her and tried to get the scissors out of her hand. We struggled, and Jason, who never could stand us arguing, jumped in. I know, Hayden, I'm sure as the sky is blue, that he was trying to get the scissors out of her hands so neither Kendra nor I would get hurt. When I eventually yanked the scissors from Kendra, my momentum sent me flying, and I jammed them into Jason's arm. He jumped back, and the scissors sliced down his arm and across his wrist, a horrible, jagged gash."

Her gaze dropped to the bloodstain. "It was an accident. I didn't mean to hurt him, but I didn't bother to stick around and see if he was okay. I took off and never looked back." With a shrug meant to be indifferent but was instead heartbreakingly sad, she slid the rug back in place. "Let's go."

He didn't need to be a profiler to see how hard this was for her, but he had to be thorough. He reached for the door to what looked like a closet. Behind him, Kate sucked in a gasp. His fingers hovered over the knob.

He'd seen torture chambers outfitted with chains, ice

picks, battery acid, and branding irons. He'd touched the final words and prayers scratched into walls by victims who knew the place where they were being held against their will would be the place they would die. And he'd heard the echo of terror that would live forever in rooms where vile bits of humanity perpetuated evil. Damn the Kendra Ericksons of this world.

His gut twisting, he pushed open the door and pulled on the cord hanging from the ceiling. Light chased away shadows, and it was his turn to suck in a breath. "It's beautiful."

She left the window and joined him in the closet doorway. "I called it Happily Ever After." Her voice was light and melodic, like sweet music. "I had forgotten all about it."

"You drew it. All of it?" He motioned to the space and asked, "Do you mind?"

"Do I mind if you look into my past? My dreams? My soul?" she asked with a sarcastic laugh. "Sure, Hayden, go right ahead."

Hayden studied her face, making sure her intent matched her words. Catching the genuine smile, he stepped into a fairy tale. Magic Markers and crayons. Hardly the tools of an artist, but the murals on the walls moved him. His gaze traveled from the magical pool to the fairy village to the pasture that housed the unicorns. A smile curved his mouth as his finger traced the green-eyed princess flying through the sky on a winged horse with a little boy with equally green eyes. He raised both eyebrows at her.

"Jason and I had a few good times," she said with an obvious fondness for the child who had been her brother. Kate had a huge capacity for feeling, for caring. Hayden had seen it in her "Justice for All" reports and in her interaction with Smokey. And she wore those feelings for all the world to see. If Maeve were here, she'd say he could learn a lesson or two from Kate.

His hand stilled when it reached the pink dragon, which lay on the ground, a silver knife arrowed in its breast.

"The dragon never got past the gate," he said softly.

"Not in Happily Ever After."

Which is where this visit should end. Hayden switched out the light and shut the door on a little piece of Kate's heart.

As they made their way down the steps, he marveled not only at her ability to express what was in her heart but at her artistic talent. He knew from his investigation into her past that she had no formal art training, but having lived years with Marissa, a trained artist, he knew good art. He also knew how that mural made him feel. He'd bought into the magic in her whimsical fairies and unicorns and celebrated the victory over the pink dragon. Kate's fairyland went deeper; it was something that moved one's soul.

*You don't have a soul.* Marissa's words.

Sometimes he felt soulless, detached from mind and heart and something deeper. But he had to in his line of work. He was the team's head guy. Hatch called him the Professor, and Parker and the rest of the team turned to him when they needed unbiased and analytical observation. He could get into the head of a criminal because he had the ability to turn off his own mind, and in order to deal with those horrors he needed some level of detachment.

With Kate more at peace than she'd been all morning, they left the house and made their way to the car when a screech sounded from under the porch.

"Look, Hayden. It's Jason's cat." Two yellow eyes shifted in the shadows. Kate held out her hand and made a soft *titch*ing sound. The cat took a furtive step toward her. "She looks horrible. I wonder when she last ate." The mangy cat, a mottled mix of orange, brown, and yellow, continued to inch forward.

A uniformed officer walked by. "Hey, there's Ellie." The officer made soft clicking noises toward the porch skirt. "We've been trying to get her for days. Here kitty, kitty."

Jason's cat ran into the shadows.

# CHAPTER ELEVEN

*Saturday, June 13, 11:30 a.m.*
*Colorado Springs, Colorado*

Shayna Thomas's eighty-three-year-old grandmother held out her blue-veined hand, raining dirt on her granddaughter's casket. That old hand shook, as did her stooped shoulders as she tried to hold back tears in eyes full of heart-shredding sadness. This was one fucked-up world when a grandma had to throw clods of dirt on one of her grand-babies' graves.

Lottie shifted in her seat in the back row of chairs next to gravesite 154-B. Eleven more of CSPD's finest, dressed in their Sunday best, were planted at and near the Forest Lawn Cemetery, the final resting place of Shayna Thomas. Her boys had also been at the Alleluia Lutheran Church looking for Shayna Thomas's killer.

Five days had passed since they'd found Thomas's bloody body and Lottie had sworn to find the SOB who was fucking with her town.

Right now they didn't have much. The fingerprints on the window were run through IAFIS, the FBI's mother of a database. No matches. She was still waiting on the DNA from the ejaculate. Contrary to all those cop shows her twelve-year-old grandson liked to watch, it took weeks, sometimes months, to get DNA results. They had that size nine shoeprint of the ugly orange- and yellow-striped shoes. And they had the woman's orthotic shoeprint.

All that added up to a whole lot of nothing.

The mourners at the gravesite stood and sang a song about walking in the shadow of death and fearing no evil. Lottie didn't fear the evil that had invaded her town. She despised it. She wanted to grab it by the balls and twist. Hard.

When the music died away, the mourners filed out, and Lottie met with Detective Traynor at one of the parking lot exits.

"You see anything, Hayseed?" Lottie asked.

Traynor shook his head. "We're taking down plates, though."

Lottie took the two-way out of her purse and radioed her other men. Nothing at the other exit. Zilch at the park across the street and the office building on the corner. Her radio squawked.

"Got a man at the gravesite," one of her men said with a catch in his voice. "Jogger."

A jogger in a cemetery? Pretty damned creepy. "You close enough for an ID?" Lottie asked.

There was a pause. "Yellow and orange shoes. Zebra-striped."

Lottie hiked up her dress and sprinted past the pond with its two white swans, past the veterans' section with its proud flags, and past a gazebo with swirly benches. A hundred yards into her sprint, the heel of her right black satin three-inch pump snapped off. She kicked off her left shoe, sending it through the air like a sleek black missile.

The center of her chest ached, and her lungs throbbed.

Her fat old ass wasn't up to this, but her heart was. She out-ran the pain, including the stab from a rock that sliced her instep. She reached the gravesite, where one of her officers had a man on the ground, his face pressed against the dry grass. She dropped to her knees. Grabbing him by the hair, she spun him toward her, ready to go face-to-face with evil.

But she got a shock. Evil didn't stare at her, fear did.

\* \* \*

*Saturday, June 13, 6:30 p.m.*
*Dorado Bay, Nevada*

Why weren't people staring at her?

Kate had spent all day with Hayden, meeting and in-terviewing people who knew Jason. She steeled herself for pointed stares and whispered talk, but today no one blinked twice at her scars. Was it because she wore the makeup and scarf? Or was it because all of Dorado Bay was focused on another monster?

"I can't believe Jason is the Broadcaster Butcher," Jason's postal carrier had said. "He was always so kind, even helped me get my truck out of the snow one day."

Likewise, Jason's neighbors, pastor, and coworkers didn't give her a second look, but they had plenty to say about Jason—everything from he enjoyed taking long hikes by himself to he didn't hang out at bars or clubs. What they didn't say was where Jason may be hiding.

"He never strayed far from home," Ike Iverson, Jason's pastor, had said. "He was dedicated to his mother and his work at Hope Academy."

Hayden, for all the dead ends, kept going with an efficient

doggedness Kate had come to expect from him. She also found comfort in it. Hayden would not stop until his mission was accomplished. If she ever needed to move heaven and earth, she knew who to call.

"You're smiling," Hayden said.

She sat in the passenger seat of the rental car as he slipped the key into the ignition, ready to pull out of the parking lot of Pastor Iverson's Living Waters Church. "Does my smile bother you?"

Hayden was such a serious sort, all work and no play. Even when she'd been focused on her broadcasting career, she took time off to play. She indulged her creative side with her jewelry and her adventurous side with scenic motorcycle rides. She squinted, trying to picture Hayden on her motorcycle. No. It would mess up his hair and wrinkle his suit.

"It's an anomaly," he explained, referring to her smile.

"And you notice anomalies?"

"I notice everything about you, Kate."

Her heart did a stutter-step as the space between them seemed to shrink. She heard the beat of his heart, breathed in spicy cinnamon, and felt a sudden heat. Surely he felt it, too. And then she remembered who this man was. He dealt in facts, not feelings, and any sensory overload was clearly one-sided, as he hadn't budged. Hell, he hadn't even blinked, so intent was his gaze. The comment wasn't a come-on, just Hayden being Hayden, the FBI profiler who sees everything.

She clicked her seatbelt in place. "One more stop today, right?"

At last Hayden blinked and cranked the ignition. "Are you sure you're up to it? I could drop you off with Evie and Hatch and do this one on my own."

Something soft and warm wrapped about her heart. Agent Perceptive really could be sweet, like now.

"No, let's get it over with." Kate was not looking forward to talking to her grandparents. The few times Kendra took Kate and Jason to her parents' lakeside mansion, the visits were uncomfortable affairs with Kendra screaming that they abandoned her and with Oliver Conlan's icy return that Kendra made her own bed and needed to lie in it.

A large man with tufts of white hair over his ears and a sharp nose opened the door. Kate stood in the shadow of a column but shifted to get a better look at the grandfather who had ignored her all of her life.

"I need to talk to you about Jason." Hayden showed the old man his badge.

"We've already talked to the police," said a thin woman with a platinum halo of hair and overly tight skin. And this would be the cold-shouldered grandmother. Kate wrapped her arms about her waist, surprised at the chill.

"I appreciate that, Mrs. Conlan, and I assure you my questions tonight will be brief."

Good. Less exposure to this ice couple meant less chance of frostbite.

Her grandparents shared a long look and nodded.

"When was the last time you saw Jason?" Hayden asked.

"Three weeks ago," Oliver Conlan said. "He stopped by to tell us goodbye."

The skin on Kate's arms pebbled, but Hayden didn't flinch. "Was he going on a trip?"

Her grandmother's shoulders sagged. "He didn't say. He just said he wanted to see us one last time."

"One last time? Did he say he was going away for good?"

"He didn't say, but he was visibly upset."

Was it that split personality concept Hayden had been toying with? Did the good, productive Jason want to say goodbye to those he loved because the evil, killing monster was taking over? But Hayden said people who suffered from this disorder could barely function.

Hayden slipped a knotted fist in his pocket. "Do you know where Jason could be right now?"

Oliver Conlan's bushy eyebrows jerked up. "That hovel of a hunting cabin is my first guess. Jason was connected to it because it belonged to his lowlife father's family."

"Did he ever talk about traveling or wanting to visit certain places?"

"Never," Ava Conlan said. "Jason seemed very content here."

"Did he have any friends, girlfriends?"

"None," Oliver Conlan said. "There wasn't a good deal to like about him. Now, if you'll excuse me, I'm done." He turned, and the mansion swallowed him.

Hayden thanked Ava Conlan, and they'd turned to leave when the old woman said, "Good night, Katrina." There was a softness, an almost wistfulness to her voice.

Kate's heart contracted and slammed against her chest, which was crazy. Why should she care about this woman who had never cared about her? She nodded at the older woman and clipped down the granite steps. Hayden's hand once again slid to the base of her spine, holding her steady.

* * *

*Saturday, June 13, 6:40 p.m.*
*Dorado Bay, Nevada*

"Fishing's stupid," nine-year-old Benny Hankins said. "So is spending all day in this stinkin' boat." He tossed a rock into the water.

"Stop throwing rocks, pea brain. You'll scare away the fish," Charlie, his twelve-year-old brother, said. Charlie didn't want to bring his kid brother out fishing, but his mom made him. *You have a good head on your shoulders. Maybe some of it will rub off on Benny.*

Charlie glared at his motionless bobber. Nothing was going to change his brother. Benny got into more trouble than anyone he'd ever met. Just last week after baseball practice, Benny stole a motorboat from old lady Milburn's dock and grounded it, ruining the blades. His stupid little brother told police he saw one of the boys from Hope Academy swimming away from the boat, but the police found Benny's baseball mitt in the hull. His brother was a thief *and* a liar.

Benny tossed in another rock. "Ain't no fish in this stupid part of the lake, *asshole*."

"Watch your mouth," Charlie said. "Of course there are fish in here. Last week Neil Parker caught a sixteen-pound mackinaw."

Benny flapped his lips in a crude sound. "Neil Parker beat you out, didn't he? That's what's ragging you, that he has a great big fish, that and the fact that BB Delinski knows it."

"Don't call her that." Charlie's hands tightened around his pole. "Her name's Belinda."

"But all you care about are her BBs. Big boobs."

"Shut up."

Benny tossed the rest of the rocks into the water. "I'm going swimming."

"Don't—"

His brother jumped into the lake. Stupid kid. This wasn't the best place to swim. Too many reeds, which could get caught around the idiot's foot.

Charlie checked his line again. Heck, no fish was going to come within a mile of his hook with Benny splashing so much. He started cranking in the line, and for the first time that day felt a tug. Charlie reeled faster. The line strained. Man, he must have a big one. Out of the corner of his eye, he noticed Benny climbing a rock. "Benny, get back here now or I'll tell mom."

"Ooooo, I'm quaking so hard my balls are gonna fall off." The twerp dove into the water.

Charlie focused on the fish, which was really fighting him now. "Benny, get over here. Come see what I got." He looked behind him. No blond head. No splashes, not even bubbles. "Benny," he called as he yanked the stupid fish into the boat and threw down his pole. "I'm going to kill you if you don't manage to get yourself killed first."

Charlie powered up the trolling motor and aimed his skiff at the rocks. "Benny!" He slapped the oar on the water. "Come out now or you'll be grounded for life."

The water remained still. Had something really happened to his brother? He was a pain and a liar, but...Charlie looked at the black mounds of rocks huddled above and below the dark blue. Did Benny hit his head on a rock? Was he caught in the reeds? Charlie tore off his shirt and kicked off his shoes. He was about to jump in when a blond head popped up.

"Gotcha!"

Charlie's heart slammed into his chest and fell to his quaking knees. When he was able to speak, he jerked his thumb and said between clenched teeth, "Get in the boat."

Benny's cheesy grin fell off. "Hey, no need to get pissy. I was just joking."

"I said get in the damn boat." Charlie yanked his little brother into the boat by the waistband of his trunks. "Sit!" But Benny remained upright. "Sit now!"

Benny shook his head. "Wh...wh...what's that?"

Charlie went to the back of the boat and reached for the motor. "What's what?"

"Th...th...that. On the end of your fishing line."

Charlie looked at the bottom of the boat, where his pole sat. He jumped back, almost falling overboard. There on the end of his fishing line wasn't a fish to beat Neil Parker's mackinaw record. It was a human foot.

\* \* \*

*Saturday, June 13, 9:40 p.m.*
*Colorado Springs, Colorado*

"You know, this peckerhead is really beginning to piss me off." Lottie aimed her index finger at the skinny, red-haired man with the yellow and orange tennis shoes. He sat behind the glass in interrogation room number three, his mouth shut. This was Greg Wullner, the man found jogging by Shayna Thomas's grave.

"Jogger taking the fifth?" Detective Traynor asked.

"Not a fucking word. Said he won't talk until his attorney arrives." She and her men spent most of the afternoon having a go at him. He was nervous and had puked twice.

"If he won't talk without an attorney, he's hiding something," Traynor said.

"Ya think?"

"I guess he isn't so stupid after all."

Mr. Stupid. That's what Lottie called Greg Wullner when she first saw the footprints, fingerprints, and ejaculate outside Shayna Thomas's bedroom window, but right now, he was more scared than stupid. He had no priors and worked as a mechanic at the local Lexus dealership. And yes,

Shayna Thomas drove a Lexus. And yes, the dealership confirmed that Mr. Stupid had worked on Thomas's car last year.

"But he's still pissing me off," Lottie said.

"I have something that may bring a smile to your face." Traynor handed Lottie a single piece of paper.

She grabbed the search warrant and let out a whoop. "If he ain't talking, maybe his home will."

Lottie and Traynor pulled up in front of the Colonnade apartment complex, and the property manager let them into 214C.

"Is this the home of a serial killer?" Traynor asked as they stepped into a cluttered living room with a flat-screen TV and a coffee table made of flattened beer cans.

Lottie lifted the lid of a pizza box. Inside was a single triangle covered with green fuzz. With her left toe, she nudged aside a pillow with crusty yellow stains. "It's the home of a man in serious need of soap and a bucket of water."

"Didn't Agent Reed say we're looking for a neat freak?" Traynor asked.

"Yep, but Reed said the trait could be manifested in only specific areas of his life. We'll need to check out his work space, his computer, and his car."

Lottie checked out the elaborate TV and DVDs, looking for anything that connected to Shayna Thomas or the TV station where she worked, but finding nothing. Just as she was about to dig into the next drawer of the entertainment center, Traynor called her into the front bedroom.

"Holy shit," she said with a hiss.

"There isn't anything holy about this room," Traynor said.

"It is if you call it a shrine."

Candids and professional photos of Shayna Thomas covered one wall. On the desk sat dozens of DVDs, all neatly labeled as Shayna Thomas newscasts. In the desk drawers they found shoes and undergarments and a straw with bright red lipstick stains.

"This creep's obsessed with her," Traynor said.

Lottie scratched a curl of hair above her ear. "But did he murder her?"

\* \* \*

*Saturday, June 13, 11 p.m.*
*Dorado Bay, Nevada*

Kate carried in two glasses of tea and placed one in front of Hayden, who sat on the sofa, his computer open on the coffee table before him. Sweet mint wafted up from the icy drink.

"Sorry it's not champagne," she said.

"Champagne?"

"To celebrate."

He raised both of his eyebrows, noticing for the first time the half grin on her mouth.

"You're not the only one who can read people, G-man." She set the other glass on the table near the recliner. "You're getting close to something. It's all over your face." He took a long sip and watched her swaying hips disappear back into the kitchen.

She was right. He was getting close to unraveling the mystery of Jason Erickson. Earlier this evening the coroner confirmed that the body found in Jason's shed was indeed Kendra Erickson. Cause of death was not a single immobilizing stab but heart failure. Kendra Erickson died of natural causes. The coroner was still working on time of death, which was harder to pin down given that the body had spent time in a frozen state, most likely in Jason's freezer.

Hayden could clearly see the sequence of events: In January, something causes Jason Erickson to snap, possibly the death of his mother by natural causes. He can't bear to lose her, so he stores her body in the freezer. When he's finally able to part with his mother, most likely after taking the prescription medication for panic attacks, he takes her to the hunting cabin and gives her a ceremonial send-off. Monthly he travels to the cabin and covers her body with the pink roses she loved. Now here's where things get less clear. Jason then goes on to systematically kill the broadcasters. Why? Is it something to do with his long-gone sister, Kate? And what happened in Colorado Springs? Why didn't he break the mirrors?

Hayden had heard from Lottie. She tracked down the man at Shayna Thomas's back window and discovered he was a bona fide stalker. Greg Wullner, whose shoe and fingerprints matched those found at Thomas's house, had pictures of Thomas and pieces of her clothing along with trash pilfered from Thomas's Lexus, all kept in a spare bedroom.

Was Wullner working with Erickson? Or if he wasn't, did he see something?

It was no wonder Kate saw something on his face. For the first time in five months, he was making headway in this investigation, getting close to getting his hands on the Butcher.

Hayden checked his watch. Lottie said she'd call as soon as she and her people finished interviewing Wullner, whose lawyer had finally showed. The numbers staring back at him told him that it was late, that he should be tired, but he was wired.

Kate came back with two plates piled high with thick

browned bread topped with thin sliced roast beef and peppers in a steamy BBQ sauce.

He took it, realizing he'd had nothing to eat since the Danish at breakfast. Given the way Kate dug into her sandwich, she was starving. So much for taking care of his witness.

He took a bite, his mouth wakening at the myriad textures and flavors, the crispy bread, crunchy peppers with tender roast beef, and sweet-sour tang of the sauce. "This is incredible. Where'd you learn to cook?"

"The corral."

He took another huge bite. Forgetting to eat while on a case wasn't new to him. Having someone cook for him was. His mouth full, he raised an eyebrow.

"You mean, after all that background research on me you don't remember 'Katrina's Korral'? I was working for a station out of Abilene and got assigned to the morning show. I wasn't quite anchor material, so they put me on features. I ended up with the segment called 'Katrina's Korral,' which was sponsored by the local beef council. Along with my chef guests, I cooked up a storm, all beef, all the time."

He took another bite and washed it down with the minty tea. "I remember now. Red apron with the longhorns on the"—he paused as an image of Katrina in the kitchen flashed through his head—"front." The points were strategically placed at the tips of her breasts, clearly sexist, and clearly memorable.

She shrugged without a blush. "I did what I had to do, and six months later I ditched the apron and started covering hard news." She licked the BBQ sauce from the side of her index finger. "But I never forgot how to wrangle a good beef dinner. By the way, you're a mess." She wiped at his chin.

Her touch was casual, but there was nothing casual about

the jolt that sparked in his midsection. His hand jerked, and a sliver of beef slid down his shirt and landed in his lap.

She laughed. It was low and sexy, rumbling at the back of her throat. She picked the beef off his thigh—a good thing because he was suddenly immobile—and pointed at the red sauce plastered across his shirt. "It's going to stain unless you get it in cold water."

Cold water. He could do with some right now. His training and common sense told him she was off-limits. His head knew that. Unfortunately, his body was having a harder time with the concept. He dropped his sandwich on his plate, walked to the bathroom, and turned on the water in the sink. As he took off his shirt, his phone rang. "Can you get that? It's probably Lottie." Red stains also streaked his undershirt, and he stripped that off, too.

He could still feel where Kate's hands touched him. Something besides spicy BBQ sauce was heating him up. Kate. Her angry shouts. Her cries. And more recently her laughs. She wasn't shy with her emotions. She was loud and boisterous, not the type to be quiet in bed. He plunged his shirts into the icy water. She was probably one of those women who made soft little sounds at the back of her throat, who threw her head back and screamed in pleasure. The BBQ sauce on his pants shifted as he stiffened.

The last thing he should be thinking about was Kate moaning and screaming in his arms. But he was. The image was clear and vivid, leaving nothing else in his head. No shattered mirrors, no voices, not even the bloody hands.

His fingers gripped the cool porcelain sink. Kate was a victim, a witness, someone he needed to protect, but she was also a beautiful, vivacious woman who lived hard and probably loved hard, too. He swallowed a groan.

The soft shuffle of bare feet sounded behind him. Attached to those feet would be curvy calves with a spray of freckles, a softly rounded butt, breasts just big enough to fit nicely in the palm of his hand. Topping her off wére those chestnut waves, so soft he could imagine burying his face in them as he pressed his body against the length of hers. One nudge, that's all he needed from her. A slant of her gaze, her body angled just a degree toward him.

He turned slowly. Kate stood in the bathroom doorway in her shorts and flimsy T-shirt. Her cheeks were flushed, and her breath came out in choppy bursts. She thrust a hand toward him, jabbing his phone in his face.

"It's the Dorado Bay police. They found Jason."

# CHAPTER TWELVE

*Saturday, June 13, 11:34 p.m.*
*Dorado Bay, Nevada*

*Jason is dead.*

When she was a child her father told her if she said something enough, believed in it enough, it would come true.

*Jason is dead.*

*Jason is dead.*

Hayden held her elbow as they joined the cluster of bodies at the edge of the lake near Mulveney's Cove.

"How did it unfold?" Hayden asked Dorado Bay police chief Mitt Greenfield.

"Local kid caught the foot while fishing. Got our boys in here a few hours ago and found the body thirty yards out near the boulders. Weighted with cinderblocks. Wrapped partially in plastic. In his wallet we found a driver's license that read Jason Erickson. Knew you and your team needed to take it from here."

Take-charge Hayden was here. Iron-faced. But there was a crack, a fissure of urgency. As for Kate, she was ready to crack, to split like fissioned atoms.

*Jason is dead.*

They walked through the darkness toward the klieg lights and a stretcher near the shore. Standing at the edge of light, she put her hand on Hayden's.

"It's over, right?" Kate said. "If this is Jason's body, everything is over. No more broadcasters killed. No more blood. No more broken mirrors." No more running.

Hayden raised a hand and placed it along her neck where her pulse slammed out a wild rhythm. "We don't know for sure if that body is really Jason's. We need to go slow."

Go slow? Was he insane?

No. He was Hayden. He'd changed into a new crisp white shirt and another beautiful silk tie, this one with cool green and blue and lavender waves. His hair was neatly combed, his shoes shiny. But they wouldn't be for long with the damp, spongy lakeshore sucking at his feet. The cluster of bodies parted as she and Hayden approached the stretcher draped with a white canvas-like sheet.

The crickets stopped chirping. The owls fell mute. Even the lake ceased its gentle drumbeat on the shore. All was silent but the mantra in her head.

*Jason is dead.*

One of the officers folded back the sheet, and a wave of putrid air slammed her. She took a step back but stared fixedly at the corpse. It was stiff, covered in a frosty-white, waxy substance. Something had nibbled away the eyes, ears, lips, and nose, making the exposed teeth—which appeared frozen in mid-chatter—the only feature recognizably human.

"His arm," she said with a catch in her voice. "Let me see the inside of his right arm."

The officer carefully pulled back the shirt sleeve, exposing a scar, a crisp white checkmark, the one she'd given him when he'd jumped between her and her maniacal mother on prom night. Her eyelids slammed shut. "It's him."

Jason was dead.

Relief. She waited for it to pour over her in glorious waves. She expected her arms to jut high in triumph, but something held her back. Was it the thought of celebrating death, even one of a killer, that left her heavy-limbed? Or was it being next to him, her attacker, the man who'd stolen so much from her with twenty-five thrusts of a knife?

A hand curved around her waist. She was a broadcast journalist who saw news feeds that would never make the airwaves: a YouTube video of a woman hanging herself from an attic rafter, a wobbly cell phone video of junior high kids kicking one of their classmates until he was comatose. But this was different. This was personal. She leaned into the smooth, warm wall of Hayden's suit coat.

Another Dorado Bay police officer approached Hayden. "Kyl Watson from Hope Academy is here. He said you asked him to come and ID the body. You still want to see him?"

Hayden nodded. Kate almost wanted to hug him for being so predictable. There were too many unfamiliar feelings ricocheting through her chest right now.

Watson wasn't alone. He'd brought his sister, Beth, her face as pale and waxen as the moon. He drew up in front of the body and swallowed. "The hair, the body size. It looks like him."

"Absolutely sure?" Hayden asked.

Watson narrowed his eyes, opened his mouth, and closed it before shaking his head.

"Lift his hair and check his ear," Beth Watson said from behind her brother.

"What?" Kyl and Hayden asked at the same time.

Beth raised a hand to the side of her head. "Jason has

a mole behind his right ear, about the size of a pea." Kyl looked strangely at his sister, but she didn't look back. One of the officers used a gloved hand and pushed back the hair, displaying a small, dark mole. "It's him."

Kyl raised his gaze to the night sky. "This is bad, oh God, this is bad. Jason is the Butcher, right? He's the man who killed those six women, all this while he worked at Hope Academy."

"We're still investigating," Hayden said.

"What am I going to tell my boys? My board?" Kyl's throat caught on the words as he slipped an arm around his sister, whose entire body trembled with silent sobs.

*Tell them Jason is a murderer, a sick son of a bitch who got the cruel death he deserved*, Kate thought about offering. It was, after all, the truth.

Wasn't it?

Her feet shifted, sinking deeper into the loamy earth. Then why didn't she feel like celebrating?

* * *

*Sunday, June 14, 12:55 a.m.*
*Colorado Springs, Colorado*

Stalker Boy looked like shit. Not just shit, week-old shit that had been sitting in the hot sun, stinking and full of maggots. Lottie knew something was squirming in Stalker Boy's gut. Time to poke it with a stick and see what crawled out.

Lottie nodded to Detective Traynor, who dropped the color photo of Shayna Thomas on the table, the one of her neck nearly severed in two.

"Not pretty anymore, is she?" Traynor said.

The stalker, Greg Wullner, turned a lurid shade of green, and she stepped back, worried he might blow chunks on her yellow snakeskin slingbacks.

"But she was beautiful at one time, wasn't she?" The detective's voice grew soft. "A face you could stare at for hours on end."

The stalker swallowed.

"But you'll never see the beautiful woman again, will you? Because this is all that's left." Traynor took out another photo, this one a close-up of her gouged-out eyes. "Brutal, wasn't it? Stabbed sixty-two times with a double-edged, eight-inch knife."

"Stop!" Stalker Boy brought a fisted hand to his mouth.

"It's hard for you, seeing these things. I can tell."

Stalker Boy nodded, gnawing his fist like a starving animal going at a bone.

"You feel bad, don't you? Like your own heart has been ripped out. Like you've been bled to death."

Stalker Boy nodded again. Saliva dripped down his arm.

Lottie nudged past Traynor. "You feel bad because you were there."

The stalker raised his head, his eyes no longer glassy. "No, I didn't kill her. I could never kill Shay."

"But you *were* there, weren't you?" Lottie edged closer to the table.

"No," Stalker Boy said.

"What about the evidence? It doesn't lie." She dropped a folder on the table. "Fingerprints." Another folder. "Footprints." Another thud. "Semen." The folders were filled with papers she had dug out of the recycling bin because lab results weren't back yet, but there was no way Stalker Boy here would know that. He couldn't take his gaze off Shayna Thomas's mutilated body.

"No, no, I didn't kill her!"

"But you were there."

The lawyer, who'd been sitting at Wullner's side, cleared his throat. "My client will not respond to that."

"Let's review the facts, Mr. Wullner," Traynor said. "We found a room full of photos, taped news segments, trash from Shayna's Lexus, and some of Shayna's clothing at your apartment." He pointed at the folders on the table. "We also have evidence linking you to the crime scene at the time of Shayna Thomas's murder."

"Frightening scenario, isn't it?" Lottie asked. "Enough to scare the stink off shit, wouldn't ya think?"

The attorney raised a hand, but Stalker Boy waved him off. "Yes."

"Speak up," Lottie said. "Can't hear you with these old ears."

"Yes, I was there."

Lottie's body tensed. "And you saw something through the window."

He nodded. "I saw a person."

Lottie took a folder from her briefcase. There was nothing trumped up about what was inside of it. She slipped out a photo and placed it in front of Shayna Thomas's stalker. Stalker. Not killer. For at this point it was possible, maybe even probable, that stalker Greg Wullner was not the murderer, but a witness.

"Is this who you saw through Shayna Thomas's bedroom window?" Lottie asked as he stared at the photo of Jason Erickson. She wanted to scream, *Okay, you lowlife, stinking, maggot-infested son of a bitch, is this the madman you saw taking chunks out of Shayna Thomas with a butcher knife?*

Stalker Boy tilted his head as if he were a great thinker. At last he said, "Absolutely not. I saw a woman."

"A woman?" Lottie rubbed at her forehead.

"Pink dress. Drab hair. She didn't look dangerous," Stalker Boy said. "I had no idea she was a killer."

"So why didn't you come forward when you heard Shayna Thomas had been stabbed?"

"I thought you'd blame me."

Okay, he was smarter than he first appeared, and the pisser was, Lottie believed the maggot. She believed he left before the Butcher whacked Shayna, because Stalker Boy was clearly obsessed with Shayna Thomas, a beautiful, *living* Shayna Thomas.

So what the hell was going on? Both Stalker Boy and the kid across the street saw a woman in a pink dress. Did she kill Shayna? Was she just the front that got the real killer in the door?

They were back to square one. No, that wasn't true. Stalker Boy may be a maggot, but he got a look at Shayna's killer's face. She scooped up the photo of Erickson and crammed it back in the folder. "Do you think you could identify this woman in Shayna Thomas's bedroom if you saw her again?"

Pain lashed Stalker Boy's face, and again Lottie realized this loser had just lost the love of his sicko life. "I'll try. I'll do anything to find whoever killed my Shay."

* * *

*Sunday, June 14, 5:10 a.m.*
*Dorado Bay, Nevada*

Kate's life on the run was over.

Six hours ago, she'd seen her attacker's stiff, bloated

body, and she'd identified the scar on his wrist. Jason was dead, and his death meant she should be at peace.

She scrubbed her hand across eyes that refused to close. So why didn't she feel relief? Why couldn't she sleep? And why was she standing in the doorway of Hayden's bedroom?

Hayden sat on the bed, his laptop balanced on his thighs, his shoes and socks on the floor near the dresser. He looked normal, almost relaxed. He still wore his suit pants, but he was tie-less, a golden wedge of skin and dark hair showing above his creamy white undershirt. She tapped the doorframe.

When he looked up, she cleared her throat. "I...uh... saw the light, figured you were still awake." Her fingers dug into the hem of her nightshirt. Hard to believe she used to make her living talking in front of a camera.

"I couldn't sleep," he said. If he was surprised to see her, he didn't show it. Stubble shadowed the lower half of his face, and the smudges beneath his eyes were inky thumbprints, but he looked intensely clear-eyed, more animated than she'd ever seen him. And very, very sexy.

"What are you doing?" Kate asked. Really, she should go back to her room, but her room was too dark.

"Looking for links." He motioned to his laptop. "We have to be sure that Jason is indeed the Butcher. Right now I'm trying to find anything that connects him to one of the dead broadcasters, hopefully Shayna Thomas. I'm waiting for the autopsy report." He looked at his watch. "They put a rush on it. Should be done within the hour."

"Best-case scenario with the autopsy?" Kate asked as she walked into his room, aglow with light from his computer.

"In my wildest fantasies we find Shayna Thomas's hair, skin, or blood somewhere on Jason's body. I'll take anything we can DNA match. More realistically, we'll find something that will lead us to whoever killed him, and perhaps that person will help us link Jason to the Broadcaster slayings."

"Are you hopeful?" She licked her lips, the word tasting odd on her tongue.

"I'm always hopeful, Kate." Hayden didn't smile often, but when he did, it carried more power than the gun tucked into the holster still strapped to his chest.

She edged to the side of the bed but didn't sit. Maybe she was here because she needed to see him smile and hear him say that good will conquer evil, justice will prevail, and all will live happily ever after. Growing up, she lived with a mother who had told her that she was ugly and worthless, who had screamed that she regretted bringing Kate into this world, who—

"Stop." Hayden set aside his laptop and reached for her hand, the nails of which were digging into her thigh.

She had no desire to pull away—just the opposite. Something, maybe the smile, drew her closer. She pictured herself sinking into his arms. "Stop what?"

"Thinking about dragons."

His thumb stroked the top of her hand, and she tried to laugh, but it came out as a choky gurgle. "You're getting into my head again."

"Honestly, you're an easy read, particularly tonight."

"Am I? Then tell me why I'm here." She finally raised her gaze to his. *Wanting to throw myself into your arms.* Smokey Joe said she wasn't a liar, and she was doing a piss-poor job of lying to herself tonight. Her world had been rocked by Jason's death, but the tremors had begun the night she invited Hayden to handcuff her to the bed in Smokey's upstairs bedroom. She'd tossed out the taunt to jolt a seemingly unshakable man, but she'd been affected, too. And until today, she'd been too deep in her self-imposed darkness to see. With Jason finally gone and the darkness giving way to something she wasn't quite ready to call hope, she was free to feel the electricity sparking between them.

Jason's death changed everything.

The pulse at Hayden's wrist slammed hers, but he quickly patted the top of her hand as if giving comfort to a frightened child. "In less than twenty-four hours you discovered both your mother and brother dead. Regardless of your feelings for them, it's a loss of your primary family unit, and you're feeling very much alone right now. You need company. I'm here."

She held up their clasped hands. "Do you think that's all you are, Hayden, a hand to hold while I travel a bumpy road?"

He paused just long enough for her to see doubt flit across the granite plane of his face. "Yes."

No, she wasn't going to let him brush off her feelings with head-talk. Still holding his hand, she sat on the edge of the bed. Her thigh brushed against his, and a tidal wave of heat flooded her body. "You feel nothing?" she asked.

A whisper of a tremor shook his hand. "I feel a need to protect you with every resource available to me and my team and with every cell of my being."

She pictured Hayden's being. No gun or briefcase. No fancy suit and shiny shoes. Just golden skin and curved muscle and rumpled, wavy hair. Her tongue darted out to moisten her suddenly dry lips. "Every cell?"

He dropped her hand as if he, too, felt the fire, and shucked his fingers through the sides of his hair, keeping them glued to his scalp. "You're a witness, a victim, and this is a job."

"A job?" A few days ago, she had made the mistake of calling Smokey Joe *a job*, and Hayden had called her on it.

A laugh, light and airy, expanded her chest and tripped over her lips. God, it felt good to laugh. "You're saying I'm just a *job*? That this…this thing between us is purely professional?"

Hayden turned his gaze to the blackness outside his window. She settled her fingertips on his shirtfront, the fabric buttery soft and vibrating with the thrum rushing through her veins. He remained a slab of marble. How could he not feel that? Was the heat purely one-sided? Maybe the upending of her world addled her brain. Maybe she *was* just a job.

She flattened her hand on his chest, ready to push away, but the rapid-fire beat of his heart slammed her palm, heated her skin. "Just a job?" she asked on a rush of breath.

He looked almost pained as he tore his gaze from the window and back to her. Hayden may pretend to be made of stone, but there was nothing cold about him as he lowered his head, his warm breath sweeping along her jaw, nothing hard as his lips brushed against hers. Her fingers dug into his shirt as she steadied herself against the barest of kisses. Three years. It had been three years since she'd been this close to someone, three years since she'd *wanted* to be this close to someone.

As if sensing her want or admitting one of his own, Hayden dug his hands into her hair and pulled her closer. The feathery touch of lips gave way to the firm pressure of his mouth. She tasted cinnamon, sweet and spicy, and heard the low moan at the back of his throat.

"Not a job," he said, his mouth not moving from hers. "Definitely not a job."

Her mouth curved against his, and a rumble rocked his chest.

Somewhere a phone rang, but Hayden, clearly no longer in work mode, didn't seem to notice. The phone let out another shriek. She snapped her head upright. It rang again. Hayden blinked. And in that blink, his face became a cold, hard slate. He grabbed the phone.

Kate drew in a long breath, attempting to cool the heat swirling in her chest. She watched him take notes as he listened to whoever was on the other end of the phone. How could he do it? Turn off his emotions in the blink of an eye? She picked at a loose thread on the quilted coverlet. Because his life was his job. He lived and breathed his work. She'd seen it the first day he tracked her down at Smokey Joe's cabin. And when this case was over, he'd move on to the next case, the next killer.

She wrapped the thread around her finger. And she'd hop on her bike and…Honestly, she had no idea where she'd go, but for the first time in three years she had freedom to move about without fear. That thought sent a different type of warmth through her body. Instead of heading out on the road right away, maybe she'd go back to Smokey Joe's cabin and make sure he got set up with a new aide. She'd help him finish all the orders for their jewelry business. She was earning a nice little nest egg that would pay for quite a few tanks of gas. Maybe she'd even see if Smokey wanted to take a trip to Las Vegas to get a new LOST MY ASS candy dish since she'd broken his old one.

Behind her, in the cottage kitchen, the landline phone rang. Maybe it was Smokey Joe calling to complain about the heat in Tucson or Maeve or both. More likely it was someone from Hayden's team, or the Dorado Bay Police, or the coroner with word on Jason's autopsy. She hurried to the phone.

"Agent Hayden Reed, please," a deep male voice said.

"May I ask who's calling?"

"Lieutenant Rhodes of the Oakland Police."

"He's on another call right—"

"Tell him to get off."

The tone irked her. Like Smokey, she did not like people telling her what to do. "He can't—"

"Tell him to get off the damned phone. He's got another one."

"Excuse me?"

"Another slaying. The Broadcaster Butcher struck here in Oakland last night."

That couldn't be right. Jason's dead, bloated body had been found at the bottom of the lake. A tremor rocked her spine, and she steadied her hand on the back of a chair. How had he managed to get in one last kill? Did he have a partner? Was a killer's accomplice still at large? Or was this some kind of copycat?

Holding a pencil so tightly it snapped, she took the lieutenant's name and number and walked into Hayden's room. He'd moved to the window overlooking the black night, his phone no longer at his ear. He stood in profile, but she could see something red and hot racing across his face. Had he learned about the Oakland murder?

She joined him at the window and held out the paper. "The Oakland police called. Jason struck again."

Hayden didn't look at the paper. Why the hell wasn't he looking at the paper? Why wasn't he taking charge and fixing things?

"Hayden, what's wrong?"

He stretched his neck as if trying to make the words flow. "Autopsy protocols show Jason's body was in that lake ten to fourteen days."

The paper slipped from her hand. "But Shayna Thomas was killed on Monday, six days ago, and there's the Oakland broadcaster who was killed last night."

Hayden rested both palms on the windowsill. "Jason didn't kill Shayna Thomas or the broadcaster in Oakland. Jason Erickson is not the Butcher." His words shot out fiery hot in the already warm room. "Jason was stabbed with an eight-inch, double-edged knife at the back of his head. Two subsequent stab wounds to main arteries bled him to death. Not only is he not the Butcher, he was killed by the Butcher."

A glacial cold, like the waters of the lake outside her window, washed over her. "The Butcher's still on the loose."

"And he won't stop until he—"

As Hayden's voice broke off, something hovered at the far edges of her mind. For nearly a week she'd lived and breathed this case with Hayden, who now stood before her, his face twisted in anger and something more unsettling: fear.

"Kills me," she said with a gasp. "He has to break all the mirrors. He has to finish the job." Her finger slid along the scar on her neck to the scar on her breast. "I'm the job he never finished. He has to kill me."

Hayden didn't argue. He couldn't. He intimately knew the Butcher.

Adrenaline shot through her legs. After a few hours of precious peace, it was time to head back to the shadowy back roads where the Butcher couldn't find her.

Before she could make a run for the door, Hayden reached for her.

Her feet tensed. Her hands fisted. Ready to fight. Ready to flee.

She expected the jingle of cuffs. Instead, skin brushed against skin as he slipped his arms around her. Every muscle in her body tightened. It would be so easy to smack away his arms, to head-butt him in the chin, to duck and run. She pulled back her arm.

His lips brushed against the top of her head, and his arms dropped to his side.

The unexpected freedom left her off balance. She grabbed the bedpost. This was one of his head games. He was giving her a choice, giving her power. Right now she could walk away, duck into the shadows.

She shifted from one bare foot to the other. But that wouldn't stop the Butcher. He would continue to kill, continue to hunt for her because she was the one who got away.

She took a single step, not toward the door but toward Hayden, and rested her cheek against the crisp coolness of his shirt, his heart beating calm and steady.

*Click.* His arms locked about her. Then came his words, delivered with a heat that surprised her. "This is one job he's not going to finish."

# CHAPTER THIRTEEN

*Sunday, June 14, 7:45 a.m.*
*Dorado Bay, Nevada*

Hayden gave the fan blade a spin. It whirred smoothly, silently, just the way it should. He fastened the mesh frame in place and double-checked the clamps, making sure the blades were covered. Everything safe.

Unlike Kate.

Metal clanked as he threw a screwdriver and pliers into the toolbox. Jason Erickson had been found at the bottom of the lake, and the Butcher was still on the loose. And when—not if—he found out Kate was still alive, he'd go after her because his meticulous method of madness demanded he finish the job.

And to the Butcher, Kate was just a job.

Hayden slammed shut the toolbox lid. Now he had two lives on the line, including the woman who had the power to wrench his mind from *his* job.

"Evie and Hatch just drove up with Chief Greenfield right behind." Kate handed him a cup of coffee, their fingers brushing. Heat that had nothing to do with the steaming brew flooded his arm.

He plugged in the fan, an arc of cool wind sweeping over his skin as Kate set down her own coffee cup with a rattle. She'd been rattled all morning, casting glances out the window and checking door and window locks. But he expected that from a woman who knew a serial killer was gunning for her. Which is why Hayden needed to focus on the job, and only the *job*.

When his teammates and the team from the Dorado Bay PD arrived, he dove in because the only surefire way to keep Kate safe was to catch the killer. "Jason is key," Hayden said. "He's not the Butcher, but he knew the Butcher and is somehow involved in the attacks. We find out more about Jason, we get one step closer to the Butcher."

"Tell us about our boy." Evie threaded her fingers together and cracked her knuckles, as if getting ready for a fight.

"Jason was raised by a mentally ill, abusive mother who showered him with warped love and despised Kate. Jason, on the other hand, adored his feisty older sister. Over the years, Jason's mother descended further into ill health, both physically and mentally. Throughout all this, Jason tried to create order and peace in his family home and his world. In the end, he failed. Even his attack on Kate was a failure."

"You still believe Jason attacked Kate?" Greenfield asked.

"Absolutely," Kate said, her jaw raising more than a fraction. "I saw the scar. I saw his eyes."

Hayden nodded. "The facts support her. Obedient and subservient to a fault, Jason attacked Kate three years ago, but he did it on someone else's orders—the Butcher's. Jason, who genuinely cared for Kate, hated himself for the attack, and he couldn't stand to see himself after he stabbed her, so he broke the mirrors. He also folded her hands to try to make peace. Finally, he left the crime scene free of traceable evidence because he was a meticulous sort."

"That makes sense," Hatch said. "But why did the Butcher order the attack on Kate in the first place?"

"If we knew that, we'd probably know our Butcher," Hayden said. "One of the things we'll be working on over the next few days is finding out who wanted Kate dead three years ago, because that same person went on to kill the seven other broadcasters using Jason's MO."

"But why did he kill the other broadcasters?" Kate asked with audible frustration.

"Two possible scenarios. One, the Butcher's a sociopath and has a fixation with female broadcasters. But I'm leaning toward number two. In this scenario, he killed the other broadcasters to flush you out. He figured once you made the connection between your attack and their deaths, you'd come out of hiding. Your strong sense of justice would demand it."

Kate rubbed at her temples. "It's so complex."

"Serial murders with this degree of success usually are," Hayden added. "The Butcher thought of everything. He killed the broadcasters, but he staged them in a way to make it look like Jason executed the kills. He meticulously thought out every detail. The Butcher planned the killings around Jason's work schedule. He followed the same MO, including the mirrors. But he missed one thing that makes me certain a different individual killed the other broadcasters."

"The knife," Evie said.

Hayden nodded. "The seven broadcasters received a single immobilizing stab wound to the neck followed by two stabs to maximize blood loss, and so did Jason. Kate didn't."

Kate ground her fist into the center of her forehead as if her head ached. "But why did he start up after two and a half years of doing nothing?"

While he'd been working on the fan, Hayden asked himself the same thing. "Perhaps he's been incapacitated for the past two years, possibly with an illness or some kind of physical restraint, like prison. Or it's possible something happened in January that escalated his fear of you. The Butcher *needs* you dead, and something triggered that in January."

"Maybe he needs to get me. Maybe we need to go fishing for him, and I'll be the bait."

"No."

She jumped to her feet. "Why the hell not?"

"Because I'm in charge of this investigation, and I said no." He pointed to her chair and waited for her to take a seat.

"Well Mr. In-Charge, you're doing a piss-poor job because seven women have died under your watch."

The words cut through his chest like a double-edged knife. But they were true. This was his watch, and the Butcher was still on the streets. He straightened his cuffs and looked Kate squarely in the eye. "And you won't be number eight."

Evie hopped up from her chair and started to pace. "Hold on, *amigo*. Kate's on to something."

Kate took a seat on the sofa next to him and placed her hand on his knee. "You said it yourself, Hayden. It's me he wants. The killings started because of me, and they can end because of me. If we let him know where I'm at, he'll come."

He pictured Kate's hand, bloody and resting on her lifeless chest, and swallowed. "No."

"Why not?" Chief Greenfield asked. "Her brother and mother are dead. It would make sense for her to come back home, and we can make sure people know about it."

"You'll control the situation." Kate's hand pressed into his thigh. "I'll be perfectly safe."

"I said no."

"Think this through, Professor. Really think." Hatch leaned back in his chair and crossed his ankles. "You've been hunting this beast for months. Maybe Kate's right. Maybe it's time to stop hunting and go fishing. We could make the whole thing very public, have a big press conference, and get her image on television screens across the country."

Hayden didn't want Kate out in the open. He wanted to keep blood off those hands.

Evie popped him on the back of the head. "Where's that big brain you're supposed to have? We're talking pure logic here. The fastest way to catch the Butcher is to dangle bait he can't resist."

Kate folded her hands in her lap. "Which would be me."

Every person in the room drilled him with a hard gaze, dared him to say they were wrong. He couldn't. This thing had started with Kate and could very well end with her. She'd already pointed out the chilling number: seven deaths on his watch.

"We're talking a press conference, Kate," Hayden said. "Hundreds of people and cameras and questions. Everyone focused on you." He forced out the words he didn't want to say. "Are you sure?"

"Damned straight I am."

In that moment, he saw the woman who'd stood in front of the camera for those "Justice for All" reports.

"What do you need me to do?" Kate asked.

*Stay safe*, he wanted to say. *And stay in my arms.* Instead he took out his computer and started to plan a fishing trip.

\* \* \*

*Sunday, June 14, 12:30 p.m.*
*Dorado Bay, Nevada*

"I like it better without the scarf."

Kate's fingers stilled at her neck, where she'd been fluffing the green silk, her gaze meeting Hayden's in the bathroom mirror.

"I like it better *with* the scarf." She yanked the fabric, making sure the knot was secure.

He walked in, and the little bathroom closed in on her. Right now the entire world felt like it was closing in on her because in less than an hour, she'd be facing the world for the first time in three years. Scars and all. She pulled in a deep breath.

Cinnamon.

Hayden was here, rock solid and at her side. She wouldn't have agreed to the press conference otherwise. She broke her gaze with him and fanned out the edges of the scarf. But that didn't mean she liked the idea of bearing her scars for all the world to see.

His hands slid along her shoulders, his touch lighter than the gauzy silk. "You have a beautiful neck." His fingers loosened the knot. How could such a big man have such a light touch? She'd felt it hours ago in that single kiss stolen in a moment of peace. The silk swished to the floor.

"Look." His insistent fingers tilted her face toward her reflection. "You can barely see them."

She forced her gaze to the scars that crisscrossed the right side of her neck and cringed. "I do."

His hands dropped to his sides, and for the second time that day, a barely contained roar rumbled his chest. "Only because you're looking for them."

"Others will too." She picked up the scarf and draped it around her neck. Of course she'd wear it, no matter how Hayden's feathery touch made her feel.

"Kate, you're a beautiful woman." His fingertips rested on her shoulders. "You don't need the scarf."

"More psychobabble stuff, Hayden. I'm totally onto you. You're trying to boost my courage before I go out in front of all those people and all those cameras."

"And if I am?"

"This is no fairy tale. You don't have magical powers, and your words won't change who I am."

He jerked her toward him. "Exactly who are you, *Kate*? And don't give me a single line of vitriolic nonsense your mother planted in your head."

She tried to pull away. He was crazy if he thought she would let her insane mother define who she was. She'd long ago escaped that dragon.

Hayden's fingers dug into her shoulders. "She was the monster, Kate, not you. You have to get her out of your head." One hand slid along her shoulder to her neck. Anything she'd been thinking, any words that thought about shooting off her tongue, disappeared. Did he feel the skip and quickening of her pulse?

Hayden bent toward her, and his lips parted, but they didn't settle on hers. He went lower, to her neck, where his breath and then his lips brushed against her heated skin.

"You're beautiful, Kate." His lips traveled down the column of her throat, along the raised, white-hot scar. His tongue flicked at the spot where her pulse hammered. Then he raised his head and sunk his fingers into the silk scarf, which he tore off. "You don't need it."

She was too stunned to argue. With trembling fingers that had nothing to do with nerves over the press conference, she switched off the light and walked out of the bathroom, Hayden at her side, the silk scarf puddled on the floor.

* * *

*Sunday, June 14, 1 p.m.*
*Dorado Bay, Nevada*

Tripods clicked to attention, fingers tapped on mics, and bodies jockeyed for the best camera angle. Sights and sounds from her past. But at this press conference, Kate wouldn't be reporting the story. She would *be* the story. She stood to the right of the podium, next to Hayden and behind two Dorado Bay police officers.

Chief Greenfield stepped up to the mic and read his prepared statement regarding Jason Erickson and the Broadcaster Butcher. Although the police chief spoke first, Kate knew the man directing this dog-and-pony show was FBI agent Hayden Reed, the same man who had sent her world out of kilter with a series of kisses. Her fingers slipped to the bare column of her throat. The skin was still ablaze.

When the chief finished his statement, Hayden took his turn at the podium. She watched his careful gestures, the occasional well-timed facial expressions, his lips. He was smooth and steady and masterful in the way he spoke. And kissed.

"We have a witness that has recently come forward," Hayden was saying, "and she has been instrumental..."

Kate didn't hear the rest of his words but focused on the pressure of Hayden's lips against her neck. On his words. *You're beautiful, Kate.*

"...she'll now issue a brief statement. Katrina Erickson."

A gasp rippled through the journalists as they crowded closer. Her feet twitched. Hayden held out his hand to her, and she reached for it. Cameras clicked and hands flew to lenses, tightening in on her face. Hayden nodded. She could do this.

On a small piece of paper in her pocket, Hayden had written what she needed to say, but she didn't need a script.

"For those of you who don't recognize me, I'm Katrina Erickson, and I'm a former news reporter for KTTL Frontline News. Three years ago I was attacked in Reno, stabbed twenty-four times by a man I have since identified as Jason Erickson, my brother."

A soft murmur swept across the crowd.

"Like most of you, I feel angry at this senseless taking of life and at the gross injustice done to my seven fellow broadcasters, and I am working with the FBI and Dorado Bay Police to find the individual responsible for these deaths."

That was the easy part. Truth always came easy to her. Her fingers dug into the podium ledge. "In the past week I have undergone memory recovery therapy and was able to recall that my brother, Jason Erickson, didn't act alone. He had a partner, the killer who you know as the Broadcaster Butcher, and I have since given details to the authorities. It is my hope that this information will aid in apprehending this killer swiftly and that justice will be served."

A display of fireworks exploded as more cameras flashed, capturing her face, which no doubt displayed her determination and her fear. The bait was set.

Now it was the Butcher's turn. How would he react? Come at her? Kill another? Her legs were shaking as she walked from the podium toward Hayden.

"Ms. Erickson, how do you feel about your brother's death?"

"Katrina, where have you been for the past two and a half years?"

She kept walking. She'd given what she could. Right now there was nothing left.

Behind her, Chief Greenfield took the podium, but she didn't hear what he said.

"Perfect," Hayden said softly.

"I need to get out of here."

Hayden put his hand at her back and guided her off stage. Chief Greenfield raised his head and asked, "You want me to take the Q&A?"

Hayden paused then shook his head. This was a crucial moment, and Kate knew he couldn't give up control. He motioned to Hatch. "Get her inside," Hayden said to his teammate, and then to her, "I'll be right there."

Inside the police station, Kate found more people, more stares. The scar along her scarfless neck burned, and she tugged her hair across her throat.

Hatch led her through the station. When she spotted a women's bathroom, she rushed toward it. She pushed open the door, but Hatch dashed in before her.

"Hatch!" She pointed to the ladies room sign.

"I'm staying with you."

She threw a glare at him then yanked open the bathroom stalls. "Look, no butchers. Give me some privacy, please."

He paused.

*Please*, her eyes begged, in a way her words couldn't.

"Okay," Hatch said on a long breath. "I'll be right outside."

When the door closed, Kate's knees gave way. Her fingers gripped the counter as emotions crashed over her. Mostly fear, because the Butcher finished every job. He would take the bait. He was on his way.

She turned on the tap and thrust her hands under the water, letting the cool stream wash over the heated pulse at her wrists. With cupped hands, she splashed water on her face. Handful after handful, she tried to wash away the stares, the fear, and the ingrained desire to run.

At last she turned off the water and fumbled for the towel dispenser. Cranking out a paper towel, she tore off a piece and blotted her face. She raised her face to the mirror, but instead of her own reflection, she saw another.

"Long time no see, Katrina."

# CHAPTER FOURTEEN

*Sunday, June 14, 1:25 p.m.*
*Dorado Bay, Nevada*

How the hell did you get in here?"

Robyn Banks, a line of blood dribbling down her shin, pointed to the narrow window on the back wall. "Hungry reporters will do anything for a story, and these days I'm hungry, Katrina, real hungry."

"My name is Kate." She wadded the paper towel and threw it in the overflowing trash can next to the sink.

"Reinventing yourself?"

Kate didn't have time for Robyn Banks and her questions or her jealously. The two had had a notorious rivalry back in her KTTL days, when Kate had uprooted Banks from the nightly news anchor spot. "What do you want?"

"A story, of course." A feral smile tugged at Robyn's glossy lips.

"You got my story."

"I got two minutes of vetted FBI propaganda."

"It's all I have."

The painted calm of Robyn's face cracked. "It's bullshit."

"There's no more. So don't waste your time or mine."

"Do you think you're going to get rid of me that easily?" Kate walked toward the door.

Robyn's red-tipped nails dug into her upper arm. "Déjà vu, huh? You and me at each other's throats. We had our share of heated moments."

"We fought like cats. Claws extended." Kate shook off Robyn's hand.

"Thirty minutes." Robyn blocked the door. "That's all I want. Your terms. You choose the location, the camera angle. Hell, I'll even let you choose the questions. Just give me an exclusive." Robyn's desperation had an almost manic tone.

Kate took a page out of the Book of Hayden. "No."

The calm ruffled Robyn even more. "You owe me the story."

"I owe you nothing." Kate stepped around her and reached for the door handle.

"You owe me your life."

Kate stopped but didn't turn.

"The night you were stabbed and bleeding to death, someone called nine-one-one." Robyn's words lost all bravado. "That someone was me."

\* \* \*

Hayden grabbed Hatch's shirtfront in his fisted hand. "Where the hell is she?"

Hatch blinked his surprise. "In the bathroom."

He let go of Hatch, forcing his heart out of his throat. "How long has she been in there?"

"Five, six minutes."

Hayden's fist twitched. "Is it five or six?"

"I'm sorry, buddy, but I forgot to set my stopwatch."

Hayden raked a hand through his hair. "Why did you let her out of your sight?"

"You want me to wait outside the bathroom stall while she pees?"

"I want you to do a better job keeping an eye on my witness."

"Your *witness*?" Hatch's eyebrows disappeared into his shaggy blond hair. "Is that what she is?"

Hayden pushed past Hatch and into the bathroom, where he almost crashed into Kate. She stood still and white, a marble statue in front of a brassy-haired woman with a bloody leg.

He grabbed his sidearm and drilled it on the woman. "Step away from her and put your hands in the air."

The woman laughed. "Oh God, you sound so FBI." She made a show of running a liquid gaze up and down the length of his body. "You look it, too."

"Hands up."

Kate placed a hand on his outstretched arm. "Hayden, it's okay. She's harmless."

The woman tilted her head, a sly smile sliding onto her red-lacquered lips. Keeping the Sig aimed at her, he whisked his left hand along her dress. No weapon.

"Feel free to search a little longer," she said with a sultry laugh.

He ignored her and asked Kate, "Who is she?"

"Robyn Banks. We used to work together at KTTL."

A broadcast reporter. The woman in the red dress had the sleek look, the practiced moves and delivery of someone accustomed to life in front of a camera—from the look of her, many years in front of the camera. An unnatural tightness stretched from the corners of her eyes, and a false fullness plumped her lips. This was a woman who had had some serious anti-aging work done.

"Did she hurt you?" He moved closer to Kate.

She shook her head. "Shocked me though. She claims to be the one who called nine-one-one the night I was stabbed."

That low simmer bubbled in his gut. "You were at Kate's house that night?"

"Fortuitous thing, wouldn't you say?" Robyn said.

His pulse spiked, and questions raced through his head. *Go slow*, he warned himself. He first needed to know if she was indeed the caller. "How did you identify yourself to the nine-one-one operator?"

"I told her I was Katrina's fairy godmother."

His pulse accelerated. The fairy godmother line was a holdback. "Why the anonymous call?"

She shrugged. "It was easier that way."

"Easier?"

"I like to cover the news, not make it."

"Why did you go to Kate's that night?" Hayden asked.

"A story, what else?" Hayden watched Robyn Banks speak. Most people lied easily with their mouths. Tougher to do with a body. "I'd just broken a story and needed Katrina's help with some sources she'd used in the past."

"And when you got there?"

She tapped her finger against her chin. "Hmmm...this sounds like official questioning."

"It is."

"I got to her house and she didn't answer. Being the curious sort I am"—she shot him a what-can-I-say look—"I walked in." The cockiness oozing from Robyn dried up. "I found her in a pool of blood in her bedroom. I knew she needed help, so I left and called nine-one-one."

"You went to a convenience store two blocks away to

make the call from a pay phone. Why didn't you call from her home phone or your cell?"

"Like I said, I like to cover the news, not be a part of it. I didn't want my prints on the phone or the call traced to my cell."

He'd run across the don't-involve-me mindset many times. "Did you see anyone at or near Kate's house?"

"No one."

Hayden drilled her with the look he saved for his most reluctant witnesses.

"I may be a hard-ass reporter, Agent Reed, but I'm not heartless. If I had any information on Katrina's attacker, anything that could have stopped those other killings, I would have come forward long before this." She raised her eyebrow and looked at Kate. "You're not the only one who believes in justice for all. Now, since you've refused me an interview, I need to get back to the station."

"One more question," Hayden said.

"For a face like yours, I'll give you two." Robyn puckered her lips.

"How old are you?"

Her shoulders stiffened. "Is it important?"

"Is it a secret?"

"Thirty-five."

He nodded. "Before you go, I need contact information."

She pulled out a business card.

"Home address, too." He handed her a pen, but she didn't take it. It hovered between them. He waited. With a scowl that sent ridges along her lipstick, she grabbed it and scribbled on the back of the card.

"I'll be in touch," he said. After she left, Hayden handed the pen to Hatch. "Have latent run prints."

* * *

*Go away!*

Kate wanted to scream at the journalists still milling about the police station as she and Hayden headed for the rental car. They all wanted a piece of her, just like the Butcher.

"Go slow, keep your face straight ahead," Hayden said against her neck. "I'll handle them."

Of course Hayden could handle the press. He'd summarily handled Robyn Banks, and for that she'd been grateful. Her head still rang with the shocking blow that her colleague had saved her life.

"No questions," Hayden said to the first reporter who got in their way. "No comment," he told the next and the next and the next.

*You got you your own personal government-issued bodyguard*, she could hear Smokey say. A smile, the first of this long and emotional day, curved her lips. The old soldier would probably love to get in on this battle.

When Hayden started the car, she noticed his face was not masked in its normal stony composure. He looked...excited.

"What did you see at the press conference?" she asked as he pulled out of the parking lot with a squeal.

Hayden pressed the accelerator. "Not what, who. Beth Watson from Hope Academy was there."

"So was half the town."

"She wore a baseball cap and big sunglasses and stood at the back of the crowd. It was obvious she didn't want to be seen."

Minutes later Hayden pulled into Hope Academy's circular drive and parked next to two cars, where two sullen-faced

youths loaded suitcases into trunks. More fallout from the
Jason Erickson bomb.

The reception area was empty, but it didn't surprise Kate,
given today was Sunday. However, a sharp thud and scream
coming from the hallway made her jump. She and Hayden
ran toward the noise. Another cry echoed on the air. They
drew up in front of the infirmary.

"You fucking lunatic! I'm going to stab an ice pick
through your brain. Gonna bite your balls off. Gonna—"

A man with black-rimmed glasses held the arms of a
wiry, towheaded boy who clutched a letter opener in his
hand. The man, who reminded Kate of a short Clark Kent,
jerked his head at Hayden. "Don't just stand there. Give me
a hand before he hurts himself."

The kid tossed his head back and slammed it into the
wall. Hayden charged in and grabbed the kid's legs, and the
man with the crooked glasses nodded to her. "Get me the syringe on my desk." She didn't move. "Dammit, I'm the boy's
doctor. I need to get him calm."

Kate handed the syringe to the man. DR. ANDREW TROW-
BRIDGE, the nameplate on the desk read.

"Noooo," the kid screamed.

"Hold him tight," the doctor said to Hayden as he jabbed
the syringe into the kid's upper arm.

"You asshole! Fuckhead!"

Kate didn't know what was in the syringe, but after another three curses, the boy slumped.

Dr. Trowbridge nodded at the cot. "Let's put him there."
Now that he wasn't flailing, the kid looked small—all bones
and angles with wide, glassy eyes.

The man righted his glasses and picked up a chart. He
checked his watch, looked at the boy, and, when the boy's
eyes closed, made a few marks on the paper. After he set

down the chart, he nodded. "Dr. Andrew Trowbridge, staff physician."

"Special Agent Hayden Reed. This is Kate Johnson."

The doctor's face remained placid. "I'll get Kyl."

"No, I'd like to speak with you."

Dr. Trowbridge studied the passed-out boy and nodded. "I have a few moments." Limping, he led them to a small conference room with a large banner that read HOPE ACADEMY. RESPECT, RESPONSIBILITY, HONESTY, COURAGE.

Hayden nodded toward Dr. Trowbridge's leg. "You okay?"

"Jimmy connected with one kick before I restrained him." Dr. Trowbridge lifted his arm and showed them a faint white scar in the shape of a bite mark. "Compliments of Frankie three months ago."

"You work with some rough boys," Hayden said.

Dr. Trowbridge pressed his fingertips together. "I work with boys who choose to take rough roads."

"And it's your job to get them on the right path."

"I'm part of the team to get them headed in the right direction. As the staff physician, I work on behavior modification strategies and implementation."

Drugged-up Jimmy, who seemed to be fighting the world, certainly needed something, Kate couldn't help but think with sadness.

"Kyl Watson mentioned that the staff worked closely together for the good of the boys," Hayden went on. "Did you work much with Jason Erickson?"

"I knew Jason, but not well. The kids liked him, and so did Kyl and Beth." The doctor tapped his fingertips together. "And let me do this as efficiently as possible, Agent Reed. Jason was of average intelligence. He lacked basic social skills and confidence. He was fatherless and had a mother who dominated him. When he first started here, she'd call him five or six times a day, but he never let her know he hated her. His health records show no instances of long-term psychiatric care or institutionalization, although he was placed on an antidepressant for panic attacks six months ago.

"I haven't observed any fetishistic, sadomasochistic, or voyeuristic behavior. Nor have I observed him harming small animals, playing with fire, or suffering nocturnal urination." After his litany, a smug smile landed on Dr. Trowbridge's face. "Did I miss anything?"

"You pretty much covered the standard arsenal of serial killer questions," Hayden said with a mask of impassivity.

"But you have more?" Dr. Trowbridge asked.

Hayden's jaw ticked. "Who would you like to see in the World Series?"

Dr. Trowbridge's fingers stilled. "World Series, as in baseball?"

"Yes."

"I don't follow baseball."

"You prefer basketball, tennis?"

"Golf."

"I see." Hayden stood. "One more question. Do you know where we can find Beth?"

The doctor's lips pulled down. "She was supposed to be here today, assisting me with Jimmy's intake. If she's not at the front desk, try the barn."

\* \* \*

The day was molten, the sky a cloudless blue. On days like this, she used to take Jason out on her father's old fishing boat. They'd putter across the crystal-clear water with only the sun beating down on them. When they got too hot and they'd emptied the thermos of lemonade she'd brought for them, they'd jump into the lake, but she'd always gone first, making sure the water wasn't too deep or lake bed littered with sharp rocks that would hurt her little brother. The memory surprised her, as did the surge of wetness lurking behind her eyes.

Jamming her hair behind her ears, she told herself she'd deal with the memories later. Right now she needed to catch up with Hayden, who was race-walking across the campus.

When they reached the barn, she heard a scream coming from a stand of trees to their right. Hayden tucked her behind him and guided them through the pines until they emerged in a small clearing, where Kyl Watson was alone with a boy, probably fourteen or fifteen.

The boy was on the ground, collapsed in a motionless heap, a yoke-type structure strapped across his shoulders and attached to a pallet piled with cinderblocks.

Watson lay on his stomach, nose-to-nose with the boy, yelling, "Get up, Nathan! Get up!"

The boy groaned and ground his face into the dirt.

Watson stayed in the kid's face. "If you can't make it to your feet, Nathan, crawl on your knees. You hear me? Crawl on your knees!"

The boy raised his head, and Kate winced at the dirt and blood and saliva coating his nose and chin. The boy heaved himself to his hands and knees only to fall back on the ground. She lunged toward the boy, but Hayden pulled her back. "It's not our place."

She glared at his hand. "When do you want to intervene? When the kid's dead?"

The kid got to his hands and knees again, let out another scream, and surged forward. The pallet of bricks jerked about six inches.

"Good job, Nathan. Baby steps. You can do it. Take those baby steps," Watson said.

Nathan let out another scream, and the pallet jolted forward a foot this time. The boy continued to move forward, blood dripping from his nose, saliva streaming from his twisted mouth.

*Heave. Groan. Scream. Heave. Groan. Scream.*

Kate wanted to scream.

Watson remained on his knees, crawling backward as the boy inched forward with the load of bricks. After what seemed like an hour, the pallet crossed a line etched in the dust. The boy collapsed. Watson gathered the kid in his arms. "You did it, Nathan. You did it. Those eight blocks represent the eight people you hurt this week with your fists or words. You took responsibility for your actions. Good job, son, good job."

Despite the blistering sun, Kate wrapped her arms across her chest as she turned from the strange scene. "This place gives me the creeps."

"Why's that?"

"It's pretending to be something it's not." She pointed to the small pond with the family of swans, to the homey yellow daffodils, and to the bright white fencing. Then she motioned to the bleeding boy. "It's a violent place. Something doesn't *feel* right."

His gaze turned thoughtful. Maybe he was finally starting to realize the power of feelings, that they could be as reliable as his beloved observation and analysis.

They returned to the barn, a two-story log building that smelled of hay and horseflesh.

Inside the door, Hayden grabbed her arm. She opened her mouth, but he shook his head and pointed up. Then she heard it, creaking boards. Hayden maneuvered through the maze of stalls to the far end, where a ladder stretched to a second-story hayloft. As he disappeared through the opening, a sharp gasp and then a woman's wobbly laugh sounded.

"Good afternoon, Agent Reed."

Battling falling straw, Kate followed Hayden up the ladder. Beth Watson sat on a hay bale, a small box in her lap.

"You don't seem surprised to see me," Hayden said.

"You spotted me at the press conference, and you want to know why I was there."

"You're a smart woman." Hayden spoke differently to Beth than he had to Robyn Banks, authoritative but tempered with gentleness. "Why were you there, Beth?"

Although only a few inches over five feet and birdlike, this woman had a strong, callused presence, as if hardened by life. "To hear what you had to say about Jason." Her pinched features smoothed, and she looked almost pretty at the mention of Jason's name.

"You cared about him, beyond coworkers, beyond friends."

She smiled. "Nothing gets by you, does it, Agent Reed?"

"Not important things."

"And my relationship with Jason was important?"

"It could be."

She stroked the top of the box. "Jason and I were lovers."

Kate frowned. Having a lover was... normal. And Jason wasn't normal. Their crazy mother made sure of that. Jason wasn't a killer, but still, he was damaged enough to allow someone to convince him to bludgeon her with a knife.

"How did it happen?" Hayden asked.

"It's complicated."

"Life usually is." He leaned against a stack of hay bales.

Beth stared out the small window that lit the loft. "As Kyl told you, Jason was a lonely young man. He needed attention."

"And you gave it to him."

"I gave him the care I give everyone in this place, but he took my friendship as something more." She blushed. It was odd, seeing this middle-aged woman rosy-cheeked. "It was just a few times, about three years ago. Jason seemed particularly needy, almost lost. He'd been unusually quiet, not smiling his normal people-pleasing smile. I reached out to him at first simply to let him know someone cared." The pink crept to her neck. "I hugged him. That's how it started, with a hug."

Two arms. Nothing more. The power of a hug. Kate swallowed.

"We made love a few more times, but I think we both knew we were using each other, him to experience passion for the first time."

"And you?"

"Getting a reminder that a forty-something woman is still capable of passion." She delivered the words with bold rawness.

"And the press conference today?"

"As I said, I wanted to know what was being said about Jason." Kate sensed a protectiveness in her words. "He wasn't a monster like everyone's been saying."

Hayden clasped his hands behind his back and frowned. "So we're finding out."

\* \* \*

*Sunday, June 14, 2:45 p.m.*
*Dorado Bay, Nevada*

"Hey, Charlie, I need to talk."

Charlie ran the comb under water and slicked it over his hair, hoping it would stay down. He was going to Belinda's house to play Guitar Hero. At least that's what she said. If things went as planned, he'd get another kiss, this one longer than the peck he snuck in yesterday. And if he got really lucky, he'd get to touch one of her boobs. Maybe both.

Benny poked him in the arm. "Hey, I said I need to talk."

"Talk. I'm listening." Charlie flattened his hair with both hands.

"No you're not. You're thinking about Belinda's big boobs."

"Shut up, twerp."

His little brother didn't shoot back a swear word. Benny had been swear-free since they'd found the foot. "Listen, Charlie, I think I know something about the uh...whole foot thing." He took a deep breath. "A few weeks ago I saw some stranger down by Mulveney's Cove. Kinda by the tree with that big ol' rope."

"So."

"Old man Mulveney's a real crab. He doesn't like anyone around his place. So maybe the stranger snuck onto Mulveney's property. Maybe he was there to uh...ditch the guy with the foot." Benny toed the base of the toilet with his sneaker. "What do you think?"

"I think you're a liar wanting more attention."

Benny kicked the toilet. "Am not!"

Charlie put his hands on his brother's shoulders. "This is

serious, Benny. That foot was for real. Someone was killed. You can't mess things up with your lies."

"I'm not lying, Charlie. I swear. I saw a guy in a car on Mulveney's land a few weeks ago."

"Okay, what kind of car?"

"I don't remember."

"What color?"

"White." Benny scratched the side of his neck. "No, silver, I think it was silver."

"Like a spaceship?" Charlie put the lid on his hair gel. "Next thing you know you'll tell me the guy in the silver spaceship was an alien and that you saw his face. Was he green? Did he have one eye in the center of his forehead and gills on his neck?"

"No. Nothing like that." Benny's voice was a squeak. This kid should give up baseball and take up drama. "I couldn't tell what he looked like. He wore a fishing hat, big glasses, too." His little brother took a step back, toward the shower curtain, as if he wanted to hide behind it. "But I think he saw me."

"He saw you?"

"Yeah, I was standing there throwing rocks, and I felt someone looking at me. What if he comes after me?"

"He would abduct you and take you to the big green alien chief." Charlie tossed the gel in the bathroom drawer. "Make sure you call the FBI and tell them in case there's a whole army of little green men headed this way."

"Don't be stupid. I said it was just one guy." Benny nibbled his thumbnail. "But maybe you're right. Maybe I should call the FBI or something."

This kid would do anything for attention. "Gotta go, little bro." Belinda was waiting.

"But Charlie!"

"Go tell your lies to Chief Greenfield."

# CHAPTER FIFTEEN

*Sunday, June 14, 3 p.m.*
*Dorado Bay, Nevada*

Hayden escorted Kate to the car. She'd been silent while he questioned Beth Watson about being at the press conference, but that wasn't unusual. Kate disliked being out in public, and he knew the press conference had been hell on her.

*And you too*, a voice inside his head added.

He didn't like dangling Kate before the Butcher, but he knew their unsub. He was smart. He'd eventually find her, and Hayden would rather be at her side when he succeeded. Kate was holding up well, but she was made of tough stuff. She'd proven that at the press conference and during her run-in with the broadcaster, Robyn Banks.

"Do you think it's significant that Beth was at the press conference?" Kate asked when they reached the car.

"Perpetrators often insert themselves into an investigation in a number of ways. Some follow the media. Some visit crime scenes. Some go as far as contacting investigators to offer to help. I once worked a case where an offender who'd raped and killed a twelve-year-old boy spent six weeks with the search teams looking for the child, who they found in the man's bathtub."

"You think *she's* the Butcher?"

"We have plenty of *shes* in this case. The boy climbing into his bedroom window saw a woman, and so did the stalker. I'm not ruling out that Beth could be our killer, nor am I ruling out that she could be an accomplice."

"Beth Watson doesn't look dangerous."

"Not for someone who's good at disguise. Think about it, Kate. One of the Butcher's hallmark traits is he goes unnoticed. He—or she—is a master of blending in, and it's likely we've already shaken hands with him. Or her."

Kate, who'd been picking off bits of straw from the front of her shirt, shuddered. "Like I said, it's a messed up world."

"Not everywhere. There are pockets of goodness, places where monsters and killers don't exist."

Inside the car, she slipped her fingers into his hair, and he jumped. Her touch was light and casual, but it rocked him to his toes. He turned to her to see if she noticed the earthquake but saw that she was frowning at him.

"What?" he asked. Was she ready to argue again about a broken, hopeless world?

She jammed a finger at his head. "There's not a single piece of straw in your hair, not a single hair out of place."

"And this is important because?"

"Because I'm trying to figure you out."

"Why?"

"Because I find you"—her lips flattened in thoughtful contemplation—"*interesting*."

"Interesting?" He slipped the key in the ignition. "I've been called worse."

"I bet you have." Kate rested her head against the back of the seat. The press conference had been grueling and exhausting for her, but he could also see relief. Today she stood in front of a crowd and cameras, scars and all. She'd fought and slain one of her personal demons.

"People have called me some interesting names," she added. "When I was six, my mother called me a hideous abomination that deserved to blister and melt in the fires of hell."

His hand fisted around the key. The words, aimed at Kate and decades old, pummeled him in the gut. "She was wrong, Kate. She was an unhealthy woman, and the stuff that came out of her was sick and vile."

She waved him off with a waggle of fingers. "I was more empowered than hurt. With all the passion and elocution of a six-year-old, I called her a pink, puky, smelly slobbo."

He laughed. "Good for you." Kate had guts. And heart. She was an amazing girl who'd turned into an amazing woman. He'd seen that at the press conference. He shifted the car into drive. And he'd felt it last night when they'd kissed. He'd been too busy setting in place the latest plan to snare the Butcher to think about that kiss, but now that the bait had been set, it was hard not to. Kate had been...Kate. Passionate and fiery. He shifted in the seat, repositioning his legs.

"That's debatable. Kendra made me eat a bar of soap. But I've been called worse." Kate slanted him a gaze. "My class-mates in college called me the class whore."

"Were you?" The question slipped out against his will, but this wouldn't be the first time he'd slipped because of Kate. That kiss. The tendons in his hand tightened as he turned the steering wheel and pulled out of the parking lot.

Her rumbling laugh drowned out the revving motor. "Nope. With two jobs and a full course load, I was too busy working. I think some of the guys I turned down started the rumor. I didn't lose my virginity until my first job out of college, in Lincoln. And there, by the way, I was called a hard-nosed, hard-ass reporter."

The tightness pulling across his entire upper body lightened as he barreled down the highway. "A truthful assessment?"

"Damn right." One of her eyebrows lifted in an impish tilt. "Okay, I spilled. Now what about you? What's the worst thing you've been called?"

He checked his watch, glad she was less tense because now that the press conference was behind them, they had a lot of work to do. "Late, and it sounds really bad when it comes from Evie. She's a fireball and knows how to swear in two languages." He smiled at her. See, he could do light. "We're meeting with her and Hatch at the cottage."

"You're changing the subject," Kate said with a cluck of her tongue. "I've been around you enough to see firsthand how you manipulate people. Beth Watson, Robyn Banks, even me." She reached across the car and slid a single finger along his jaw, and if he hadn't been belted in, he would have jumped. "You hoodwinked me, Hayden. With that kiss on my neck." The finger landed on his lips with a soft tap, and he swerved to avoid the shoulder. "Not that I'm complaining. It was good. And good for me. I was so preoccupied with that kiss I didn't go into fight-or-flight mode before the press conference. You are the master." She settled her hand back in her lap. "And now that I've reaffirmed your greatness, surely your ego's propped up enough to talk. So what's the worst thing you've ever been called?"

This woman was getting under his skin. And into his head. Because he'd just missed the turn-off to the cottage. He slowed the car, waited for a split in traffic, and spun a U-turn. He turned onto the dirt road, his hands gripping the steering wheel. And still Kate waited. "Soulless," he finally said.

She laughed, a sound so loud and unexpected that the car swerved. "Whoever said that obviously didn't know you," she said with an audible smugness.

Marissa, his former wife, had called him soulless, and he never argued. "Some weeks I feel soulless, the weeks I get by with a few hours' sleep, the weeks I hole up in a room analyzing evidence and reports and witness interviews. Makes me wonder if I'm more machine than man."

"You are not a machine, Hayden Reed."

He rotated the steering wheel and got the car back to the center of the dirt road. "You sound so sure."

"I know you."

"Really?"

"You have passion for your work, such purpose and conviction. That doesn't come from college textbooks or stuff you learned at the FBI Academy. It's an inner spark, something many people call a soul." Her face grew serious. "It's pure logic, Hayden. Without a soul of your own, you couldn't combat the evil souls of this world and win."

* * *

"Really, Hayden?" Kate asked as Agent Efficient flung back the shower curtain. "Is this really necessary?"

Hayden slipped his gun into its holster. "The press conference was more than two hours ago. The Butcher could be anywhere."

"He's obviously not in my bathtub, so do you mind?" She pointed at the door, and with another sweep of his eagle eyes, he left. Finally.

When they had arrived at the cottage, Hayden had insisted on performing an armed walk-through of every room. When she went to change her clothes, he triple-checked her window and stood outside her door until she came out in her cozy shorts and T-shirt. And when she decided to go to the bathroom, he was on her heels. She rested her balled fists on the sink.

If she weren't so pissed off, she'd find humor in the irony that was her life. For the first time in years she was attracted to a man. She was trusting him and sharing a bit of her heart and soul. But the guy she had feelings for didn't have *feelings*, or at least that's what he thought...or wanted everyone to think. He called himself a machine, and to a certain extent he was. She pictured the switches in his head.

*Flick.* Conversation about souls shut down.

*Flick.* Investigation into Butcher turned on. Power level: High.

And there was nothing she could do about it, except help him with the investigation.

Kate found Hayden at the kitchen table, hunkered down before his laptop. Without looking at her, he pointed to a spreadsheet and stack of markers.

"Highlight in yellow anyone who made actual death threats against you," he said. "Green is for those who made other threatening remarks, and blue is for anyone you feel had a grudge against you but never vocalized it."

Analytical, methodical Hayden was at it again, this time wielding neon-colored highlighters. And the crazy thing was, she found comfort in the whole thing. As she picked up a yellow highlighter, she wondered how much of her attraction to Hayden was because she felt safe with him. Without him she could never have stood in front of the crowd and cameras.

She flicked off the lid and ran her finger down the first column of the spreadsheet. When Hayden first connected her attack to the Butcher slayings, he'd done a significant amount of research into every aspect of her life in his effort to track her down, including an exhaustive study of her job. He'd put together a spreadsheet of every story she'd worked on for five years before her attack, and her job was to determine who on this list wanted her dead.

The first name that came to mind wasn't in one of Hayden's neat columns. She chewed the cap of the highlighter.

Hayden, whose face was hidden behind his computer screen, didn't look up. "Who?"

*No, Hayden. You can't read my mind.* "Kendra. She hated me, told me so on a regular basis, and she said frequently she wished I'd never been born. Plus, she had Jason under her thumb."

"Your mother was at a low level of functioning. She didn't have the ability to plan and execute an attack."

"How about Robyn Banks? You saw the love between us today. And she was at my place the night of my attack. You don't think she's lying about why she came, do you?"

"She came to see you about a story, but that wasn't the complete truth."

"Why do you say that?"

"Her right hand twitched."

"And everyone whose right hand twitches is lying?"

"Not necessarily, but it's an indicator for her. When she told me she was thirty-five years old, her right hand twitched. She was lying. She's forty-three."

"Did she lie about anything else in the interview?"

"No, that's it."

He was amazing, and she was surprised it took him five months to find her. But to her credit, she'd covered her tracks

well. "You, Hayden Reed, are not a normal man," she said
with equal parts awe and irritation.

He finally looked up from the computer, a hint of a smile
curving his lips. "Have I just been insulted?"

He was joking. *Joking.* This man was driving her insane.
Just when she was ready to accept that his heart was made
of steel, he'd prove he was human. She shook her head, not
trusting herself to speak. Hell, she didn't trust herself not to
launch herself into his arms. Because then she'd drag him
into her bedroom, handcuff him to the bed if needed, and finish what they'd started last night when she'd learned Jason
was dead and her nightmare was over.

Smokey Joe was right. This was a crazy world.

She caught Hayden staring at her, his eyes warm, like liquid mercury. No, there is no way he could tell that she'd been
thinking about handcuffing him to her bed. No. Way. Neither had a chance to say anything because Evie and Hatch
arrived, and for the first time in a long time, Kate was happy
for the extra people crowding in on her.

Smooth-talking Hatch had set up interviews with four of
the boys at Hope Academy, and Hayden told her to get ready
to go. He was still trying to re-create Jason's days prior to
his murder.

She stayed seated at the table. "I'm not going." The academy made her uneasy.

"You're not staying here alone," Hayden said in that authoritative tone that made her want to pull a Smokey and hit
him upside the head with a log.

"I'll stay with Kate," Evie offered. "You and Hatch can
take care of the interviews. You're better at the whole people
thing than I am. I prefer to work with things that go *boom*."
The female FBI agent winked at Kate.

"Do you have your cuffs?" Hayden asked Evie.

Kate gritted her teeth. At that moment, she had another surge of strong feelings for Hayden, and not the warm and fuzzy kind.

"What for?" Evie asked, looking in confusion from her to Hayden.

"To cuff Kate to the refrigerator," Hayden said. The side of his jaw ticked in a quick spasm, and she wondered if he was thinking about her stretched out on the bed asking for handcuffs. An almost imperceptible red flushed the skin above his collar, and her own neck warmed.

Hatch laughed.

"He's not joking," Kate said.

Evie, who looked like she weighed half as much as Hayden, smacked him with the back of her hand on his chest. "Calm down, big guy, she's not going anywhere. You can trust me to take of her."

"I know." Hayden slid a hand along his tie, which hung askew. "I also know *her*." With a sigh, he stood before her. He was close enough to run both of her hands through his annoyingly neat hair. "The stakes are higher, Kate. Your face has been on televisions across the country. The Butcher knows you're alive and that you're right here."

She touched his hair, not to mess it up, but to...hell, she didn't know. "I know."

"Then you know you have to stick with Evie, do whatever she says."

"Yes." Of course she knew it, but that didn't mean she liked it. Here was yet another person who would be watching her, controlling where she went and what she did.

Hayden pushed back a lock of hair that plopped over her forehead, but she didn't fight the touch. She didn't want to. "I'll be fine," she said.

After a few final directives to Evie, Hayden and Hatch

left the cottage. The minute the door shut on his broad shoulders, the air changed, thinning, making breathing more difficult. Kate forced in a deep breath.

"He's really not bad, not once you get to know him," Evie said.

*Once you get to know him.* Kate had said that same thing about Smokey. She had learned to put up with the old soldier. She had called him yesterday and got the good news that both Maeve and her home were still in one piece.

"You need me to come out there, Katy-lady?" Smokey had asked. "You need me to give G-man a good boot in the butt?"

*Only if you can boot him into my bed.* And how stupid was that thought?

She turned back to Hayden's spreadsheet and focused on something less disturbing: who from her past wanted her dead.

For the next hour, Kate studied the names and in her mind reviewed the hundreds of sources and subjects she'd interviewed for her "Justice for All" reports. Frankly, there were plenty of people on this list who could have wanted her dead. Her investigative reporting pitted her against dubious characters, everyone from drug dealers to death-row inmates. Did one of these purveyors of injustice convince Jason to attack her? Or was it a coworker? Neighbor? Old lover? For three years, she'd worked hard at putting her past behind her, and this trip down memory lane was hell.

She started to pace before the great wall of glass. Evie sat at the kitchen table, drinking her third cola and banging away on Hayden's laptop. Hayden had said Evie was the SCIU's bomb and weapons specialist. Evie struck her as an explosive type, Latin in temperament and looks. Long, dark hair pulled into a tumbling I-don't-give-a-rat's-ass knot sat atop her head, and her full, red lips looked well-suited to popping off. Small and thin, Evie was a little Latin firecracker, but anyone who could hold her own against the towering ego and personality of a man like Hayden had to be tough.

After what seemed like her fiftieth pass through the living room, Kate noticed Evie close the laptop.

"Let's go for a walk," Evie said.

Kate stopped in the middle of the great room. "I officially adore you."

Evie laughed. The sound surprised Kate. Petite Evie's laugh was low and throaty, like a person who knew smoky bars and how to swig cheap whiskey.

Without a word between them, Kate and Evie struck off down the path that curved along the lake. Kate had changed into a pair of long pants and slipped on a long-sleeved overshirt, and a sticky pool of sweat gathered between her shoulder blades. She'd be a hell of a lot cooler if she'd take off the shirt, but she wasn't ready to expose that part of herself to the world. She'd done enough self-exposure at the press conference and to Hayden.

Hayden. He may no longer be at her side, but he was still in her mind. The machinelike man who never slept. The quiet, contemplative thinker who spent hours in the heads of killers. But he was also the man who looked in awe at her version of happily ever after, heated her blood with a kiss, and called her beautiful. And still, she didn't feel like she knew him because Hayden didn't let other people get close.

"Hayden grew up without a mom."

Kate snapped her head toward Evie, who walked beside her, the wild knot of hair bobbing at the side of her head. "Excuse me?" Where had Evie's comment come from?

"You were rolling the bottom of your T-shirt." Evie bent

and picked up a handful of stones. With a flick of her wrist she skipped a stone across the lake. Four bounces.

Kate's fingers knotted in her shirt fabric, and a half grin twisted her lips. "Hayden says I'm an easy read."

"He's seriously brilliant," Evie said. "You know that, right? His brain is amazing."

And so are his hands and those golden arms. And lips. She couldn't forget those lips.

"The things he sees and connections he makes, it's crazy, Kate, but in a good way. In a way that saves lives." Evie skipped another stone, this one bouncing seven times. "At the Box, we're supposed to pretty much be equals. We all have our areas of specialty. We're teammates, but Hayden, he's at a different level." Evie fingered the stone in her hand, the rock weaving between her fingers. "If anything ever happened to Parker, Hayden would take over the team."

She could see Hayden heading up one of the world's elite crime-fighting teams—the Apostles, she'd heard someone call them. "Which would make him God."

Evie laughed again and untangled the stone from her fingers. "Don't tell him that. Hayden's damn near perfect and knows it." She skipped another stone.

"What happened to Hayden's mom?" Kate asked. Machines didn't have moms. Little boys did. Kate went to that place in her head, that creative section of her brain she tapped to make angels and fairies from stones, and tried to picture little-boy Hayden. Baseball. He probably played something like catcher. She could see balls coming at him fast and furious, and he never missed a one. Definitely fishing. He was patient, not minding those long stretches of silence because he was comfortable in his head. And something to do with art. She didn't think he was an artist, but he wore all of those exquisite, hand-painted silk ties. Something in him appreciated color and texture and artistic composition.

"She died of cancer when he was six," Evie said.

"And his dad?"

"Career military."

"I see."

Evie let loose another whiskey laugh. "You've been spending too much time with him, *amiga*."

In silence, they strolled another hour, turning around at some point, and, to Kate's relief, Evie didn't force a conversation. Some day Kate would be able to converse like a normal person, chatting about the weather and about what fish were biting.

"You don't talk as much as Hatch," she told Evie.

"My mouth has a tendency to get me in trouble," the little FBI agent said with a wry grin. Kate chuckled.

They passed a small cabin, still wearing its winter storm shutters, when Evie stiffened beside her. "Bend down and pretend to refasten the strap of your sandal."

"What?" Kate asked. A hush fell over this part of the lake, where the alder and fir trees thickened.

"Bend down. I need to change places with you."

"Why?"

"Someone's following us."

The sweat soaking her shirt froze. She'd been dangled like bait. Was the Butcher about to bite? She squatted and refastened her sandal strap.

"Don't look panicked," Evie said. "He's not close enough to strike. He's just beyond the tree line."

She tugged at the strap, the blood at her wrists pulsed hard and fast. "What do we do?"

"Can you run?"

Kate wanted to laugh. Hell yeah, she could run. "Just give me the signal."

Evie reached into the back of her waistband. Kate stood. Every muscle in Kate's legs was tense and ready to sprint.

"See where the bushes open in about thirty yards? That's where we're going to take off. Straight up the rise. Don't leave my side. This could be a trap to get you alone."

"Okay."

When they reached the clearing, Evie dropped her skipping stones. "Now!"

Kate tore up the rise after the FBI agent. A shadow at the tree line shifted, and a flash of blue ducked into the dense foliage. Her feet pounded the sandy, granite soil. She slipped once, twice, as they raced toward the trees. Just ahead, someone huffed out ragged breaths and thrashed through the brush. Their prey was slow and clunky.

And she was born to run.

She kicked up her speed, pushing Evie to a full-out sprint.

They reached the tree line. A group of squawking jays erupted from a stand of alders. Kate jumped and stumbled over a semi-exposed boulder. She careened back, her butt smacking the ground.

Evie skidded to a stop. Whoever was in the bushes continued to run.

"Go after him," Kate said. "Go!" She stood, a twinge in her ankle.

Evie stared wistfully through the forest, the thrashing growing softer. "Can you walk on it?"

Kate gave her ankle a spin. Achy, but she had full mobility. "It's fine. Let's go." She hobbled toward the trees.

Evie pulled at her arm. "He's too far gone, and I don't want you running on that ankle."

"Then run after him yourself."

"And risk the wrath of Hayden?"

Hayden. He wasn't here, but he was.

"Did you see anything?" Evie asked

"Blue sleeve. What about you?"

A frown marred Evie's lips. "Blue baseball cap. Average build. Couldn't even tell if it was a male or female."

"Should we check for footprints or something like that?"

Evie shook her head. "It's getting dark. I need to get you inside."

Kate didn't argue, mostly because she agreed. With the dark easing in, shadows started shifting and night sounds kicked up. The Butcher was out there.

Glad to see the cheery yellow cottage, she hurried up the porch steps but skidded to a halt when she reached the door. Something shiny and gold winked at her.

A necklace with a tiny bottle of shimmering dust hung from the door handle.

Her breath jackknifed in her throat and she slammed her fist into the door.

# CHAPTER SIXTEEN

*Sunday, June 14, 10:40 p.m.*
*Dorado Bay, Nevada*

Directly below the fist-sized hole in the cottage's screen door, Hayden counted seven drops of blood. Something hard and sharp spiked at the back of his head. "Where is she?" he asked Evie.

"In the bedroom." Evie's fingers pressed into the tense flesh of his arm. "She's fine, Hayden, but she won't talk. She hasn't said a word since she saw it hanging from the door."

Hayden held out his hand.

Evie handed him a gold chain necklace with a tiny green glass bottle. Gourd-shaped, the bottle had a cork lid and gold filigree curved along the bottom and was filled with shimmering bits of gold.

"Dusted it," Evie said. "No prints."

"Contents?"

"Appears to be regular craft glitter, the kind my nephews use on all those macaroni Christmas ornaments I put on my tree every year. But you need to ask Kate. She recognized the necklace in a big way."

"Did you see anything, anyone?" Hayden asked.

"*Nada.* I scrubbed the cottage. All doors and windows are locked."

Hayden motioned to Hatch, who knelt in the driveway studying the gravel. "Call Chief Greenfield and get an extra car posted on the lake tonight. Then check out the grounds. Talk to the neighbors and see if they saw anyone here at the cottage. Evie, you hit the houses along the side of the lake, find out if anyone saw your mystery guy with the blue baseball cap."

After his teammates left, Hayden found Kate in her bedroom, putting the last of three Bugs Bunny bandages on the knuckles of her right hand. He centered himself in the doorway. "There's a *what's-up-doc* comment somewhere in here, but I'm not sure how it goes."

Kate gathered the bandage wrappers and ground them into a tight ball before tossing them in the trash. "You're lousy at jokes."

"I know." He dangled the green and gold bottle between them. "So let's talk about this instead."

She tossed the bandages into the first-aid kit and slammed the lid, rattling the contents.

"Kate," he said. For all her fiery fight and anger, he saw what simmered beneath. "Why are you afraid of this necklace?"

Her eyes squeezed shut, as if she didn't want to see him or that necklace. Then her shoulders sagged, and she sunk onto the edge of the bed, her hands clenched between her knees. He sat next to her, placing the bottle on the dresser directly across from them. For a while, they both stared at it.

"It's pixie dust," she said at last. "Or at least that's what my father told me when he gave me the necklace when I was five. He said if I sprinkled it on my pillow I'd fly off to wonderful, magical lands during my dreams." She huffed out a snort. "He lied." Her knees pressed into her knotted fingers, the Bugs Bunny bandages stretching into grotesque caricatures. "He's here, Hayden. The Butcher is here. He put that necklace on the door."

Hayden slid his hand over hers, intertwining their fingers. "He can't hurt you. I won't let him." He reached over and forced her gaze toward him, away from the necklace.

Kate pressed her lips together, as if contemplating arguing with him, but she shook her head and closed her eyes. With the fight gone, she looked smaller. He moved closer, his leg brushing hers. He wanted to draw her into his arms again, but she wasn't ready. He could tell she needed to talk.

She took an uneven breath. "The night of my junior prom, the night I left Kendra's home for good, I stopped long enough to take three things with me. Yep, three things to start a new life." She opened her eyes and pointed to the necklace. "That was one of them. Stupid, wasn't it? A bottle of pixie dust from a father who didn't care. And I kept it close for the next twelve years. I always wore it under my shirt or carried it in my pocket, a reminder that I make my own magic. I was wearing it the night Jason attacked me, but when I woke at the hospital, it was gone. I asked the staff if it was with my clothing, but no one remembered seeing it. It wasn't in my home, either. I figured maybe it got lost in the ambulance or possibly in the ER when they brought me in. At one point I had the crazy memory that my attacker had taken it. But in light of it showing up on the front door, it's not too crazy, huh?"

He shook his head. "The necklace was a souvenir, proof that Jason 'killed' you."

"He's here." A tremor warbled in her throat. "He was at our front door. He followed me along the lake."

Hayden slipped an arm over her shoulder. "And he's not going to get you."

"He got past armed guards at the hospital. He—"

"No, Kate, not this time." He pulled her to him, her shoulder pressing into his chest where his heartbeat picked up speed. "I know this man, Kate. I've been in his head. Right now he wants to frighten you because he wants you to run. But you're not going to run because I won't let you."

Kate's shoulders squared, and if she weren't so visibly mad, he'd laugh. Kate wore her emotions on her sleeve. A flash of anger because he told her what to do. Fear that a madman traipsed across their front porch. And...he looked harder, searched longer. At last he saw it. Trust.

With a shake of her head, she unwound herself from his arms and sunk onto the bed. "Fine, Hayden. I'm not going to run." She grabbed a pillow and punched it before tucking it under her head.

The depth of trust, especially from a woman who didn't trust easily, shook him. But then again, so much about Kate shook him. Her fighting spirit, her laugh, the fact that her hand so often slid along his leg, his hair. Even now one hand fiddled with the edge of the pillow while the other absently stroked his knee. She stared at the ceiling, her eyes wide, and her mouth in a scowl.

Thanks to the Butcher's calling card, sleep would be hard to find tonight. He knew her predicament. He'd be up most of night. The Butcher was in his head and making noise. Kate rolled her shoulders and shifted to her side as if trying to get comfortable. He imagined a night without the noise, without the monsters poking around his head.

She punched her pillow again, a little growl escaping her lips.

He kicked off his shoes.

*You shouldn't be in bed with a witness.*

*This woman clouds your judgment.*

But his body paid no heed to the voices in his head as he stretched out alongside Kate.

She stiffened. "Hayden, for Pete's sake, I'm not going to run."

"I know." He pulled her shoulders against his chest and tucked her head under his chin. "You're going to sleep."

She grew oddly still then melted into his chest. At least one of them would get some sleep tonight.

\* \* \*

*Sunday, June 14, 10:55 p.m.*
*Dorado Bay, Nevada*

He took off the sun-faded hat and the vest that smelled of fish. It was one of his better disguises. It looked so…legitimate. The hat with its sixteen hand-tied flies and the vest with the pockets holding vicious little hooks were legitimate in the broader sense because tonight he'd gone fishing.

He hated to give up the necklace Katrina wore so close to her beating heart, the one Jason obediently slipped from her neck and brought to him the night he was supposed to kill her. The necklace was supposed to serve as proof positive Katrina was dead.

Tonight it served as a little calling card.

Agent Reed, however, called it a souvenir. He'd heard Agent Reed talking about "souvenirs" to one of the detectives after the Provo slaying. Reed said the Butcher took some mementos from the victims or their homes. He thought of that precious little container of red in his freezer, compliments of the beautiful, brown-haired broadcaster in Oakland, which, when used in the correct amounts, would last exactly one month.

What a bloody mess Provo had been. The police, sheriff, and local FBI were like the Keystone Kops. No one knew what the others were doing and who was coming or going, which is why it had been so easy for him to slip into a coroner's jacket and observe firsthand what Reed was doing to find Katrina. The coroner tech disguise had been another good one.

He was a master of disguise. He could be anyone he wanted to be.

Butcher.

Baker.

Candlestick maker.

Even a dragon.

He blinked away the red hiss of steam. It wasn't time for the dragon, not yet.

He looked at the clock, which had just turned to eleven. It was time. He must do things in the right order, always in the right order. He flicked the monitor switch.

The monitor had to be checked every day at eleven a.m. and eleven p.m. Until six months ago he had checked the monitor only once a day, but that had been a mistake, one that cost him what he wanted most.

Six months ago Katrina came back to Reno at 1:20 a.m. She snuck into her condo under the cover of night and left seven minutes later. He didn't know what she was doing or why she was there. No, the important thing was that she was still alive, and so were the secrets she knew.

The three black-and-white images on the screen—no, four, as of tonight at 9:57 there were four cameras in place—flicked on, and he settled into the chair and watched. He ig-

nored the images of Katrina's condo in Reno, Kendra and
Jason's Dorado Bay front porch, and the KTTL building in
Reno. Instead he focused on the image from the newest camera he'd set up, the one that showed the little yellow cottage
on the lake.

\* \* \*

*Monday, June 15, 9:30 a.m.*
*Carson City, Nevada*

The next morning Hayden stood before the weed-choked
path leading to the Victorian house with the busted porch
swing and considered calling Kate. But he'd called an hour
ago, and both Evie and Hatch reported that Kate, ensconced
in the cottage, was safe. After finding the necklace last night,
an agitated Kate fell asleep and barely moved all night. He
knew because he'd spent much of the night awake, watching the woman in his arms. He wasn't worried that she'd run
or that the Butcher would attack. He held her in his arms
because...He scrubbed his palm along his face. No logical
reason came to mind, which is why he needed to get Kate
out of his mind.

The walkway ended at a flight of four sagging steps that
led to an intricately carved pair of double doors streaked
with peeling pale blue paint. Neglect hung in the air, dusty
and flat. Hayden pushed the doorbell button.

Robyn Banks's house was in the historic district of Carson City, which featured a collection of rambling Victorian
mansions and cottages in various states of grandeur. He
rang the bell five more times before it cracked open, fram-
ing a wedge of a short, thin man in a red morning coat

with gold-threaded peacocks. He had bare feet and dirty toenails.

"I'm looking for Robyn Banks," Hayden said.

Hidden by the gloom of the big old house, the man belched out a long, whiskey-drenched breath. "Hmmmm. The more apropos question is, Is Robyn looking for you?"

"Is she here?" Hayden asked with a sharp bluntness. He had no time for drunks.

The man in the ridiculous coat moved to shut the door, but Hayden shot out his hand and shoved the door wide open. "Where is she?"

At the bright wave of brilliant sun, the man blinked, at least the eye not covered in an eye patch. "Indisposed. Predisposed. Take your pick."

Hayden flashed his creds. "Would you care to rethink your answers to my questions?"

The man pushed away Hayden's wallet. "I care to—"

"It's okay." Robyn Banks stepped out of the shadows.

"Oh, dearest Robyn, we are anything but okay." The man's cynical laugh curled the air as he disappeared into the bowels of the dark Victorian.

Robyn motioned him inside without a word. Heavy drapes covered the windows, and Hayden had a hard time making out the house's layout and furnishings as she led him to a room just off the entryway. The room held a card table with a computer and a single folding chair.

"You're certainly fast, Agent Reed." She motioned for him to take the chair while she rested her backside on the table. "Efficient, too. I expected to see you, but not so soon."

"I'm trying to catch a killer, Ms. Banks." Hayden, who sat in the metal chair, folded his hands in his lap. "So I'll get straight to the heart of my visit. I ran your fingerprints against those found at all the Butcher crime scenes, and we got a match. At Katrina Erickson's condo."

"No surprise there." She waved a red-tipped finger at him as if scolding. "I already told you I was there that night to talk to Katrina about a story."

"Cut the act, Robyn. We're both on deadlines, and we don't have time for drama."

Her hand fell to her side. "What do you want?"

"The truth. I want to know exactly what happened when you went to Katrina's house the night she was stabbed, and I don't want the *Reader's Digest* condensed version about you walking in, seeing the bloody body, and running to call nine-one-one. I want the other details. Like why your prints were found on a highball glass in Katrina's dishwasher. And what you really saw that night."

* * *

Robyn could lie, a task she did quite well. She'd done it in the past when it suited her or Mike. But Hayden Reed saw everything. Those sharp eyes would shred her to pieces if she lied to him. And that would hurt like hell. She'd taken hits lately, hard blows that bruised her to the bone.

She gathered her thoughts as she walked to the brocade-covered window. "Katrina and I both worked the news desk that night. She went home right after we signed off, and I came by about an hour later to talk about a story she'd worked on. When she didn't answer the door, I walked in."

"Front door?"

"Yes, it was unlocked. I was about to call out her name when I heard a scream from upstairs." The words clung to her throat with sharp barbs. "The scream chilled my blood, and I froze." Even now cold terror gripped her.

"Did you recognize any voices, hear any words, names?"

"Mostly grunts and screams. Although one time I heard Katrina yell, 'You're not going to kill me you son of a bitch!' Hard to forget something like that."

"And when you could move, what did you do?"

"I ran to the coat closet in the hall and shut the door." She watched as Agent Reed's impassive mask fell off. "Yes, not your usual reaction, but you mustn't forget, I'm a reporter. A story was breaking, and I planned to cover it. About that time the first mirror shattered. Then came the rest, thirteen, fourteen crashes. I lost count. Eventually everything quieted until I heard someone walk past the closet and out the front door."

"How many sets of footsteps did you hear?"

"One."

"And after you heard the door close, what did you do?"

"I waited. Eventually I went to Katrina's bedroom." Dust fluttered in the air as her fingers dug into the curtains. "She wasn't moving; blood was everywhere, red foam bubbled on her lips, so I could tell she was breathing."

"And..."

"I went to the bathroom and threw up. Then I stopped in the kitchen and poured myself a scotch. Straight. In case that makes a difference." She let go of the drapes and shook her head. "No, not the smartest thing to do, given Katrina's physical state and her immediate need for medical attention, but I'll blame it on the shock of hearing a madman bludgeoning a colleague."

"A man? What makes you think it was a man?"

"I don't know. I just assumed an attack that grisly would be made by a man."

"And you saw nothing? No one?"

"No. With a shot of liquid courage under my belt, I

drove to the convenience store and called nine-one-one. That's it."

"So you went home and remained silent."

"Because nothing I saw would help the investigation."

"And…"

"And because it scared the hell out of me."

To her relief, Agent Reed stood and straightened the cuffs of his shirt. "One more question," he said. "Who's your roommate?"

Robyn was prepared to talk about Katrina Erickson but not about Mike Muldoon.

"Ms. Banks, who is the man who answered the door?"

She thought about lying, but there was that little issue of public records. "My husband."

\* \* \*

*Monday, June 15, 4 p.m.*
*Dorado Bay, Nevada*

Hayden had just come back from Carson City, where he had met with Robyn Banks, and Kate figured he must have won the sparring match. His gray eyes flashed triumphantly as he flipped open his laptop.

She, on the other hand, was going stir crazy. She'd been cooped up in the cottage all day, Hatch and Evie taking alternate watch over her. Hayden's colleagues buried themselves in work, either on the phone, on their computers, or rushing out to meet with people. She spent the entire day pacing the airless living room.

"Can we go out?" she asked Hayden who pecked on the keyboard. "Take a drive?"

"No."

She appreciated Hayden's doggedness, as she knew that kind of passion would get the Butcher, but right now, she needed a break. "Why not?"

"Mike Muldoon."

A breath caught in her throat. "Muldoon?"

He looked up from his laptop. "You know him?"

"Not personally, but I covered his story in a 'Justice for All' report for KTTL."

Recognition dawned on Hayden's face. "That's it. I've been wracking my brain all the way here trying to remember where I'd heard that name before. Muldoon was the pension administrator convicted of fraud and embezzlement and the subject of one of your last 'Justice for All' stories."

"Why are you interested in him? He was in jail at the time of my attack."

"Which is why I didn't investigate him when I first ran across him. Given the fact that Jason was most likely operating on someone else's orders, Muldoon now is a viable suspect. I need to find out if Muldoon and Jason were connected in any way."

"But Muldoon's still in jail. I think the judge handed him a five- to ten-year sentence."

"He's out and living with Robyn Banks."

"Robyn Banks? What the hell is he doing with her?"

"They're married."

Kate shuddered. "I can't see that."

"It's not a pretty sight. Apparently, all is not well in the Muldoon-Banks household. I need to find out when he got out of jail."

As Hayden continued his calls about Muldoon, Kate continued pacing. Did Mike Muldoon have something to do with her attack? Did he know Jason? Her feet moved faster as she considered the scenario Hayden laid out. Jason attacked her on someone's orders. That someone was the Butcher. The Butcher went on to kill seven broadcasters and Jason. The pixie dust necklace proved the Butcher was here and still wanted her. The only lead Hayden had to work with was a woman in a pink dress. And this is where more questions began. Was the woman in the dress the Butcher in disguise or an accomplice? If a female accomplice, could it be Beth Watson? Hell, why not Robyn Banks? Was it possible Mike Muldoon was the Butcher?

The rustling of paper interrupted her thoughts. Hayden left his computer and offered her a bag. "For you. I picked it up on my way back from Carson City." He smiled, looking oddly pleased with himself.

Growing up, she never received gifts from her mother for her birthday. Her grandparents never sent her Christmas presents. She wasn't used to getting gifts, which is why she hadn't been able to take Smokey Joe's one-winged tourmaline angel. She regretted it now. Crusty and gruff by nature, Smokey probably didn't give many gifts.

Hayden had tucked his gift in a plain brown paper bag. She wondered what kind of present he'd give her. Definitely something thoughtful—he spent way too much time in his head—and probably perfect. He had a lock on that, too.

Fingers tingling in silly anticipation, she reached in and took out a box of oil pencils and a sketch pad. She hadn't touched drawing materials in years. The tingle in her fingers morphed into sparks. Yes, definitely perfect.

\* \* \*

*Monday, June 15, 7:30 p.m.*
*Dorado Bay, Nevada*

Hayden pulled in front of the Grab-a-Chick restaurant, an outdoor eatery just off Main Street, and ushered Kate to a picnic table with a single occupant.

"Glad to see me, Pretty Boy?" Sergeant Lottie King wrapped him in a bear hug.

Hayden laughed out loud and returned the hug, and that's when he knew something was seriously wrong in his world. Maybe he was in some altered state of exhaustion caused by more than a week of snatching two and three hours of sleep a night, because he wasn't acting normally. First, he had bought Kate a set of oil pencils, not because it would help her psychologically deal with her troubled childhood and not because it would be a safe activity to keep her occupied as he and his team tracked down the Butcher. He bought them for her because he wanted to see her smile. There was no logic in that and no logic in hugging Lottie, other than he was glad to see the Colorado Springs police sergeant.

Kate sat on the bench and held out her hand to Lottie. What a difference a week made. That Kate could walk into a public place and make eye and skin contact with someone proved she'd come a long way since he sat bleeding at Smokey Joe's kitchen table.

"Time for a meeting of the minds?" Lottie said.

Time for his world to stop spinning off its axis. He motioned to the waitress and ordered three sets of wings, rings, and iced teas. After the waitress left, he asked Lottie to fill them in on the Thomas investigation.

"Still got the stalker under lock and key. He insists he had nothing to do with Shayna Thomas's murder, and he's sticking to the story that a gray-haired woman in a pink dress walked into Thomas's bedroom at the time he'd finished jerking off and decided to head home. We had one of our best sketch artists draw a composite. Over the next few days I'm hoping to flash it around here and get some nibbles." She took it out. "My stalker said it's not quite right, but he couldn't tell the artist where to change the damn thing."

Hayden studied the sketch, which depicted a gray-haired woman with a high forehead and recessed chin. He certainly didn't recognize the woman. "Would you mind if I got one of my teammates, Berkley Rowe, to talk with your stalker and create a sketch?"

"Another Apostle?" Lottie nodded. "Bring her on. At this point I'll take Jesus Christ. Got him on speed dial? 'Cause this case could use a miracle or two."

\* \* \*

"We're getting closer. I can feel it." Kate crossed her arms over her chest as she watched Sergeant King drive out of the Grab-a-Chick parking lot.

"There you go, *feeling* things again." But Hayden said it with that half grin she'd seen a few times in the past few days. "And for the record, I agree. The Butcher's here, and we're going to find him."

"And there *you* go again," she said, "wearing your Mr. Hopelessly Optimistic hat."

He opened the door for her. "I'd rather be a hopeless optimist than one in denial."

She smirked. "You are so wrong if you think I'm an optimist at heart, and I can prove it."

"Good. I like proof."

"If I were an optimist, I'd continue to argue with you about this topic, but I'm not. Just like I know I can't move a mountain, I cannot and will not shake your belief that justice will prevail and that good guys will always win. So why bother? I'll just shut up and move on to something else."

"That shouldn't make sense, but it does." Hayden shook his head and laughed. "We've been spending too much time together."

They pulled out of the parking lot. True. Other than a few hours with Hatch or Evie, she'd spent almost an entire week with Hayden. It was strange, being so close to another person. She was close to Smokey, but that was different because he couldn't see her.

*But he could.*

He may not have been able to see her scars, but her friend had sensed that she needed money and suggested the online jewelry store because he wanted to use his new computer. He saw the times she desperately needed to move and would demand she take him for a drive on her motorcycle so *he* could have some fresh air. She wondered if Maeve was taking him on drives through the desert and letting him sleep with open windows.

"Smokey's fine," Hayden said. "I talked with Maeve on my way to Carson City."

She didn't bother to growl in frustration. "How did you know I was thinking about him?"

"The bridge of your nose bunches."

She wondered what she looked like when she thought of Hayden, because she'd been thinking a good deal about him, and she wondered if he'd been thinking about her in ways not connected to the Butcher case. He wasn't fazed by her broken past and didn't see her scars. He'd held her in his arms last night—two golden bands that made her feel safe and right. Hayden was controlling and obsessed with his work, but he *felt* right. Last night was proof. Despite the gift from the Butcher, she'd fallen into a deep, worry-free, anger-free sleep. And he felt something, even if he wasn't ready to admit it.

She lifted her face and enjoyed the almost-cool wind rushing in through the open car window. A nice, inky darkness spilled across the sky, except where the half-moon peeked from a thin layer of clouds. The steady whir of tires spinning on asphalt comforted her. She didn't want to go back to the cottage on the lake. She knew what would happen. She'd go to bed and try to sleep, and Hayden would sit with his case notes and not sleep.

"Slow down," she said, jerking her hand to the left. "Turn there."

Hayden let up on the gas. "What's wrong?"

"Nothing. Turn and take this road."

"Why?

"I want to go for a drive."

"Where?"

"Nowhere. Everywhere." She threaded her fingers through her hair and let the warm wind slip through the waves. "Just drive."

"You want to *just drive*." In the moonlight, she could see the tick along his jaw.

"You have a problem with that?"

He kept going straight, toward the cottage. "I have a problem with aimless, purposeless activity, and a drive right now is not the wisest use of my time."

She slammed her open palms on the dash. "Dammit, Hayden, do you always have to use your time wisely? Is it part of your super agent oath? Or is it just you? Can't we do something for once that isn't on your schedule?"

He rubbed at the space between his eyebrows. "Kate."

She knew he'd never admit it, but he was tired, too, tired of the investigation, tired of chasing evil. "Please, Hayden, just drive."

And maybe he was tired of arguing with her. He hooked their rental car off the highway onto the next dirt road. They followed a series of switchbacks that climbed a mountain thick with pines. As they rose, the night air cooled. Small pebbles pinged the underbelly of the car, a melodic night music. She lifted her hair, coaxing the air to massage the muscles along her neck.

The movement felt deliciously good. The stagnancy of her days, the feelings of being trapped, the crazy hot-cold feelings for Hayden, all of it ceased to exist as the car ate up miles along the glorious back roads of the untamed wilds of northern Nevada.

Until Hayden stopped the car.

She frowned. "What's going on?"

"The road ended."

She looked up. Indeed there was no more road, just the shimmery blue-black waters of Lake Tahoe. Now that the car was still, she realized that the heat still clung to the night, and she realized exactly where they were.

A laugh tickled the back of her throat. There was a madness to the laugh, an impossible-crazy madness.

"What?" Hayden asked.

The laugh bubbled out. "You honest to God don't know where you drove us?"

His face lined with agitation. It looked so good on him. "No, I was *just* driving."

"Well, Agent Reed, you drove us to Crawford Point."

"What's so special about Crawford Point?" He jabbed the darkness with his hands.

"This is Dorado Bay's version of Lovers' Lane. Ever make out in a car, Agent Reed?"

His hands stilled. Technically, every inch of his body stilled. "No."

"Want to?" She'd meant for it to come out as a breezy joke. It hadn't. A ridiculous breathiness clung to her words. The question was foolish, given that Hayden labeled her and filed her away in the witness-victim-who-needs-protecting category of his well-ordered brain.

So call her a fool.

Hayden stared into the blackness. "You'd run, Kate Johnson, if you knew what I wanted to do with you."

The air between them arced as if a storm had rolled in.

"Maybe I wouldn't." They'd been dancing around a slow-burning fire for days. Technically, she'd been dancing, and he'd been trying to convince himself the fire didn't exist. But she saw glowing bits in his gray eyes, like banked coals. "Maybe I'd want to stay right here." *In your arms.* "Tell me, Hayden, what's going on in that mind of yours."

He released the steering wheel but kept his hands suspended in midair. Then he reached for the gearshift as if ready to throw the car in reverse, but stopped. It was odd, seeing Hayden struggle.

At last he unbuckled his seatbelt. His hands cupped either side of her face, and he pulled her toward him. His slate-gray eyes, the ones that followed most of her waking and sleeping moments, darkened and warmed. A heat of her own uncurled from her core, and she wanted to throw herself into his arms. But she'd done that already on the night they found Jason, and that got them nowhere. The next move needed to be his. He needed to go slow, to think things through, and she wanted him enough right here and right now to wait.

He inched forward, his lips brushing her temple. "I think about kissing you here."

Her throat spasmed in a deep swallow, and she jammed her hands beneath her thighs.

His feather-soft lips glided along her jaw. "And here."

She balled her hands into fists.

His mouth slid along her neck. "And here." He slipped her overshirt down her shoulders and rained a series of faster, firmer kisses there. Why didn't he just run a match along her skin?

"But most of all," his lips hovered above hers, "I think of kissing you here."

A delicious surge of heat swelled inside her as their mouths collided. She unleashed her hands and dug them into the perfect folds of his hair. A very un-Hayden-like groan rumbled between them, and she slid her tongue along his lower lip. She tasted impatience, urgency. What happened to *go slow*? Laughter arched her neck.

Right now she didn't want slow either. She wanted her world rocking and spinning, wonderful movement, with Hayden at the wheel. He must have felt the same way, for his mouth pressed harder, and his tongue slid past her lips. His hands fell to her shoulders, where he pushed down the straps of her camisole. Her own hands dropped to his shirt, the soft-crisp Egyptian cotton silky between her fingers, his heart hammering against her palm. She tugged at the exquisite fabric.

A bright light sliced between them.

Hayden sucked in a breath and reached for the gun strapped across his chest.

# CHAPTER SEVENTEEN

*Monday, June 15, 10:00 p.m.*
*Dorado Bay, Nevada*

Put down the gun!"

Blinded by the sharp beam of the flashlight, Hayden couldn't see the body behind the light, nor did he recognize the voice, but he recognized the tone. He placed his Sig on the car dash. "Yes, officer."

Next to him, Kate giggled.

"Step out of the car," the officer continued. "Both of you. Keep your hands where I can see them."

Hayden's back teeth ground down, and he raised his hands in the air, even though he needed to straighten things below. The officer opened the door, and Hayden stepped out of the car. Still fighting laughter, Kate exited the passenger side.

"Now get on the ground, spread eagle," the officer continued.

Time to end this. "Get the light out of my face."

The officer did. Hayden blinked once. Twice. He studied the officer, a young kid with curly dark hair, a name badge that read K. Garcia, and a Dorado Bay police uniform. With his hands still raised, Hayden said, "Inside right pocket of my jacket. FBI."

The kid didn't move.

"Reach into my pocket, Officer Garcia. Take out the creds. Now."

The kid did as Hayden said, and when he opened the small wallet, Garcia swallowed hard. "Holy shit, sorry about that Agent Reed. We're running extra patrols tonight, you know, the Butcher and all." The kid ran a hand through his hair. "Damn, I can't believe I actually got to meet you. Chief said you work for Parker Lord, *the* Parker Lord, and that you guys are all over the Butcher, going to get him any day."

Hayden held out his hand. "My wallet, please."

"Oh, here you go. Hey, really, I'm sorry. You can go back to"—he looked at Kate who slipped back on her overshirt—"to what you were doing. I mean, I..."

"Thank you," Hayden said with a dismissive nod.

The dry grass crunched under Officer Garcia's feet as he hurried back to his cruiser.

The car pulled away, the spray of gravel loud in the silent night, but not loud enough to cover the start-and-stop laughter bubbling from Kate.

He said nothing, his feet moving one step after another toward her.

"Your hair's sticking up," she said as she ran her fingers along the sides of his head. The fingers lowered to his chest. "And your shirt's untucked. Agent Reed, *you* are a mess. I'm afraid your reputation might be shot."

He ran the pad of his thumb against her swollen lips, against the faint red chafe along her neck. "What about yours?"

Her lips twisted in a cynical arc. "Mine's shot to hell already."

He reached for her hand and flattened it against his chest. "Do you feel that?" Could this woman, who felt everything so deeply, feel his heart threatening to burst out of his chest?

Her sharp smile fell away, and she nodded.

His other hand slid around her waist and curved around her hip. He pulled her to him, crushing her against his arousal, which hadn't abated despite the appearance of Officer Garcia.

*This is wrong. She's a witness, a victim of the vilest killer you've ever hunted. She needs your protection, not your body raging with hormones.* The voice, his own, boomed in his head.

*But it's right.* Another voice, also his own, countered.

"I want to finish this," he said, his voice raw with truth and desire.

"Me too."

He took a breath, lowered his lips against the top of her head, and said, "Not here."

They rushed to the car, and he drove straight to the cottage. No lazy meandering, no whimsical turns. As he helped her out of the car, he took her hands. "This is your last chance to say no."

"Why would I do that?" Her lips parted in a husky laugh.

Because this was crazy. Because he was in the middle of the biggest case of his life. Because she was a witness. Hell, she was the target. Plus there was the issue of focus. When he was with Kate, he lost focus, his world became less orderly, and he drove without a destination.

Logic dictated he shouldn't be taking her to his bed.

The hell with logic.

He pulled her into the curve of his arm and rushed up the

steps. He put his hand on the door just as something crashed inside the cottage.

"Down!" Hayden pushed Kate to the floor and flung his body on top of hers.

* * *

"There's glass at six and nine o'clock." Kate swept the bits of broken vase littered across the living room floor.

"Sorry, Katy-lady. Made a real mess, didn't I?" Smokey pulled a hand across his lined face. "Guess I'm tired. It's been a long day."

"I agree." Maeve carried a small trash can from the kitchen. "The plane got into Reno after eight. Then we got lost."

"*You* got lost," Smokey said.

"Using directions *you* got off the Internet." Maeve held out the trash can, and Kate dumped in the glass from the vase Smokey accidentally knocked off the fireplace mantel.

"I'm blind, lady. Why the hell are you having me get us directions?" Smokey's lips dipped in a jagged frown, but he shot a wink in Kate's direction.

"We should have waited until morning to drive here," Maeve added as she held out the trash can for the last dustpan full of glass.

"And leave Kate alone another night?" Smokey flapped his lips in a growly snort. "I don't think so."

"Joseph, she's hardly alone." Maeve took the broom from Kate. "Hayden's with her. He's keeping her safe."

"And a piss-poor job he's doing. Took me less than two minutes to break into this place." Smokey aimed a shaky finger at Hayden, who stood like a marble statue, his elbow resting on the fireplace mantel. "Hear that, G-man? Two minutes to jimmy the lock on the side door. Plus the alarm didn't go off because it wasn't set."

Hayden dug a fisted hand in his pocket. "Kate has been with me or my people the entire time she's been away from you."

Yeah, she'd been with him all right, Kate mused, and if not for Smokey and Maeve's arrival, she'd be even more with him right now. Heat surged from the V of her legs to her cheeks. But the man who'd been rocking her world in the front seat of a car was not the same one standing starched and steady next to the fireplace. Shirt tucked. Jacket straight. Smooth hair.

Kate tapped Smokey's forearm. "Clear. The recliner is two feet to your right."

Smokey stomped past her but didn't sit. "Why the hell did you let her go on TV like that? Where's your brain, G-man? Now everyone, including the Butcher, knows where she's at."

"That's the idea, Smokey." Kate sat on the couch, her knees still wobbly. Hell, her world was still wobbly, thanks to Hayden.

"The Butcher isn't the type to take a sniper shot at Kate from far away, nor is he strong enough to take on me or any of my people," Hayden explained in that clear, patient tone of his. "He's physically and intellectually inferior. He'll only get Kate if he finds her alone. And from here on out, there's no way I'm letting her out of my sight."

*But what about your hands?* Kate wanted to ask Hayden. She still felt those hands on her skin and did a double-take on her arms and shoulders to make sure there weren't fresh slash and burn marks striped across her flesh.

Maeve took a seat next to Kate on the couch. "I told

Joseph you were all right, but he insisted on coming. He threatened to hijack a plane if I wouldn't bring him here."

"And don't think I wouldn't do it." Smokey's sightless eyes narrowed.

Kate shook her head. It was crazy, but she could picture her friend hijacking a plane.

"It's late." Hayden lowered his arm from the fireplace. "We'll talk in the morning. Maeve, you can take my room. Smokey, we'll put you in the spare."

"And you?" Maeve asked. "Where are you going to sleep?"

Hayden didn't look at Kate. "I'll take the couch. I have work to do tonight."

Why did that hurt? Why the hell did it hurt that Hayden, when given the time to think and analyze, chose work over her? She knew him. She knew the kind of man he was. It shouldn't hurt that he didn't want to share her bed tonight, but it did.

She showed Maeve and Smokey their rooms, all the while wondering if Hayden's about-face had anything to do with the appearance of his mother-in-law. Was she a reminder of the ex-wife who had died just over two weeks ago?

*It doesn't concern you.*

Thank you Special Agent Hayden Reed for that little reminder.

The sheets cooled her heated skin as she slipped into bed. It was well after midnight, but Hayden sat in the living room working. She was so physically aware of him, where he was, how he moved. It was as if her nerve endings extended past her skin and reached out to him in some crazy out-of-body experience.

*I want to finish this*, Hayden had said under the cover of lake darkness.

*Then why aren't you here in my bed?* she wanted to scream.

Hell, this wasn't her, sitting around and bemoaning the hand she'd been dealt. She threw off her bedsheet, but when she reached the door, her hand hovered above the handle. With a deep breath, she inched the door open a crack, a wedge of light cutting the darkness of her room. Hayden sat on the sofa hunched over his computer. His suit coat hung on the back of a kitchen chair, but his tie, this one with beautiful splashes of sage green and black, still circled his neck.

Perfect. In any light he was so perfect it took her breath away.

She flattened her hand against her throat, where her heart hammered, her fingers brushing the raised, jagged lines of her flesh. Her heart plummeted. For a moment, in the moonlight in the front seat of a car on a lane for lovers, she'd almost forgotten the scars existed.

She closed the door, snuffing out the crack of light, and crawled into bed. Alone.

* * *

Hayden stared at his computer screen. And saw Kate.

He closed his eyes. And saw Kate.

He saw the heat in her face, the passion in her eyes, and the want on her lips. Which was all good and fine. He was a master observer, a man who saw everything. Felt nothing. Yeah, that was supposed to be him.

The kicker was, he felt it. *Felt* her.

Where was the dispassionate evaluator? Where was her protector?

He'd disappeared. In the front seat of a car.

He slammed his computer shut and bolted up. Thrusting his hands in his pockets, he paced in front of the fireplace. What had he been thinking?

*That you want her. More than you've wanted anything. Or anyone.*

His feet almost stumbled. Whose voice was that?

He started pacing again. It was someone who didn't know what he was talking about.

He wanted the Butcher, the man who had killed at least seven human beings in an evil, vicious manner, who had flaunted his victories in the face of a good and right world, who had mocked beauty and justice. The reign of bloodshed must end, and it wouldn't happen as long as his attention strayed to Kate Johnson, which told him exactly what he needed to do next.

He plunked back on the couch, his body a heavy hunk of lead. His eyes ached, as if they'd been scratched by steel wool. He'd never been so tired in all of his life.

He lifted the computer screen and went back to work.

\* \* \*

*Tuesday, June 16, 1:40 a.m.*
*Dorado Bay, Nevada*

He sat at the chipped Formica table and sipped his coffee. He should be sipping champagne right now, but they didn't have any at the Bear Down All-Night Diner, which smelled of rancid grease and overripe bananas.

"Hey, cable guy, you want another piece of pie?" The bony waitress with the cadaver eye sockets flashed him her teeth and the inside of her thigh.

"No thanks." He waved her off. Why didn't she just jerk up that short denim skirt and flash him her cunt and scream, *You wanna piece of this?*

And for the record, no, he didn't want pie or her cunt.

At one time he had, a long time ago, before he'd learned to recognize these types for what they really were. And he'd gone on to kill many of them.

The first one was a waitress much like this one. He was working as a dishwasher and screwed up the courage to ask her out. She said no. An unfortunate choice. She died behind the restaurant dumpster with a knife used to cut cherry pie. He masturbated with her blood.

Others followed, eight to be exact, all waitresses or whores with hopeless eyes and hapless lives, like the waitress at the Bear Down—he squinted through the glasses he didn't need—Mandy. Yes, like Mandy here who wanted to sell him pie and her body.

Today he saw her for what she was, a twenty-something meth user with bad skin and an express ticket to an early grave. Certainly not worthy of him.

He deserved better. He *had* better.

He had Katrina Erickson exactly where he needed her, right here in Dorado Bay. Agent Reed had done his job and more. All he had wanted the FBI agent to do was find Katrina Erickson, but the man with the shiny badge had gone above and beyond the call of duty and brought her right here to his doorstep.

And soon she would be at his feet, the blood flowing from her.

He tossed a ten-dollar bill on the table and walked outside the stinking Bear Down to the cable repair truck he'd sat in for two hours outside the yellow cottage as he waited for inspiration.

He'd always been a man of inspiration. His work was inspired and admired.

Inspiration hit a few hours ago as he watched Hayden Reed and Katrina Erickson rush up the steps to that cottage, the scent of sex and sweat so strong it made him gag.

*Whore!*

But her whore's blood would soon be let. To appease the dragon. The dragon's tongue unfurled at the back of his throat.

He climbed into the cable repair truck and grabbed a small spiral notebook from his pocket and a pen and started a shopping list.

*Shovel*
*Duct tape*
*Chicken wire*
*Plywood*
*Water bottles*
*Bananas (brown okay)*

# CHAPTER EIGHTEEN

*Tuesday, June 16, 4:50 a.m.*
*Dorado Bay, Nevada*

Kate wore a yellow scarf. Nothing else. Her green eyes were steamy, the points of her breasts erect, her legs long and sleek as she ambled from her bedroom to the couch. She stood close enough for him to touch.

*Go slow*, Hayden warned himself.

"Why the scarf?" he asked.

"I was thinking about using it later. To tie you up." She smiled. "More comfortable than handcuffs, don't you think?" She slid her hands along his bare abdomen and lowered them to his hips. He was as naked as she. He must have fallen asleep after he'd taken a shower. But this, this was a problem. Maeve and Smokey slept just feet away in the cottage bedrooms.

"They won't hear us." Kate ran her fingers along the inside of his thighs. He jerked and swelled.

"Now you can read minds?" he asked, trying to keep his voice calm.

"I can read yours." She pulled him toward her and rested

her forehead against his. "You want me, Hayden. You want me." *Me. Me. Me.*

Her words banged against his head, his heart, every naked inch of him.

*Me. You want me.*

Yes, he did. He reached for her.

*Me. Me. Me.*

His eyes flew open. He was on the couch in the cottage. Fully clothed and fully erect. Someone was banging on the front door. He stumbled to the door and stared at Officer Garcia, the kid who'd found him pawing Kate in the car.

"Sorry to wake you, Agent Reed, but the chief wants you at the station. A kid's missing, and the disappearance may be Butcher-related."

The fog of his dream-filled sleep lifted. "A kid?" He must have heard incorrectly.

"Yep. Little Benny Hankins, the nine-year-old whose brother found the foot on the end of his fishing line, has been missing almost twenty-four hours." The foot that belonged to Jason Erickson, who was killed by the Butcher.

Hayden slipped into a clean white shirt, grabbed a tie, and flung it around his neck. Then he reached for a sheet of paper. The pen stilled as he thought about the note he needed to write Kate just in case she got up before Hatch or Evie got there.

*I'll be back in a few hours. Please stay in your room and wait for me, wearing nothing but a yellow polka-dot scarf.*

He settled for: *Hatch is on his way. Do NOT leave this house. Do NOT open the door.*

He also ducked into Smokey's room and picked up the gun. Hayden had noticed the bulge last night in the old man's baggy jacket. He wasn't surprised the vet brought his own brand of protection. He cared for Kate, and he'd do anything to keep her safe. He'd take a man like Smokey Joe on his team any day. Back in the living room, he placed Smokey's Ruger next to the note.

\* \* \*

There were too many people in the Dorado Bay police station. Too many officers, too many reporters, too many people in tears.

"Where is he?" Hayden searched for a twelve-year-old kid who liked to fish.

A detective led him to the station's break room, where he found Charlie Hankins sitting on a couch next to a vending machine. The kid held an unopened package of M&Ms. This was Charlie Hankins, the older of the two brothers who'd been fishing and discovered Jason Erickson's foot.

"Hey there, Charlie, I'm Special Agent Hayden Reed."

Charlie nodded at him, his hairless jaw hard, his eyes unblinking. Hayden plinked three quarters in the vending machine and bought a giant-size Snickers bar. He dragged a folding chair from a nearby table and set it a few feet in front of the kid. He sat. Eye to eye. Man to man.

"Doing okay?" Hayden asked.

The boy nodded.

Hayden unwrapped the candy bar and took a bite. He chewed slowly, thoroughly. Then he took another bite. That's when Charlie opened his package of M&Ms and poured a few into his mouth. One fell to the ground. They both ignored it. When the bag of M&Ms was empty, Charlie wadded it in his fist, his knuckles white and tight.

"It's my fault my brother's missing," Charlie said. "I should have listened to him. Benny tried to tell me the killer might be after him."

Hayden folded his empty candy bar wrapper and tucked it in his pocket. "Charlie, the first thing you need to know is you're not the only one Benny told about seeing the car by the lake."

The boy's head shook and so did the tears swelling in his eyes.

"Your brother told three other people about seeing that car, including his baseball coach. No one, including an adult, believed him. Benny had a history of telling stories. You and everyone else had a reason to doubt him."

"But I shouldn't have. I should have listened and done something to keep him safe."

"The other thing you need to know is you aren't responsible for other people's actions, not your brother's or anyone driving by the lake. You understand that, Charlie? You can't control other people. There's one person you can control in this world. Who is it?"

Charlie stared at the candy wrapper in his hand. "Me."

"That's right." Hayden held out his hand, and Charlie loosened his fist and dropped the crumpled paper onto his palm. "Don't ever forget that."

Hayden put the crushed wrapper in his pocket and took the digital recorder out of another. He didn't need the little machine, as he wouldn't forget anything the kid told him, but it made everything look more official. The kid needed to feel like he was doing something important.

"I need your help."

Charlie sniffed and nodded.

"You need to think real hard about what Benny said about the man in the car."

Charlie's jaw quivered. "I wasn't paying attention. I was razzing him about seeing little green aliens."

"I bet you were paying more attention than you thought.

You're a smart guy, Charlie, I can tell. You have a good head." Hayden tapped his own head. "The brain is an amazing thing. Let's see what it can do. First, I want you to close your eyes. Picture your brother on the day he told you about the car by Mulveney's Cove." Charlie's face scrunched into a hard frown. "Do you have the picture in your head?" The boy nodded. "Good. You keep saying Benny talked about a man. Are you sure he said the person driving the car was a man?" If this kid mentioned a woman in a pink dress, he'd...Hayden blinked. He didn't know what he'd do.

"Yes," Charlie said, "it was a man. I'm sure of it."

"Good. What did the man look like?"

"Benny said he was wearing a cap and glasses. No, not a cap, a fishing hat." Charlie opened one eye. "Is...is...that important?"

"Yes. You're doing great, Charlie. Now think back to your conversation with Benny. Did he say anything else about the man?"

"That's all."

"Was the man alone?"

Charlie gnawed on his bottom lip. "I don't remember."

"Did Benny mention anything about a woman, an older one with gray hair?"

"Alone. I'm pretty sure—no, I'm sure Benny said it was just the guy."

"What did Benny say about the man's car?"

"It was light colored. Maybe white or silver."

"Anything else? A license plate? Clean or dirty? Was it running? Making any noise?"

Charlie's forehead and mouth and nose scrunched. Finally, he shook his head.

"Do you remember where Benny said the man with the car was?"

"Mulveney's Cove." The boy's eyes brightened. "By the tree with the rope. In the summer a bunch of us guys sneak over to Mulveney's place and use the rope to jump into the lake. We like it because the place is kind of outta the way, and we can do some crazy stuff without worrying moms and stuff. We are usually naked." Charlie's lip curled in disgust. "That was lame, wasn't it?"

Hayden snapped off the recorder. "You did well, Charlie. You gave me more than I had ten minutes ago. And most importantly, you gave me a place to look for evidence, which no one else has been able to do. You know what I'm talking about, right?"

"You're going to the rope swing near Mulveney's Cove to look for tire tracks or footprints or stuff."

"Exactly. And that kind of stuff is far from lame."

"Are you going to find my brother?"

"I'll do everything within my power."

"Everything? You promise?"

Hayden squeezed the boy's slumped shoulder. "I promise."

While the Dorado Bay Police Department ramped up the massive manhunt for nine-year-old Benny Hankins, Hayden continued his own hunt for the Butcher. He intended to go back to the cottage where Hatch was now with Kate, Maeve, and Smokey Joe, but Evie joined him at the station with news that changed his plans.

"I spent the night getting cozy with your Mike Muldoon. Creepy eye patch, but interesting fellow," Evie said. "Kate's right. Until the pension fraud scandal, he was a fine, upstanding citizen. He was young, successful, wealthy, but quiet, almost shy. He wasn't a joiner, not a member of the chamber, young executives club, or even a gym. He spent most of his spare time collecting."

"What?"

"Pretties." She took out pictures of the artwork seized from Mike Muldoon's home. "Most of the paintings were Impressionists, whatever that means. There were also some statuary pieces, quite a few bronzes, all costly. He also liked beautiful women." Evie hauled out pictures of Muldoon with a leggy red head and a blonde with bright blue eyes. Both attractive, especially next to his blandness. "He didn't get serious with either, and he never married until the day before he went to jail. Court records show he and Robyn Banks tied the knot right before U.S. Marshals whisked him away."

"Interesting timing."

"Yes, timing is very interesting when it comes to Mike Muldoon, who got out of jail on January third of this year."

Hayden darted toward the parking lot before Evie had time to take a breath.

The first Butcher slaying occurred on January nineteenth.

* * *

*Tuesday, June 16, 9:15 a.m.*
*Dorado Bay, Nevada*

Kate stood in the doorway of the cottage, her mouth a twisted grimace.

"I won't take it," she said to the uniformed officer holding a hissing, foul-smelling cage. "Not now. Not after you give it a bath. Never."

"Please, Ms. Johnson," the Dorado Bay police officer said. "The animal shelter people said they are going to put her down. They said Ellie's too violent. She attacked two volunteers."

"Then maybe she needs to be put down."

"Kate!" Maeve and Smokey cried in unison.

"Don't *Kate* me." She shot both of them a dirty look, extra heat, since Smokey couldn't see. "And stop looking at me like that, Smokey. I'm not the bad guy here. This screwed-up cat belonged to Jason, a very sick man who once tried to kill me. Who knows what he did to this animal?"

"Actually, the neighbor said she was a good cat and that she'd never been a problem until a few weeks ago when Jason disappeared," the officer said. "I think maybe she misses him, and Ellie here seemed to like you the day you were at the house. You were the only one able to get within three feet of her without her going ballistic."

"But I don't like cats," Kate said with a snap. "No, that's not right. I like cats. I just don't *do* cats. I don't *do* pets. Period. They take too much time and too much work." Kate lifted her palms in the air. "Tell me, Smokey, what am I supposed to do when I'm done here? Get a cat carrier and hitch it to the back of my bike?"

"Leave her with me. Don't mind no animals."

The cat hissed and rocked the cage. "Smokey, she'd claw your eyes out."

"Not like I need 'em."

Kate let out an exasperated groan.

Maeve squinted into the stinking cage. "Ellie does look...difficult."

Kate didn't do difficult, either, which is why she wasn't going to have anything else to do with Hayden Reed. Last night he'd been ready to drag her into his bed, but in the light of day, he'd got back in control. And therein lay the issue; Hayden was too much of a control freak to be a part of her life.

"I'm sorry, officer, but Jason's cat is not my responsibility."

The officer shook his head at the scraggly cat. "Had to try, Ellie." He nodded at Kate. "But if you decide you want her, get to the shelter by Saturday. That's when they will put her down. Come on, Ellie."

The cat hissed and jabbed a paw, claws bared, through the wire mesh.

\* \* \*

*Tuesday, June 16, 11:30 a.m.*
*Ely, Nevada*

When Kate talked to him of a shattered, ugly, hopeless world, Hayden insisted it was only broken in places. This was one: unit three of the Ely State Prison.

"You really think Muldoon has something to do with the Broadcaster Butcher slayings?" Wally Shepherd, the warden of Nevada's maximum security correctional facility, asked as they made their way down a hallway smelling of pine cleaner and angry men.

"Do you?" Hayden countered.

"Muldoon was an odd one. But of course, he didn't really belong here. Wasn't a maxer."

"Exactly how did a man convicted of pension fraud and sentenced to five to ten years in minimum security end up in max?"

"Bad timing? Bad luck? Who knows?" The warden scratched a mole on his neck. "Beds were full at NNCC, so they brought him here for a temporary stay, but we never got a transfer order on him. So he lived with the lifers until he timed out on early parole."

"What type of prisoner was he?"

"In the beginning he was a real whiner. He whined about the food, the beds, and the razor wire blocking his view of sunsets." The warden laughed. "Didn't like the view. Can you believe that? Told him this ain't no Holiday Inn, but after the green bologna incident, he quieted down."

"Green bologna?"

"Yeah, Muldoon was a real prima donna until about his third month. Around that time he refused to eat his bologna sandwich because it had some green on it. He threw it across the room and damn near started a full-scale riot, but my guards shut it down before there was too much damage. During the ruckus, Muldoon got his eye poked out with a spoon. He quieted down after that. We never heard another complaint. I guess going *mano-a-mano* with the lifers around here straightened him out."

More like broke him. Muldoon may have entered this place as a white-collar criminal, but he'd left a broken man.

The maze of hallways ended at a heavy metal door. The warden punched in a code, but before he opened it, Hayden asked, "Did you pull up the visitor's log on Muldoon?"

"Yep. No one named Jason Erickson ever signed in to see him. The only visitor he ever had was his wife, Robyn Banks."

"What did you find in Muldoon's phone records?"

"Just a few calls to and from Banks. Not even calls to an attorney. The entire time he was here in prison, the only person he ever communicated with was his wife." Which meant that if Mike Muldoon gave the order to kill Kate, it came before he was imprisoned or was routed through Robyn Banks.

No one outside the prison provided any links between Muldoon and the broadcaster slayings, and Hayden hoped he'd have better luck with someone on the inside, like Albert

Brown. Brown was serving two consecutive life sentences for the murder and rape of the five-year-old girl who lived next door to his granny. He'd been holed up in ESP unit three for ten years. For two of those years, Mike Muldoon had lived in the cell next door.

"What'll I get if I talk 'bout Mikey?" Brown's arms, covered in a tattoo of sutures running from his wrist to shoulder, rested on the metal bars of his cell.

Hayden stood in the hallway across from the cell, one hand in his pocket. "The knowledge that you could save the lives of innocent women." He had to try.

"That ain't worth shit."

*You ain't worth shit.* The thought slammed into Hayden with a fierceness that blistered the backs of his eyelids. The hand in his pocket folded into a fist. Anger would get him nowhere with Albert Brown. He refocused, realigned, and relaxed his hand.

Hayden knew what oiled the gears of a man like Brown. "What do you want?"

Brown rubbed two fingers along his chin, mocking thoughtful consideration. "I'm here for the long haul, so comforts are my gig. I like things that take the"—he smiled, a gold canine tooth glinting under the harsh, institutional lighting—"edge off this place."

Hayden didn't blink. "It's yours."

"Damn, you must be a mighty powerful man. You run the FBI or something?"

"Or something. Tell me what you know about Muldoon."

"Okay, here's the shit on Mikey. He kept pictures of girls, lots of pictures, but they weren't from the titty mags. Muldoon liked faces, had hundreds of them in a shoebox, tore them out of magazines, newspapers, and department store ads. He'd look at his faces for hours. I asked him one time why he collected faces. You know what he told me?" Brown shook his head in disbelief. "He said, 'They're beautiful.' That's it. Nothing else. Is that fucking weird or what?"

In his head, Hayden was wording the search warrant request on Mike Muldoon's home. "Did you recognize any of the women?"

Brown ran his tongue over his gold tooth. "We ain't talked payment yet. I like beef, maybe a little surf to go with it, and a Bud. You think you can swing the Bud?"

"Bottle or draft?"

"Hot damn. Yep, one of them faces Muldoon slobbered all over belonged to that newscaster who got all cut up a few years back."

"Mike Muldoon had a picture of Katrina Erickson?"

"Yep."

"How can you be so sure?"

"I asked him about her because she seemed to be one of his favorites."

"Favorites?"

"Yeah, he used to talk to her, call her 'my pretty green eyes.'"

\* \* \*

*Tuesday, June 16, 12:15 p.m.*
*Dorado Bay, Nevada*

Rose Heber dropped a saliva-covered hunk of leather on her daughter's bed.

"That is so disgusting." Her daughter swatted the shoe onto the floor. "What is it?"

"The end of your softball career."

Her daughter dropped the teen magazine she'd been reading. "What?"

"I found Duchess chewing on it, and I told you last week if you let Duchess tear up one more set of cleats, your softball days are over. No more cleats, no more softball."

Her daughter scrambled off the bed. "Noooo! I can't leave the team. We're in first place."

Rose pointed at the twisted mass of leather. "You got an extra sixty bucks for a new pair of cleats?"

"No."

"Then instead of playing ball, you'll be playing with Duchess. The poor dog's bored. That's why she spends all day chewing things."

"Wait!" Her daughter picked up the mangled shoe. "This isn't my cleat. It's too small."

Mother and daughter looked at the Great Dane pup, all feet and spindly legs and soaking wet, a long lake reed entangled in her collar.

"Looks like she's been down by Mulveney's Cove again," her daughter said.

Rose took the mangled baseball cleat. "The missing little boy. Benny Hankins." Rose breathed out. "He'd been on his way to baseball practice at the park near Mulveney's Cove when he disappeared. Oh, God!"

# CHAPTER NINETEEN

*Tuesday, June 16, 2:00 p.m.*
*Dorado Bay, Nevada*

Dozens of cars lined the dirt road snaking from Mulveney's place to the lake, mocking the NO TRESPASSING signs posted every twenty feet. Hayden parked his car behind a Dorado Bay police cruiser marked K-9 UNIT.

"Maybe it's not the little boy," Kate said, her voice a soft warble. "Maybe..."

Hayden put his arm around her, pulled her close, and kissed the top of her head. Her pain for a little boy she'd never met reminded him of how deeply she felt. When they received news that Benny Hankins's baseball cleat had been found near the tree with the rope at Mulveney's Cove, she joined him in racing out the door.

As he and Kate made their way to the shoreline, he spotted Lottie.

"You got here fast," Hayden said.

Lottie flashed him her cheetah-print stiletto. "Got my running shoes on."

At the water's edge, they flagged down a Dorado Bay police officer.

"Dogs found Benny's baseball bag in the bushes," the officer said. "It wasn't buried, just tossed aside, which is a good thing, right? I mean, the Butcher is a meticulous guy. If he did something to Benny, he wouldn't leave the bag lying around, would he?"

"It's possible." But not probable, although Hayden didn't express that out loud. The Butcher was careful in his broadcaster slayings, adhering to the ritual and order that bound them. Nine-year-old Benny wasn't part of the ritual. He was most likely a set of eyes that saw too much; therefore the killing and disposal of his body wouldn't be as conscientious.

One of the divers in the lake surfaced and called out, "We spotted blocks."

Despite the heat, Kate wrapped her arms about her chest, and he edged closer to her, the skin of her upper arm as cold as the deep blue lake water. He didn't feel cold. Just numb.

A moment later, the diver reappeared and dipped his head.

Silence rippled over the search-and-rescue workers gathered at the cove. Kate leaned into his side. On his other side, Lottie let loose a growl. No, he wouldn't make the assumption. Not yet. He wouldn't believe that boy was dead until he had proof positive. Fifteen minutes later a pair of divers placed a small body on a tarp on the shore. Juvenile male. Three feet tall. Thin. Sandy blond hair. Skinned left knee.

"Jesus H. Christ," a man Hayden knew to be Benny's baseball coach said with a choke. "It's Benny."

The silence exploded into soft murmurs and not-so-soft sobs. The sounds pounded Hayden's head, but he focused on the body, on the victim, on this possible link to the Butcher.

"Turn him over," Hayden instructed one of the officers.

Even before the officer turned over the stiff, bloated body that had once been a little boy, Hayden knew what was there: a single puncture wound at the base of the skull.

Kate's fingers dug into his arm.

"The son of a bitch. The goddamned, baby-killing, son of a fucking bitch!" Lottie quaked so hard, it rocked his body. Or at least he thought it was Lottie.

"He's a beast, a monster," Kate said, tears streaming down her face. He drew her to his chest, and small, hot tears for a boy she didn't know soaked his shirt. Yes, Kate felt deeply.

And right now, so did Hayden.

He tried to focus on the case, on the need for prompt and thorough response and investigation.

Instead he saw himself sitting down with Benny's twelve-year-old brother, Charlie.

*I'll do everything within my power*, Hayden had promised Charlie Hankins. His words slammed into his chest.

Kate's arm tightened around his waist, and when he looked down, she was staring at him. "You okay?" she asked.

Hayden started to nod, but a single word rushed over his lips. "No."

Kate settled her forehead against his chest and murmured, "Me neither."

\* \* \*

*Tuesday, June 16, 11:30 p.m.*
*Dorado Bay, Nevada*

Kate didn't know what frightened her more, the fact that the Broadcaster Butcher had killed a nine-year-old boy or the fact that Hayden had lost his jacket.

She and Hayden had spent all afternoon and much of the night with the search team, scouring Mulveney's Cove and the land surrounding it, looking for anything that would lead them one step closer to the Butcher. She had followed Hayden as he questioned homeowners and boaters and swimmers and joggers, desperately seeking information that would help them find the Butcher before he sunk his knife into another innocent body.

Their futile efforts left her angry at the horror and injustice of Benny Hankins's death, frightened that the desperate Butcher was getting closer, and shocked that Hayden's stoic façade cracked. His jacket was missing. He took it off sometime during the search and forgot where he placed it.

Now jacketless, Hayden unlocked the door to the cottage. Darkness greeted them, as did a soft snore rumbling from Smokey's bedroom. Hayden took off through the house, checking Smokey and Maeve's rooms along with the back and side doors. When he came into the living room, he switched on the light, set his computer on the coffee table, and slipped off his tie. For a moment she thought he'd let the slip of brightly colored silk fall from his hand to the floor, but he laid it carefully across the armrest of the sofa.

"Are you going to bed now?" he asked.

She listened to his words, *really* listened, trying to figure out if there was something else behind the question. Was this his way of saying, *It's been a bitch of a day, and I need to talk?* or, *Dammit, Kate, help me forget that today I saw a nine-year-old's bludgeoned body.*

Because right now, that's what she was dealing with. Every inch of her body ached for that boy and his family. She wanted to expunge the evil that descended upon them. A fast, hard ride on her bike would help. She fiddled with the hem of her shirt. So would another tumble in the front seat of the car with Hayden.

As for Hayden, she couldn't tell what was going on in his little pinky, let alone his head. Hell, since when had she been able to make sense of anything in this screwed-up world?

"Goodnight, Hayden." Now that felt comfortable, normal. Don't know what to do? Run.

Hayden tugged on the cuffs of his shirt. "I'll check your room."

This, too, was good—Hayden the Efficient at work, taking care of her, taking care of the world. So he lost his jacket. No big deal. The world wasn't falling apart.

Although he'd repeatedly said the Butcher was too weak to attack her in the presence of others, Hayden checked her closet and under her bed. He pushed back the curtains, tugged on the lock, and jammed the small stick deeper into the window groove. She thought he'd turn away and march out, but he paused before the glass, as if mesmerized by the golden lake beyond her bedroom window.

She studied his reflection. Was he thinking about the dead boy? About the Butcher? About his missing jacket? His face remained impassive. But then his body shifted a fraction and his forehead leaned against the windowpane.

The tiny movement stilled her heart. For the past week, Hayden had offered her comfort. He had said and done things that helped her find strength. He had kept her sane, possibly alive, but here in her bedroom with his back to her, he'd just proved he wasn't a rock. Moonlight streamed in through the window, painting streaks of gold through his black hair. He looked tired, but that was nothing new. Right now he looked...alone.

"Hayden?" What could she say? *Stay. I want to take you in my arms and hold you. I want you to hold me, and maybe to-*

*gether, the two of us can pretend to be whole.* She clasped her hands behind her back and settled on, "Don't leave me alone, not tonight." There. She'd play one of his head games, appeal to the rescuer in him and make him think she needed him.

A long breath streamed from his mouth and fogged the glass. "Is this what you want?" he said to the glass.

"It's what I *need*." And it was the God's honest truth. She needed him right now.

Hayden faced her, and she bit back a gasp at the message in his eyes. *I need you, too.* It grew clearer with each step he took through the slivers of moonlight toward her.

"Are you sure?" His lips barely moved.

She laughed. "Oh, God, Hayden, you're being thorough again."

"Obscenely." He kept his face a serious mask, but something bright glinted in those heavy-lidded gray eyes.

She thought about the feel of his lips on her neck, his fingers as they raced across her breasts, the swirls of warmth in her midsection. Her body didn't lie. Nor did she. "Yes. I want this. I want you."

His fingers trailed up her arms. "I dreamed about you last night."

She swallowed. "You did?"

His hands meandered along her shoulders to her neck, his thumbs tracing circles where her pulse pounded. "You were wearing a yellow polka-dot scarf." The corners of his mouth tilted up. "Nothing else."

Her knees gave way, but she was saved from melting to the floor by his arms, which he wrapped about her waist. Her hands pressed into the silky smooth cotton of his shirt, and his mouth captured hers, taking away her breath, her thoughts, her fears.

His tongue dipped past her lips, and he backed her toward

the door, their hips and legs moving in tandem. "Smokey has good ears," Hayden said as he pressed her against the door until it clicked shut.

"Is this going to get loud?" she asked with a half laugh, half shudder of desire as she thought of Hayden—quiet, controlled Hayden—letting go.

A groan—a delicious, un-Hayden-like sound—thrummed against her mouth. His fingers traveled to her shoulders, where he slipped off her overshirt, which he placed neatly on the top of the dresser. One by one, he stripped off her garments and placed them on the dresser. With each new bit of skin revealed, he took his time, savoring each inch, with his hands, his mouth, his eyes. Careful. Methodical.

She wanted to shout, *Stop going so slow!*—but she didn't.

Instead she forced her hands to move slow as she took her turn at undressing him, even though an almost frantic need pulled at her. In the moonlight, his bare skin was more exquisite than his handmade shirts. Smooth, soft, perfect. And so right under her hands. She arched into him, molding her body against his. Hands roamed along heated skin, mouths traded sighs and delicious groans, and when he slid into her, her body shook in exquisite pleasure followed by a delicious and unexpected peace.

\* \* \*

*Wednesday, June 17, 7 a.m.*
*Dorado Bay, Nevada*

A warm, soft cleft cradled him.

He stiffened. So fast and hard, like he was twenty years younger. All hormones, no brain cells.

His eyelids flew open. Kate. In his arms. In his mind. But not in his dreams. Oddly enough, he couldn't remember having dreamed at all last night. Not of Kate. Not of the Butcher. And not of voices from his past.

He checked the small clock on the nightstand. Another shocker. He'd slept six hours straight.

His arms tightened around Kate, and he pulled her bare bottom into his lap. Her hair smelled of lemons, her skin of sex. He nuzzled his face against the soft waves of her hair.

Last night had been imprinted in his mind. The moonlight setting her pale skin aglow. The almost unbearable sweetness of her breath as she let loose tiny gasps against his lips. The feather-soft brush of her fingers sliding over his chest and below. He ran his hand along her hip, and she gave a satisfied sigh and snuggled deeper into him. It would be so easy to spend the next few hours—frankly, the next few days—in bed with her. He ran a hand through his sleep-tousled hair. He could still feel Kate's fingers in his hair, leaving sparks in their wake. Ten little lightning rods, jolting his skin and forcing him to acknowledge feelings he thought he'd never have.

But he shouldn't be thinking of Kate's ten fingers.

As he climbed out of her bed he thought of nine bodies.

The Butcher had upped his body count to nine, almost double from five in just one week: seven broadcasters, including Shayna Thomas in Colorado Springs and the broadcaster in Oakland; Jason Erickson; and nine-year-old Benny Hankins.

\* \* \*

*Wednesday, June 17, 4 p.m.*
*Dorado Bay, Nevada*

A screech tore from somewhere in the yellow cottage. Kate dropped Hayden's laptop on the bed and ran to the kitchen, her heart in her throat and an all-too-familiar fear at her back.

Smokey, who must have been napping, stumbled from his room. "What the he-ell was that?"

Maeve stood at the sink, trimming the stems from a handful of wildflowers. "I'm not sure, but it came from the back deck."

Hatch, who'd been sitting at the kitchen table, took out his gun. Even though he motioned her to stay back, Kate followed him onto the deck. To her surprise, he pocketed his gun.

"You, Miz Kate, have a visitor," Hatch said.

"Who?" she asked, trying to see around him.

"I think the correct term is *what*?"

Behind Hatch on the deck railing crouched the ugliest, angriest creature she'd ever seen.

"Ellie," Maeve said from behind her.

"That devil cat?" Smokey laughed. "Must have busted out of prison."

Ellie hissed at them.

Maeve patted Kate on the shoulder. "You know, there's just not a lot to like about that cat."

Kate laughed. There was nothing to like about Jason's cat. Not only was it the scraggliest, dirtiest thing she'd even seen, it stunk and wore a perpetual frown on its smushed face.

She waved the air with the back of her hands. "Go away."

The cat stared at her with narrowed eyes. She shook her

head and went inside. Another mangled cry sounded. Then, avoiding the smile on Maeve's face, she opened the refrigerator and took out chicken from last night's dinner.

Kate took the bowl to the deck and put it on the railing. At first Ellie backed up, the fur at the back of her neck standing on end, but after sniffing the air, she pounced on the bowl, wolfing down the food without bothering to chew. Kate settled onto the deck and hung her legs over the side as she watched the attitudinal cat.

"What are you going to do with her?" Maeve asked as she came out with two glasses of iced tea.

Kate shrugged. "She probably won't stay."

Maeve set the tray on a small table and handed Kate a glass. "Probably not. But she does look better, less feral." Ellie, having inhaled half a chicken, sat on the deck rail, licking her paws and swiping them over her head. "Her coloring's beautiful, if you can get past the rough edges."

For a moment, Kate stared at her reflection in the bay's crystal-blue water. She had her share of rough edges, but last night Hayden called her beautiful. More importantly, in his arms and in his bed, she'd *felt* beautiful.

Maeve sat next to her. "Hayden seemed well rested today."

*Earth-shattering sex will do that to you.* Her lips curved then froze as Kate snapped a gaze to Hayden's mother-in-law, her face heating. This isn't the kind of thing you talked about to a man's mother or, in Hayden's case, the closest thing he had to a mother.

Maeve slipped off her shoes and dipped her toes in the water. "Kate, it's obvious Hayden cares for you." Kate almost dropped her iced tea, and Maeve laughed. "You look surprised. Hayden isn't one for words about his feelings."

"That's an understatement."

"You realize, don't you, that he doesn't know what he's feeling half the time, but I've seen him watching you." Kate reached up to the curl at the side of her head, but Maeve placed her palm on Kate's hand and pushed it down. "Looking at you, Kate, not the scars and not at all that baggage you carry around."

"I don't have baggage." She was just the opposite. No ties. No roots. She looked at Ellie, who was running a rough tongue along her back haunch. No pets.

Maeve made a clucking sound. "How do you feel about him?"

*Like I want to tumble every hair on his head and tear off his custom-made suits and shirts until he's standing in front of me as naked as Michelangelo's David.* A warm wash crept up her neck.

"Not something you want to talk about to his mother-in-law, hmmmm? You don't need to. I can see it. I'm happy for him and for you."

"This thing between us, Maeve, it's nothing serious."

"I think Hayden could do with a little less serious in his life, don't you?"

With the tip of her toe, Kate made circles in the water, rippling the blue glass surface. "Has he always been so intense, so hell-bent on fixing the world and all of its problems?"

"For as long as I've known him. I think that's why he married Marissa. He wanted to take care of her, and she definitely needed to be taken care of."

"I'm sorry about the accident. This must be a difficult time for you."

"It is, but having your friend Joseph around helps, and, of course, there's Hayden. He took care of the funeral, insurance, and all the details of death. Despite everything they went through, he remained a devoted husband right to the end."

"Husband?" Kate's toes stilled. "I thought you said their marriage ended years ago."

"It did. For the last seven years Marissa had been living in a long-term care facility for patients with mental disorders, and during all of those years, she was unresponsive. But Hayden, he tried. For seven years he tried to reach her. He worked with doctors and medications and alternative therapists. Last month he decided to do what I'd been begging him to do for years. He decided to get a divorce. He finally gave up hope."

\* \* \*

*Wednesday, June 17, 5 p.m.*
*Dorado Bay, Nevada*

Lottie was too tired to swear. She slipped the sketch back in the plastic sheath and left the Boathouse.

She'd been in Dorado Bay two days, flashing the sketch that Berkley Rowe from Parker Lord's team made of the woman Stalker Boy had seen in Shayna Thomas's bedroom. The town had ten thousand summer residents, and she had pressed the flesh with at least a quarter of them. The latest batch included the happy hour revelers in the Boathouse Bar and Grill. None of the bar-goers recognized the woman, but a few commented that she looked "familiar."

Lottie's sore feet pounded the paved path that curved around this portion of the lake. She could still hear the laughter and clinking of glasses from the raucous people in the bar. She wouldn't be relaxing anytime soon, not with the Butcher killing nine-year-old babies. Lord give that little boy's grandma strength. And Lord give her strength to keep walking this lake with Berkley Rowe's sketch. Right now this sketch, which Stalker Boy said was a dead ringer, was the key to finding the Butcher. The woman in the pink dress, seen by both the stalker and the boy across the street, was either the killer or knew the killer.

Speaking of killers, her navy blue satin wedges were biting into the swollen flesh of her feet. She probably should think about switching to more practical shoes.

To her right, milky white beach sand stretched along the path all the way to the next restaurant about one hundred yards up the lake, perfect therapy for a pair of tired, old bare feet. She rested her hand against a pine tree for balance, lifted her right foot, and unfastened the skinny strap on her right shoe.

Her toes dug into the warm, silky sand. Maybe the doc was right. Maybe she should toss out every shoe over three inches high. And maybe she should start exercising and lay off the homemade candy. She wanted to see every one of her grandbabies get their doctorates.

She heaved her torso toward her left shoe and unfastened the strap. Her fingers froze. Behind her was a pair of clunky black shoes. Out of the corner of her eye she saw something bright and silvery slice the air. She lunged to the right, but not before a blade struck her back. Pain engulfed her torso. She fell, her head slamming into one of the tree trunks.

# CHAPTER TWENTY

*Wednesday, June 17, 6:15 p.m.*
*Dorado Bay, Nevada*

For the first time since Hayden had met her one week ago, Sergeant Lottie King looked old, like a grandmother of seven and a seasoned cop who'd seen too many bad guys doing too many bad things over too many years. She lay in exam room three of the Bayside Medical Center, one bandage over her right temple and another across her neck and shoulder. Her feet were bare.

"Damn, I'm glad you're here, Pretty Boy," she said when he stepped into the doorway of the exam room. Her mouth dipped into a snarl, and she jabbed a finger at the door. "Time to get back to work." She swung her legs over the side of the table, but the movement must have made her dizzy, for her cocoa-colored skin paled, and she swooned.

Dr. Gray settled her back on the crinkly paper. "I've already advised Sergeant King that she should go to a hospital in Reno for further observation, as we're not equipped here for overnight stays." He gave the woman on the table a stern look. "But she politely declined."

*Probably with a few well-chosen expletives*, Hayden thought. "Exactly what happened?" he asked the doctor. He'd been on his way back to the cottage after spending the day at Hope Academy and Mulveney's Cove when he received the call from Hatch that Lottie had been attacked while visiting bars along the lake with Berkley's sketch.

Dr. Gray picked up the chart at the foot of the exam table. "Sergeant King received a single laceration to the deltoid, four inches, but I'm not too worried about that. She's a strong woman." He winked at Lottie, but she refused to look at him, her arms knotted across her chest. The doctor's face grew serious. "I'm a little more concerned about the concussion. She'll need supervision tonight, someone to watch for vomiting and make sure she stays hydrated. She took a hard fall."

Hayden's chest tightened. No, every part of his body tightened, including his fists. The Butcher got to Lottie, a police officer with superior reflexes and years of training. How was their unsub doing it?

Hayden jammed his hand in his pocket.

*Take it slow. Observe. Analyze. Evaluate. Begin by studying the victim. Comb through the crime scene. Interview witnesses.*

*There won't be any witness.*

*Get out of my head!*

He must have said something because the doctor took a step toward him. "Are you okay, Agent Reed?"

He unclenched his fist. "I'm fine."

Dr. Gray took out a pad of paper and scribbled something on it before handing it to Hayden. "Here's a scrip for a painkiller. Have her take it as needed." He turned to Lottie. "And you, Sergeant King, bed rest for a minimum of twenty-four hours, and then limited work, understand?"

Lottie glared. After the doctor left, Hayden handed Lottie her shoes. "He was right behind me. You hear that, Pretty Boy? That butchering SOB was right behind me, and he got away. I want to get my hands around his prick and pull till his eyes bulge out."

"You're sure it was him?" Hayden asked. This was a bold move, an attack in the middle of the day at a public place. "The Butcher isn't bold." He was a coward and weak and pathetic, but the Butcher was getting desperate, and desperate people did desperate things.

"I'm sure it was him," Lottie said. "His shoes were dead ringers for the ones the orthotic shoe man back in Colorado Springs showed me."

"Give me the details."

Lottie slipped her shoe on and fumbled with the thin strap. "I'd spent the afternoon flashing the picture of the woman in the pink dress, showed it to hundreds of folks. I figure the Butcher must have wanted to shut me down."

"Because you're onto something." He brushed aside her hands and buckled her shoe.

"Ya think? So I bend over to take off my shoe, and while I'm there, I see those ugly orthotic shoes. Then out of the corner of my eye, I see a knife. I get my fat ass out of the way, but not before he gets a piece of me. I probably would have gotten him, too, but I fell and cracked my damn head."

"Did you pass out?"

"I must have for a few minutes because when I came to, he was gone, and a cocktail waitress on her way to work was kneeling beside me. She helped me to the bar, where I called Chief Greenfield."

"You keep saying *he*. Are you certain it was a man behind you?"

Lottie's pasty face faded to a lighter shade of gray.

"Damn this aching head. I forgot to tell you about the dress."

"The person who attacked you was wearing a dress?"

"Not a pink one. It was green, with yellow flowers. One of them granny dresses, but the dress isn't important. The legs are. They were hairy and thick. I swear there was nothing girly about the legs I saw."

Finally, a puzzle piece he'd been searching for. "We're chasing one person. Not two. A master of disguise." He could see it now. The Butcher dresses up as a woman, gains entrance to the victims' homes, perhaps with a story about a broken-down car or a lost dog. Once inside he pulls the knife on them from behind and immobilizes them. Then he kills.

The images in Hayden's mind grew crisper and clearer.

* * *

*Wednesday, June 17, 7:35 p.m.*
*Dorado Bay, Nevada*

Kate frowned at the scraggly orange and black pile of fur and bones in her lap. She'd come out to the porch to get away from all the people inside—Lottie, back from the medical center; Smokey and Maeve; Hatch and Evie; and Hayden, especially Hayden—but Jason's cat, Ellie, was determined Kate wouldn't be alone. The cat had slinked out from under the porch, eyed her for ten minutes, then stomped her way onto the porch swing next to Kate. Ellie now rested in her lap, buzzing out a purr that sounded like a chainsaw with carburetor issues.

As she stroked the cat, Kate watched the blood-red sun sinking in the sky and knew Hayden would soon demand she come inside. And when Hayden demanded...She shook her head and stared out at the peaks of the Carson Range, which tonight were gray-green sentinels against the red-gold sky.

Inside the cottage a steady stream of voices continued to chatter and laugh. Kate ran her fingers through the cat's matted hair and wondered if she would ever be able to sit in a room full of people without feeling like such an outsider. Although, to her credit, she had made serious headway the past few days. She held real conversations with Evie, Hatch, and Maeve. But not Hayden.

She ran her knuckles over Ellie's head, and the cat purred louder. Damn Hayden for not telling her about Marissa, and damn her for feeling hurt over it. After all, neither one of them wanted anything serious, and their fling would end as soon as the Butcher was found, but she deserved to know that he was *married* up until three weeks ago.

A crack of light slipped through the front door, followed by the one person she didn't want to see.

"What's that?" Hayden shut the door quietly behind him.

She continued to stroke Ellie, refusing to look at him. "My cat."

"You own a cat now."

"Ellie seems to have come to that conclusion."

Hayden sat on the swing, and she inched to the far side, Ellie grumbling but not moving out of her lap.

"You shouldn't be out here alone," Hayden said.

An exasperated puff fell from her lips. "I'm not. You've been parked two feet from me at the window for the past thirty minutes."

"You saw me?"

"No, Hayden, I *felt* you." She dug both hands into Ellie's fur and kneaded. "Of course I saw you. You rarely leave my side."

He laid a hand on her leg, which she didn't realize had been shaking. "I told you I'd keep you safe."

She pushed away his hand. "Stop it."

"Stop what?"

"Being nice. I'm trying to be really pissed off at you."

"Why?"

"Because..." She struggled for words, not because she didn't know them, but because there were too many racing through her head. *Because I want to know why you didn't tell me you were married, why you tried so hard, so long, to make your marriage work, and why the hell I care?*

Hayden slid closer. "What's wrong, Kate?"

"Stop it!"

A rush of air spilled over his lips. "What am I doing now?"

A half growl, half laugh rumbled in her throat. "Being Hayden. Taking care of the world with utmost efficiency and aplomb." He opened his mouth but she waved him off. "And I'm having problems with it because I have problems. Period."

In the cottage behind them, laughter erupted. He turned toward the graying mountains. "I'm sorry. I should have made other arrangements for everyone."

"Yeah, there are a lot of things you should have done." And before she could stop herself, she added, "Like tell me you never divorced Marissa."

There. The words hung suspended between them, tight and electrified.

His jaw hardened.

"We both know there's nothing serious between us," she said, "just sex. And we know it's not going anywhere. You have your job, and I have...I have places to go." Her feet kicked at the porch floor. The swing creaked and swayed.

"But I deserved to know that you never divorced your wife."

His gaze remained straight ahead, stonelike. "It's complicated."

"Well, there's a new one. *Life is complicated.* Yeah, Hayden, I know a little about how complicated life can be, and you know that because you know everything about me. But I don't know anything about you. I don't know your favorite color or if you're a dog or cat person. I don't know anything about your family or why you stayed in a marriage that was broken beyond repair."

Hayden ran his hand along the crisp pleat of his trousers. "Marissa lived in a mental institution for the past seven years." He leaned forward and rested his elbows on his knees, his chin on his knuckled hands. "She'd been diagnosed as bipolar in her teens. Maeve and her husband got her therapy and on meds and tried to help her have a normal life. Marissa did, in part, but there were some rough times."

Hayden's words continued to come out slowly, as if he were pulling them from a place he didn't visit often. "Marissa and I met in college, and I knew relatively soon that she suffered from a mental illness, but I saw her anyway. She was an artist and very much a free spirit. I told myself that we balanced each other. We got serious, and Maeve tried to talk me out of marriage, but I loved the color Marissa brought to my life, and I wanted to help her be whole and happy."

Hayden's voice trailed off, and she couldn't help but add, "Out to save the world."

"Out to save one soul." He started the swing swaying. "Ours wasn't a typical marriage, but we did okay. She stayed on her medication, and in the beginning we avoided high-stress situations. Marissa was a painter. She worked mostly on textiles, specializing in silks. Quite a few galleries were displaying her work, and she was starting to get regular commissions, but for all her artistic talent, she continued to have dark moments, always coinciding with the times I left for training or an extended investigation." The exquisite fabric of his custom jacket bunched along his wide shoulders.

"My work was hard on her," he continued. "I worked long hours and brought my job home. It killed her. Almost." His knotted hands dipped. "She tried to kill herself three times. All three times happened while I was away for work. The last time..."

The night grew silent, and even Ellie stopped purring, but Kate didn't think Hayden noticed. He wasn't here, not all of him. As for her, she was very much here, watching this new and different side of Hayden. She placed her hand on his knee.

"The last time..." Kate prompted, not because she wanted to know, but because she sensed that he needed to tell her.

"The last time she tried to kill herself, Marissa slit her wrists, and with her own blood, made handprints all over our bedroom. Hundreds of red handprints." He lowered his eyelids, and Kate knew undoubtedly he'd seen the image thousands of times. "And in her own blood, she signed it and addressed it to me. It was her final piece of art."

The mountain air grew thinner. Hayden visibly struggled for breath. It was obvious he had never forgiven himself. She reached for him. He stood.

"After her last suicide attempt, Marissa's parents and I decided she needed full-time care. She lived in the home for seven years. She didn't recognize Maeve, her doctors, or me. She sat and stared out the window, except for three weeks ago, when I told her I was going to put in motion plans for a divorce. Even though she didn't communicate, I thought she needed to know. Apparently she understood. An hour after I left she stole the car keys from a staff member and drove off a cliff. The authorities ruled it suicide."

Kate could feel his anguish and guilt, something he probably hadn't shown to anyone, including Maeve, Hatch, or his other teammates. And beyond the guilt, she saw something even more telling. A loss of hope, a hard concept for a man like Hayden to stomach. And so hard for her to see, because Hayden was a man who believed justice would always prevail. At heart, he was a man of hope.

She put down Ellie and joined him at the railing. "Hayden, I'm so sorry, for both you and Marissa."

She reached out to him, but he turned and motioned her back toward the front door. "Time to go inside."

"No. Not yet."

"Kate," he said to the door. "It's getting dark. There's a killer on the loose, and you need to get inside."

"I will." Before he could move, she slipped her arms around his waist. With surprising ease, she turned him to face her. "But first, this."

She locked her hands behind his neck and pulled him toward her. He didn't resist. There was nothing slow, nothing gentle, as their lips collided and tongues tangled. This kiss was very much about the here and now. It consumed her, pushing away sorrows of the past and fears of the future. Hayden must have felt it too, for he leaned his backside against the railing and pulled her to him.

"Feel better?" Kate asked when they finally came up for air.

"I feel something," Hayden muttered between a laugh and a sigh.

"Excellent." She tapped him on the butt and pointed at the door. "Time to get up close and personal with all of these people you invited into my life."

With a satisfied smile, she followed him into the cottage, but when the screen shut, a shriek tore across the darkened porch. Kate's eyes plunked closed, and another shriek sounded. She opened the screen. Ellie strutted in, her crooked tail high in the air.

* * *

*Wednesday, June 17, 7:35 p.m.*
*Carson City, Nevada*

"Goodbye, bitch." Robyn Banks threw a photo onto the fireplace grate and watched flames leap across Katrina Erickson's face.

Robyn discovered the shoebox full of photos the first night her husband was released from prison, the night he drank himself into a stupor and she kept him from drowning in his own vomit. She ended up unpacking the small duffel he brought home from prison, including the box of photos. Until now, she'd pretended they didn't exist.

Robyn smelled Mike before she heard him. The scent of cheap whiskey with a double shot of despair curdled her stomach.

"You shouldn't touch what isn't yours," Mike said with a heavy slur as he snatched the shoebox from the mantel.

"It's time to get rid of them, Mike." Robyn tried to take the box from his hands, but he wouldn't let go. "You're out of prison. You've served your time. You need to move on with your life."

"Move on with my *life*?" He swung a hand wide in the grand gesture of a ringmaster. "*This* is a life?" A boozy cackle reverberated through the big, empty room.

"Stop it!"

"Angry tonight?"

Yes, she was livid about this ramshackle house, her flailing career, and the downward spiral of her sorry excuse for a husband. She took a deep breath, trying to push aside her growing anger. "If you're not up to a job, you can at least try to work on yourself. Your probation officer gave you the name of a therapist, and when you're ready, I have that list of jobs—"

"Jobs?" Mike hooted. "Who, my dear, wants to hire a money man who stole hard-earned pennies from a bunch of retirees forced to live on canned beans for the rest of their lives?"

His pompous edge sliced into her, but she fought the urge to jab back. "You can get work outside of finance. People change careers all the time."

His lips twisted in a grimace. "And what the hell am I supposed to do with a goddamn felony hanging around my neck and one fucking eyeball?"

She looked at the smoldering photo, at the flames leaping and crackling, charring the paper image of Katrina Erickson, and she looked at the man who promised her a future in hell.

She sunk onto the floor in front of the fireplace. "We can't go on like this, Mike. KTTL is letting me go. I sent out a few resumes." Her trembling hands flattened on the fireplace hearth. "Nothing."

His moment of manic ugliness disappeared as he tucked the box under his arm. "Sad thing, isn't it? An aging broadcaster trying to stay in the bright lights. But bright lights show all the flaws and wrinkles, don't they?"

She flinched. He wanted to hurt her because he was hurting. She kept telling herself that over and over. Prison skewered him, and all those little holes festered, oozing puss and hatred.

\* \* \*

*Wednesday, June 17, 11:50 p.m.*
*Dorado Bay, Nevada*

A broad-shouldered figure stepped into the blackened frame of her bedroom door, and Kate's breath caught in her throat. "How's Lottie?" she asked.

Hayden took off his coat and hung it in her closet. She almost laughed at the absurdity of that exquisite coat next to her T-shirts and leathers. He loosened his tie. "I just woke her to check on her, and she told me if I touched her again, she'd make sure I never fathered a child."

Kate tried not to smile. "I assume she used more colorful words."

"You assume correctly." He sat on the edge of the bed. Something warm and tingly feathered out from her heart.

She shrugged off the shiver that rocked her body and focused on Hayden, trying to gauge his mood. After he spilled the story about his wife's suicide and his own guilt and sense of hopelessness over the whole thing, Hayden spent the rest of the evening at work, phone to his ear and hands on his keyboard. She came to bed an hour ago, but she hadn't been able to sleep. She was too busy thinking about Hayden and trying to figure out what was going on under that granite façade.

She didn't know, but she knew how she felt. She pushed back the bedsheet and reached for his tie, sliding the piece of silk from his neck. "You should probably get some sleep," she said.

"I should."

She pulled his shirt out from his pants and dipped her fingers beneath the silky fabric. "You look exhausted."

"I am."

"Can I do anything to help?" She slid her hands along the flat, hard plane of his abs and then followed with her lips.

"What you're doing is fine."

\* \* \*

Kate woke hours later to a razor-sharp hiss coming from the foot of her bed. She raised her head and found Ellie standing near her feet, baring her teeth at the bedroom door.

Kate blinked. Hayden lay next to her, sound asleep, his face unlined, his breathing even. A soft tap sounded on the door, and Ellie hissed again.

The tap sent Hayden bolting up, his hands circling her. She pushed him away and smiled.

"It's just someone at the door," she said. "Lottie probably needs something."

Hayden slipped into his trousers and opened the door to Maeve, who stood there, her eyes wide and her hands trembling.

"Sergeant King?" Hayden asked. "Is she okay?"

"She's fine," Maeve said. "It's Smokey. He's gone."

# CHAPTER TWENTY-ONE

*Thursday, June 18, 6:20 a.m.*
*Dorado Bay, Nevada*

Gone?" Kate's heart lurched to her throat, making the single word a raspy croak. "What do you mean Smokey's *gone*?"

"I checked the back deck, the front drive, and the lakeside path," Maeve said. "No signs of him. I'm worried."

Hayden dipped his arms into the shirt he'd worn last night. "Did you check with Lottie?"

Maeve nodded. "She hasn't seen him, either."

Hayden bolted into Smokey's room, and Kate followed. The old man's wrinkled brown leather slippers sat at the foot of the bed. The warm breeze that had kicked up yesterday blew past the strips of muslin over the screen.

"The window," Kate said with a heavy breath of air. "He always sleeps with the window open." Kate ran to the window, her head swimming when she saw two drops of red splattered on the sill.

Hayden grabbed the pillow from the bed and sucked in a breath. Maeve screamed. And Kate saw red. Literally. Slick, bright red coated the pillow.

Lottie came running, wobbly and barefooted.

Kate looked at Lottie, Maeve, and Hayden. Anywhere but at the blood on Smokey Joe's pillow. She tried to stop the words, but they came out cold and hard. "The Butcher."

Hayden took her icy hands in his. "We don't know that."

The ice moved from her hands, up her arms, and across her chest. The cold fogged her brain and slowed her blood. She thought of Smokey, his old, wrinkled body pummeled by the Butcher's knife. Two hands reached for her, and two arms clanked around her. No. She pushed back the arms, but Hayden didn't let go.

"We'll find him, Kate. Smokey Joe is a tough man. He knows how to survive."

The cold split her in half, tore open her chest, but the blood didn't flow, because it froze solid. She couldn't shake her head, couldn't even speak and tell Hayden he was dead wrong.

\* \* \*

*Thursday, June 18, 11:45 a.m.*
*Dorado Bay, Nevada*

The world as Hayden knew it had turned into a giant grid, measured off in distinct sections and assigned to the ever-growing mass of volunteers descending on Dorado Bay in the hunt for Joseph "Smokey Joe" Bernard.

The midday sun pounded Hayden as he stood at a picnic table in the public park that served as the search's command center. More than 150 searchers combed the pine forests and boated through the reedy waters of the lake. Word spread quickly that a seventy-four-year-old blind man disappeared, leaving behind a pool of blood.

Chief Greenfield joined Hayden at the table. "Just sent out the ground dogs, and I'm waiting for the water-trained Labrador to arrive from Tahoe City. Herb and his crew are out at Mulveney's Cove."

Hayden refused to see the image of Smokey's bloated body lifted out of the chilled waters that recently yielded Jason Erickson and Benny Hankins.

"My people talked to the sheriff's department and to officials at Incline Village and Crystal Bay," Chief Greenfield continued. "Has your guy arrived yet?"

Hayden shook his head. "MacGregor should be here within an hour." This morning, after an hour of searching for Smokey Joe and finding nothing, Hayden called Jon MacGregor, the SCIU's missing and endangered child expert, and his teammate hopped on Parker's private jet. No questions asked. Before joining Parker Lord's team Jon MacGregor worked for the FBI's Crimes Against Children Division and gained worldwide recognition for his efforts at finding the lost.

"Glad to have the expertise," the chief said, "because if we lose another one to the Butcher, I'll have a riot on my hands. This fellow has my town more nervous than a pack of rattlesnakes in a room full of rocking chairs." The police chief pulled off his hat and ran a hand through his sweat-soaked hair.

They had plenty to be sweating. Smokey had been missing nearly six hours, and they had found nothing more than a few drops of blood and that red-soaked pillow.

"How did he do it?" Greenfield crammed his hat back on his head. "You were less than twenty feet away, and I had patrols running by the cottage every hour last night. The neighbors saw nothing. My men saw nothing. How did the Butcher drag Mr. Bernard out the window and get him out of there without leaving a sign? Damn, sometimes I think we're chasing a ghost."

"He's not a ghost, but he knows how to fit in." This was another key piece of the puzzle. The Butcher was not extraordinary in any way. He was gray, tan, shades of twilight. He shifted unseen through shadows. "As I see it, he was dressed in a manner that wouldn't draw suspicion—a garbage worker, a gardener, the cable guy. He may even have dressed himself up as one of us."

"A cop?" Greenfield asked.

"Anything's possible with the Butcher. He could be impersonating a cop, a reporter, a cleaning lady. We've probably talked to him already. It wouldn't surprise me if he were out with the search team right now."

The chief's ruddy face whitened. "You really think he'd be that bold?"

Hayden's blood bubbled. "Bold? No, the man's a coward, unable to show his own face, but he's getting desperate."

The chief shook his head and walked off, mumbling something about getting all the search-and-rescue volunteers to sign in to a master roster.

Hayden left the search command and made his way back to the cottage, where he spotted Lottie drinking coffee and pacing back and forth across the porch. The Colorado Springs sergeant was still shaky this morning, and she was antsy to get outside and look for Smokey. She stayed put only when he told her he needed someone he could trust to watch over Kate.

Kate. What was he going to do about her? She hadn't said a word all morning. She sat in a kitchen chair, staring at the crystal-blue water with that hissing cat on her lap. Kate was wrong. He did have the capacity to feel, and right now a low, hard ache throbbed in the middle of his chest.

"Any news?" Lottie asked as he walked up the steps.

"Nothing." He dipped his head toward the cottage door. "How's Kate?"

"Beating the shit out of herself. You better get your ass in there before she knocks herself unconscious."

Inside the cottage Hayden tossed his jacket on the couch where Kate sat with Ellie and squatted before her. "We'll find him."

She shook her head, tears streaking her face and dampening the cat's fur. He'd never seen her cry before. Those tears hurt him more than when her head had slammed into his mouth and her elbow had jabbed his ribs.

"Kate, we have more than a hundred people looking for Smokey. We'll find him and bring him back to you."

"We also have a pillow soaked with blood." Kate turned a hard stare on him. "You of all people know how important blood is to the Butcher."

"This may not even be a Butcher attack."

"And you're living in a fantasy world!"

"Anything is—"

"Hayden, do you believe the Butcher came into this house and kidnapped Smokey Joe?"

He didn't want to say it, but he did. "Yes."

"The Butcher doesn't leave survivors."

"Lottie survived."

Kate's eyes welled with a fresh batch of tears. "Sergeant King is a trained cop, not a seventy-four-year-old blind man." Her voice cracked.

"Smokey's a fighter."

"Exactly. He's a soldier, a man who survived eighteen months in a North Vietnamese underground prison no bigger than a closet. He knows how to fight. To survive. Hasn't it occurred to you we heard nothing last night? Nothing! And you don't miss anything, G-man. Smokey Joe wouldn't go quietly, not unless the fight had been taken from him."

No. Hayden still had hope, and he'd hang on to that hope until he had proof otherwise. "Come outside, help me look for him."

Kate dug her hands into his shoulders. "You don't get it, do you?"

"Get what?"

"He's dead, Hayden. Smokey's dead."

\* \* \*

*Thursday, June 18, 12:15 p.m.*
*Dorado Bay, Nevada*

Smokey Joe had put up a good fight. Too good. He studied his right eye in the mirror, the one the old man had slammed with his age-spotted fist. The eye was red, swollen, just like his lower lip, which Smokey Joe had butted with his knobby head.

He was surprised the old guy was so fast and strong. Pretty sharp hearing, too. Smokey woke when he got within a foot of the bed, his knife raised. The former solider dove at him, getting him in the eye and the lip. But he had spent the past six months fine-tuning his knife skills and with a quick thrust had silenced Smokey Joe, who now lay in a very *special* grave at the edge of his property.

The grave had been brilliant, a four-by-four hole big enough to hold one shrunken old man in a fetal position, although he wasn't done with him, not yet.

He turned from the mirror to the mask sitting on his office desk. He ran his fingers along the green and black sequins he'd fashioned into dragon scales. Good thing the fundraiser tomorrow night was a masked, black-tie affair. The swelling in his lip would probably decrease, but his eye would be black and blue for a few days. Hayden Reed would notice it. Hayden Reed noticed everything.

A soft chuckle escaped. Well, almost everything.

G-man—he loved Smokey's name for the uptight FBI agent—hadn't noticed that he wasn't really who he said he was. Only one knew his true identity, the green-eyed woman who'd once believed in justice for all.

He pushed aside the scaly green mask he'd spent hours crafting and picked up the other one he just started working on. This one was fashioned out of white satin, with long white ribbon dangling from one corner. In the other corner, he dabbed a dot of glue and picked up the tiny, one-winged teal angel. A broken angel. How appropriate.

*  *  *

*Thursday, June 18, 12:30 p.m.*
*Dorado Bay, Nevada*

"I'm not going to go, Hayden. It's a waste of time—mine, yours, and the hundred people you have looking for Smokey. He's dead." Kate planted her feet on the kitchen floor and wondered if Hayden would bolt across the table, pick her up, and throw her over his shoulder. She could see he was trying to control his temper. He stood before her, jacketless, his shirtsleeves rolled up, and a lock of hair loped across his forehead.

"You're not staying here alone," he insisted with a matter-of-factness that made her want to scream.

"So get one of your fancy-suited buddies to stay with me."

Hayden jammed his hands into his trouser pockets. "I'm not going to waste a man babysitting you when he could be out looking for Smokey Joe."

"I'll lock the doors and stay by myself."

He pushed in the kitchen chair. "I'm not going to let you sit around feeling guilty."

She raised both hands and jabbed them at her chest. "Why the hell shouldn't I feel guilty? My best friend just got sliced by a butcher who really wants to get at me. The Butcher always finishes the job. He breaks the mirror. He kills all the broadcasters."

Hayden jabbed a finger at her. "Stop right there. You are not responsible for Smokey's disappearance."

"And where's the turnip truck you just fell off? You know damn well Smokey wouldn't be here if it weren't for me. How can you say I'm not responsible for his death?"

"He's not dead!" So much heat from cold Hayden. Too bad it wouldn't do any good.

"We've already beat that dead horse."

He went after her, and his fingers dug into her arm. "You didn't force Smokey to get on that plane from Tucson and come here. Kate, look at me, listen to me." His fingers pressed harder. "You can't control what other people do. There's only one person whose actions you're responsible for."

Something snapped. Maybe it was the tension of the Butcher getting closer. Maybe it was the load of guilt over Smokey's death. Maybe it was Hayden and his damned jacketless chest. But she laughed, just threw her head back and let a long, bitter laugh ring through the kitchen. "Oh, that is too much coming from you, the man who thinks he's responsible for the world." She cleared her throat and lowered her voice. "I am super agent Hayden Reed. Bring me the lost, the lonely, the torn, the tangled, the blind, and the buried, and I shall fix them all." The steam rose, hissing and blinding. "Well, here's a news bulletin, G-man. You're not God. You're not even close. You're a man, just a man, one that eats and sleeps and breathes and bleeds like the rest of us lowly, broken bits of humanity, so stop pretending you're so damned perfect, because you are one screwed-up human being, just like me. No, you're worse, because you don't admit it. Smokey's dead. The bad guy won."

"Smokey's alive, and my team will find him."

She lifted her arms in frustration and bewilderment. "You still believe. I don't know how the hell you do it, but you still believe."

"Excuse me?"

"In justice, Hayden. You still believe in justice. You still have hope." Her arms dropped to her side. "Which makes you a fool."

Hayden let go of her arm and took a step back as if he'd been punched in the stomach.

A not-so-small bolt of self-inflicted anger jabbed at her chest. Chalk one up for Kate Johnson. Another shot straight to the heart. But her own heart was in shreds. Smokey Joe, her best friend, was dead. She steadied herself by placing a hand on the kitchen table. She could admit that now, call him what he was, someone she cared about.

Like Hayden. That's why she didn't want him heading out into the woods to hunt for a killer. "The Butcher's creating a different, more daring order, Hayden. He could kill you."

"He won't."

"How do you know? How do you know he won't take you from me? Smokey's gone. I can't bear to lose you, too."

He tilted his head, as if confused.

"Dammit, Hayden, for a guy who sees everything, you're blind." She closed the space between them and grabbed one of his hands. "I'm worried about losing you because I love you."

He settled his hand on the table, as if suddenly unsteady. "You what?"

She blew out a long breath and forced herself to look him in the eye. "Despite your ego and obsession with work and controlling ways, I've fallen in love with you."

He didn't turn away. Instead he squinted harder, as if he were trying to see into her soul. He opened his mouth but was saved from continuing the conversation when Evie and Hatch barreled through the cottage's front door, followed by Lottie.

"Jon MacGregor's here," Lottie said with a whoop. "He's at the command center, and he has everyone hopping. Man, you boys sent from God don't mess around."

Hatch rushed by them and sat at the table in front of Hayden's computer. He started blasting away at the keys. Lottie hoofed down the hallway toward the room she'd been in last night, muttering something about needing more comfortable shoes.

Evie motioned to Hayden. "Jon reminded everyone how crucial the first twenty-four hours are, and he's escalating things. He wants you at the command center, *pronto*. I'll stay with Kate."

As an excited tension filled the air, Kate watched Hayden's lined face smooth. His head and heart were getting back on the job, and he was much steadier on his feet.

After jotting notes, Hatch closed the computer and hopped up from the table. Lottie rushed into the kitchen, wearing a pair of Maeve's boxy white tennis shoes. Hayden pushed back his sleeves and turned toward Kate. His gaze locked on hers, and he put a hand on either side of her face. And then he planted a hard kiss on her lips. In front of everyone. Hatch. Evie. Maeve. Lottie. She was fairly confident her heart skipped a half dozen beats.

"Come on, Pretty Boy, stop swapping spit and get your ass in gear. Smokey's out there, and we're going to find him."

"We'll talk later," Hayden said with a serious nod.

She sunk onto the kitchen chair, wondering what the hell had just happened between them.

# CHAPTER TWENTY-TWO

*Thursday, June 18, 12:45 p.m.*
*Dorado Bay, Nevada*

Hayden took off at a run toward the command center. He needed to talk to Jon MacGregor, the SCIU's missing person's specialist, about Smokey Joe, but he was also getting away from Kate.

Kate. Hotheaded, passionate Kate. She lingered on his lips. Stoked his fire. Called him a fool. She'd gotten under his skin and made him feel things he'd never felt. Anger. Heat. Yeah, a lot of heat. And something deeper. But now was not the time for deep. As promised, he'd talk to her later. About what she said. About what he didn't. Yeah, he'd been a fool all right, but not for hanging on to hope that Smokey Joe was alive. But that was for later. After he found Smokey Joe and the Butcher.

Hayden wasn't paying Kate lip service when he said he believed Smokey was alive and that the Butcher had him. He was certain the Butcher would use Kate's friend to trap her, and that trap would be much more enticing if it featured live bait.

MacGregor, Hayden learned when he joined his teammate at the command center, was of a similar mindset. "Got a bird coming in from Reno and a mounted group from the south shore. I've expanded the search radius and have two boats at Mulveney's Cove," Jon said with a heat that matched the fire in his eyes. "I'm going to find Mr. Bernard and then help you nail the son of a bitch who took him."

MacGregor was the SCIU's white knight, noble and tenacious, and damned good at what he did. His teammate had personally tracked down more than one hundred missing and endangered children. If anyone could find Smokey Joe, Jon could. He would.

"Now tell me what you know about the Butcher," his teammate said. "I know you've been in his head."

* * *

*Thursday, June 18, 1:05 p.m.*
*Dorado Bay, Nevada*

Heat shimmered on the water, giving it the golden cast that led to its name. As a child, Kate had hunted for treasure in these cold waters. Now divers hunted for Smokey Joe's body.

Smokey's dead body.

She sat on a boulder overlooking Mulveney's Cove, a uniformed Dorado Bay officer next to her and Evie at water's edge. Kate shivered as she thought of six gray cinderblocks weighting Smokey to the bottom of the lake. But Hayden and Jon and more than two hundred searchers insisted Smokey Joe was alive. Were that many people right?

The thought flashed briefly in her head, and she figured

Hayden was getting to her in more ways than one. He was a man who believed in justice, one who would never give up hope. Her fingers traced her lips, lips he had touched with his, which promised he'd return so they could "talk." She wasn't sure she wanted to go there, wherever *there* was.

She pressed her lips together and waited. Any minute now one of the six divers looking for Smokey would pop his head up and nod. And she'd cry a river of tears. No, a lake. Tears she hadn't been able to cry for the brother she once loved, the father who loved and left, and the mother incapable of love. Because Smokey Joe was her family, and now he was gone.

A loud harrumph sounded behind her, and she turned with a start. "What are *you* doing here?"

"We're here to help search." Oliver Conlan, her grandfather, gave her a stiff nod and motioned to the three men standing next to him. "This is Clive Tyndale, piloted a VMO-6 chopper over the coastal waters of Korea. Next to him is Ron Whitfield, ran recon near Phuoc Vinh in Vietnam. And the baby here on left is Pastor Ike Iverson, saved a lot of souls in Saudi Arabia during Desert Storm."

Kate stared at the soldiers standing before her, wondering what she was supposed to say to them. *Go home. Smokey's dead.*

But Hayden kept insisting Smokey was alive, that the Butcher wouldn't kill him until he got to her. She rubbed at the center of her forehead.

"Where do you want us?" her grandfather asked. She noticed a hot fire in the cloudy blue of his eyes, just like the heat in the other three men's eyes. The fire spoke of war and survivorship, something she was sure she'd see in her own eyes if she ever looked at her reflection.

She pointed to Evie near the shore. "Ask her."

He nodded and turned, the three men following him, but before Oliver Conlan got too far, she called out, "What about you? Where did you fight?"

Her grandfather turned, his chin inching up a fraction. "Bataan."

\* \* \*

*Thursday, June 18, 7:40 p.m.*
*Dorado Bay, Nevada*

"It'll be dark in an hour." Kate always welcomed the dark, the black cover of night that hid her scars. Tonight she despised it. "Most of the searchers will probably stop."

"I'm sure some will stay out all night," Maeve said. They sat at the kitchen table in the cottage looking at the uneaten casserole from one of their lakeside neighbors. "The divers didn't find Smokey's body in Mulveney's Cove, so it's possible he's still out there, alive. Agent MacGregor is bringing in a helicopter with those big light beams."

Kate's hands trembled, and she tucked them under her thighs.

"I heard Pastor Iverson is holding a candlelight ceremony tonight," Maeve went on. "Partly to honor the little boy who died and Jason, but also in hope for Smokey."

Maeve was trying to take the edge off the pain of losing her best friend, but it was there. Razor-sharp. Covered with blood.

A picture of Smokey's crimson-soaked pillow flashed through her head. "He's dead, Maeve. No one could lose that much blood and still live."

"Evie said head wounds, even minor ones, bleed more

easily than cuts on other parts of the body. It's possible he survived the attack and is waiting out there for us to find him."

Kate's vision blurred. She thought there were no more tears, but they came, and so did visions of Smokey Joe.

*Hey Katy-lady, let's open a jewelry store. Make us buckets of money.*

*I can teach you to shoot.*

*Leave the cat with me. I can take care of her.*

Smokey was a tough man. He'd survived Vietnam and battled colon cancer and won. He was beyond tough. He was all she had.

Within the past week she had learned that her mother and brother were dead. Her grandparents wanted nothing to do with her. And Hayden. She loved him, but he couldn't return the feelings because half the time he didn't even know how he felt. She was very much alone in this world, and for the first time in her life, the heaviness of that reality crushed her. Ellie rubbed against her ankle, and she scooped the cat into her lap.

She pictured the candlelight ceremony that would take place in a few hours. She'd seen plenty in her "Justice for All" days. She'd stood shoulder-to-shoulder with mourning mothers and praying preachers and lovers who refused to give up on love, all carrying little white tongues of light meant to be tiny beacons of hope, lighting the way for the missing to come home.

*Can't see a damn thing, lady. Why the hell would you show me anything?*

She laughed at the scratchy old voice. If the Butcher had him, Smokey was probably giving him hell, maybe even warning him that G-man and God himself were on his tail because Smokey would never give up. He believed safety pins could hold a man together long enough to get to a doctor. He believed a blind man could run a computer-based business.

*Don't tell me what I can and can't do!*

On feet that slowly picked up speed, she went into the dining room, where Hayden sat at the table, his laptop in front of him and a phone at his ear. He was working around the clock in his efforts to fix the world.

She put down Ellie and held out her hand. "I need the keys to the rental car. I'm going into town." He opened his mouth, but she held up her hand. "Just give me the keys."

He blinked once then stood. Hayden Reed had the amazing ability to read a person, because with one quick look at her, he realized there was no way she was backing down.

They sped through the night to Dorado Bay's downtown district and retail shops. "Where do you want me to stop?" Hayden asked when they reached the first stoplight.

"Not sure. Head down Main."

"Do you know what you're getting?"

"Not exactly."

His jaw tightened and ticked.

"Does the lack of direction bother you, Agent Reed?"

His shoulders bounced in a shrug. "I'm getting used to it."

Two minutes later she pointed to a gift shop sandwiched between a bakery and a store that sold only white clothing. "There, that should work."

Hayden parked the car and followed her inside, but he didn't say a word. He watched, an observer to his core. She knew he was also trying to figure out what the hell she was doing, but there was nothing logical, nothing reasonable about her actions right now. She made her purchase and hurried back to the car. "Home," she said as she settled her bundle in her lap.

They were both quiet on the drive back to the cottage. Nor did he say anything to her as she took her purchase to the back deck. She dragged one of the Adirondack chairs to the point where the two eaves butted together and a small overhead hook hung. To his credit, Hayden didn't offer to help.

She needed to do this on her own.

She peeled back the tissue paper cushioning her purchase and, climbing onto the chair, hung the wind chime from the hook. The warm breeze slipped through the silver chimes, sending a soft call through the black night. Smokey Joe might not be able to see candlelight, but he had amazing ears.

* * *

*Thursday, June 18, 10:55 p.m.*
*Dorado Bay, Nevada*

"How's your head, Lottie?" Kate asked.

"My hard ol' noggin's fine."

"And your feet?"

Lottie had started limping about an hour ago.

"Still kicking."

Agent Jon MacGregor's search for Smokey Joe continued. Hayden's teammate and Chief Greenfield worked up a comprehensive search-and-rescue plan that now included more than two hundred searchers who believed they would find the old blind man. Alive.

And count her among them.

She walked next to Hayden, his hand in hers, and she marveled at the simple act. She'd never held a man's hand before, not as a teen whose mother refused to let her date, not as a college coed who'd been slammed with a reputation for hotter and heavier things, and not in her broadcasting days, when she hadn't had time for holding hands. The simplicity of the gesture had been lost on her until now.

Hayden squeezed her hand, and she rolled her eyes, a part of her wondering how the hell he knew she was thinking about him and his damn hand, but she stopped wondering when she heard a series of shouts beyond the hill they crested.

Hayden took off, dragging her with him. At the top of the hill stood a thick stand of pines, where more shouts were chiming. Hayden led her through the trees, guided by a host of bobbing lights.

They stopped when they reached more than a dozen searchers gathered around a fallen log. Next to the log was a depression in the earth, and at one end, sticking out of the dirt, was half a human foot.

# CHAPTER TWENTY-THREE

*Thursday, June 18, 11 p.m.*
*Dorado Bay, Nevada*

The shallow grave rested in a small stand of sugar pines. In less than two seconds Hayden knew that it did not house the remains of Joseph "Smokey Joe" Bernard.

"It's not him, Kate. The grave's too old." He took her trembling shoulders in his hands and tried to force her gaze from the partially unearthed body. He knew the minute Kate hung up the wind chime that she had a glimmer of hope, and he wouldn't let that faint light die. "That grave has been there too long, months, maybe years." He half expected her to argue, but she didn't. She slumped against him, and her sorrow and relief washed over him, through him.

"What do you make of it?" Lottie asked.

Dorado Bay PD had marked off the area around the grave with tape. A police photographer finished taking pictures, and two officers with shovels gently pried the dirt away from the body. Hayden found the location of the grave particularly telling, as it was located in a dense wood past a hard-to-cross ravine. "If it weren't for the intense manhunt for Smokey, that body would never have been found. Someone wanted that body hidden."

"But it looks like *something* got to it before us, probably a bear or a coyote." Lottie wagged her head. "Wonder who it was?"

Hayden stared at the foot, and at the leg slowly being revealed, but instead of flesh and bone, he saw a number. The Butcher had claimed nine bodies already. Was this number ten?

Anger spiked at the wall of his chest. He didn't even try to control it. He breathed it in, letting it move like oxygen through his veins.

Chief Greenfield stood at the foot of the grave. Unlike his men's faces, the chief's face wasn't touched by horror or sadness. A weary resignation lined his features.

Hayden motioned for Lottie to keep an eye on Kate as he made his way to the chief. "Who is he?"

"I don't know for sure," Chief Greenfield said.

"But you have a very educated guess."

The chief leaned back on the heels of his cowboy boots. "Eddie Williams. Fourteen-year-old kid who disappeared twelve months ago from Hope Academy. According to Kyl Watson, Eddie arrived at the academy in late spring and fled after his first full week. Watson reported it immediately. We searched for the boy, but we never found him. The mother was devastated, then angry. She blamed Eddie's disappearance on the academy and said her son called her the third night he was there and complained about passing out when he'd been forced to drag a pallet of bricks for punishment."

"The mother did nothing?"

"At the time, she told herself it was tough love, and that's what her boy needed. She's been beating up herself ever since."

The officers raised the body, partially wrapped in a blue tarp, from the ground, releasing the scent of rotting flesh and damp earth. One of the Dorado Bay detectives folded back the tarp, exposing a partially decomposed face. Hayden saw immediately that it wasn't an old man or a full-grown woman. Teenage boy with buzzed red hair. The question now was, was this death Butcher-related?

"Turn him over," Hayden directed the officers.

They rotated the corpse, and relief washed over Hayden. No puncture wound along the back of his neck.

"Not one of yours," Chief Greenfield said as he ground his boot into the earth. "One of mine." The chief turned from the grave and told one of the detectives, "Get out to Hope Academy."

* * *

*Friday, June 19, 7 a.m.*
*Dorado Bay, Nevada*

Kate stood in the cottage kitchen, listening to the wind chime. Early this morning, the wind had picked up, sending the long silver chimes dancing and a soft tinkle through the cool morning air. The weathercaster reported a storm coming in on the heels of the wind. She curved her hands around a cup of coffee.

Smokey didn't do well with storms. They tore through his joints. When the Butcher took him, her friend wore only thin pajamas. Was Smokey cold? Kate pictured the old man aiming a shaky fist at the Butcher, demanding a blanket. She held on to that image, a cold, shaking, mad-as-hell Smokey.

Hayden walked into the kitchen, buttoning the cuffs of his

neatly pressed white shirt. He had spent part of the night at
the teenage boy's gravesite, but eventually came back to the
cottage and snagged a solid four hours of sleep in her bed.
She, too, managed to push aside her worry about Smokey
and slept peacefully in Hayden's arms.

"Ready?" Hayden took the cup of coffee she held out,
and his lips rested briefly on her cheek. How domestic, *normal*, she couldn't help but think.

"Let's go." But going no longer meant running. Today going meant doing something to find Smokey Joe.

Kate had called Agent MacGregor earlier for an update
on the search, but Hayden's colleague had been in a meeting.
She was anxious to talk to him.

As they headed out the door, Kate nodded toward her
bedroom. "Your suit coat. You left it in the closet."

"No time," Hayden said.

She didn't argue.

They found Agent MacGregor at the Dorado Bay police
station in one of the conference rooms. He leaned over a
large topographical map of Lake Tahoe, which was covered with small colored dots. Like Hayden, Agent
MacGregor was dark and tall, but unlike Hayden, Jon
MacGregor was whipcord lean. He wore a sharp edginess,
and an excited energy brightened his intense face. There
was nothing cool or polished or reserved about Jon
MacGregor. He wore his strength and passion on the outside for the world to see.

Agent MacGregor put his arm around her shoulder. "The
bad news is that last night we found nothing. The good news
is that last night we found nothing." He gave her shoulders a
quick squeeze, turned back to the map, and began to explain
the current search efforts to Hayden.

Kate didn't hear his words because she was too busy trying to understand Agent MacGregor's hug. It was a hug from a friend, even though he didn't know her. She reasoned he was Hayden's trusted colleague and friend, and she... 

Exactly what was she to Hayden? His witness? The Butcher's target? The woman who ruffled his hair? Who made him *feel*? Who professed her love?

Even with Smokey missing and the Butcher getting closer, she couldn't get her mind off Hayden. He'd forced his way into her life, and she'd tried to run, fast and far, but right now, the only place she wanted to run to was his arms, because in the comfort of his arms, the world looked a little less broken.

She focused on Agent MacGregor, who was saying, "Fifteen minutes ago one of the dogs found a blood spot about a hundred yards down the road from the cottage. I'm getting it typed, getting tire tracks made, and checking with residents in the area to see if they remember seeing a car."

Kate could see Hayden's mind at work, the pictures that were flashing through his head. Planning, thinking, working. In control of everything.

Even her heart.

No matter how far and how long she ran, she couldn't escape the fact that she loved Hayden Reed, a man who may not even know how to love.

After the update with Jon, she and Hayden searched for Chief Greenfield to get an update on the boy found in the sugar pines.

Unlike Hayden, Chief Greenfield hadn't slept last night. He wore the same wrinkled beige uniform, muddy cowboy boots, and a haggard weariness. "Got a positive on the body," the chief said. "As I expected, it's Eddie Williams, the Hope Academy student who went missing a year ago."

"And you have something else," Hayden said with his

non-question thing. His people-reading skills continued to amaze her.

"We found footprints on the tarp wrapped about the body."

Kate remembered that Sergeant King's people had found prints outside Shayna Thomas's house in Colorado Springs. The sergeant was particularly interested in tracking them down.

Hayden must have been thinking the same thing. "An orthotic?"

"Nope. Size nine hiking boot, one that matches a pair of shoes worn by Jason Erickson."

Kate stiffened. "My brother? Are you saying my brother had something to do with this boy's death?" Over the past few days, Kate had started to make peace with her brother, who she was sure had been manipulated by the Butcher, and she couldn't imagine him killing a child.

"I'm saying we found a footprint on the tarp that matches a pair of Jason's boots."

"It's likely that your brother didn't kill this boy," Hayden said. "We've already established that he didn't have that kind of mentality or even ability. The more likely scenario is he buried the body on someone's orders."

"Whose?" she asked.

Chief Greenfield jammed his cowboy hat on his head. "Our detectives went to the academy early this morning. As expected, no one fessed up to knowing anything about Williams's disappearance and death, at least everyone we talked to. Kyl Watson, the director, was conveniently missing."

\* \* \*

*Friday, June 19, 7:30 a.m.*
*Dorado Bay, Nevada*

Hayden maneuvered past three news vans and a handful of other media vultures circling the gates of Hope Academy. Kate was still at his side. There was no way he'd trust her with anyone else now. The Butcher was closing in. Hayden could *feel* it.

They found Beth Watson in the lodge at the front desk, which was abuzz with phone calls. Her pinched, birdlike features were ruffled; her movements jerky and frantic. When the phone stopped ringing, she turned to them.

"My brother's not here," she said with a curtness meant to prod them back out the door. This was a woman close to coming unglued. Right now, he needed her together.

Hayden rested his elbow on the reception counter and leaned in. "I need to talk to Kyl."

"I said he's not here."

"Beth, I need to find out what Jason Erickson had to do with Eddie Williams's death." He held out both hands, palms facing upward. "For me this isn't about placing blame on your brother. It's about finding a killer." Specifically, Hayden needed to find out who ordered Jason Erickson to help move that boy's body. Jason was taking orders from someone, and that someone could be the Butcher. "Do you know where your brother is?"

Her teeth dug into her bottom lip. "I wish I did."

Hayden could see her concern, fear, and panic. "When was the last time you saw him?"

"Last night around midnight. He was up with one of the boys who had had a rough night. Dr. Trowbridge ended up giving the boy a sedative."

"What was your brother's state of mind last night?"

"You've seen Kyl. He's worried sick about this place, about the boys, about the ones whose parents have taken them out and about the ones who are left. Last night he was a nervous wreck."

"Do you know where he may have gone?"

"No. This place is everything to him." The phone at her elbow rang, but she ignored it. "Do you understand that, Agent Reed? Hope Academy is more than a job. It's his home, his life. It's all he has. I can't imagine him leaving it. I can't imagine him doing anything that would jeopardize it." The phone continued on in a shrill cry.

"Is Dr. Trowbridge available?"

"He's not seeing anyone this morning but parents. With Kyl gone, Dr. Trowbridge is trying to get things in order for the fundraiser tonight, trying to calm parents, trying to keep things running around here."

"The fundraiser is still on?"

"Without the fundraiser, the academy is gone." This came not from Beth, but from Dr. Trowbridge, who had entered the lobby behind them. "No, Agent Reed, it's not the ideal timing, but the board has decided to stand behind our current program, and it appears our supporters also want to proceed with the fundraiser. Now if you'll excuse me, I need to pick up one of the board members from the airport."

* * *

Hayden was quiet as he tucked Kate into the car and came around to the driver's side. He had a soul-deep need to keep her away from this place, from anything ugly or harmful. As he ducked into the driver's side of the car, Kate let out a soft cry.

She raised a shaky hand to the dash. There rested a white satin mask with feathery angel wings on either side and long ribbons fastened to one end, attached to a long stick. At the corner of an eye hole sat a small, teal-beaded angel with only one wing.

"It's Smokey's." Her voice trembled. "He carried it everywhere with him."

"You're sure?" He shouldn't have asked. He didn't need to. He knew the Butcher. Intimately. The Butcher wanted Kate, and he'd taken the one thing in this world she valued. Smokey. This was proof.

"It's a message, isn't it, from the Butcher?"

"Yes, he has Smokey, and he wants you at the fundraiser tonight." He pointed at the angelic mask. "This is his invitation."

# CHAPTER TWENTY-FOUR

*Friday, June 19, 11:15 a.m.*
*Reno, Nevada*

**N**o one bothered to say goodbye.

Robyn Banks had dedicated eighteen years to KTTL, and as she walked out of the newsroom, past the set, and through sales and marketing, no one said a word. She was nothing, here at KTTL or anywhere else. None of the resumes she sent out had drawn a nibble. She was a forty-three-year-old broadcast journalist no one wanted to put in front of the camera.

The parking garage was full of cars, empty of people. Everyone was working but her. What was she going to do? About work? About the house? About the shell of a man who was her husband?

Should she run away like Katrina Erickson? No, she wanted nothing to do with the bitch who was responsible for her current hell.

Robyn jammed her keys into the ignition and yanked her car out of the parking space she'd used for eighteen years and sped toward Leroy, the ancient security guard who tacked more than a hundred pictures of his grandkids and great-grandkids on the back wall of his guard booth. As she slammed to a stop at the booth window, her stomach lurched at the sight of all those smiling faces.

What really made today worse was that she was facing it alone. No faces smiled in her corner of the world. No one would tell her that things would be all right or that life would go on. Her throat swelled.

She pictured Mike, or at least the man he was before prison. So much had been taken from him, from her.

"Hey there, Miss Banks," Leroy said. "I heard you was leaving today, and I got something for you." He rummaged below the counter. She didn't rush him. Who wanted to rush home to a crumbling house and crumbling husband?

Plastic crinkled, and the security guard stuck his hand through the open glass window. "Got you a little going-away present. I know how you like them."

She stared at the cellophane package filled with a dozen chocolate peppermints.

"It ain't much." Leroy winked. "But I thought you'd like a few for whatever road you're headed down next."

No, it wasn't much. Not a big party. Not a sending-off bonus. Not even a group-signed greeting card. But it was something. Something in her miserable, pathetic excuse for a life.

"Thank you," she said around a tsunami of gratitude in her throat because Leroy had offered something. And as she drove home, she thought about that *something*.

Her life with Mike wasn't what she expected or even wanted, but it was *something*, and right now, it was all she had. *He* was all she had. He might think he was nothing, but she didn't. Not yet. She wasn't ready to give up hope.

"Mike!" She hopped out of her car and ran into her run-down house. Maybe they needed to give up the ruins of their old life, of this house, and strike out down new roads. She raced up the steps, almost tripping on the torn runner. "Miiiiike!"

She ran into Mike's bedroom, where stale air and gloomy shadows greeted her. She turned on the light, expecting to find him passed out in his chair, but the chair was empty, and so were his bed, his bathroom, the kitchen, and every other room in the creaky Victorian. Her husband was gone.

On lead-lined feet, she went back to his bedroom. How far "gone" depended on one thing. She opened the bottom drawer of his dresser, rummaged past the oxfords he never wore anymore, and found the box he'd hidden there.

With trembling fingers, she slipped through the pictures of his faces, and just as she expected, the ones of Katrina Erickson were gone.

* * *

*Friday, June 19, 11:30 a.m.*
*Dorado Bay, Nevada*

Cool gusts of wind and the promise of rain to a region that had for months been blanketed in sun and heat greeted her as she and Hayden left the Dorado Bay police station. She wrapped her arms around her chest and wondered again if Smokey was cold.

She felt calmer now, but still shaken. By leaving the mask with Smokey's one-winged angel, the Butcher finally made his move. Tonight he wanted her at the Hope Academy fundraiser, because tonight he would attempt to finish the job.

The mask sent Hayden into a whirl of activity. All morning he'd been at the station with Hatch and Evie making plans. Those plans included bringing in Parker Lord and others from his Maine-based SCIU team.

As they hurried through the parking lot toward the car, a broadcast reporter Kate recognized from one of the Reno network affiliates fell in step next to Hayden.

"Agent Reed," the reporter said, "is it true Jason Erickson's footprint was found on the tarp surrounding the dead Hope Academy student, Eddie Williams?"

"No comment," Hayden said.

"Does the Williams boy's death have anything to do with the Broadcaster Butcher?"

"No comment." They reached the car, and Hayden tucked her inside.

"A trusted source has informed me that Hope Academy director Kyl Watson is missing. Is it true that you questioned Watson previously in Butcher-related—"

"Dammit, I said no comment!"

The reporter took a step back, and Kate watched in stunned silence as Hayden got in the car.

"You swore," she said.

Hayden gunned the engine and pulled out of the parking lot. "And…"

"I've never heard you swear."

He turned to her and frowned. "Is there some point to this?"

"The point, Hayden, is you're upset."

"Of course I'm upset." He slapped his hand against the steering wheel. "I have eleven dead bodies, the latest belonging to a fourteen-year-old boy, which may or may not have anything to do with the Butcher. I have a seventy-four-year-old blind man bludgeoned and snatched from right under my nose. How many more dead bodies will I find before I get this son of a bitch? How many more will he kill before he sinks a knife into you?"

The rambling admission, more so than the Butcher's one-winged angel message, sent a stiffening resolve through Kate's spine. Hayden, the rock, was on shaky ground, but he didn't need to be. She'd been to hell and gotten banged and bruised along the way. In the end, she found a way out, sometimes running, sometimes fighting, but she survived.

"We're going to get him." She ran her fingers through the soft, black folds of his hair mussed by the wind. "We're going to get the Butcher, and we're going to get Smokey Joe."

Hayden's head leaned into her cupped palm. "Is that hope I hear?"

She pictured tough old Smokey Joe. Another survivor. "Damn right."

As they drove from the station toward the lake, some of Kate's resolve faltered when she realized they weren't going back to their lakeside cottage but to the pricey estates to the north. A kick of panic jolted her as he pulled the car into the drive of her grandparents' mansion.

"Why do we need to see *her*?" Kate asked. Her grandfather was out searching for Smokey Joe, and she had no desire to visit the woman who had left her and Jason at the mercy of their sick mother and turned the entire town of Dorado Bay against her father.

"We're not visiting your grandmother," Hayden said. "We're here to see Parker."

"Your boss?" She turned wide eyes on him.

"Parker and the rest of my team arrived an hour ago. They're here to help me with tonight's grab."

"But why *here*?"

"This is where the Hope Academy fundraiser is being

held," Hayden continued, ignoring the fact that she was digging her heels into the cobbled drive as he dragged her to the stone-lined doors. "Your grandparents have been financial supporters of Hope Academy for a number of years, and this year they're co-chairing the fundraiser." He caught her gaze. "And they just put up a twenty-thousand-dollar reward for anyone with information leading to Smokey Joe."

"Why would they do that?"

"For you."

She rubbed at the ache between her eyes. "Don't go there, Hayden."

"They're not monsters, Kate. They're good people. During the hunt for Smokey Joe, I spent some time with your grandfather. Jason and Kendra's deaths have been hard on them. They realize you're all they have left."

"I'm nothing to them."

"In your eyes, maybe so, but we can discuss your family dysfunction later." He knocked on the door, which was opened immediately by Kate's grandmother.

"Agent Lord is on the east patio," the older woman told Hayden. "He's waiting for you."

In a quickness that surprised her, Hayden sprinted through the house, leaving her alone with her grandmother. *Aren't you supposed to protect me?* Kate wanted to scream at his retreating back.

She stared at Ava Conlan, who stared back, her carefully powdered face unmoving, her coiffed hair stiff. The older woman could give stone-faced Hayden a run for his money.

"How is the search for your friend going?" Ava Conlan asked in a cultured voice, honed by scads of money and a social status unparalleled in all of Dorado Bay.

"Still going."

"Oliver says they'll find him. They won't leave a man behind." For a moment, the older woman's gaze softened, and Kate wondered what it would be like to have a grandmother in her life.

Kate pressed her lips together. Smokey Joe was all the family she needed. "I'd like to join Hayden and the others."

Ava Conlan nodded and led her into a huge ballroom. The house was probably ten thousand square feet and, on a normal day, a showplace with its fine furnishings and art. But today it wore an extra glittery party face. Black and gold bunting flounced the doorways, and large gold pots with creamy white flowers dotted the floor. Gold Mylar balloons with curling gold ribbons floated high on the ceiling.

As they clicked through the ballroom, a heavy silence pressed on them.

"How—"

"Do—"

They spoke at the same time.

"Go ahead," Ava said.

"How many people do you expect tonight?" Kate asked.

"About five hundred. Even with the bad publicity, it sounds like people still believe in the academy."

"Do you?" Kate asked, wondering how someone like her grandmother would support having fifty troubled boys living nearby.

"When the academy first opened, most of us on the lake were opposed to it. Honestly, we were worried about our property, even our lives. They get a lot of rough boys through there." Her carefully plucked brows knitted. "But the more we saw, the more we realized the amazing success the academy had with turning lives around." Her lifted face suddenly lined, and Kate wondered if she was thinking about her daughter, Kate's mother, who had never been able to turn her life around from its destructive course.

Kate realized the other woman was openly staring at her. She wanted to pull her hair across her face, but she stood straighter and thrust out her chin.

"You don't look like your mother," Ava said.

"I'm nothing like her."

"No, you're not. You're stronger." She twined her thin, pale fingers. "But you need to be careful, Kate. This Butcher, he's a monster." She shivered and inched to Kate's side.

Kate didn't like this conversation or the closeness. "Where are Hayden and Agent Lord?"

Ava Conlan pulled herself together and let out a husky laugh. "Parker Lord is everywhere."

"What?"

"I take it you haven't met Hayden's superior." The older woman's eyes glinted like the gold balloons overhead. "This way."

Kate found Hayden on the patio with Hatch, Evie, and a half dozen people she didn't recognize. Everyone was focused on Hayden except for a man sitting at the patio table and staring at her with an enigmatic smile. For a moment, everything blurred but him. Black hair, dusted with silver at the temples, sat atop his head in wind-swept waves. He wore a navy polo shirt with some kind of nautical emblem on the pocket. His jaw spoke of arrogance, his chiseled nose of strength, and his eyes of confidence.

This had to be the legendary Parker Lord, and her grandmother was right: He had a power that screamed, *I am captain of the seas, master of the universe.*

He winked at her.

She blinked and for the first time noticed he was sitting in a wheelchair.

When Hayden was done talking, he took her hand and introduced her. He was so casual about it. She could do this.

She could be around normal people and act like a normal person.

"We've actually met before," a man Hayden introduced as Finn Brannigan said. He wore black jeans and a black T-shirt and moved with the grace of a cat. "Jewelry heist at the Atlantis Resort four years ago. I was the JAG specialist you interviewed for your 'Justice for All' report."

She stared at him, and a hazy memory started to come into focus. The Atlantis was a ritzy resort and spa in Reno, and their penthouse suites housed the highest of the high rollers as well as their jewel-decked spouses. "Yes," she said with a smile of recognition. "You were the agent who re-created the crime by reenacting the thieves' escape route. You went out onto the ledge of the twenty-seven-story building and crawled down a rope. Everyone, including the livid hotel manager, was afraid you'd fall."

"Pretty good, huh?" Agent Brannigan said, but he really meant *It's so good to be bad.*

Before she could answer, the patio doors swung open and out stepped Dr. Trowbridge, followed by her grandmother, who was wringing her hands.

"Get out." Dr. Trowbridge pointed at Hayden and jerked his thumb over his shoulder. "You have no reason to be here."

"I do if I plan on catching a murderer." Hayden's hand knotted, the pressure intensifying on her fingers.

"Not during the fundraiser," Dr. Trowbridge said. "The academy is relying on this event to bring in money to keep our doors open for the next year. We can't have you and half the FBI wandering among our guests looking for a serial killer. Your presence will jeopardize the academy's future."

"You're worried about me jeopardizing your damned

fundraiser?" Hayden took a step toward the doctor, but Hatch grabbed his arm.

Kate, along with everyone else on the patio, turned to stare at Hayden, who was visibly shaking. And swearing. He looked like a cannon ready to blast the Hope Academy doctor.

"A man known as the Broadcaster Butcher has left a clear signal that he'll be here tonight, at this fundraiser," Hayden said. "And I'll be here, waiting for him."

"This is a private affair, by invitation only," Trowbridge insisted. "Since our good director, Kyl Watson, has gone AWOL, I'm the one handing out invitations, and you don't get one. There is no way you are going to link Hope Academy to the Broadcaster Butcher."

Hayden threw off Hatch's hand and took a step toward the doctor. Dr. Trowbridge drew back a fist.

"Fifty thousand dollars a head. Four heads." The words stilled the entire room, and everyone turned to Parker Lord, the man who'd spoken. "Hayden, Hatch, Evie, and Kate. Those four get admittance into the fundraiser, and I pay Hope Academy two hundred thousand dollars."

Hayden gave a single stony nod. Hatch flashed his megawatt smile and chucked an arm around Evie. "She cleans up real nice," Hatch said with a wink. Evie elbowed him in the ribs.

A struggle played out on Dr. Trowbridge's face, and eventually the $200,000 won. "Three agents." He looked at Kate. "And her. But no guns."

Hayden shifted, but both Hatch and Finn reached out and grabbed him by the arms.

"It's a deal." Parker Lord wheeled off the patio.

* * *

*Friday, June 19, Noon*
*Dorado Bay, Nevada*

"Dammit to hell!"

Smokey Joe threw the broken water bottle on the ground. That was the third shovel to take a dump on him. He squatted and ran his fingers over the muddy floor of his underground prison. Where the hell was his last water bottle? He needed to make another shovel.

A day and a half ago, that son of a bitch Butcher snuck into his room through an open window, and before Smokey could rally the troops, the Butcher whacked him in the mouth with the butt of something hard and followed with a thwack to the side of the head. Smokey ran his fingers along the crusted blood at his temple and chin. Didn't hurt no more.

Smokey didn't need no eyes to tell him he was in an underground hole—three and a half feet square and four feet deep—and that the top was covered by plywood weighted with a foot or two of dirt. He'd found six bananas and four water bottles in one of the corners and felt a slight but steady stream of fresh air coming from a small mesh-covered hole above him. He heard mallards and not-too-far-off motorboats, so he figured he was close to the lake. He also figured he'd been in the hole going on two days. Two times birds started yammering, telling him the sun rose, but only once did bullfrogs and crickets make a racket.

At last he found the final water bottle and poured the few remaining drops into his mouth. When it was empty, he bit into the base of the bottle and made a small hole. Then with his old, muddy hands—nothing shaky 'bout 'em now—he tore at the hole, peeling back the plastic bit by bit. This one probably wouldn't last too long either, but it didn't matter. He'd keep digging. He'd done it before, and back then it had only been his sorry old butt on the line.

"You haven't got me yet, Butcher Boy, and you ain't gonna get my girl." Smokey gouged his plastic shovel into the three-foot wormhole he'd been working on for two days. "I'm coming, Katy-lady. Just you hang on and stick with G-man. Old Smokey's coming for you."

# CHAPTER TWENTY-FIVE

*Friday, June 19, 4:10 p.m.*
*Reno, Nevada*

Home sweet home." Kate tried to keep her voice light, but it wavered as she stood at the front door of her Reno condo, trying to get the courage to slip her key in the lock.

Hayden motioned to the two-story ground-floor unit with the walled private patio. "Nice place. You could have sold it for a considerable sum. Why did you hang on to it?"

"Honestly?"

*Shoot straight or ditch the rifle.*

Hayden nodded.

"This is my home, the first real home I ever had, and I guess a part of me wanted to hang on to it in case I ever felt safe enough to come back."

"More hope?"

"Or stupidity." She laughed, but the sound died off as she aimed the key at the lock and missed.

Hayden held out his hand, and she handed him her key. Good, let Agent Efficient help her get what she needed, and then they'd go. He turned toward the door but didn't insert the key. Instead he squinted, frowned, and plucked a small round object from above the door jamb.

"Is that what I think it is?" Kate asked.

"A camera to watch you coming and going." Hayden fisted it in his hand. "Set up no doubt by the Butcher."

Fear burrowed in her chest as she tried to comprehend someone so consumed with finding her that he'd set up miniature cameras at her home. And he must have seen her when—"The trigger. Oh, my God, Hayden. I'm the trigger." Guilt, an icy, heavy avalanche, almost knocked her over. She steadied herself against the patio wall. "The Butcher made his first attack six months ago, and you said something happened to trigger that attack. It was me. In January, I came here to get some jewelry to sell, and he must have seen me. It's just like you said. Realizing I was alive, he must have killed the other broadcasters, knowing that I would have to come out of hiding because I could never live with myself if I let the injustices against those women go unanswered."

Hayden slipped the disk into his pocket. "But he won't get you. Let's get the dress and go."

Kate didn't argue. After Hayden unlocked the door, she hurried up the steps into the master bedroom, refusing to look at the brown stain of her own blood and terror and anger indelibly imprinted on the carpet. She threw open her walk-in closet and rummaged past the suits to the back, where she kept her formal wear. She took out three full-length dresses. The first, a sapphire velvet gown, was too low in the front. She studied the black with the jet beads, but the sleeveless sheath would show too much of her arms. Finally she held an emerald green charmeuse with a high waist and cap sleeves.

"The green," Hayden said. "Definitely the green." She

spun and found him sitting on her bed, his legs stretched out in front of him, his back against the headboard.

"Why the green?" She held up the shimmery fabric with the flowing skirt and low back.

"It's my favorite color."

"You like *green*?"

"Is that a crime?" For the first time since his run-in with Dr. Trowbridge, Hayden smiled. The sight sent a brilliant light through the dark, dusty room.

She shrugged a laugh. "You're just not a *green* kind of guy."

He shook his head like a parent amused with a precocious child. She knew she and Hayden were fundamentally different. He was an analytical control freak and she was...She clutched the dress to her and sunk onto the edge of the bed. She didn't even know who she was anymore.

"I'm not green," he said. "Okay, then what color am I?"

She squinted. "Something practical. Black. Brown. Maybe camel."

"Nope." He reached for her. "I'm definitely a sucker for green." He ran his finger along the side of her face then nodded to the wad of emerald charmeuse in her hands. "Wear it. It matches your eyes."

She hugged the flimsy fabric to her chest. "Tonight I'll be in a room with a killer who needs me dead."

"And I'll be right beside you." Hayden was a large man, but he moved with surprising agility as he landed a deep, hot kiss on her lips.

When she pulled away, she steadied her hands on his chest. "Is that a classic case of courage delivered with a kiss?"

"No. That was purely primal on my part. It happens when I'm lying in a bed with you."

She took a deep breath. She'd handled dragons as a child, dealt with barracudas like Robyn Banks in broadcast news, survived twenty-five stabs wounds, and she got Hayden Reed to tap into and act on primal feelings. She was ready for tonight, for a cocktail party with a butcher.

*  *  *

*Friday, June 19, 7 p.m.*
*Dorado Bay, Nevada*

"Damn, Pretty Boy, you look good in a tux."

Hayden ignored Lottie's smack to his butt and held out the cufflinks.

She took one of the links and threaded it through the buttonhole of his right cuff. "Are your guys ready?"

"Hatch and Evie are already at the Conlan mansion. Parker has men set up at the estates on either side. Chief Greenfield has roadblocks all along the bay roads."

The old police sergeant turned him around and secured the other cufflink. "You be careful. You might look like a million bucks, but you're still flesh and blood under this fancy suit." She straightened his tie.

"You, too. I've arranged for one of Chief Greenfield's men to go out with you tonight." Lottie gave herself a clean bill of health, and she planned to spend the evening flashing around the sketch of the "woman" seen by Shayna Thomas's stalker. The difference now was that she'd be telling everyone that this was a man disguised as a woman.

Lottie placed both hands on his chest and pushed him away. "Kate's right. You're a control freak."

"No, Lottie, I care about you."

The sergeant waggled her eyebrows at him. "You got an older brother hiding somewhere who likes old bags with great shoes?"

Hayden laughed. "No, but if I did, I wouldn't hesitate to introduce you."

At that moment, Kate and Maeve walked out of the bathroom, and his heart dropped to his knees. He was sure of it, because they were knocking with a steady beat as he looked at the fairy-tale version of Kate. Here, in the early twilight, she looked like something out of her closet mural, Happily Ever After. Her creamy skin peeked out from the brilliant emerald of the long, flowing dress that hugged her slim curves, and in her hair, hanging in loping curls about her face, were tiny iridescent pearls.

"Let's go," she said when it became obvious he was gaping at her.

He nodded. Go. They needed to go.

Kate remained silent as they drove toward the glittering mansions on the lake. It was like first-date jitters, but to the $n$th degree. Their date tonight was with a butchering serial killer.

As they passed the road leading to Mulveney's Cove, Hayden recognized a car heading to the water. "There's Jon. I want to check in."

Lakeside, they found Jon dispatching an elite SAR group from Phoenix.

"No news," Jon said as they joined him at the water's edge. "But we won't stop until we find him, and we're going to find him. Alive."

Kate did the unthinkable and hugged Jon, whispering against his neck, "I know."

On the way back to the car, Hayden recognized another face, a smaller one without Jon's hope. Charlie Hankins sat on an outcropping of rocks overlooking Mulveney's Cove, tears streaming down his face.

"Oh, Hayden." Kate grabbed his hand. "That kid's miserable. Please go over and say something to him."

The kid's hunched shoulders were carrying something heavier than the weight of the world. "I don't know what to say to him," Hayden said. *Sorry for letting you down. Sorry for not finding your brother before the Butcher did.*

"That's crazy. You always know the perfect thing to say and do."

"Kate…" he started.

She thumped him on the chest. "Just go."

He shook his head. "I can't leave you."

"I'll glue myself to Jon. Go."

She gave him a little push, and his feet slogged through the lakeside muck toward Charlie Hankins. He climbed the back of the rock, which was covered in dried fish innards and lichen. The boy picked at the frayed edge of his cut-off shorts but didn't say anything as Hayden sat next to him. Clearly, Charlie's heart was breaking, and he felt guilty as hell. The hard part was knowing what to say. For once there were no voices in his head, no logical thoughts processing in his brain.

"I heard the funeral's tomorrow," Hayden said.

Charlie tossed a rock into the red-gold waters of the bay reflecting the setting sun. "Yeah. You gonna be there?"

"I'd planned on it. That okay with you?"

Charlie tossed in another rock. "Yeah."

Hayden picked up one of the rocks and tossed it in the water, a soft *kerplunk* harmonizing with the fading day's chirps and buzzes. He tossed in seven more before Charlie turned his tear-stained cheeks to him. "I have these dreams at night where I find him, the killer, in Benny's room, and I

take Benny's baseball bat and hit him over the head. Again
and again and again until…until…there's nothing left. Is
that okay to feel that way?"

The ripples in the water stretched farther and farther.
"Yeah, it's okay to be angry, because that means something
deeper is going on. You're hurt or sad, probably a little of
both. Feelings are okay. They prove you're human." And
lately, Hayden had felt very human.

* * *

*Friday, June 19, 8:30 p.m.*
*Dorado Bay, Nevada*

Robyn Banks tore off the check for $1,000 and handed it to
the birdlike woman at the door of the Conlan mansion. The
woman from Hope Academy took the check and smiled, although she wouldn't be smiling tomorrow when she tried to
cash it. That little piece of paper would bounce higher than
the gold balloons floating in the cathedral ceilings of Oliver
and Ava Conlan's front entryway.

"Do you need a mask?" The woman pointed to the array
of feathered, sequined, and bejeweled face coverings.

Robyn hadn't thought to bring one. She'd left her home
in Reno focused only on finding her husband, who'd crawled
out of his hole of despair to go after Katrina Erickson. "Yes,
I'll take the red one." The crimson mask sported a single red
plume jutting jauntily from the right side.

Robyn slipped the red silk confection over her face and
entered the ballroom, where hundreds of masked partygoers
mingled. A string quartet played in the corner, and waiters in
black pants, white shirts, and various animal masks threaded

through the guests with sparkling flutes of champagne and artfully arranged finger foods.

One of the waiters offered her a glass of bubbling liquid, but she declined. How easy it would be to get stinking drunk right now, which she guessed was the case with Mike. She searched the masked faces, trying to spot the tottering, drunken fool, because she knew he'd be here in search of Katrina.

Funny, how everything kept coming back to Katrina.

When Robyn arrived home from her final day at KTTL with a bag of chocolate peppermints and the grand idea of leaving with Mike and starting a new life, she'd discovered that he'd left without her. And he must have started off the journey already pickled, for she'd found an empty fifth of scotch next to his wallet and his cell phone. The last text he'd sent had been to Katrina to agree to meet her at 9 p.m. at the Hope Academy fundraiser.

What a stupid, stupid fool. Her husband was on the hunt for Katrina Erickson, but she had to stop him before someone found out who he really was. Her fingers wrapped around her purse, home to her 9mm handgun.

\* \* \*

"Do you see Kyl Watson?" Kate asked as she and Hayden found a quiet spot in the corner of the Conlans' bustling ballroom. She and Hayden had walked the floor for the past hour, Hayden taking a mental inventory of the guests, but it was hard with so many masks. Her own mask, the white one with the one-winged angel, scratched her nose, but that single angel gave her hope that Smokey Joe was still alive.

"I don't think Watson is here yet," Hayden said. "But

Dr. Trowbridge is. He's the one in the mask with the silver glitter."

The short man with the Clark Kent build ground his hands together behind his back. "Looks a bit uncomfortable, doesn't he?" Kate noted.

"Kyl Watson is the people man, the one who connects to the boys, the staff, and the donors. Dr. Trowbridge, on the other hand, is the head, the brain responsible for working out programming to turn troubled boys into productive members of society. He hates stuff like this, and if the academy weren't on the brink of closing, he wouldn't be here."

A tall blond man wearing a gold sequined mask with three purple jester points in stiff velvet flashed her miles of brilliant white teeth. "Was that Hatch?" she asked.

"Yep. Evie is by the musicians. She's wearing the red-sequined mask with the devil horns."

"Do you recognize anyone else?"

Hayden pointed out the mayor, the publisher of the local paper, Pastor Ike Iverson, and two casino owners who had vacation homes on Dorado Bay. "Anyone who's anyone in this town is here tonight. I spotted Chief Greenfield earlier following Dr. Trowbridge."

Knowing that the chief and Hayden's teammates hovered nearby gave her comfort, as did the fact that Parker Lord and another half dozen agents were stationed at the neighbors' properties while Chief Greenfield's men were manning roadblocks.

Outside, a steady rain started to fall, and the wind rattled the glass panes of the tightly closed patio doors. The long-awaited storm had landed and broken the back of the heat wave.

A waiter with a green dragon mask strolled by with a tray of steaming appetizers. "Shrimp?" he asked.

Both she and Hayden shook their heads, and she forced a deep breath to calm her heaving stomach. "The Butcher's here, Hayden, I feel it."

Hayden's gray eyes shone through the simple black satin mask he wore. "Me too."

* * *

He set the empty shrimp tray on the kitchen counter and picked up a new tray, this one piled with sparkling champagne flutes. Before he balanced it on his left hand, he slipped a tiny piece of paper under the glass in the second row, third from the right.

"Are you sure you can carry those?" the headwaiter asked. "I noticed you limping as you walked the room with the shrimp."

"I'm fine." Thanks to all that earth moving he did for Smokey's underground prison, his leg was bothering him again. But other than that, he was very, very fine. Tonight the heavens would toast him, for he would finally put an end to Katrina Erickson.

"Okay, get out there. The toast is in five minutes."

Lightning fired the sky as he adjusted the green dragon mask. The lights flickered off, but it didn't matter. A flame flickered within, burning hotter, burning brighter.

The lights flicked back on. It was time.

He wound his way through the crowd, occasionally handing out glasses of champagne, but he made sure no one took the glass in the second row, third from the right. That alone was for Katrina.

He spotted her next to the ever-diligent Agent Reed, who would not leave Katrina's side tonight—he smiled—well, not without good reason. Reed was good, and few could match the FBI agent in wits and strength. He for one would never try to take on Hayden Reed, for he knew his physical limitations. That in itself was a strength that would serve him well tonight.

No, there was but one person in the room tonight who was stronger than Hayden Reed. The beautiful woman in the green mermaidlike dress with pearls woven through her hair. Katrina Erickson was stronger than all of them. She had the power, and thanks to one of her "Justice for All" reports, she knew his secret. It was right there on one of Agent Reed's carefully constructed spreadsheets, but no one had been smart enough to follow the trail to him.

As he drew nearer, the heat flicked higher, hissing and curling at the back of his throat. It would be a shame to see her dead because, like Agent Reed, she was a good one, not a weak, sniveling whore like his mother and the eight prostitutes he'd killed. Katrina was beautiful, smart, and strong, and he would use all that against Agent Reed.

"For the toast," he said, handing agent Reed a glass of champagne. "And for you, madam." He handed Katrina the glass from the second row, third from the right.

\* \* \*

A small slip of paper slid into her hand. It had been under her champagne glass. Her head snapped up, and she searched for the waiter with the dragon mask who'd handed it to her, but he'd vanished.

The storm rattled the windows, and the lights flickered again. The room fell into darkness. Some partygoers gasped. Seconds later, the lights flashed back on.

"Attention everyone," her grandmother said. The older woman stood at a podium at the front of the room with Dr.

Trowbridge and the Hope Academy board. "I'd like to welcome you all..."

But Kate didn't hear anymore. She took the note and unfolded it. *Meet me at the boathouse in ten minutes. If you're late, Smokey Joe dies. If you bring G-man or any of his friends, Smokey Joe dies.*

Smokey! He was alive. This note proved it. How else would the Butcher know *G-man* was Smokey's pet name for Hayden? With this note the Butcher finally reached out to her.

But she wouldn't be meeting him alone. All her life, she'd been on her own, until now, when she'd finally found a man she could count on. Hayden would come up with a plan to free Smokey, trap the Butcher, and stop global warming all in one swift move.

An insane laugh bubbled in her throat. She wasn't alone, she wasn't running anymore, and they were about to find Smokey Joe. She tugged at Hayden's arm, but he was oddly still, focused on the patio door. She tugged again, but he held up his hand.

The door swung open. Wind and rain poured in. Someone at the back of the room screamed. A boy stumbled through the doors, his face lined with terror and his Hope Academy T-shirt covered in blood.

# CHAPTER TWENTY-SIX

*Friday, June 19, 9:20 p.m.*
*Dorado Bay, Nevada*

Hayden saw everything at once.

Kate's grandmother dropped her champagne glass. Dr. Trowbridge turned from the podium and bolted toward the door. Hatch whipped off his jester mask and took off after the doctor. The blood-covered Hope Academy boy slumped to the floor in front the patio doors. Evie ran toward him. And beside him, Kate swayed.

He slung his arm around her to keep her from collapsing to the ground, and he knew she was wondering if that blood belonged to Smokey Joe. Was this it? Was the Butcher making his move? Had he made his move? Hayden needed to talk to that blood-covered boy. He ran a frantic gaze about the room and spotted Kate's grandfather elbowing his way through the crowd.

"I'll take her. You see to the boy," Oliver Conlan said. Hayden hesitated, his gaze locking with Kate's grandfather's just long enough to see what he needed to see.

He moved Kate into her grandfather's arms and pointed

at Kate's grandmother, who'd left the podium and made her way through the stunned crowd. "Get Parker on the phone and get him in here. And you," he nodded to Kate's grandfather. "Don't let her out of your sight." Kate was in good hands. Love was the fiercest of protectors.

He ran to Evie and knelt over the boy, who lay in a puddle of rainwater pinked by blood.

The kid stared at the slick red coating his hands as he moaned, "Too much blood, too much blood."

Hayden grasped the boy's shoulders. "Are you hurt?"

The boy's chin trembled. "No, not me. The blood, it's... it's Mr. Watson's. I found Mr. Watson."

"Is Mr. Watson hurt? Has he hurt someone? Where is he?"

"I got a c...c...call telling me to check the loft in the barn, and I found him, d...d...dead. Someone shot him. Blew off the back of his head." The boy shook from head to toe. "Blood and brains, oh God, it was everywhere."

Hayden gripped the boy's shoulders. "Someone called you and told you to check the barn? Who?"

"I...I...I don't know. Blood, too much blood. Too much!" The kid let out another moan and broke into body-wrenching sobs.

Hayden moved his hand to the boy's head and rested his fingers in his hair. "See if you can track down Chief Greenfield," Hayden said to Evie. "I don't know where the hell he is, but he was here earlier, and as soon as you can, get to that barn."

"You think the Butcher made the tip-off call?"

"Yes." Because this was all part of the Butcher's plan. Hayden could see it now. The Butcher was trying to create chaos, and in that chaos, he'd make a move. He turned to check on Kate, who still stood between her grandparents, two eagle-eyed bookends.

"Where are you going?" Evie asked.

"To find out why Dr. Trowbridge felt the need to flee."

Hayden made his way through the packed ballroom, now buzzing with hushed and not-so-hushed voices. He didn't need to go far in his hunt for Trowbridge. He was sprawled in the Conlans' drive with Hatch's knee in his back.

Hatch yanked Hope Academy's doctor to his feet and got in his bone-white face. "Talk, asshole."

\* \* \*

Kate tried to take off after Hayden, but her grandparents closed in on her, so close she could barely breathe. Her hand fisted around the note from the waiter. Hayden needed to know the Butcher had made contact with her. She looked for Hatch or Evie, but Evie had just left the ballroom with the bloody boy, and Hatch had disappeared after Dr. Trowbridge.

She had no idea what was going on, but she didn't care. She cared about Smokey and finding Hayden so they could go to the boathouse. She rushed in the direction of Hayden, but her grandfather grabbed her arm.

"You're staying here." Her grandfather's eyes narrowed.

"I need to go after Hayden."

"You're not leaving this room."

"But—"

"Hayden's orders."

The old man, who'd never stood by her in the past, was standing strong now. Damn him. But her anger fizzled when she saw the worry in the old man's eyes, even more intense than when he and his fellow soldiers were searching for Smokey Joe. Hayden was right. Her grandparents cared.

"Look," she said, "one of the waiters slipped this note to me. The Butcher has Smokey and wants to meet me at boathouse." She looked at her watch. "I'm supposed to be there right now. I need Hayden."

Her grandfather looked at the note, his great white bushy eyebrows dipping with a frown. "*You* will stay here. I'll find Hayden."

Fighting words teetered on her tongue, but she didn't have time to fight. Smokey didn't have time for her to fight. "Fine. I'll stay, but get Hayden. Now."

Her grandfather bulldozed through the ballroom crowd, and her grandmother moved closer, slipping her arm about Kate's waist. The touch sent way too many feelings through her, but she didn't have time for feelings. She closed her eyes and tried to picture Smokey. Was he frightened? Fighting? Tired? Hurt? Giving the Butcher hell?

Her frantic gaze shot around the room again. Why had Hayden left her? Her grandmother's hand tightened on her waist. What if her grandfather couldn't find Hayden in time? What if . . . Oh, God, she didn't have time for what-ifs.

Kate headed for the patio door, but her grandmother stopped her with a surprisingly hard jerk. "I've lost my daughter and my grandson this week, and I'm not going to lose you, too." Her grandmother looked ready to take on an army of dragons. "If you take one more step, I'll have half a dozen of these guys on you in seconds."

Kate's mouth fell open. Where had this warrior been two decades ago when she'd had to face one pink dragon on her own? But she didn't have time to ask questions. *Think*, she told herself as her eyelids slammed shut. What would Hayden do? Or Hatch or Evie or Parker Lord?

Her eyes flew open. "It's important to take care of those you love, right?" She was surprised at the catch in her voice.

Her grandmother's artfully stretched face didn't budge, but the air around them quivered. "Yes."

Okay. Now. For Smokey Joe. She threw her arms around the older woman and gave her a hug. Two arms. *Her arms.* The touch moved her more than she wanted to contemplate, but she didn't focus on it. Hugs had the power to stop wars. They also had the power to momentarily stun lonely, guilt-ridden grandmothers.

"I have to go to Smokey. Tell Hayden to hurry. And go find Parker Lord and Chief Greenfield. Tell them all I'll be at the boathouse."

\* \* \*

*Friday, June 19, 9:30 p.m.*
*Dorado Bay, Nevada*

More than ten thousand drummer boys banged on the inside of Lottie's skull, and her feet were killing her. She was a sorry piece tonight, but not half as sorry as the Butcher would be when she got her hands on him.

She banged again on Louella Bollinger's front door. Louella was the sixty-seven-year-old president of the Bluelake Golden Girls Dance Line. She was also the proud owner of one butt-ugly pair of size eight and a half wide orthotic shoes that matched the prints found in Shayna Thomas's backyard.

While she was out flashing that sketch of the "woman" Shayna Thomas's stalker saw, Detective Traynor had called with the news that Louella Bollinger, who lived on the west shore of Dorado Bay, had a prescription filled for the shoes. Coincidence? Hell, no. Although it was highly unlikely that sixty-seven-year-old Louella was at Shayna Thomas's house in a pink dress, Lottie sure as hell wanted to know who had access to that woman's shoe tree.

She and the Dorado Bay police officer Hayden assigned to babysit her stood on Louella's front porch, banging on the door.

"I'm coooooming," a voice from within the house crooned. The door opened to a tall, slim woman with rhinestone-studded cat-eye glasses and snow-white hair.

"Mrs. Bollinger, I'm Lottie King of the Colorado Springs Police Department, and I'm following up a lead on one of the Broadcaster Butcher slayings. We've learned a suspect at one of the crime scenes was wearing orthotic shoes that match a pair prescribed to you." She held up a picture of the black, chunky shoes. "Do you own a pair of these?"

The woman shook her head, the rhinestone chain of her glasses tinkling against the eyeglass frame. "Heavens no. I wouldn't be caught dead in those." The woman waggled her foot, which was encased in a pair of Via Spiga pumps, candy-apple red with double tassels.

"You've never had an orthotic shoe prescribed to you?"

"Never." She pointed her toe and kicked, her foot coming to within an inch of Lottie's nose. "These hoofers are in great shape."

Lottie walked away wondering who the hell faked Louella Bollinger's prescription.

* * *

As Kate ducked into the rain-soaked night, sirens wailed and lights flashed near the front of her grandparents' mansion. Good. The police had arrived, and Parker Lord and his people were probably storming the front door, too. It was all good.

And any minute Hayden would join her. Her grandfather should have found him by now. She had to trust them, believe that good would conquer evil, that they'd come through for her, that she didn't need to do everything on her own.

She had hope. That she'd be safe. That Smokey was still alive.

Sheets of rain plastered her dress to her body as she made her way toward the boathouse, her heels sinking into the sodden earth. Technically, she couldn't see the boathouse through the deluge, only the bug light mounted on its face.

Was the Butcher waiting inside? Was Smokey Joe?

She slipped on the slick path and fell to her hands and knees, mud splashing her. She heaved herself back up.

At that moment, the yellow bug light went out along with every other light along the bay, leaving the night liquid black. The wind must have knocked down a power line. She wanted to laugh. No problem. She was okay in the dark and knew how to use it to her advantage.

Feeling her way, she found the hedge that separated her grandparents' property from their neighbors' and ducked behind it. She looked back over her shoulder, wondering where Hayden was. When she saw nothing, she inched forward. When she got to within five yards of the boathouse, she squinted, searching for a human shape, but she saw no one.

Then she heard something behind her, coming from the house. Footsteps.

\* \* \*

Hayden wanted to slam a fist into Dr. Trowbridge's mouth. The Hope Academy physician had clammed up, refusing to speak until his attorney arrived.

"Give me an hour with him," Finn said. "And I'll get the story. You want to watch?"

"No, I need to get back to Kate." He'd been away less than five minutes, and he told himself she was safe with her grandparents, that the older couple would protect the granddaughter they loved. He ran to the Conlans' foyer just in time to see Kate's grandparents rush out the front door. Alone.

Anger knotted his fists, his gut, but not his tongue. "Where the hell is Kate?"

Just as Oliver Conlan opened his mouth, two men stumbled around the side of the house, one in handcuffs.

* * *

"What the hell are you doing here?" Kate asked.

Robyn Banks was close enough now that Kate could see a full grin spread across her former rival's face. "Oooo, you were always so good about asking the right questions. A real ace reporter. And a pretty face to go with it. Ever think about getting into broadcast news?"

"Stop being an idiot, Robyn, this is…" Kate's words died off as Robyn reached into her purse and pulled out a gun.

"I am anything but an idiot."

Kate took a step back.

Robyn lifted her arm. "Don't even think about running, Katrina, not this time."

Kate froze. Where was Hayden? Why wasn't he coming to help? Had her grandfather been unable to find him? Could anyone hear her above the screeching wind?

Robyn leveled the gun at her chest.

"I'm not sure what you want or why you're here, but you'll solve nothing by shooting me."

Robyn's smile fell away. "I'll get justice."

"Justice?"

"You ruined my husband's life. You broke him." She and the gun drew closer.

"How did I break Mike Muldoon?"

"Because of your investigative report he lost everything. His money. His art. His job. His right eye. His freedom." Robyn stopped five feet in front of her. "And in prison, he lost his spirit. He was repeatedly beaten and sodomized by the criminals in that place. You can't imagine what that does to a man who wanted only a life of beauty. And you, Katrina Erickson, are responsible for what he became." Robyn's hand trembled.

"And what's that?"

"You're a smart newswoman. Look at the facts."

Thunder pounded the night. A second later, a brilliant streak of lightning lit up the sky, and she saw Robyn's face. Clearly. Terror and horror and sadness and shame.

Kate's knees buckled. "Your husband is the Butcher?"

"Give the smart woman a chocolate peppermint." Robyn's finger moved toward the trigger. "Mike has been consumed with you from the moment you first broke his story. It was sickening, his obsession with you. I'm sure he planned to kill you. But now I must put an end to the killing before someone finds out Mike is the Butcher. And that means killing you. With you dead, his hunt is over."

Something shifted in the shadows. Her heart skipped. Hayden?

A flash of silver.

Robyn Banks swayed. The gun fell from her hand. Her body hit the ground at Kate's feet, a knife sticking out of the back of her neck.

A man, the waiter with the green dragon mask, stepped out of the shadows. She opened her mouth, but something cold and hard hit her temple, and she saw black.

# CHAPTER TWENTY-SEVEN

*Friday, June 19, 9:45 p.m.*
*Dorado Bay, Nevada*

Look who I found skulking in the bushes." Chief Greenfield dragged a cuffed man with his head hanging low up the steps of the Conlan mansion. The chief yanked back the man's head.

Hayden tore his attention from Kate's grandparents and stared at Mike Muldoon, who looked and smelled like a rat drowned in a barrel of whiskey. Streaks of red shot through the drunk man's eyes, and he wore the ratty red morning coat with the gold peacocks.

Chief Greenfield reached into the man's pockets and took out a handful of pictures, all of Kate. Hayden stopped breathing.

"I found these on him," the chief said. "I asked him what he was doing here, and he said he was here to see Katrina, that she'd called him and invited him here for an interview."

Muldoon's face cracked in a boozy grin. "She's been after me for years." He executed a clumsy bow. "So I finally decided to give her what she wants—me, in the flesh."

"Where is she?" Hayden asked. "What the fuck did you do with her?"

"Nothing. We haven't had a chance to swap air kisses yet."

Hayden lunged for Muldoon, but Chief Greenfield pulled him back. He spun to Hayden's grandparents. "Where the hell is Kate?"

Oliver Conlan put his arm around his wife. "She ran off to the boathouse to meet with the Butcher. He slipped her this note. She took off a few minutes ago but said she needs you."

The note was a hot coal in his hand. *Meet me at the boathouse in ten minutes. If you're late, Smokey Joe dies. If you bring G-man or any of his friends, Smokey Joe dies.*

Hayden shrugged off the chief and grabbed Muldoon by his collar. "Where the hell's Kate?"

Muldoon sputtered, and his face grew as red as his velvet collar.

"Hayden, hold on, there's something you should know," Chief Greenfield said. "I checked Muldoon and his car and I didn't find a knife."

"No knife?" The Butcher would never approach Kate— or anyone—without a knife. He was a weak son of a bitch who managed to kill his prey only through carefully planned scenarios. He wouldn't take on Kate without a knife.

"I think Muldoon is telling the truth," the chief said. "I think someone pretending to be Kate sent him a message to come here tonight. The only things I found on him were a hair comb and a mirror."

The hole where Muldoon's right eye should've been jerked in a grotesque wink. "I wanted to look my best in case Katrina brought her camera crew."

Hayden released the vile human being that was Muldoon.

Think. Analyze. This drunk couldn't be the Butcher. But someone called Mike Muldoon to meet with Katrina, just like someone told the Hope Academy boy about the dead body in the barn.

More chaos. Meant to divert him.

Hayden elbowed his way through the ballroom and into the storm-torn night. His Italian lace-ups sunk into the mud, and an airborne flood washed down on him, trying to slow him, but failing.

He hopped over ground lights that weren't working and crashed through low-lying shrubs as he raced through the darkness. As he neared the boathouse he spotted a mound on the ground near the hedge.

*Noooo*, a voice inside cried. Or did the animal-like cry really tear up his throat and into the howling night?

The closer he got, the more red he saw. It ran in rivers along the sodden ground, covered the body, and trickled from the body's neck, where someone had planted a silvery knife.

He dropped to his knees and took the body in his hands. It was a woman, but it wasn't Kate. The relief was so great, so overwhelming, it was shameful.

The others—Hatch, Evie, Finn, Chief Greenfield, Oliver Conlan—reached him. "It's Robyn Banks. She's alive, but just barely. Oliver, stay with her and call the medics."

Hayden jumped up. "Finn, search the boathouse. Evie take the beach to the right, Hatch you take the left. Chief, take the grounds."

"Where are you going?" Oliver Conlan asked.

*To my own private hell.* Which was exactly what life would be if the Butcher killed Kate.

\* \* \*

*Friday, June 19, 10 p.m.*
*Dorado Bay, Nevada*

Smokey Joe's fourth—and final—water bottle shovel had busted to hell three hours ago. That's when he started using his hands. The shaky old things weren't letting him down.

The earth was getting softer, sandier. Like a gopher, he'd dug himself a wormhole three feet straight out, and then he'd started clawing up. He got past them planks of wood the Butcher put on top of his underground prison. He could tell by the change in the sound as he dug.

With raw stubs of fingers, he dug harder, faster. At last his right hand broke through the earth into the cold, rainy air. He raised a fist in triumph.

Mission accomplished.

He widened the wormhole and heaved himself out, gulping in fresh air. He called out and heard nothing but wind.

No problem.

He crouched low to the ground. He heard rain on the lake. Arms outstretched, he found a tree. Dropping to his knees, he felt around the base. Moss. He'd found north. He put his hands flat on the ground and waited. Within minutes he sensed a rumble. A road to the west. Road meant cars. He had gained consciousness when the Butcher dragged him from a car into a house (he heard the refrigerator humming and smelled lemon furniture polish) and along a back deck of some type. He had a damn good idea where he was.

His hands groped along the forest floor until he found a tree branch about three feet long, the width of a baseball bat. He'd rather have his Ruger, but the stick would do.

"I'm coming Katy-lady."

* * *

*Friday, June 19, 10:20 p.m.*
*Dorado Bay, Nevada*

Kate woke to a strange hissing sound, like a snake whispering in her ear. She opened her eyes a slit. Bright light. Her eyelids slammed. Had someone taken a sledgehammer to her skull?

Was that someone the Butcher?

She'd gone to the boathouse to meet the Butcher. Robyn Banks had greeted her instead and explained that her husband, Mike Muldoon, was the Butcher and that Kate needed to die to free Muldoon. But someone had stepped out of the shadows—Muldoon?—and sunk a knife into Robyn's neck, and that same person had slammed something against Kate's head.

Kate tried to raise her hand to the back of her head, but a thin, sharp cord dug into her wrists.

"There's no blood, if that's what you're searching for."

The voice was so close, she jumped. Slowly, she forced her eyes open.

She was on the floor of a kitchen she'd never seen before, her arms bound behind her, her green charmeuse dress tangled about her legs. The electricity was still out, but a half dozen candles flickered at regular intervals throughout the room.

A man sat in a chair at the kitchen table. He held a knife to a stone slick with oil. The hissing sound wasn't a snake but the rasp of a knife against a whetstone.

"I used my favorite knife on Robyn Banks, but there was no time to pull it out," he said with a casualness that sent her inching back on the cold tile floor. "I think this one, with a little sharpening, will suffice. I'm glad you're here. This way I can take my time, really enjoy our last moment together."

He was the waiter from the fundraiser, dressed in a black tux and still wearing the green dragon mask. This was the Butcher they'd been chasing and who'd been chasing her, the man who'd taken her best friend.

She pushed back the pain behind her eyes. "Where's Smokey Joe?" she demanded.

"Oh, he's close by. Very close."

"I want to see him. Now."

"You were always such a sucker for underdogs, weren't you? But then, you are one yourself. Especially now."

He knew her well, which meant he had the upper hand. But not for long. She had to find Smokey Joe or at least stay alive until Hayden found her. She was sure the dogged, passionate FBI agent she'd given her heart to would find her and Smokey.

"Where are we?" Kate shifted, getting her legs underneath her.

"My house."

"Where's that?" With her hands tied and her wet gown twisted about her legs, balance would be difficult, but she could do it. For Smokey. For Hayden.

"We're across the bay." His voice was familiar, his tone conversational. "How's your head, by the way?"

"How did we get here?"

"So full of questions. It's what got you in trouble in the first place." He held the knife to the candle, and it glinted. He put down the whetstone and capped the tiny bottle of oil that sat on the table. "But to answer your question, I knocked you out and dragged you to a boat, one with an electric motor. Convenient that the wind kicked up and sped us on our way across the bay."

"Who are you?"

"I'm glad you finally asked." He took off the mask and she gasped. It wasn't Robyn Banks's husband, Mike Muldoon. Staring at her was Dr. Daniel Gray, or at least some distorted version of him. He looked nothing like the kind-eyed man at the medical clinic who'd attended to little Pammy and Sergeant King.

"Some people call me the Butcher." The knife still in his hand, he stood and pushed in the kitchen chair. "Some people call me Dr. Gray, but you know who I really am. And that, Katrina Erickson, is going to cost you your life."

She had to keep him talking because Hayden was on his way. "I thought Robyn Banks said her husband was the Butcher."

"That woman isn't too smart, is she? Mike Muldoon is a lost cause, although I can see how she might suspect him. He really is obsessed with you, one of the most beautiful creatures ever to walk this earth." His gaze slid over her, and she shivered. "But I did find Muldoon useful tonight. Right now he's creating havoc at your grandparents' house, as is a blood-covered boy from the academy—havoc that has your orderly, methodical Hayden Reed and his team going absolutely, positively ballistic."

"How did you manage that?"

"A few phone calls and meticulous timing, and presto, mass chaos, and of course you had to do your part. Being the purveyor of justice that you are, the staunch voice of the underdogs and oppressed of this world, you couldn't help but come for Smokey Joe. On your own, no less. How convenient."

"Where's Smokey?"

"Just outside that back door, in a grave, but no worry, lovely Katrina, he's still alive, because I needed him alive until I got you."

"I'm here. Let him go."

"You are hardly in a position of power." He ran the length of the blade along his thumb.

"What's your real name?"

"Come now, Katrina, don't tell me you've already forgotten me."

"I don't even know you."

"Does the name Dustin Root ring a bell?"

She wracked her brain. Nothing.

"How about Robert McRay?"

She shook her head. Nothing familiar about that, either, but it was hard to focus on anything but that silvery knife drawing closer and sending her heart racing in a dizzy panic. But she had to stay calm. Like Hayden. Calm, analytical, thorough Hayden. "Refresh my memory, please."

"Robert McRay called you three years ago and left a message that he had a lead for one of your 'Justice for All' reports. You were in the middle of the Mike Muldoon story, so you called him back and left a message that you'd touch base with him soon."

She thought back to that time. She'd been working the Muldoon story for a solid month, and she'd been knee-deep in interviews with defrauded investors and the U.S. Attorney's office. She'd been hell-bent on getting Muldoon himself in front of the camera. It's possible she got a tip that she put on the back burner, one that…

"The pregnant woman," she said with a rush of recognition.

"Ahhh, so you do remember."

"I remember a man calling and leaving a message that a

doctor killed his pregnant wife and unborn child. I don't remember the details, but he was distraught."

"That would be Robert McRay. He was distraught, *very* distraught and very desperate." The Butcher stopped two feet in front of her, his knife now within striking distance.

She swallowed, forcing her heart to slow. "Tell me about the man. I want to hear his story. I want to hear *your* story."

"It's not a pretty one, not a fairy tale, but your life hasn't been much of a fairy tale either, has it, Katrina? We're alike in that respect, aren't we? Both victims of dragon mothers."

She nodded, anything to keep him talking, and that's when she heard something. The click of a door. The man didn't appear concerned. Was she imagining the sound? Had Hayden found her?

"What's your story?" she asked.

"Tough childhood. I had a whore for a mother who shared me with her customers, but I survived by pretending I was someone else somewhere else. Eventually I killed her and others like her, all worthless whores."

"And no one ever suspected you?"

He motioned at the mask on the floor. "Let's say I became very good at becoming other people and wearing disguises. The police never knew quite what they were chasing."

"You're not a real doctor."

"No. But Dr. Daniel Gray does exist, or he did. Unfortunate for him that he found me butchering a whore in the alley behind his pissant little clinic in Vegas. But fortuitous for me because I was able to become Dr. Gray, who was just about to move to the quiet little town of Dorado Bay and open a small medical clinic." He smiled. "You look doubtful. You've always been so expressive, Katrina, but yes, I impersonated a doctor, stitching up cuts, setting broken bones. It's amazing what you can learn from the Internet, but of course I sent all the serious cases to Reno."

"Until Robert McRay's pregnant wife."

"Yes, by the time the fool got her to me, she was in serious distress. I did my best, but it was too late to life-flight her to Reno. Robert McRay was devastated beyond reason, and he blamed it on me. He tried to rile the Dorado Bay police and state medical board, but they didn't bite. All bought into the masquerade."

"But McRay refused to give up," Kate said. "He called me to investigate you for one of my 'Justice for All' reports. I never got around to following up before Jason attacked me."

"Exactly, and we both know how good you are. Lucky for me, I got to him before you two officially touched base."

"You killed Robert McRay."

"He's in Mulveney's Cove." Dr. Gray/the Butcher/Dustin Root shook his head. "Funny thing, he hasn't popped up yet."

A creak and a shuffle sounded. She'd been so engrossed in this madman's story that she'd forgotten about hearing something. Hayden? She had to keep the Butcher talking. "So you talked Jason into killing me."

"It was pathetically easy. Jason was so easy to manipulate after your mother's death."

Kate sucked in a breath. "My mother died three years ago?"

"Yes, it appeared to be a heart attack." He winked at her. "But I'm not a doctor, so I'm not sure. Anyway, when I got to Jason's house, she was dead. And Jason was pretty far gone, too. From what I learned he kept his mother's body in the freezer for more than two years. Sick little boy. He wanted to keep her close, but when I started killing the broadcasters and using the exact same attack he'd made on you, he must have gotten scared and moved the body to the hunting cabin. Horrible, huh? He couldn't let go of the mother he loved."

Kate pictured the iced blood in the bottom of Jason's freezer. "And you used that love to get him to attack me."

"After I discovered that Robert McRay had contacted you about the death of his wife and child, I knew I had to get rid of you, but unlike the whores I'd killed before, you were well known. Your death would be front page news. I'm good, but I didn't want to take any chances of getting caught. So I told Jason *you* killed Kendra Erickson, that you'd come back to town to punish your mother for hurting you as a child. I even gave him the knife."

She had to keep him talking. "And the other broadcasters? Why kill them?"

"To get to you, of course. When you disappeared off the face of the earth, I harbored the hope that you'd died, but after I saw you in the surveillance video six months ago, I knew you still lived and had to die. Since you're such a big fan of justice, I knew killing innocent women would flush you out of your hidey-hole. Took me awhile, but eventually it did." He clapped his hands in front of his chest. "Yay, me."

Where was Hayden? He always wanted to go slow, to be absolutely certain. She needed him now.

She wet her lips. "But why make the Broadcaster Butcher attacks so similar to my brother's attack on me? Why the broken mirrors? Why the multiple stab wounds?"

"Initially to cover my tracks. Better to let the authorities chase Jason than hunt for me. But it gave me a little bonus because Agent Reed and his brilliant mind made the connection between the attacks and eventually led me to you, which was the intent from the beginning." He spun the knife in his hand. "But you've stalled long enough, Katrina. It's time to die."

She backed up into the cupboard doors and couldn't go any farther. She could dive at him, head-butt him as high as possible, and try to keep the knife away from vital organs.

At the same time he raised his knife, a shadow crossed the doorway and a wet, muddy shape appeared. Her chest almost exploded.

She wanted to yell, *Run! Fast and far!* But the old soldier wouldn't. He was ready for war.

"Five steps forward. Two to the right. Aim at two o'clock. Swing hard. He has a knife."

\* \* \*

*Friday, June 19, 10:40 p.m.*
*Dorado Bay, Nevada*

"How the fuck did he get away!" It wasn't a question. It was a roar torn from the volcano in Hayden's chest.

He stood in the grand foyer of the Conlans' lakeside mansion. An army of searchers, including his teammates, hunted for the Butcher and Kate, and all came up empty.

Evie rushed from the kitchen. "Just confirmed with the caterer, one of the waiters is missing. No one seemed to know his name or where he came from. He was the one wearing the green dragon mask."

A master of disguise. That's what Hayden was dealing with, and the dragon had Kate.

Frustration and anger and fear erupted. "So how the fuck did he get away, and where did he take her?"

"Calm down, Hayden," Parker said. "You're not thinking

clearly, and we need you to think. This is your case. You've lived it, breathed it. You know this man better than anyone."

Hayden closed his eyes, trying to clear away the raging red that blinded him, but he couldn't. All he saw was Kate and those green eyes that finally shined with hope.

"I know shit!" Hayden opened his eyes, only to find himself facing the mirror in the Conlan foyer. He balled his fist and slammed it into the image of his face, shattering the mirror.

He welcomed the slice of pain, the trickle of red. Better his hands than Kate's.

"Dammit, Hayden." Evie yanked a table runner off one of the foyer tables and wrapped it around his bleeding hand. "You're not going to do Kate any good acting like an idiot."

"Evie's right," Hatch added. "Focus on what you do, Professor. Look at your facts. Look at those pictures in your head."

His other hand fisted and he raised it.

Finn Brannigan grabbed that fist and got in Hayden's face. "Tell me she's dead, Hayden. Look me in the eye and tell me the Butcher got her. Tell me you see Kate's body still except for the blood pouring out of her." Finn grabbed him by the front of the shirt. "Tell me, dammit!"

The picture refused to come into focus. "No. She's not dead."

Parker lifted a single index finger, getting everyone's immediate attention. "Glad we got that settled. Mrs. Conlan, find someone to stitch up Agent Reed's hand. Hayden, let's review what you know."

Ava nodded, then stopped. "I'll find Dr. Gray. He's supposed to be here tonight."

Hayden kept his hand above his heart as he pushed back the emotion and tried to tap into his logical, analytical side.

It took six deep breaths to find it. "We found no signs of the Butcher or Kate by the boathouse, but that's no surprise, given the rain and the Butcher's propensity for leaving nothing behind. The officers posted on all the roads leading out of the Bayside Estates have seen no cars. The Butcher is physically weak, most likely with some kind of foot problem as evidenced by the orthotic shoes. He couldn't be far unless—"

"What?" Hatch asked.

"The lake. He escaped by boat."

"The storm has whipped the lake into a frenzy," Chief Greenfield said. "No sane person would try to run a boat on that."

"We aren't dealing with a sane person." As blood dripped from his hand, Hayden flipped through his mental notes on the Butcher. They were dealing with a man who found power in blood, who was a master of disguise. "His ability to disguise himself is his biggest strength. He was able to trick his way into each of his victim's homes."

*The Butcher got to me twice after the first attack!* Hayden's knees threatened to give way. The voices had been silent lately. And now he heard Kate's.

*He stood at my bedside. He came into the recovery room. He. Held. My. Hand.*

*The lead detective said there was no way any unauthorized personnel could have gotten in.*

Which meant the Butcher disguised himself as medical or law enforcement personnel.

He opened his mouth but stopped short when Lottie burst through the front door, wearing a pair of soggy white tennis shoes and a snarl on her lips.

"Okay Mr. FBI Hotshot," she said, pointing her finger at Hayden. "I need your hotshot take on something." She told them about the bogus orthotic shoe prescription for Louella Bollinger. "Who the hell faked the prescription?"

Ava Conlan ushered a paramedic into the room. "Hayden, this young man will look at your hand. I couldn't find Dr. Gray."

Hayden grew still as the paramedic unwrapped the table runner bandage and blood splattered to the floor.

Dr. Gray. The snapshots flashed through his head. The man who'd been limping after he'd been kicked by two-year-old Pammy. The man who quietly joined in the search for both Smokey and little Benny Hankins. The man who'd been Jason Erickson's doctor and wielded power over him.

Parker was right. He had all the information.

# CHAPTER TWENTY-EIGHT

*Friday, June 19, 10:45 p.m.*
*Dorado Bay, Nevada*

**N**ow he's three feet to your right, crouched low, knife in his left hand." Kate kept her voice calm as Smokey Joe and the man known as the Butcher circled each other in the kitchen lit only by candles.

She stood next to the cupboard, her damn hands still tied behind her. "Watch it, Smokey, he just stepped to the left. Knife at four o'clock."

"Sorry team we make, huh, Katy-lady?" Smokey Joe said with a smile that cracked the mud on his face.

Yeah, they were a team, and they could beat this guy. The key was getting the knife out of the Butcher's hand. If only Smokey could keep his attention while she slammed him from behind. Smokey Joe seemed to sense her plan. He jabbed a three-foot stick at the Butcher. "Come on, Butcher Boy, try and take me now, you who can only take on sleeping old men, little boys, and women."

The Butcher stilled, his face growing red. Kate could see the fire swirling behind his eyes. Like a dragon. The dragon was completely focused on Smokey's taunting words, on the little jabs of Smokey's stick.

Kate sprung from the cupboard and lunged for the Butcher. He stepped aside, and she flew across the room, hitting the floor with a thud. Her teeth sunk into her tongue, and blood spurted out her mouth.

"Kate!" Smokey cried out.

She spat out the blood and turned, expecting to see the Butcher's knife hovering above her. But to her horror, it wasn't. The sickle of silver was aimed at the blind man.

"Duck right. Roll!" Too late.

The Butcher's knife slashed into Smokey Joe's chest.

"Noooo!" she screamed as blood soaked through Smokey's muddy shirt. She struggled to her feet. "Smokey!"

He didn't answer.

Everything had stopped. The storm outside. The humming refrigerator. Her heart. Even the Butcher stood eerily still, fixated on the bloody knife. Again she realized how mesmerizing he found blood.

*Run!* She could make it down the hall. She could flee into the night. They were on the lake. The part where the houses were few and far between. She could get to the road. Find a car. At the very least she could hide in the darkness.

But was Smokey really dead? His eyes were closed, his chest painfully still. No. He couldn't be dead. He was a survivor, like her.

Rage built inside, a monstrous, ugly rage. Her hands still bound behind her back, she rushed again at the man called the Butcher and screamed, "You're not going to beat us!"

\* \* \*

*Friday, June 19, 10:55 p.m.*
*Dorado Bay, Nevada*

Even before Evie stopped the car, Hayden hopped out and tore up the front steps of Dr. Daniel Gray's secluded lakeside home.

"Kate!" Hayden cried as he bolted into the dark house.

"Here! In the kitchen."

With hands and heart leading the way, he stumbled through the dark toward Kate's voice. "I'm coming." At last he saw a faint flickering light. He skidded to a stop in a large kitchen lit by candles, and he saw red. Everywhere. On Kate's hands, on Smokey's chest, and on the knife sitting on the floor.

Kate, who with bound hands was pressing a dishtowel against Smokey's chest, said, "He heard you pull up and just left through the kitchen door."

Hayden headed for her, but she waved him off with a growl. "I'm taking care of Smokey. You go get the Butcher."

He couldn't see past her red hands.

"Dammit, Hayden, I have everything under control. Run!"

He took off through the kitchen door into the rain. He still couldn't see five feet in front of him.

*Use your head.* Parker's voice.

He needed to think this through. This is what he did. Dispassionate evaluation. With Kate safe inside he could stop thinking with his heart and start using his head.

Slick pine needles covered the area. Dr. Daniel Gray walked with a limp, and he could never get far in this terrain on a night like this. The man needed a car, but Hayden's rental was blocking the garage. Or a boat.

The wind howled and waves pounded the shore as Hayden ran toward the lake. Not only could he not see a thing, he couldn't hear anything, either.

But he *felt* something. His gut—Parker talked often of leading with the gut, but up until now, Hayden didn't understand it—told him to keep running toward the lake.

Like a blind and deaf man, Hayden stumbled through the storm, and when he reached the water's edge, a flash of lightning in the black liquid night revealed a small boat fifty feet off shore. It struggled against the waves and wind.

Hayden kicked off his shoes, threw off his jacket, and dove into the icy water. But unlike the boat that struggled on the top of the water, he stayed under, kicking and surfacing only to grab occasional breaths. Below water he controlled his breathing, his strokes, and his kicks. He was an underwater missile.

When he neared the boat, he silently broke the surface. Gray sat at the stern, fighting to keep the craft heading straight into the rolling, angry waves. Hayden placed his shoulder near the bow of the boat and kicked. The boat swerved, and instead of cutting perpendicular into an oncoming wave, it ran parallel. A wall of water crashed down on Gray.

Hayden's hands clawed around the boat's ledge, and he pulled himself halfway out of the water. The boat tipped, and he heaved himself into the hull.

Gray crawled around the bottom of the boat and grabbed an oar. He tried to lift it, but another wave pummeled the small vessel, and he lost his balance. Hayden lunged for him. They crashed into the bottom of the boat. Hayden's hands circled the man's throat.

Gray opened his mouth but couldn't cry out.

The volcano in Hayden bubbled and shot fire. It overflowed and burned. Never before had he wanted to kill, but God help him, he wanted to now. He tightened his fingers around the man's neck. For little Benny Hankins, for the seven broadcasters, for Robyn Banks, for Kate's brother, for Hope Academy's Kyl Watson, and for Smokey Joe. But most of all for Kate.

The pathetic excuse for a man shook and mewed like a newborn kitten. He had no knife, and from the look in his eyes, no hope. Death right now would release him from the reckoning that awaited him, for justice would be swift and brutal.

Hayden pulled in a breath, the oxygen cooling, not fanning the fire.

"Okay, you fucked-up son of a bitch." And this one was for Lottie. "I'm taking you in because I want you to meet someone who's going to nail your ass to the splintered seat of a cold dark cell where you'll never see the light of day."

Warm liquid washed over Hayden's foot, and he smelled urine. The Butcher's chest heaved in sobs.

Hayden, with the pathetic heap of the man he knew as Dr. Daniel Gray at his feet, got the boat back to the shore, where Hatch, Evie, Finn, and Jon MacGregor waited for him along with Chief Greenfield and a dozen of his men. And Lottie.

"You got our man, Pretty Boy," Lottie said as Chief Greenfield shut the door on the police cruiser holding the man known as the Broadcaster Butcher.

"*We* got our man," he corrected her. It had been a team effort, and no small part of that had been Kate. "Where is she?"

"Kate's fine," Lottie said. "Not even a scratch. She went to the hospital with Smokey, who's headed for surgery. The Butcher gave him a nasty chest wound, but it missed all the major organs. Robyn Banks is also alive and in surgery."

Kate was safe. Smokey, too. That's all he needed to know.

The rain and wind continued to wreak havoc on the night as they got into his rental car and drove to the Dorado Bay police station. Maeve, who was on her way to the hospital in Reno, stopped by with a dry suit and a hug. He took a shower in the station's locker room and put on his clean suit but no shoes, which he must have lost somewhere near the lake.

With bare feet, he took care of all the paperwork that was needed to put evil like the Butcher in jail. Chief Greenfield confirmed they'd found a surveillance system trained on locations connected with Katrina Erickson, and in a small freezer in the basement of Gray's lakeside home, they'd found two small containers of blood, already typed and confirmed matches to that of Shayna Thomas and the broadcaster in Oakland.

Dorado Bay police found Kyl Watson's body in the loft of the Hope Academy barn, his head nearly severed from his neck. Dr. Trowbridge, with counsel present, admitted that Eddie Williams did die at the academy during one of their extreme physical conditioning exercises, and he and director Kyl Watson mutually decided to hide the body, as they knew their work would be shut down if the death became known.

After six hours, Lottie thwacked Hayden on the shoulder. "Ain't no more *i*'s to be dotted or *t*'s to be crossed. Time to call it quits, Pretty Boy. We both need a bit of beauty sleep."

"Yeah." Sleep, with Kate in his arms. He closed his laptop.

"I'm gonna find me a motel for the night, but I'll check in with you before I go. You make sure you tell Kate and Maeve goodbye for me."

"I will." They'd reached the door to the station. Sometime during their paperwork marathon, the storm had passed. The early morning air, still dark, was cool and damp, fresh and clean. He helped her into the car and shut the driver's side door, but he didn't walk away when she started the engine. "Oatmeal raisin cookies," he said.

"Huh?"

"You, Lottie, are like oatmeal raisin cookies, soft and sweet, but with a spicy kick."

Lottie's deep laugh rumbled as she pulled away.

Hayden got into his rental car and picked up his phone. Chief Greenfield had told him earlier Smokey came through the surgery and was feeling good enough to pick a groggy fight with the chief nurse. Kate had been there with the old man the whole time.

It was *his* time now. He picked up his phone.

Maeve answered, but her voice sounded worried.

"What's wrong?" Hayden asked. "Is it Smokey? Are there post-op complications?"

"It's Kate. She left."

"Left?"

"A few hours ago, right after the doctors upgraded Smokey's condition to good."

"Where did she go?"

"I...I don't know. I didn't get a chance to ask her. She just disappeared. She didn't even say goodbye to Smokey."

She had run away. Again.

His head slumped forward and rested on the steering wheel. Kate was the first to admit there was something more between them. He knew that now. He needed to tell her that he loved her and that he wanted her in his life. He wasn't good at letting people in, but he'd find a way.

The tires squealed as he backed out of the parking lot and cut across the median. He had no plan, no logical thought processes, just the fiery need to find Kate. At the yellow cottage, he tore through every room. She was gone. Packed up.

*She left you.* The voice was a small snicker.

*No, she wouldn't leave you. She loves you.*

He chose to listen to the second voice. Back in his car, he started to hunt once again for Kate Johnson.

\* \* \*

*Saturday, June 20, 5 a.m.*
*Dorado Bay, Nevada*

The cry was low and tortured. It came from the porch that wrapped around Kate's childhood home.

"Where are you?" Kate knelt in the mud, a flashlight in her hand as she squinted into the darkness under the porch. Night still hadn't given way to dawn, but a soft glow hovered on the horizon.

Another cry sounded, and she aimed her flashlight to the right, and there, staring at her with wide eyes and a battered right ear, was her cat.

"Ellie," she said with equal parts irritation and affection, "I've been looking for you for hours."

The cat blinked.

"Come on, girl," she said in a softer tone. Poor thing. She'd been left on her own at the lake cottage, and when no one showed, the cat must have run to the one place where she felt safe. "Come here, Ellie, I'll take you home. Get us both cleaned up." The cat just sat there.

Home? Was that her condo? Smokey Joe's cabin? She didn't know where that was anymore, but she knew she needed to get off her bike and rest for a while. Somewhere. But not alone.

She had . . . a cat.

She laughed out loud. She had a cat.

She had Smokey Joe, who was on the mend in a Reno hospital. She had her freedom, because Hayden had hauled the Butcher off to a cage.

And Hayden. She had Hayden.

But the poor man didn't realize it yet. The man wasn't good at feelings, but she was. She loved Hayden Reed, and she'd fight to get him.

"Come on, Ellie, I'm cold and hungry and tired, and we need to find Hayden before he takes off."

Ellie let loose another strangled cry, inched out of her muddy crawl space, and gave Kate a hiss. Kate laughed and scooped her into her arms. "Okay, you're tired, too. Let's get out of here."

They got as far as the driveway when a car pulled up.

Hayden got out, and a surge of warmth flowed through her entire body. He looked perfect, in command, as if he hadn't battled a madman last night. Hayden wore one of his exquisite suits. Every hair on his head was in place. Today's tie was red with black swirls. But no shoes. She laughed.

His steps weren't sure or purposeful. And his eyes—so many questions seemed to swim in those gray depths. "I thought you ran away."

She shook her head and tried to smile. "I can't run anymore. I have a cat." *But do I have you?* It was on the tip of her tongue. But for once, she held back her words.

*Go slow. Be patient.* She'd learned much from the man she loved.

He didn't say it. Instead he held out his arms to her, and she didn't hesitate. She threw herself at his chest. His arms clamped around her, their bodies pressing together in a moment that she wanted to last forever.

Ellie, trapped between them, screeched.

Hayden drew back his chest but lowered his mouth to

hers. The kiss heated her chest and fogged her brain. He pulled her closer, tighter. It stirred up frothy desire low in her belly and sent a throaty sigh over her lips. So thorough. That kiss was so obscenely thorough. And right. Never before had anything felt so right.

When he finally pulled himself from her, Hayden cupped her cheeks with his hands, forcing his gaze on her. "I'm pretty screwed up. You realize that, right?"

"Me too," she said.

"I'm obsessive about my work."

"Me too. It's what started this whole thing."

"And the touchy-feely stuff," he slid a hand along his tie and shook his head, "it's tough for me."

"I can help."

Any steel left in his gray eyes fled, and he lowered his head.

Ellie hissed.

A soft laugh fell from his lips. "And just so you know, I'm not a cat person. Or a dog person. I'm too busy with work."

"I'm sure Ellie's willing to work with you on that one." Kate held out the cat to him. Ellie hissed and jumped to the ground, her crooked tail high in the air.

"She might need some convincing," Hayden said.

"I'm all over that, too." Hand in hand, they walked to the car. When Hayden opened her door, Ellie jumped into the backseat. "Where are we going?" she asked.

Hayden slid into the driver's seat, and a frown settled on his lips, quickly replaced by a half smile. "I'm not sure."

# EPILOGUE

*Tuesday, June 30, 7:48 a.m.*
*Mancos, Colorado*

Kate set a steaming mug of coffee on Smokey's placemat in the number three spot, right where he liked it. She placed a plate of cinnamon toast with a fat pat of butter in the center. "Come back to Reno with us."

"Why the he-ell would I do that?" Smokey grabbed his steamy coffee and took a long swig. It had been almost two weeks since the surgery to repair the stab wound that had nicked his left lung, and he was getting back to his cantankerous old self. Two days ago, the aide he'd hired gave his notice after Smokey Joe "accidentally" wiped the man's personal computer. Of course this was after the aide refused to learn how to use the bread machine.

"We want you to live with us," Kate continued, "because we love your genteel manner and sweet nature."

Smokey snorted a laugh and set down his cup. He seemed to stare at the steam as if reading a message from a smoke signal. At last he turned his sightless eyes to her. "You and

G-man got a good thing going, and good things, Katy-lady, with a little work turn into great things. You don't need me to complicate things."

These past two weeks with Hayden hadn't been easy. Fiercely independent, they were still learning how to be a couple, but Hayden had moved to Reno.

"Except for Maeve, Tucson is just a place to store my suits," he'd said. "I'm rarely home."

True. Last week, Hayden had been called in to profile an individual believed to be running a sex slave ring in San Francisco, and before that he had been in Washington, DC, profiling the sender of a series of ricin-laced letters sent through the U.S. Postal Service. But to her surprise, he'd called daily. And on the day she'd interviewed for a position to work as the media relations liaison for a Reno-area non-profit, he had commandeered Parker's jet and its captain, and flew home for a celebratory dinner.

"Celebratory?" she'd asked as she grilled two T-bones that night while he poured champagne. "Isn't that a bit premature?"

"You'll get the job," he said with a smile. Agent Know-It-All had been right. After a delicious dinner then dessert in bed, he hopped on the jet back to DC. The next day the recruiter called and offered her the job. Today, she finally found the nerve to say yes. And tomorrow, she and Hayden would start house hunting in Reno.

"You're right. Hayden and I have a long way to go before we get to the doorstep of Happily Ever After, so why not go to Tucson? Maeve said she wouldn't mind putting up with you a while longer. Go, just for a few weeks. She needs the company."

"That bossy thing?" Smokey picked up his toast and aimed the point at her. "I don't need people telling me what to do, including you." Smokey didn't want to be a burden to anyone, but he couldn't live alone.

The old soldier had dug his way out of an underground prison and helped Hayden catch Dustin Root, aka the Butcher. He was healthy, and yesterday, before the aide left, he told her Smokey Joe hadn't had a single nightmare. Maybe because the old solider had completed the mission. She wrapped her hands around her coffee but didn't drink. Smokey Joe had been her hero. He had saved her in more ways than one.

"But I need you," she said. Just like she needed Hayden. "Who's going to help with the jewelry store? You expect me to work two jobs while you sit around and play dominoes?"

"Stop your yammering, Kate. That new aide I hired will be here any minute, and I need to find that damned bread machine book." He hopped up from the chair and started rooting around one of the kitchen drawers. "Now git outside and check on G-man. He should have the shed doors fixed by now. Also have him take a look at the bottom step on the porch. I damn near broke my leg on it the other day."

Outside Kate found Hayden wearing a tool belt and using a screwdriver to test the hinges on Smokey's newly installed shed doors. He pressed the two doors together, and they clicked into place.

"A perfect fit," she said.

He turned with a smile. "Well?"

"I couldn't close the deal," she sat on the bottom step, which was indeed loose. "I'm afraid all you get is me and the cat."

Hayden tucked the screwdriver into the tool belt and joined her on the bottom step. "All I need is you."

"But I'm going to keep trying. Eventually, he'll admit that he can't keep chasing off aides, and he can't live alone."

"Is that hope I hear?" Hayden asked with a grin.

"Probably."

*Escape is impossible.*

*Please see the next page for a preview of THE BURIED by Shelley Coriell.*

# CHAPTER ONE

Momma was wrong.

Good things didn't happen to good girls.

Tears seeped from Lia Grant's eyes, and she inched a bloodied hand to her cheek and brushed away the dampness. She couldn't see the tears. Or the blood.

Too dark.

But she felt the slickness running down her palms and wrists, the slivers of wood biting into the fleshy nubs of what was left of her fingers, and the heaviness pressing down on her chest, flattening her lungs.

Yes, Momma was wrong. Bad things happened to good girls.

A scream coiled in the pit of her stomach and clawed up her throat, but by the time it poured over her lips, the cry was little more than a strangled gasp. She had so little left. Little fight. Little air. Little hope that God would protect good girls who did good things.

She always tried to be a good girl, just like Momma

wanted. Church every Sunday. Straight A's in her first year of nursing studies. A job as a volunteer greeter at the Cypress Bend Medical Center. But that was so far away from the dark, cold place where she now lay.

In a box.

Underground.

Somewhere on the bayou.

She breathed in the rot of the swamp, a steamy mixture of death and decay. In the world above, kites and warblers cried and gators splashed. A chunk of earth fell onto the top of the wooden box that encased her trembling body.

"Let me out! Please let me out!" She beat her fists against the rough-hewn lid of her tomb.

The thud of damp earth momentarily stopped. "I'm afraid that would be against the rules," a faraway voice said.

*Rules?* There were rules that governed bad people doing bad things?

Lia clawed and kicked. Screamed and swore. Eventually she cried. Then prayed. She prayed for help, prayed for air, and when she realized the bad would win, prayed that after death she'd be in a good place for good girls.

She didn't know how long she'd been in the wooden box, but she knew it would be over soon. She inched her arms above her head, trying to ease the ache in her lungs, and when she did, something clattered, like bones rattling in a coffin. Was it a hand? A foot? An elbow?

Dear God, she was falling apart.

Her fingers slid over something cold and hard, small and square. Not a bone. More like a deck of playing cards. Did the devil who'd buried her alive want her to amuse herself as she suffocated?

Her fingers, sticky with blood, slid over the small box. No, not playing cards. A phone. A whisper of breath caught in her throat. Had her captor dropped a phone? Would a phone work underground? Her trembling fingers fumbled with the power button. A joyful cry tumbled over her lips. Light, glorious light, glowed on the face.

"Momma, oh, Momma, I'm here. Your good girl's here." Lia Grant reached up from her cold, dark grave and with bloodied fingertips punched in Momma's phone number.

* * *

Grace: 345. Bad guys: 0.

Grace Courtemanche always kept score. A relatively easy task at this point in her career.

"Hey, counselor, one more picture." A photographer from the Associated Press motioned to her as she stepped away from the microphone centered on the steps of the county courthouse.

Grace turned to the photographer and smiled. Lips together. Chin forward. Left eyebrow arched. Her colleagues called it her news-at-eleven smile, and tonight it would be splashed across televisions and newspapers throughout the Florida Panhandle, right next to the stunned mug of Larry Morehouse. Morehouse, the former commander-in-chief of the state's largest ring of prostitution houses masquerading as strip clubs, had just been slammed with a few not-so-minor convictions: conspiracy to engage in prostitution, coercion, money laundering, racketeering, and tax evasion. As lead prosecutor, Grace had dealt the blows, swift and hard, and she'd loved every minute of the fight.

Her step light, she made her way through the buzzing crowd to the offices that housed the team of prosecutors from Florida's Second Judicial Circuit. She pushed the elevator button that would take her to her third-floor, garden-view office and to Helena Ring. Ring was the twenty-four-year-old meth user who gave birth to a son in a roadside rest stop off Highway 319 and tossed the newborn in an underground toilet to die amid human waste. *Florida vs. Morehouse* was over, and she couldn't wait to dig into *Florida vs. Ring*.

As she waited for the elevator, the phone at her waist buzzed. Call display showed *Restricted Number*. She jabbed her finger at the keypad and banished the call to voicemail where it would be saved so she could forward it—and the six others—to the sheriff's department. The calls had started months ago when the Morehouse camp had approached with her a bribe, suggesting they all shoot for a deal down. She laughed then and now.

With the elevator once again stuck on the second floor, she spun on her gray slingbacks and took the stairs. Inside her office she reached for the light switch but stilled when a man sitting in silhouette on the windowsill bent in a sweeping bow.

"I shall buy you furs and diamonds and place chocolate bonbons at your feet," her boss, Travis Theobold, said.

She switched on the light and slipped out of her jacket. "I'm sure your *wife* will take issue with that."

"Nah. She knows you too well." His eyes were bright, his grin boy-next-door appealing. A deceptively young-looking man with a mop of carrot-colored hair, her boss served as the state attorney for Florida's Second Circuit. He had an ease with people that she had never quite mastered, not that she needed it. There were people-pleasing politicians like Travis, and there were people like her, people who didn't care about getting votes, just getting bad guys what they deserved.

"Damn, Grace, you buried that son of a bitch and made us look brilliant."

Some called her a justice-seeking missile. Those with

less tact called her the Blond Bulldozer. In her youth her father had simply called her a winner. For the briefest of moments, she raised her gaze heavenward and allowed the corners of her mouth to tilt in a grin that wasn't practiced, a little girl smile that came from a heart some defense attorneys claimed she didn't have.

*See that, Daddy, I won.*

"Why don't you knock off for the day? Come to Jeb's and celebrate?" Travis asked.

She placed her jacket on the back of her chair and fired up her computer, concentrating on the soothing hum. "Can't. Helena Ring needs my immediate attention."

She reached for her computer mouse. Travis cupped his hand over hers. "I've taken you off the Ring case. She tried to shake off his hand, but his fingers tightened. "It's about the bribe."

"You mean the one Morehouse's people offered and I didn't take?"

"We received detailed information on a bank account in Nevis in your name. It includes two six-figure transfers from one of Morehouse's companies."

In her dreams. Until payday she had a whopping fifty-six dollars in her bank account. "This is clearly a twisted case of identity theft."

"I agree, and when we're done investigating, I hope to rack up a few more counts against the Morehouse camp, but for now, I need you on *vacation*." He held out his hand. "Keys please."

"You're serious?"

He waggled his fingers.

A cold tightness stole across her chest. Ten years ago when her personal life had taken a beating, this job had been her refuge, a safe place to land.

"Work with me on this," Travis said with a cajoling smile. "Take a few days' vacation."

Her computer stared up at her with its giant, unblinking black eye. In the ten years she'd worked at the SA's office, she hadn't taken a single vacation day. "Exactly what do people *do* on vacation?"

Travis laughed. "Doesn't construction on Graceland begin soon?"

*Graceland.* She hadn't heard that one, but she liked the sound. Grand and stately. There'd been plenty of talk in Cypress Bend about her new home project, a two-story Greek revival slated for construction on the old Giroux place, twenty prize acres of land on the Cypress Bend River near Apalachicola Bay. Grace had been a player in a bidding war for the plumb parcel, and she'd won.

*Another win, Daddy. See it?*

Travis had a point. It might be good to be home for a few days to oversee construction. "Earth movers start clearing tomorrow morning," she said.

"So go home, drink champagne, and celebrate that you, dear Grace, are living the dream, that you are one of the privileged souls who get everything you ever go after."

For the briefest of moments a face with eyes the color of a summer sky flashed into her head. No, not everything. She flattened her hands on her desk, but before she could say anything, her phone vibrated again. With a frown she sent the call from the restricted number to voicemail.

"Another crank?" Travis asked.

"Seven calls this afternoon from the same restricted number."

"And you'll report this to the sheriff?"

"Of course." She was independent, not stupid.

"Seriously, Grace, be careful out there. Your new place is

remote, and with Morehouse in jail, his people are riled. As someone counting on your continued brilliance to boost my career, I need you safe." Travis hopped off the windowsill and slung his jacket over his shoulder. "Keep me and the sheriff's office posted, and even though you'll be on vacation, I'm expecting you at the oyster roast on Saturday. Amanda would tie me up and roast *me* over the coals if you didn't show."

"I'll be there." She was a member of the SA team, and this was the annual get-together where all were expected to attend, and she was certainly good about living up to expectations.

"With or without a guest?" A grin slid across Travis's lower jaw.

Like he didn't know. "Just me."

Travis chuckled. "You're being forewarned. Amanda will be in game mode. Finding Grace a man is one of her favorite games."

"I don't need a man."

"Of course you don't need anyone, but my lovely wife thinks you need a bit of light and color in your drab gray life." With a widening grin, her boss flicked off the light. "Now get out of here and start vacationing."

Her boss's footsteps fading, she reached for her mouse. If she was going on vacation, she'd take a few files on baby-killer Helena Ring with her to tackle during down time. She keyed in her log-in information and clicked enter.

*Denied.*

She rekeyed the information.

*Denied.*

She laughed. After ten years, her boss knew her well. "Okay," she told the doorway where her boss's footsteps faded. "I'm going on *vacation*."

Grace grabbed her jacket, her fingers digging into the gunmetal gray fabric. This morning when she picked it out, she thought the shiny gray contrasted nicely with her charcoal-colored silk tank and pearls, but in the faded afternoon sunlight seeping through the window blinds, it looked flat. For a moment she stood motionless, surrounded by a veil of gray. Was her life a drab, monochromatic gray?

She gave her head a shake. Far from it. She pictured her new land, lush and green, and of course there was Allegheny Blue. A growl rumbled in her throat. Who could forget her new roommate?

As she headed for her door, her unknown caller buzzed again. Cranks thrived on reaction, but she might as well see what information she could get for the sheriff's office. "Hello."

A pause stretched along the line followed by a sharp intake of breath, almost a gasp. She was about to cut off the crank call when a voice said, "G…g…grace…is… is…that y…y…you?" The voice was soft and female, low and raspy.

"This is Grace Courtemanche."

A muffled sob answered her.

"Who is this?" Grace demanded.

"I…I've been trying to reach you, b…b…but no one answered. Got your voicemail. Over and over. Why didn't you p…p…pick up the first time? Why?"

"Who is this?"

A wheeze rattled, followed by another sob. "L…Lia Grant."

"Listen Lia Grant or whoever you are, I—"

"It's cold. And dark. I can't breathe. Help me, Grace. Help meeeee!" Hollow rattling sounded, like stones rolling about a wooden box.

Grace's irritation gave way to anger. "I don't know who you are or what you want—"

"Help. I want help. I'm in a b...b...box. Underground." What kind of sick joke were Morehouse's minions playing now? The voice softened to a whisper. "Help me, Grace. Please...help me..."

The breathy words rushed through Grace, cold and dark, an icy shade of black. Maybe this wasn't the Morehouse camp orchestrating another crank call meant to unnerve her. Maybe this was a woman in serious trouble. The cold puddled in her feet, freezing her in place.

The caller coughed then let out a labored sigh. "Tell Momma I...I tried to be a g...g...good girl. I tried..." Seconds ticked.

"Lia?" Grace asked.

No words, just a faint, whisper of breath.

"Lia!"

No one answered.

Grace slid a finger along the scattered pearl necklace circling her throat. She didn't know Lia Grant, had never heard of Lia Grant, and there was absolutely no reason for Lia Grant to call her if she were in any kind of trouble.

*Help meeeee!*

The call ended, cutting off the faint breathing, and her cell phone face went dark.

In Grace's ten years with the State Attorney's office, she'd heard fear and terror in the voices of victims who'd been violated and in the whispered truths of the witnesses who'd come face-to-face with evil. And there was something about that voice, something grave and desperate and to her horror, real.

Her fingers quaking in an uncharacteristic tremor, Grace dialed the sheriff's office.

# CHAPTER TWO

*Gulf of Mexico, Off Florida Coast*

Hatch Hatcher adjusted the jib, propped his bare feet on a five-gallon bait bucket, and tilted his face toward the sun-soaked sky. He had steady winds, low chop. Should be straight-line sailing. At this rate, he'd arrive in New Orleans with time on his hands.

He ran a hand through his hair. Too long. He should probably get a trim before his presentation in the Big Easy. He was giving a talk to regional law enforcers on crisis negotiations and would be representing Parker and the team. He reached into the cooler at his side and pulled out an icy longneck.

Or maybe he'd skip the haircut and visit old friends. Natalia lived in New Orleans. Clara, too. Yeah, Clara, a woman who loved to laugh...on the beach, on the dance floor, in his bed. He loved to hear a woman laugh. He loved everything about women, the sounds, the smells, the taste. He uncapped the beer. His was a good life. A job he loved, beautiful women in every port, and plenty of free time to travel the world on a boat called *No Regrets*.

He raised his longneck, toasting the sun and sea, when his satellite phone rang. Caller ID showed a number from Cypress Bend. The bottle froze midway to his mouth. He knew one person in Cypress Bend, but she wanted nothing to do with him. She'd made that clear ten years ago when she'd sent him sailing from Apalachicola Bay. His fingers tightened around the beer bottle, the veins in his forearm thickening and rising.

Nope. Not going there.

He pushed away the past. Gathered in the peace.

Always peace.

Whoever was calling from Cypress Bend was not Grace Courtemanche, and whoever it was could wait. He took a long draw of the icy brew. Mackerels would be biting at sunset, and a slab of butter and frying pan waited in the galley below. As he reached for his fishing pole, the call went to voicemail, and he noticed the blinking light on the phone, indicating other messages, including one from the Box, headquarters for the FBI's Special Criminal Investigative Unit. His team. That call he couldn't ignore.

"Hey, Sugar and Spice, miss me?" Hatch said when his teammate Evie Jimenez answered the phone. Evie was the SCIU's bomb and weapons specialist, and he loved getting her fired up.

"I refuse to feed your gargantuan, testosterone-fueled ego," Evie said. "You may have every woman east of the Mississippi charmed by that syrupy drawl, but not me, *amigo*. Speaking of feeding your ego, we got a call from Atlanta PD. The kid you talked into giving up his boom box at the high school got a seriously mentally ill designation. He's in a treatment center and getting his life back together. One of the Atlanta news stations also called. They want to do a feature on you."

"Tell 'em I'm on assignment." Hatch's role as a crisis ne-gotiator was simple. Get in. Defuse. Get out. He didn't need media attention that often came with his line of work. "Park around?"

"Yep, but he's in the communications room with some techie. Computer crashed again."

Hatch grinned as he took another swig from his beer. The Box was a huge glass, chrome, and concrete structure on the rocky cliffs of Northern Maine, and while the SCIU's official headquarters looked like a high-tech, ultra-modern marvel, it had a notoriously cranky computer system.

"I'm returning his call," he said. "You know what he wanted?" Evie paused, which sent warning sirens blaring through his head. His hot-blooded Latina teammate rushed into life like a firestorm. Evie never paused for anything. "Okay, Sugar and Spice, what's up?"

Another beat of silence. "Have you checked your e-mail?"

"Not today." Honestly, not for a few days. His work often featured long, intense moments of negotiation with men and women in the throes of crisis, insanity, rage, or a soul-sucking combination of all three. So when time allowed, and, hell, even when it didn't, Hatch set sail, which is why he ended up with Parker Lord's team. His boss understood his need to disconnect and recharge. He'd just spent the past week anchored near the sugary sand dunes of Islamorada in the Florida Keys hunting for buried treasure and fishing for mahi.

"Then you haven't heard about Alex?" Evie continued.

"Alex?"

"Alex Milanos." The quiet stretched on. "Your son."

A burst of laughter shot over his lips. "Good joke." He was careful about these things, and he had been since the age of fourteen when he'd discovered the gift of a woman's body. He had no desire to be tied down by anything or anyone. He simply didn't do long-term commitments, and his disastrous relationship with his old man had cured him of any parental longings.

"This isn't a joke, Hatch. A woman from Cypress Bend contacted the Box and insisted on talking to you. Parker finally took her call. Her name is Trina Milanos, and she claims her daughter, Vanessa, knew you, as in the biblical sense, and that Vanessa's thirteen-year-old son is yours."

Hatch studied an icy bead on his longneck as if it were a tiny crystal ball. Vanessa Milanos? He couldn't picture a face. The name didn't ring a bell either, and he certainly didn't associate it with Cypress Bend.

Cypress Bend was Princess Grace's kingdom.

Grace Courtemanche was royalty, and he told her that every night as they lay intertwined on the deck of *No Regrets*, drenched in sweat and moonlight, too impatient to make it to the berth below.

But this call from Cypress Bend had nothing to do with Grace Courtemanche. Some other woman was setting forth the claim that he had a thirteen-year-old son. He did the math. The timing could work. In his college days, he spent a number of summers on St. George Island, one of the barrier islands below the Florida Panhandle. He taught sailing to kids at a posh summer camp, and before the summer of Princess Grace, he had a string of women on his boat and in his bed. But he was careful about these things. He didn't do children. Hell, ten days out of the month he didn't do responsibility.

"With the risk of being blunt, I don't leave bits and pieces of me around," he told Evie.

"That's part of the problem. It sounds like Vanessa

Milanos wanted a piece of you, any piece, and she admitted to her mother that since she couldn't have you, she'd settle for a part of you. She sabotaged your efforts at protection. Take a look at the picture in the e-mail. Kid's your spitting image. Same shaggy blond hair. Same baby blues. Same killer dimples. Plus Parker, being Parker, had a rush DNA test done." Evie paused. "It's a match, *padre*. He's your son."

*Your son.*

Hatch's throat constricted, and he stretched his neck, trying to ease the way for words. As a crisis negotiator, words were his tools, his constant companions, always at the ready.

"Hatch, you still there?" Evie asked.

He forced the rest of his beer down the tight, dry column of his throat.

"There's more, Hatch," Evie added. "The granny needs you in Cypress Bend *pronto*. It appears your son has gotten himself into serious trouble. He's in jail."

\* \* \*

Grace needed a bomb. Nothing fancy. Nothing complicated. Just something with the ability to blow up the attitudinal Ford compact she now called her own.

"'Nother dead battery, Miss Courtemanche?" The security guard that prowled the government buildings clucked his tongue as he walked up beside her.

"This month it's the starter."

"Man, you didn't have problems like this when you owned that fine Mercedes. Now there was a car."

Grace didn't want to think about her Mercedes, a late-model, high-powered, *mechanically sound* silver coup. She'd sold it earlier in the year along with her luxury condo and her parent's estate, all so she could afford the Giroux place.

No. It was the Courtemanche place now. *Her* place.

"You need some help, counselor?" the security guard asked.

*Help meeeee!*

Grace shook off the voice. After four months with her persnickety compact, she'd become a master of cheap DIY car repair. "I'll take care of it, Armand, but thank you."

She took the hammer from her glove box and banged on the starter. After a half dozen tries, her car turned over, and she puttered out of the parking garage, all the while the voice echoing through her head.

*Help meeeee!*

"I did," she said as she pulled onto the highway. She'd given details of all nine calls from "Lia Grant" to Deputy Will Fillingham, stressing that the girl genuinely sounded distressed. Then she'd checked her personal and work contact lists but didn't find any Grants. She didn't have a call-back number. What else could she do?

Five miles outside of Cypress Bend and with Lia Grant's voice still echoing through her head, Grace turned her car onto the rutted road that wound into the swamp and led to a one-bedroom shack with a sagging front porch and rusted metal roof. Feathery cypress branches filtered the retreating sun, but even the seductive cover of lacy shade couldn't soften the wretchedness of her new home.

She made her way up the rickety porch steps and tripped over a knobby column of white. Another bone, this one a grisly joint speckled with bits of dried flesh.

"Dammit, Allegheny Blue, how many of these things do you have?" An ancient blue tick hound sprawled in front of the door opened a cloudy eye. Upon seeing her, he heaved himself up, plunked across the porch, and rested his head against her leg. Drool dribbled onto her foot. She nudged him away with her knee. "Don't even pretend we're friends."

With the tips of her index finger and thumb, she picked up the bone and tossed it into a trashcan on the porch. It clunked and rattled among the dozen already there. She slammed on the lid and turned to the dog. "No more bones." The dog licked his lips, sending a line of drool whipping across her legs. "And stop drooling. You're making a mess."

The dog followed her inside where she reset the alarm, not that the tiny shack held anything of value. Most of her furniture and home electronics were in storage. But her boss was right that her home was remote, a good half mile from her closest neighbor, hence the security system. Smart women watched out for themselves.

Was Lia Grant smart? Did she fail to watch out for herself? The walls of her shack moved in closer, and she shrugged out of her jacket. Was the terrified-sounding caller really in a box, underground?

Grace set her jacket and computer on the kitchen table, forcing herself to stop thinking about the woman. With Blue at her heels, she filled the dog's food dish with dry chow, softened with warm water. When he looked at her with drooping eyes that had seen way too many doggy years, she sighed, went to the refrigerator, and took out a piece of cooked bacon. "You're going to die of clogged arteries." She crumbled the bacon into his bowl. "You realize that, don't you?"

Allegheny Blue plopped his nose in the food dish and started eating. Slow and steady. She didn't dislike animals, but she didn't have time for them, especially those that took an ungodly amount of maintenance.

She opened the refrigerator door again, a wave of icy air washing over her.

*It's cold...Help meeeee!*

Grace slammed the door. If that cry for help wasn't real, she'd been played. And the chilling fact that no one played state attorney Grace Courtemanche swept through her decrepit kitchen.

"What now?" she asked Allegheny Blue.

The dog continued to inhale his food, but her father answered.

*Winners do, Gracie, and doers win.*

Grace picked up her phone and called Jim Breck, the internal security chief and her go-to guy with a local cell phone company. The SA's office regularly turned to him for wiretaps and call records.

"Counselor Courtemanche, why does it not surprise me that you're working after hours?" Jim said when he answered his work phone.

She laughed. "Because like you, Jim, I love my work and have no social life. Did Deputy Fillingham contact you this afternoon for a call search?"

"Not yet."

Figures. Fillingham was new to the force, green, and probably trying to figure out how to work the sheriff's office resource directory. "I need to know the subscriber's name and contact information on a series of calls I received."

"Got the paperwork?"

No, and she wasn't likely to get a subpoena, not while on *vacation*. She tucked a curved end of her hair behind her ear. *Help meeeee!* "This isn't an official investigation," she said, trying to keep her tone neutral.

"Sorry. Can't move forward without a subpoena."

She tucked a wing of hair behind the other ear. Sometimes you had to bulldoze past a few roadblocks. "I received nine calls from a stranger begging for my help. This whole thing could be a series of crank calls from friends of a convicted felon who's been harassing me for the past few months." Her shiver of unease morphed into a gnawing fear. "Or it could be a young woman in grave danger and who's running out of time. I'm seriously leaning toward the latter."

Jim said nothing.

"Come on, Jim. You've worked with me for years. You know my track record."

"Let me see what I can do," he finally said. An excruciating two minutes later he came back on the line. "Interesting."

Without a subpoena, they were walking a fine line, but she was grateful to finally be doing *something*. "Can you verify the subscriber's name?" Grace asked.

"No."

"Can you verify the subscriber's address?"

"No."

No surprise there. "Can you verify that it was a prepaid phone?"

"Yes."

"And let me guess, the subscriber is listed as Mickey Mouse."

Jim cleared his throat and said with a cough, "Clark Kent."

It fit the MO in the other Morehouse communications: phone calls and texts made from untraceable prepaid phones. But Lia never mentioned Morehouse, and more importantly, she sounded genuinely terrified.

Much like Allegheny Blue and his search for bones, Grace couldn't let go. "Where was the phone purchased?" As this wasn't subscriber information, she knew Jim could speak freely. Clicking sounded on the other end of the line.

She tapped her fingers against her pearls.

"Retailer in Port St. Joe."

"If I give you the time of the calls, can you tell me the location?" She rolled her shoulders and flexed her wrists, a warm-up of sorts, like in tennis.

"Caller didn't activate GPS functionality, but according to the Call Data Record, the call came off the Cypress Point cell tower. It's an omni site that covers a three-mile section. Topo map shows swampland, a handful of high-end resort properties, and a few residences."

Like hers. Her shack was located on Cypress Point. Lia Grant's call had been made within three miles of her home. Significant or coincidental?

After thanking Jim, she tapped her fingers on the base of her keyboard, itching to do something. Normally she'd work. Grace could always lose herself in her cases, give herself over to the consuming fire to battle the bad. She'd been drawn to the prosecuting end of criminal law because she wanted to fight bad guys who'd haunted much of her childhood.

"They're everywhere," her mother used to say on her *difficult* days. "The bad guys are on the streets, in our neighborhood, beneath our home." Her mother's delicate fingers would claw into Grace's ten-year-old shoulders. "They're watching me, following me, touching me while I sleep. Make them go away, Gracie, please, please make them go away."

She'd take her mother's trembling hand and lead her around the house, turning on lights and shooing away shadows. "They're gone, Momma. The bad guys are gone." Grace never knew if her words or the tumblers of scotch that always followed soothed her mother.

Ten years ago when Grace joined the SA's office, Grace

discovered her mother was right. Bad guys were everywhere. Jamming her hair behind her ears, she began typing.

She didn't need the subscription databases and law enforcement contacts afforded to her as a member of the SA's
office. Using the almighty Google, she searched the terms
"Lia Grant" and "Florida," and a dozen hits turned up, including one about a young woman who lived in nearby
Carrabelle. Within fifteen minutes Grace had a full page of
notes on the nineteen-year-old nursing student and member
of her church volleyball team, including a current address
and phone number.

After eight rings, a groggy voice came on the line. "'lo."

"Lia Grant, please."

"Lia's not home yet." *Yawn.* "Who's this?"

"Grace Courtemanche. She called me this afternoon."
Nine times. "I'm returning her call."

"You spoke to Lia today?" Something rustled, and when
the voice spoke again, all fuzziness was gone. "If you talk to
her again, tell her to get her ass home. Last night she had a
volunteer shift at the hospital, and she borrowed my car. She
was supposed to have it back to me by ten this morning so I
could make it to my summer school class. Didn't happen. I
called her a dozen times, but she never returned my call, and
I missed my chem exam. I'm gonna kill her."

Grace looked at the photo she'd found on Lia's church's
website. The young woman had stick-straight brown bangs
and hair bobbed at the shoulders, a big toothy smile with
a slight overbite, and a tiny cross pendant around her neck.
Was this sweet-looking girl the same one who made those
scared-as-hell phone calls?

After asking a few more questions, Grace hung up and dialed the hospital where Lia worked as a volunteer. The clerk
at the twenty-four-hour information desk verified Lia had

not shown for her volunteer shift. "Quite odd for Lia," the chatty woman said. "Although she's young, she's a responsible little thing, a real good girl."

*Tell my momma I... I tried to be a g... g... good girl. I tried...*

Had Lia Grant really been buried alive in a box underground? With a phone? Near or on the Giroux place? Grace knuckled her temples. It sounded insane. Just like Larry Morehouse thinking she'd take a bribe and deal him down. And just like her mother who believed bad guys lived under their house and stole her jewelry. Yes, insanity lived in this world.

She called the sheriff's station and left word for Deputy Fillingham to contact her immediately, but in the meantime, the bulldozer would keep rolling. Grace reached for her purse. The lump of dog snoring under the kitchen table opened one eye.

"You're not going with me." She dug out her keys and headed for the door, the dog at her heels. "You shed and drool and you stink." She opened the door and tried to slip out, but the dog lumbered past her, a slow-moving avalanche. "Dammit, Blue! Get back here."

The dog plodded to her car where he sat near the passenger-side door. For some reason she couldn't even begin to fathom, Blue didn't like her going off at night alone. Tonight she didn't want to fight. It would take too much time and energy that should be spent on Lia Grant, whoever she was. Scratch that. *Wherever* she was. Grace opened the passenger door, and as the old dog heaved himself in she mumbled, "The vet said you're supposed to be dead by now."

This time her car started, and she slipped through the night to the hospital where Lia was scheduled to volunteer. Despite the dark, it didn't take her long to find a small blue hybrid. Grace checked the license plate number Lia Grant's roommate had given her. A match.

"This is too easy," Grace said to Allegheny Blue as they got out of the car.

Locked car. No obvious car damage. Under the car near the back driver's side tire she spotted something white and knobby. A picture of one of Allegheny Blue's bones flashed through her head. She shook off the gruesome image, squatted near the tire, and pulled out a purse. Inside was a wallet with a driver's license. Bangs and a toothy grin with a slight overbite looked back at her.

*It's cold. And dark. I can't breathe. Help me, Grace. Help meeeee!*

The plea brushed across the back of her neck with a chill at odds with the steamy night. Where the hell was Deputy Fillingham? Grace reached for her phone to call but was interrupted by an ear-piercing sound. Allegheny Blue stood at the back of the car, his body quivering, his tail whipping the air, his neck arched in a night-splitting howl.

She ran to the back of the car and found him spotted up on a smear of red slashed across the bumper.

# THE DISH

## Where Authors Give You the Inside Scoop

### From the desk of Lily Dalton

Dear Reader,

Some people are heroic by nature. They act to help others without thinking. Sometimes at the expense of their own safety. Sometimes without ever considering the consequences. That's just who they are. Especially when it's a friend in need.

We associate these traits with soldiers who risk their lives on a dangerous battlefield to save a fallen comrade. Not because it's their job, but because it's their brother. Or a parent who runs into a busy street to save a child who's wandered into the path of an oncoming car. Or an ocean life activist who places himself in a tiny boat between a whale and the harpoons of a whaling ship.

Is it so hard to believe that Daphne Bevington, a London debutante and the earl of Wolverton's granddaughter, could be such a hero? When her dearest friend, Kate, needs her help, she does what's necessary to save her. In her mind, no other choice will do. After all, she knows without a doubt that Kate would do the same for her if she needed help. It doesn't matter one fig to her that their circumstances are disparate, that Kate is her lady's maid.

But Daphne finds herself in over her head. In a moment, everything falls apart, throwing not only her reputation and her future into doubt, but her life into danger. Yet in that moment when all seems hopelessly lost...another hero comes out of nowhere and saves her. A mysterious stranger who acts without thinking, at the expense of his own safety, without considering the consequences. A hero on a quest of his own. A man she will never see again...

Only, of course...she does. And he's not at all the hero she remembers him to be.

Or is he? I hope you will enjoy reading NEVER ENTICE AN EARL and finding out.


Best wishes, and happy reading!

*Lily Dalton*

LilyDalton.com
Twitter @LilyDalton
Facebook.com/LilyDaltonAuthor

♥ ♥ ♥ ♥ ♥ ♥ ♥ ♥ ♥ ♥ ♥ ♥ ♥ ♥ ♥

*From the desk of Shelley Coriell*

Dear Reader,

Story ideas come from everywhere. Snippets of conversation. Dreams. The hunky guy at the office supply store with eyes the color of faded denim. THE BROKEN, the first book in my new romantic suspense series, The Apostles, was born and bred as I sat at the bedside of my dying father.

In 2007 my dad, who lived on a mountain in northern Nevada, checked himself into his small town's hospital after having what appeared to be a stroke. "A mild one," he assured the family. "Nothing to get worked up about." That afternoon, this independent, strong-willed man (aka stubborn and borderline cantankerous) checked himself out of the hospital. The next day he hopped on his quad and accidentally drove off the side of his beloved mountain. The ATV landed on him, crushing his chest, breaking ribs, and collapsing a lung.

The hospital staff told us they could do nothing for him, that he would die. Refusing to accept the prognosis, we had him Life-Flighted to Salt Lake City. After a touch-and-go forty-eight hours, he pulled through, and that's when we learned the full extent of his injuries.

He'd had *multiple* strokes. The not-so-mild kind. The kind that meant he, at age sixty-three, would be forever dependent on others. His spirit was broken.

For the next week, the family gathered at the hospital. My sister, the oldest and the family nurturer, massaged his feet and swabbed his mouth. My brother, Mr. Finance Guy, talked with insurance types and made arrangements for post-release therapy. The quiet, bookish middle child, I had little to offer but prayers. I'd never felt so helpless.

As my dad's health improved, his spirits worsened. He was mad at his body, mad at the world. After a particularly difficult morning, he told us he wished he'd died on that mountain. A horrible, heavy silence followed. Which is when I decided to use the one thing I did have.

I dragged the chair in his hospital room—you know the kind, the heavy, wooden contraption that folds out into a bed—to his bedside and took out the notebook I carry everywhere.

"You know, Dad," I said. "I've been tinkering with this story idea. Can I bounce some stuff off you?"

Silence.

"I have this heroine. A news broadcaster who gets stabbed by a serial killer. She's scarred, physically and emotionally."

More silence.

"And I have a Good Guy. Don't know much about him, but he also has a past that left him scarred. He carries a gun. Maybe an FBI badge." That's it. Two hazy characters hanging out in the back of my brain.

Dad turned toward the window.

"The scarred journalist ends up working as an aide to an old man who lives on a mountain," I continued on the fly. "Oh-oh! The old guy is blind and can't see her scars. His name is . . . Smokey Joe, and like everyone else in this story, he's a little broken."

Dad glared. I saw it. He wanted me to see it.

"And, you know what, Dad? Smokey Joe can be a real pain in the ass."

My father's lips twitched. He tried not to smile, but I saw that, too.

I opened my notebook. "So tell me about Smokey Joe. Tell me about his mountain. Tell me about his *story*."

For the next two hours, Dad and I talked about an old man on a mountain and brainstormed the book that eventually became THE BROKEN, the story of Kate Johnson, an on-the-run broadcast journalist whose broken past holds the secret to catching a serial killer, and Hayden Reed, the tenacious FBI profiler who sees past her scars and vows to find a way into her head, but to his surprise, heads straight for her heart.

"Hey, Sissy," Dad said as I tucked away my notebook after what became the first of many Apostle brainstorming sessions. "Smokey Joe knows how to use C-4. We need to have a scene where he blows something up."

And "we" did.

So with a boom from old Smokey Joe, I'm thrilled to introduce you to Kate Johnson, Hayden Reed, and the Apostles, an elite group of FBI agents who aren't afraid to work outside the box and, at times, outside the law. FBI legend Parker Lord on his team: "Apostles? There's nothing holy about us. We're a little maverick and a lot broken, but in the end we get justice right."

Joy & Peace!

*Shelly Oriel*

♥ ♥ ♥ ♥ ♥ ♥ ♥ ♥ ♥ ♥ ♥ ♥ ♥ ♥ ♥ ♥

*From the desk of Hope Ramsay*

Dear Reader,

*Jane Eyre* may have been the first romance novel I ever read. I know it made an enormous impression on me when I was in seventh grade and it undoubtedly turned me into an avid reader. I simply got lost in the love story between Jane Eyre and Edward Fairfax Rochester.

In other words, I fell in love with Rochester when I was thirteen, and I've never gotten over it. I re-read *Jane Eyre* every year or so, and I have every screen adaptation ever made of the book. (The BBC version is the best by far, even if they took liberties with the story.)

So it was only a matter of time before I tried to write a hero like Rochester. You know the kind: brooding, passionate, tortured...(sigh). Enter Gabriel Raintree, the hero of INN AT LAST CHANCE. He's got all the classic traits of the gothic hero.

His heroine is Jennifer Carpenter, a plucky and self-reliant former schoolteacher turned innkeeper who is exactly the kind of no-nonsense woman Gabe needs. (Does this sound vaguely familiar?)

In all fairness, I should point out that I substituted the swamps of South Carolina for the moors of England and a bed and breakfast for Thornfield Hall. I also have an inordinate number of busybodies and matchmakers popping in and out for comic relief. But it is fair to say that I borrowed a few things from Charlotte Brontë, and I had such fun doing it.

I hope you enjoy INN AT LAST CHANCE. It's a contemporary, gothic-inspired tale involving a brooding hero, a plucky heroine, a haunted house, and a secret that's been kept for years.

*Hope Ramsay*

♥ ♥ ♥ ♥ ♥ ♥ ♥ ♥ ♥ ♥ ♥ ♥ ♥ ♥

# From the desk of Molly Cannon

Dear Reader,

Weddings! I love them. The ceremony, the traditions, the romance, the flowers, the music, and of course the food. Face it. I embrace anything when cake is involved. When I got married many moons ago, there was a short ceremony and then cake and punch were served in the next room. That was it. Simple and easy and really lovely. But possibilities for weddings have expanded since then.

In FLIRTING WITH FOREVER, Irene Cornwell decides to become a wedding planner, and she has to meet the challenge of giving brides what they want within their budget. And it can be a challenge! I have planned a couple of weddings, and it was a lot of work, but it was also a whole lot of fun. Finding the venue, booking the caterer, deciding on the decorating theme. It is so satisfying to watch a million details come together to launch the happy couple into their new life together.

In one wedding I planned we opted for using mismatched dishes found at thrift stores on the buffet table. We found a bride selling tablecloths from her wedding and used different swaths of cloth as overlays. We made a canopy for the dance floor using pickle buckets and PFC pipe covered in vines and flowers, and then strung it with lights. We spray-painted cheap glass vases and filled them with flowers to match the color palette. And then, as Irene discovered, the hardest part is cleaning up after the celebration is over. But I wouldn't trade the experience for anything.

Another important theme in FLIRTING WITH FOREVER is second-chance love. My heart gets all aflutter when I think about true love emerging victorious after years of separation, heartbreak, and misunderstanding. Irene and Theo fell in love as teenagers, but it didn't last. Now older and wiser they reunite and fall in love all over again. Sigh.

I hope you'll join Irene and Theo on their journey. I promise it's even better the second time around.


Happy Reading!

*Molly Cannon*

Mollycannon.com
Twitter @CannonMolly
Facebook.com

❤ ❤ ❤ ❤ ❤ ❤ ❤ ❤ ❤ ❤ ❤ ❤ ❤ ❤ ❤

## From the desk of Laura London

Dear Reader,

The spark to write THE WINDFLOWER came when Sharon read a three-hundred-year-old list of pirates who were executed by hanging. The majority of the pirates were teens, some as young as fourteen. Sharon felt so sad about these young lives cut short that it made her want to write a book to give the young pirates a happier ending.

For my part, I had much enjoyed the tales of Robert Lewis Stevenson as a boy. I had spent many happy hours playing the pirate with my cousins using wooden swords, cardboard hats, and rubber band guns.

Sharon and I threw ourselves into writing THE WIND-FLOWER with the full force of our creative absorption. We were young and in love, and existed in our imaginations on a pirate ship. We are proud that we created a novel that is in print on its thirty-year anniversary and has been printed in multiple languages around the world.

Fondly yours,

*Sharon*
*&*
*Tom Curtis*

Writing as Laura London

♥ ♥ ♥ ♥ ♥ ♥ ♥ ♥ ♥ ♥ ♥ ♥ ♥ ♥ ♥ ♥

*From the desk of*
*Sue-Ellen Welfonder*

Dear Reader,

At a recent gathering, someone asked about my upcoming releases. I revealed that I'd just launched a new Scottish medieval series, Scandalous Scots, with an e-novella, *Once Upon a Highland Christmas*, and that TO LOVE A HIGHLANDER would soon follow.

As happens so often, this person asked why I set my books in Scotland. My first reaction to this question is always to come back with, "Where else?" To me, there is nowhere else.

Sorley, the hero of TO LOVE A HIGHLANDER, would agree. Where better to celebrate romance than a land famed for men as fierce and wild as the soaring, mist-drenched hills that bred them? A place where the women are prized for their strength and beauty, the fiery passion known to heat a man's blood on cold, dark nights when chill winds raced through the glens? No land is more awe-inspiring, no people more proud. Scots have a powerful bond with their land. Haven't they fought for it for centuries? Kept their heathery hills always in their hearts, yearning for home when exiled, the distance of oceans and time unable to quench the pull to return?

That's a perfect blend for romance.

Sorley has such a bond with his homeland. Since he

was a lad, he's been drawn to the Highlands. Longing for wild places of rugged, wind-blown heights and high moors where the heather rolls on forever, so glorious it hurt the eyes to behold such grandeur. But Sorley's attachment to the Highlands also annoys him and poses one of his greatest problems. He suspects his father might have also been a Highlander—a ruthless, cold-hearted chieftain, to be exact. He doesn't know for sure because he's a bastard, raised at Stirling's glittering royal court.

In TO LOVE A HIGHLANDER, Sorley discovers the truth of his birth. Making Sorley unaware of his birthright as a Highlander was a twist I've always wanted to explore. I'm fascinated by how many people love Scotland and burn to go there, many drawn back because their ancestors were Scottish. I love that centuries and even thousands of miles can't touch the powerful pull Scotland exerts on its own.

Sorley's heritage explains a lot, for he's also a notorious rogue, a master of seduction. His prowess in bed is legend and he ignites passion in all the women he meets. Only one has ever shunned him. She's Mirabelle MacLaren and when she returns to his life, appearing in his bedchamber with an outrageous request, he's torn.

Mirabelle wants him to scandalize her reputation.

He'd love to oblige, especially as doing so will destroy his enemy.

But touching Mirabelle will rip open scars best left alone. Unfortunately, Sorley can't resist Mirabelle. Together, they learn that when the heart warms, all things are possible. Yet there's always a price. Theirs will be surrendering everything they've ever believed in and accepting that true love does indeed heal all wounds.

I hope you enjoy reading TO LOVE A HIGHLANDER!
I know I loved unraveling Sorley and Mirabelle's story.


Highland Blessings!

*Sue-Ellen Welfonder*

www.welfonder.com